CAT on the RUN

IN
CAT OF
DEATH!

Text and illustrations copyright © 2023 by Aaron Blabey

All rights reserved. Published by Scholastic Inc., *Publishers since 1920.* SCHOLASTIC
and associated logos are trademarks and/or registered trademarks of Scholastic Inc.
This edition published under license from Scholastic Australia Pty Limited. First
published by Scholastic Australia Pty Limited in 2015.

The publisher does not have any control over and does not assume any
responsibility for author or third-party websites or their content.

978-1-338-83182-5

10 9 8 7 6 5 4 3 2 1   23 24 25 26 27 28

Printed in Italy   183
First U.S. printing 2023

AARON BLABEY

CAT on the RUN

IN CAT OF DEATH!

Scholastic Inc.

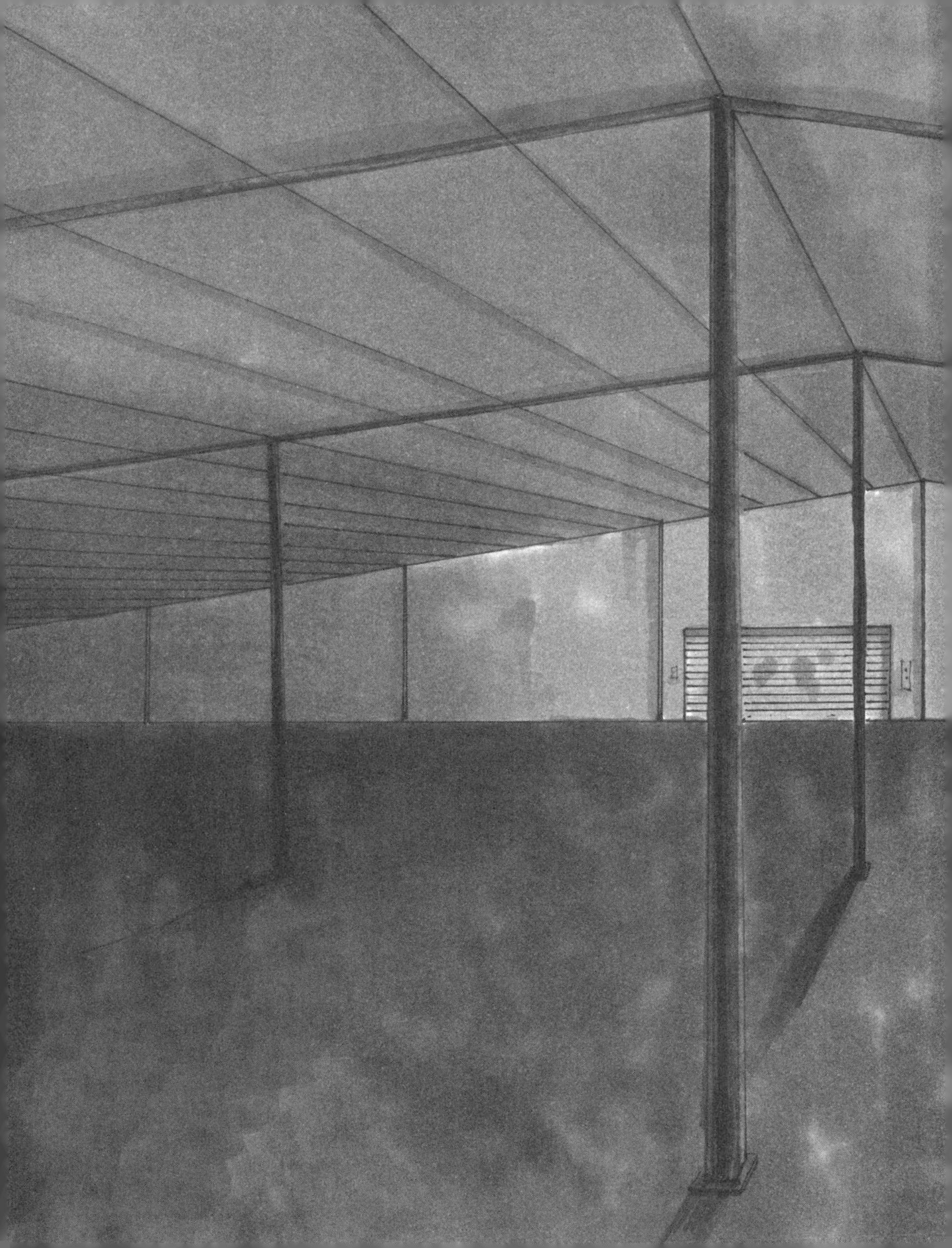

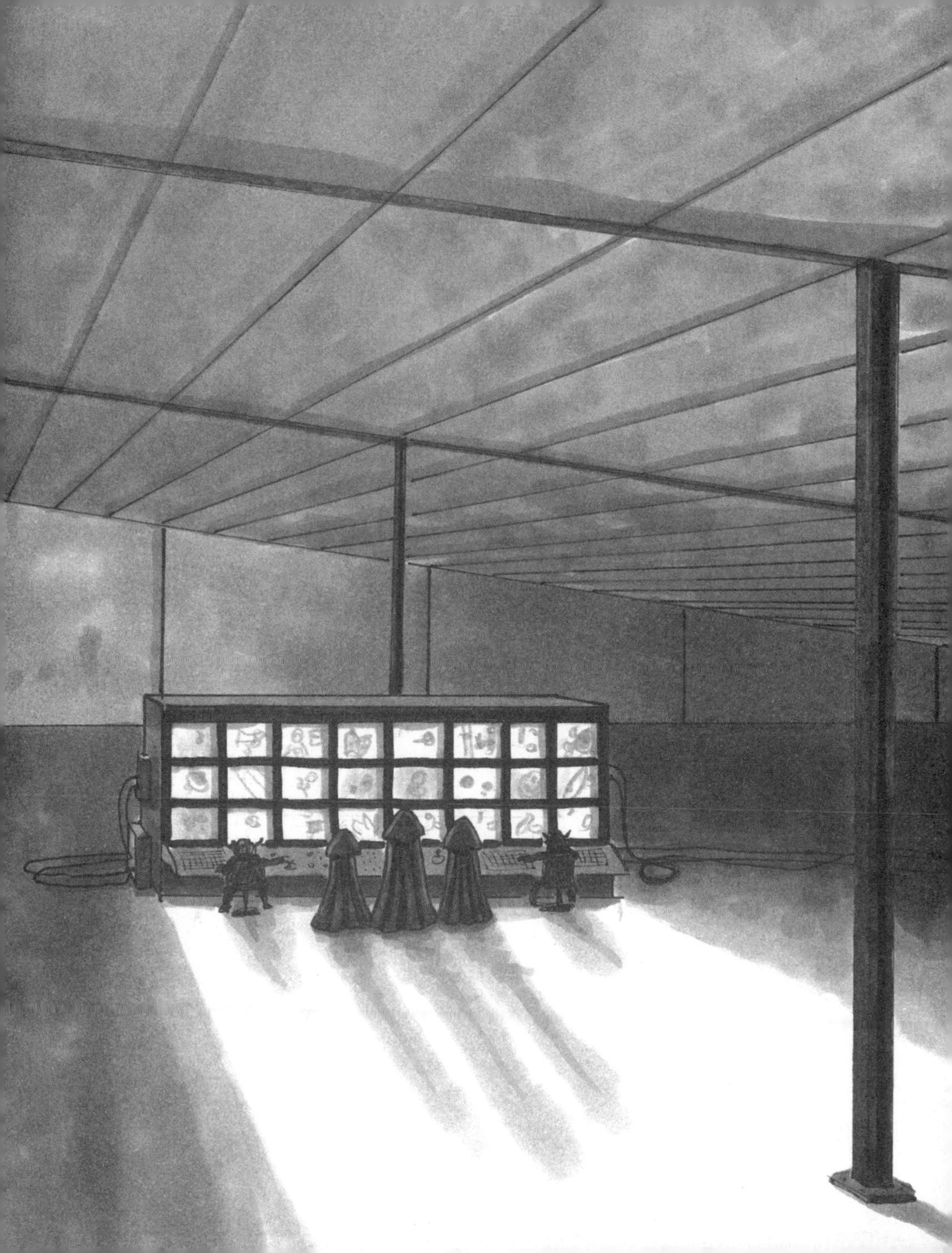

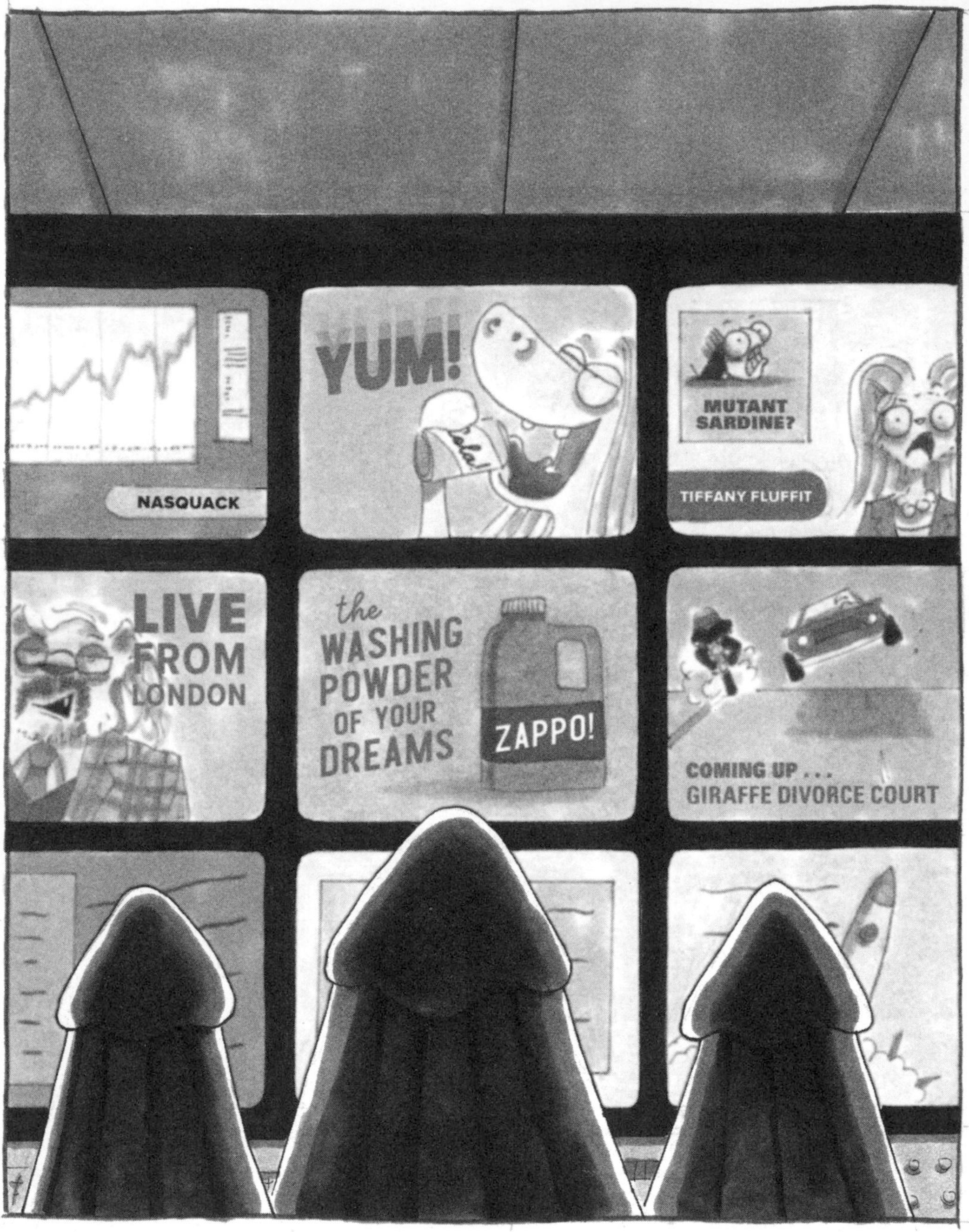
NASQUACK
YUM!
MUTANT SARDINE?
TIFFANY FLUFFIT
LIVE FROM LONDON
the WASHING POWDER OF YOUR DREAMS
ZAPPO!
COMING UP . . .
GIRAFFE DIVORCE COURT

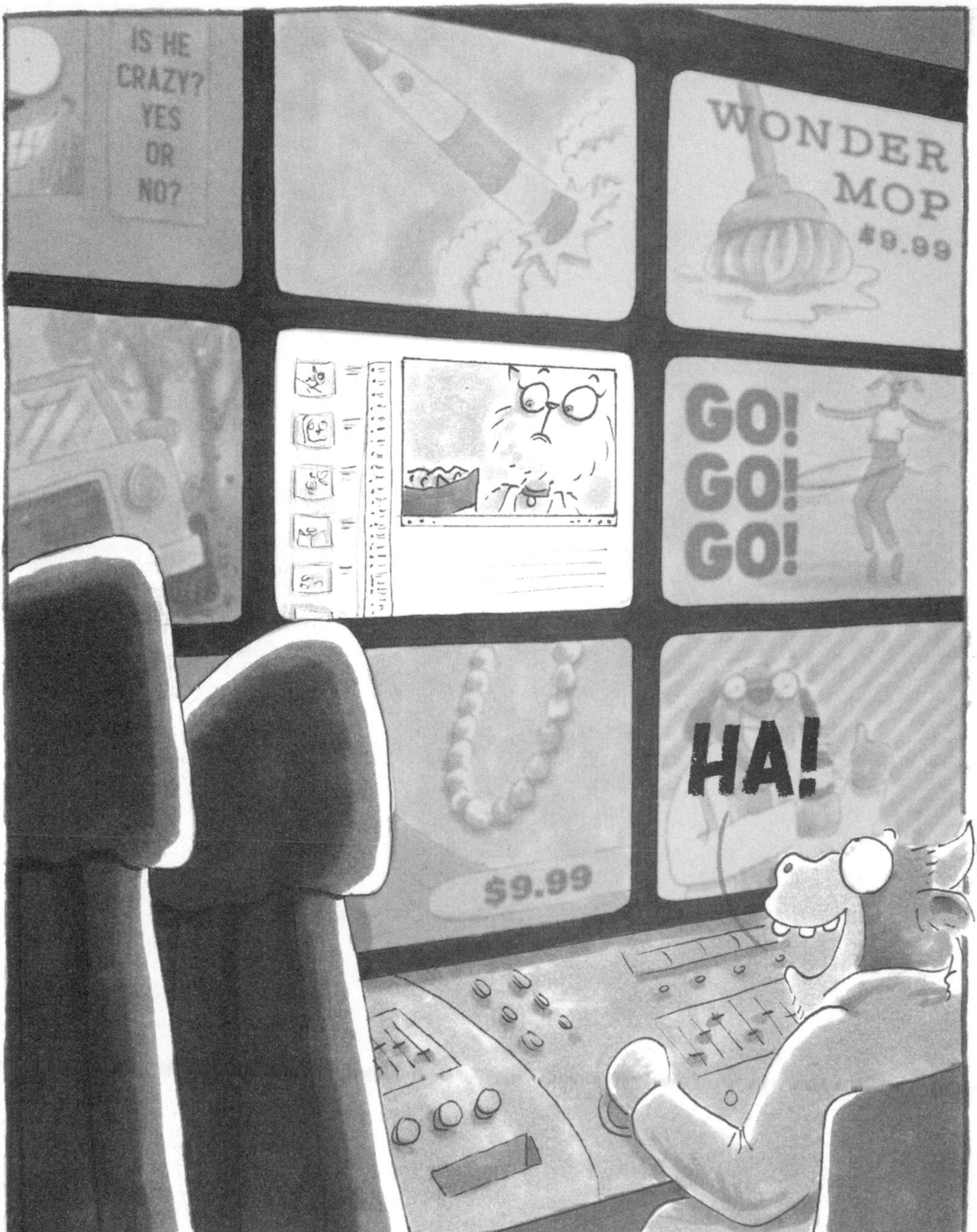
IS HE
CRAZY?
YES
OR
NO?
WONDER
MOP
$9.99
GO!
GO!
GO!
HA!
$9.99

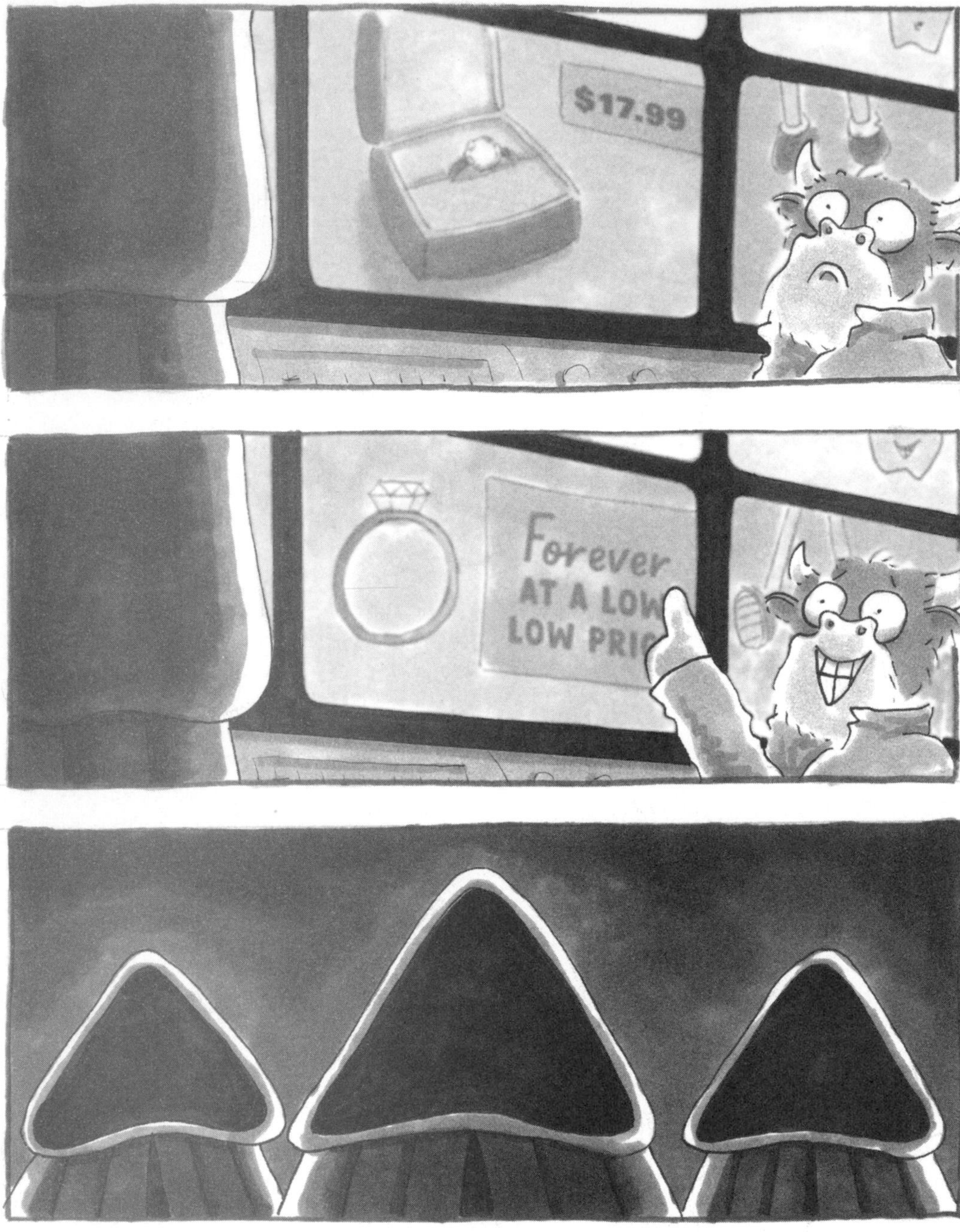
$17.99
Forever
AT A LOW
LOW PRIC

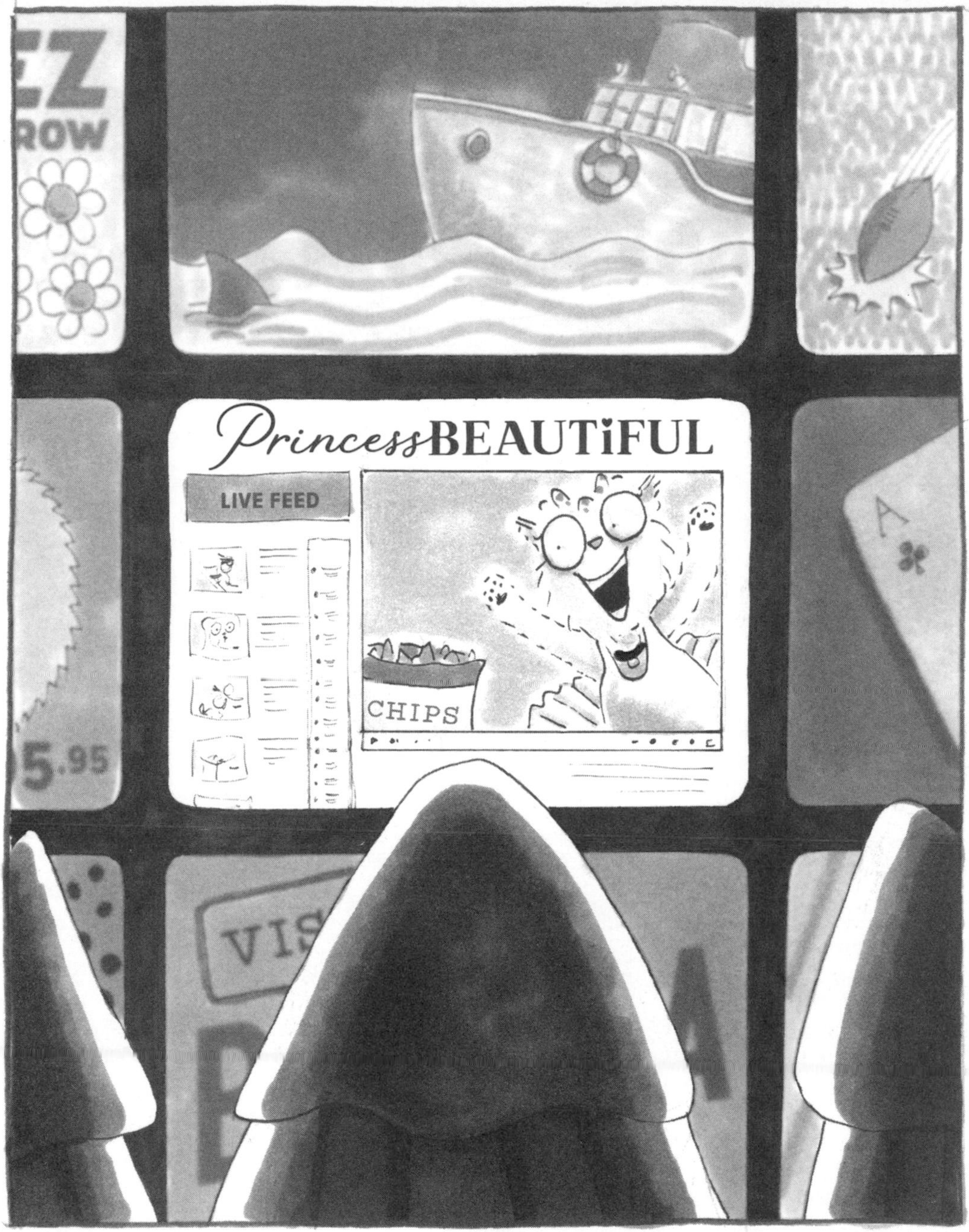
EZ
ROW
Princess BEAUTiFUL
LIVE FEED
CHIPS
5.95
VIS

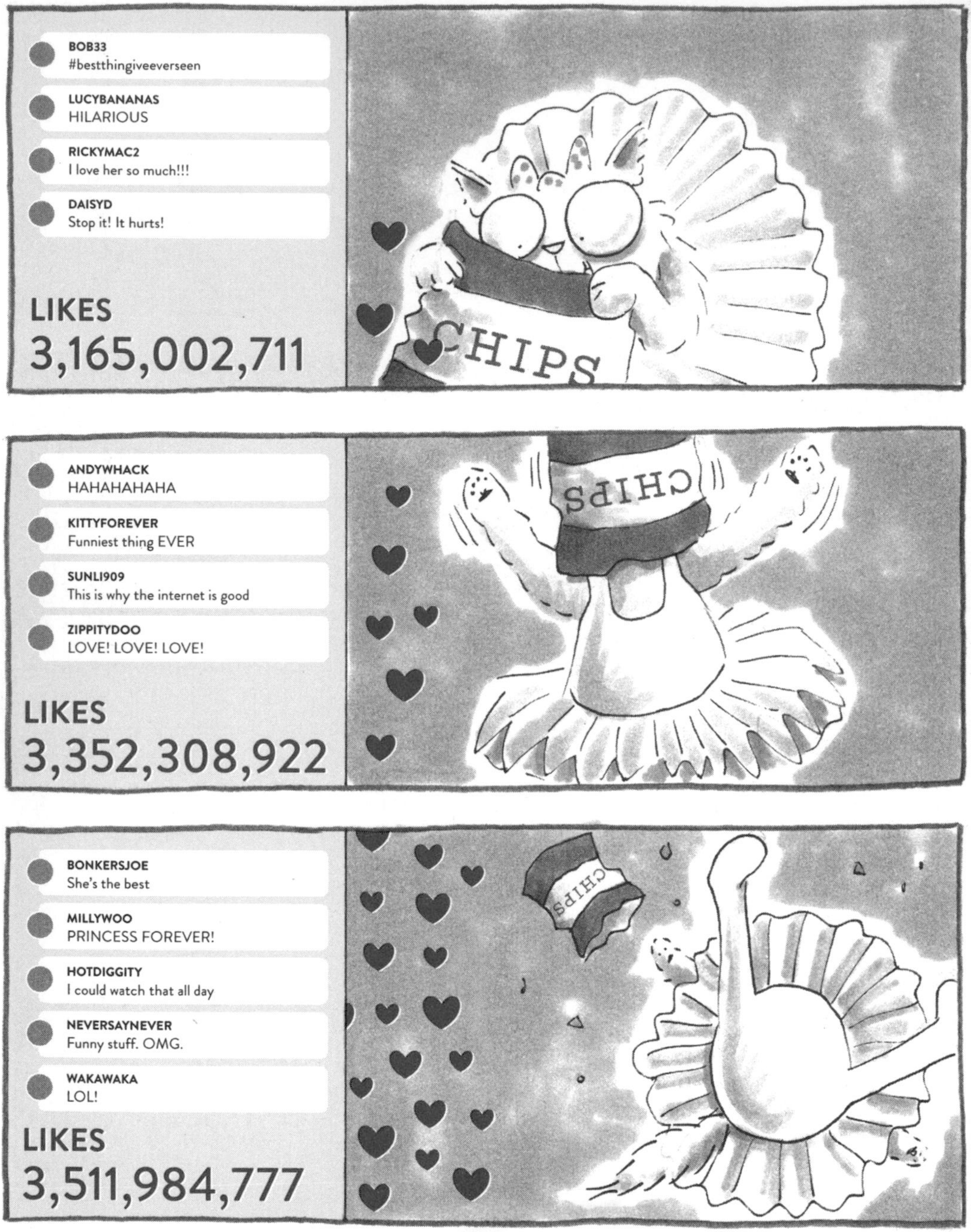
BOB33
#bestthingiveeverseen
LUCYBANANAS
HILARIOUS
RICKYMAC2
I love her so much!!!
DAISYD
Stop it! It hurts!
LIKES
3,165,002,711
CHIPS
ANDYWHACK
HAHAHAHAHA
KITTYFOREVER
Funniest thing EVER
SUNLI909
This is why the internet is good
ZIPPITYDOO
LOVE! LOVE! LOVE!
LIKES
3,352,308,922
CHIPS
BONKERSJOE
She's the best
MILLYWOO
PRINCESS FOREVER!
HOTDIGGITY
I could watch that all day
NEVERSAYNEVER
Funny stuff. OMG.
WAKAWAKA
LOL!
LIKES
3,511,984,777
CHIPS

LIKES
3,712,002,137

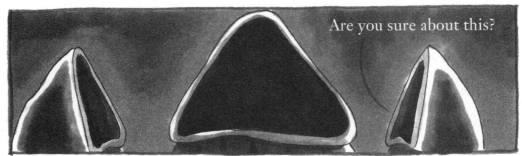

Are you sure about this?

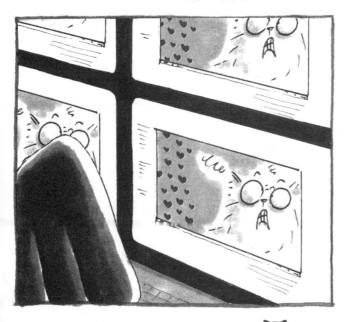

Oh yes.

Princess
BEAUTIFUL

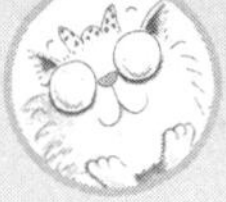

Princess Beautiful

2.2 billion subscribers

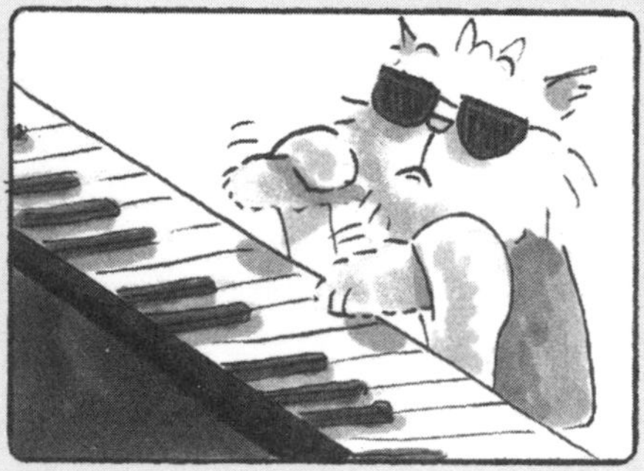

Boogie Woogie Kitty

2.7 billion views

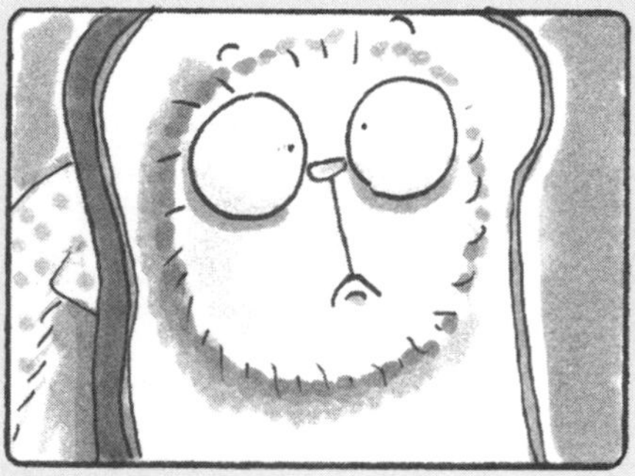

Bread Head

2.3 billion views

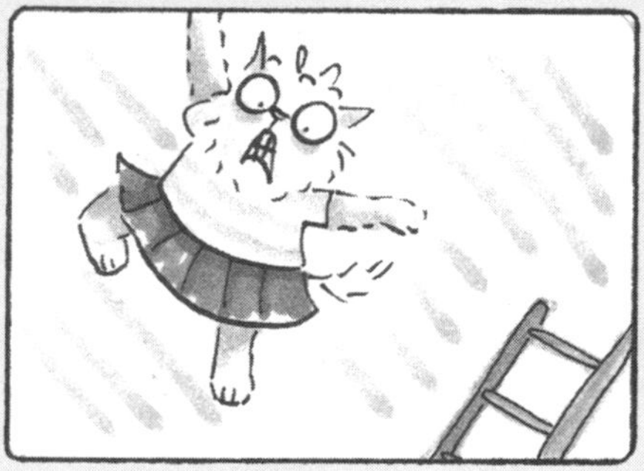

Hang in There!

3.3 billion views

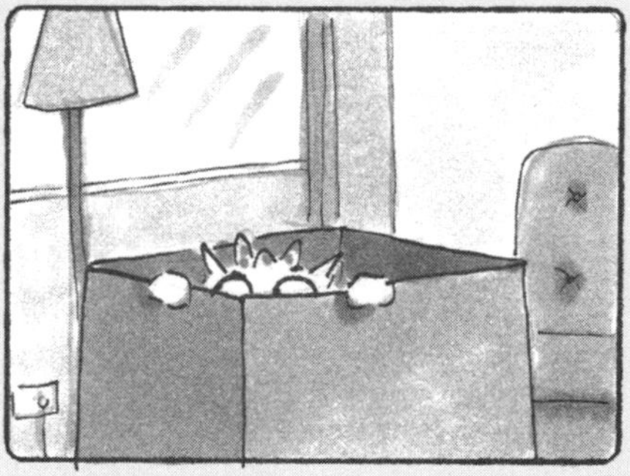

Box O' Trouble

2.9 billion views

THE WORLD'S #1 CAT VIDEO STAR!

VID-E-GRAM CHANNEL

SUBSCRIBE

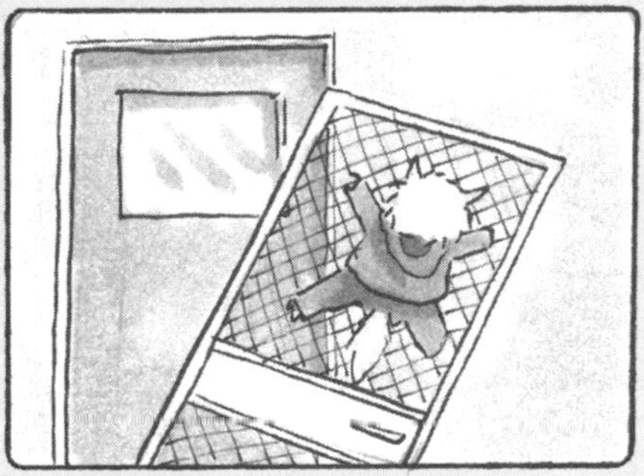

Screen Door Capers

2.8 billion views

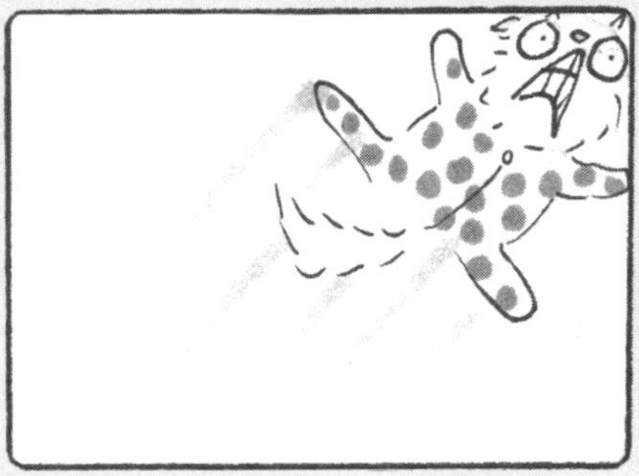

Uh-Oh

3.1 billion views

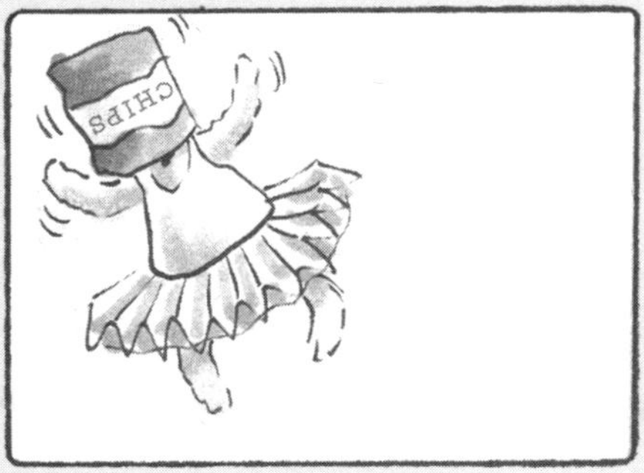
CHIPS

The Chips Are Down

3.7 billion views

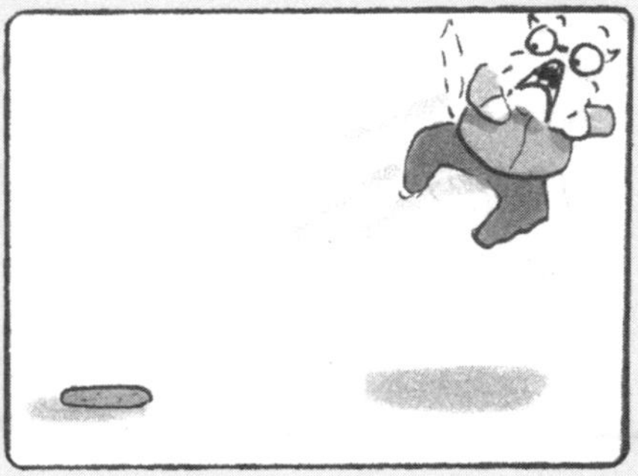

Cucumber Freak-Out

3.1 billion views

She's perfect . . .

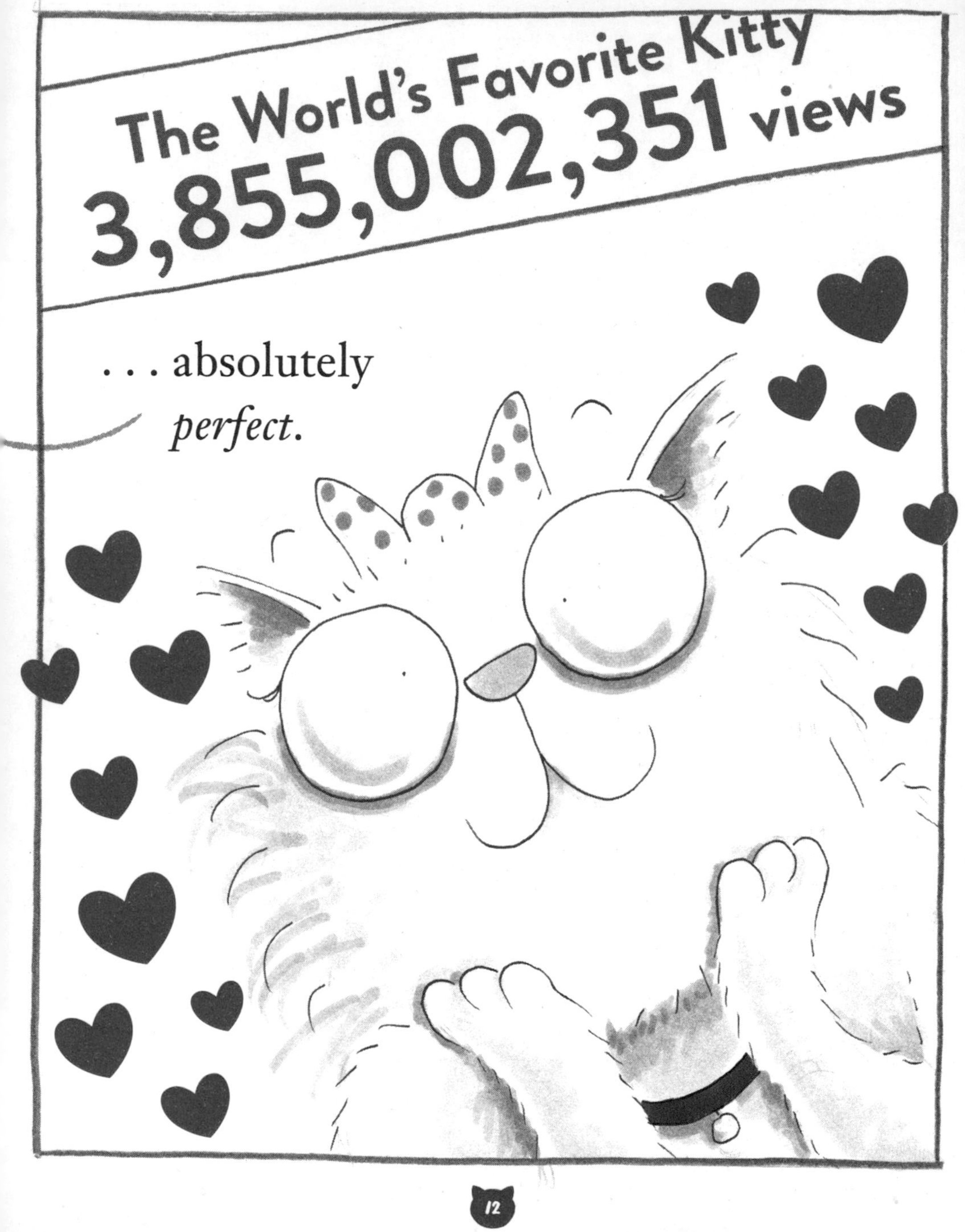
The World's Favorite Kitty
3,855,002,351 views
. . . absolutely
perfect.

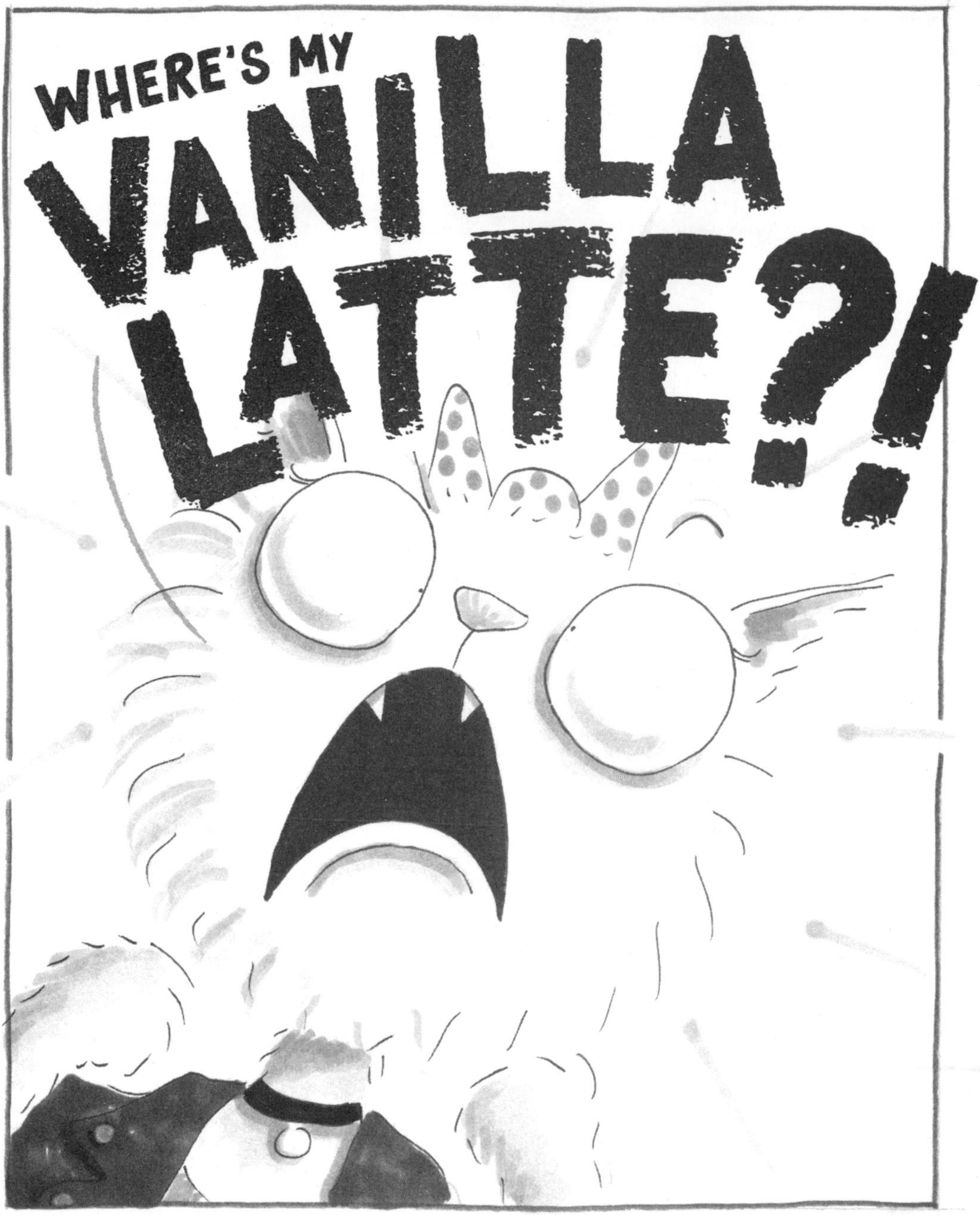
WHERE'S MY VANILLA LATTE?!

One

#1 AIN'T EASY

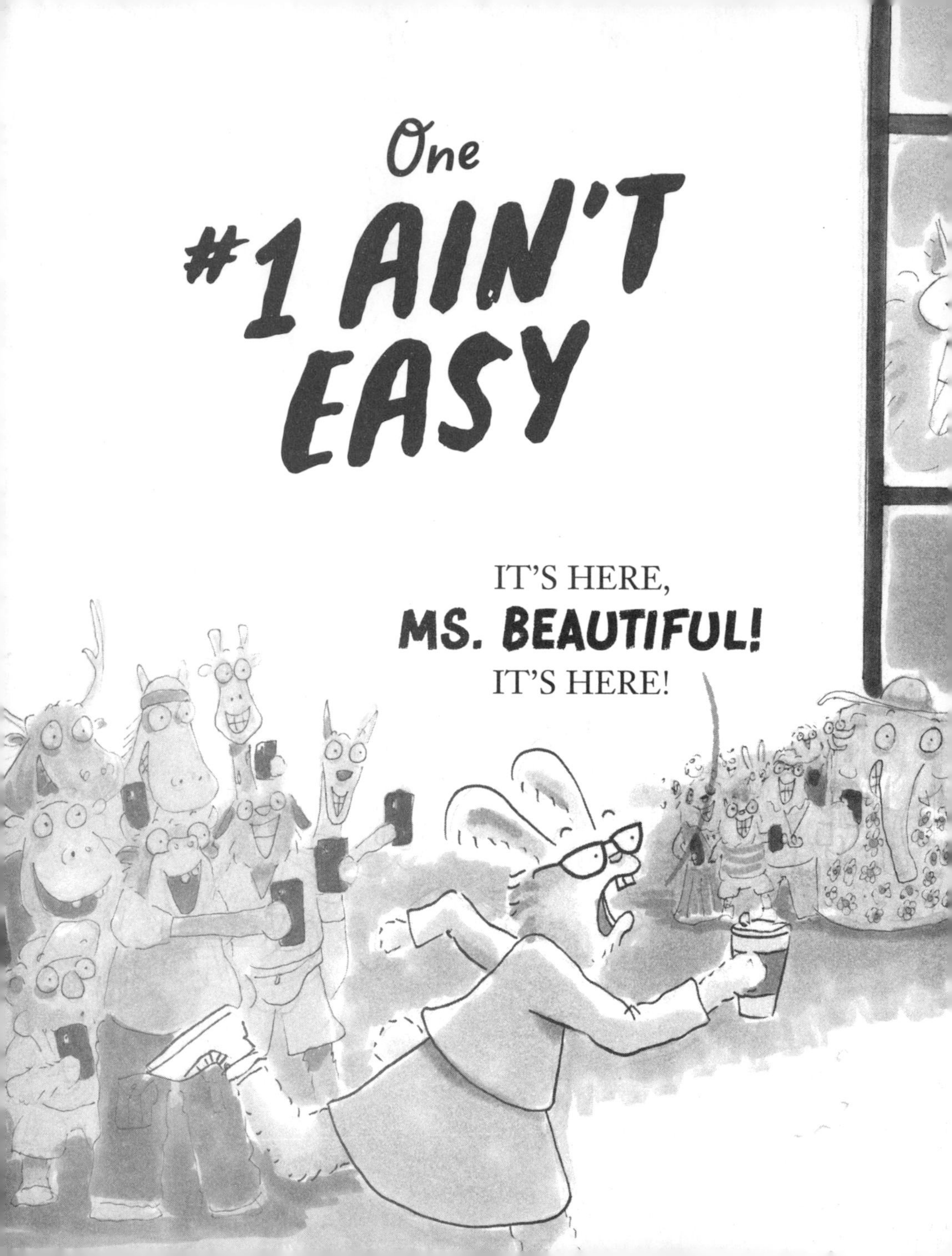
IT'S HERE,
MS. BEAUTIFUL!
IT'S HERE!

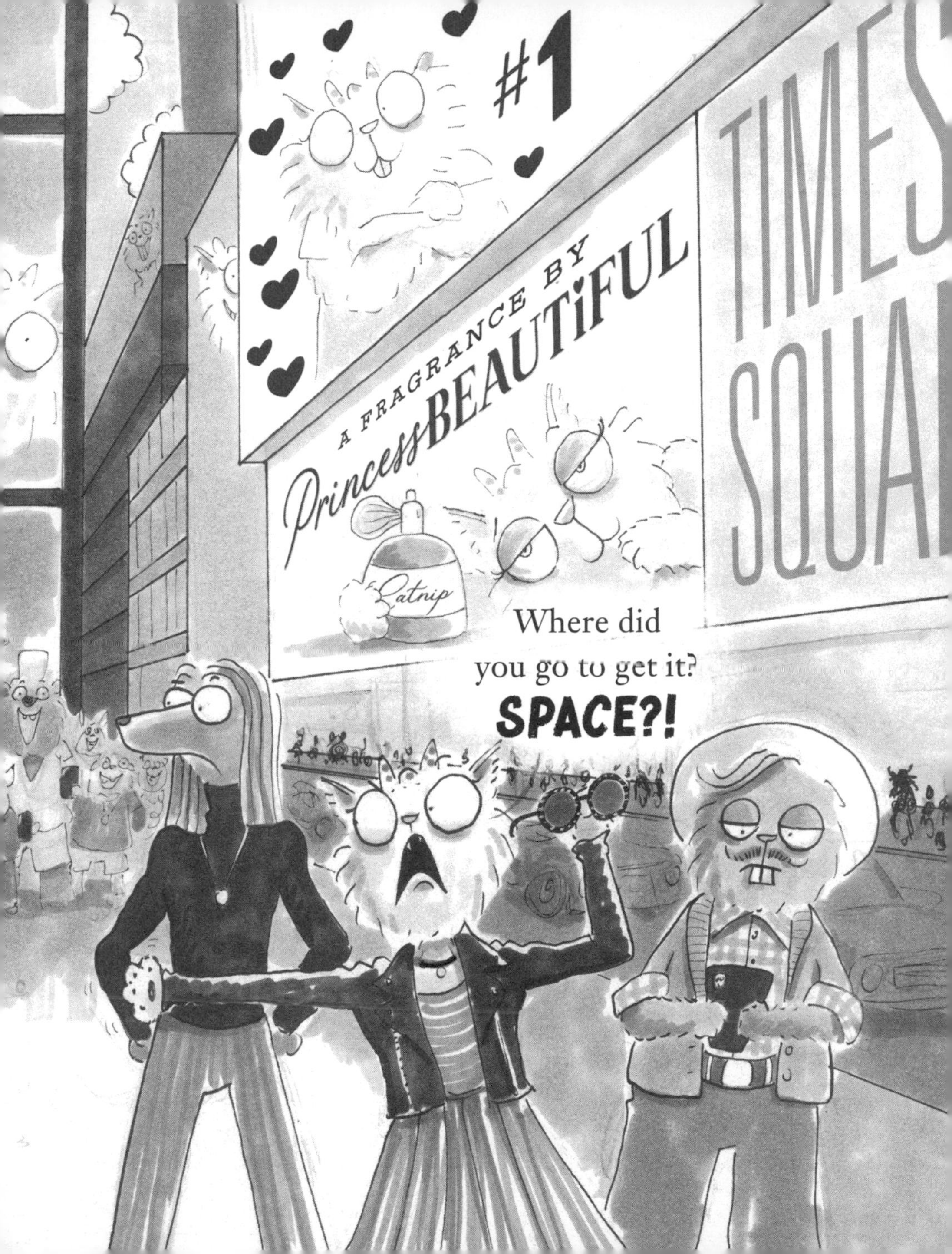
#1
A FRAGRANCE BY
Princess BEAUTiFUL
Catnip
TIMES
SQUA
Where did you go to get it?
SPACE?!

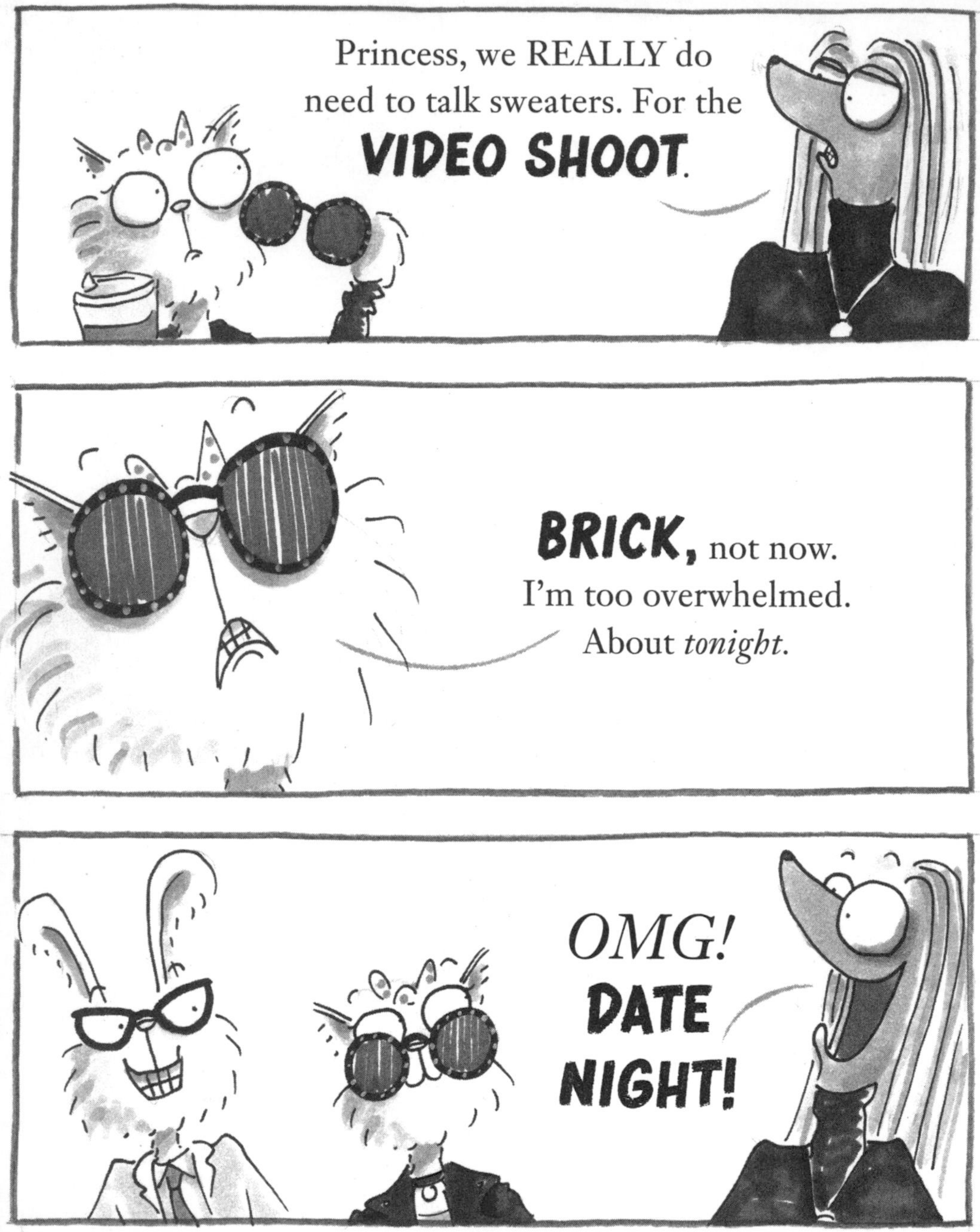

Princess, we REALLY do need to talk sweaters. For the VIDEO SHOOT.
BRICK, not now. I'm too overwhelmed. About *tonight*.
OMG! DATE NIGHT!

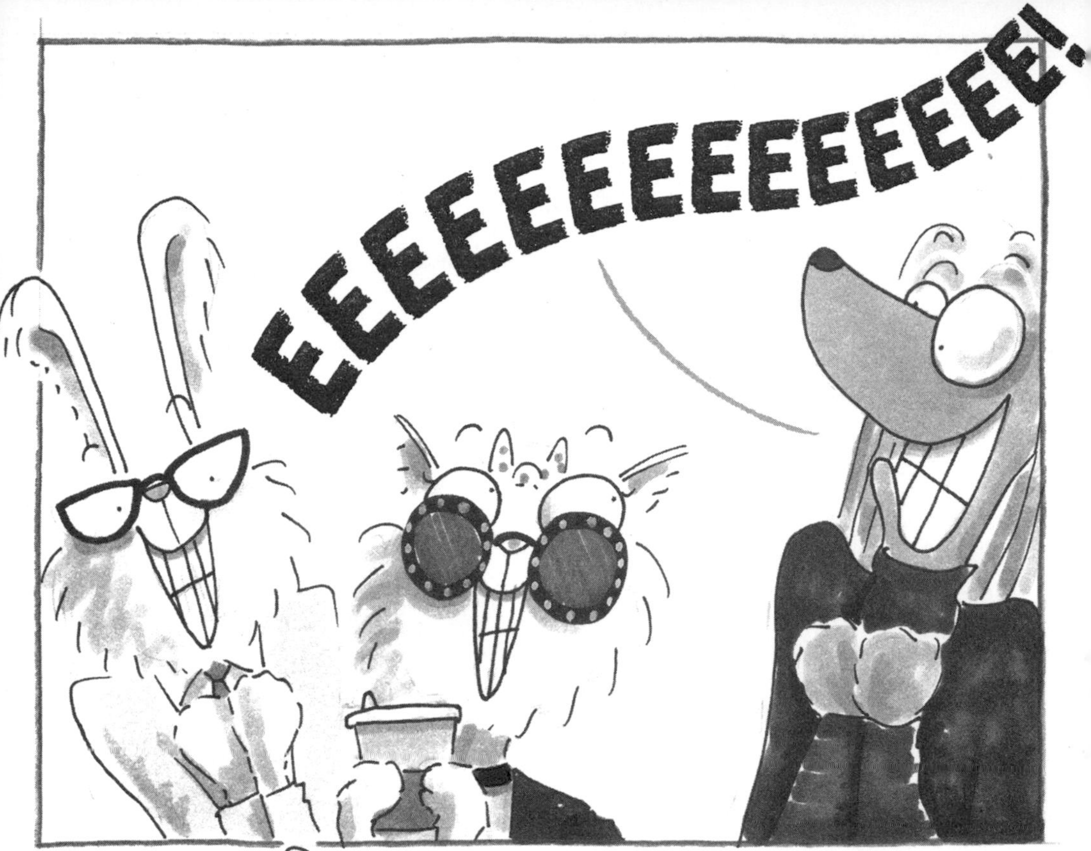
EEEEEEEEEEEEEE!

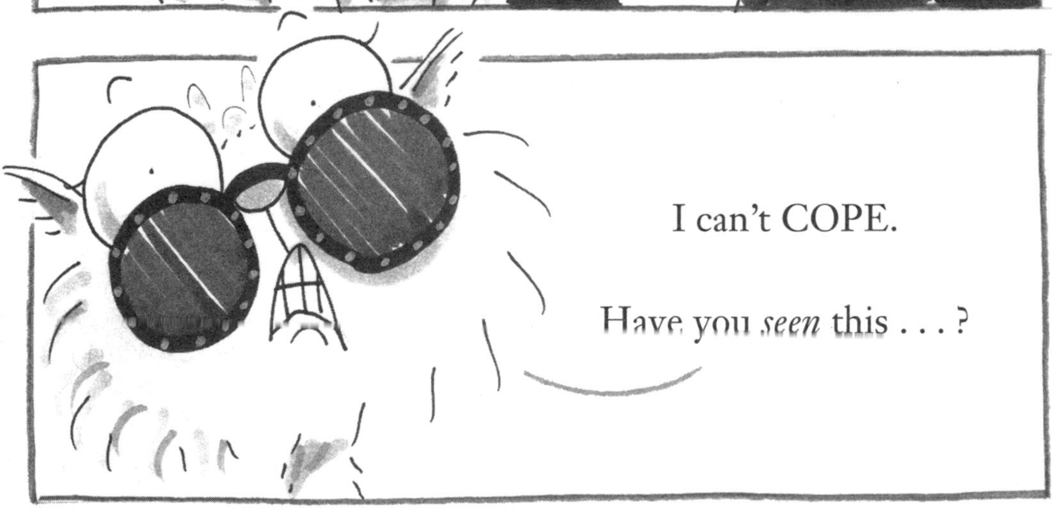
I can't COPE.
Have you *seen* this . . . ?

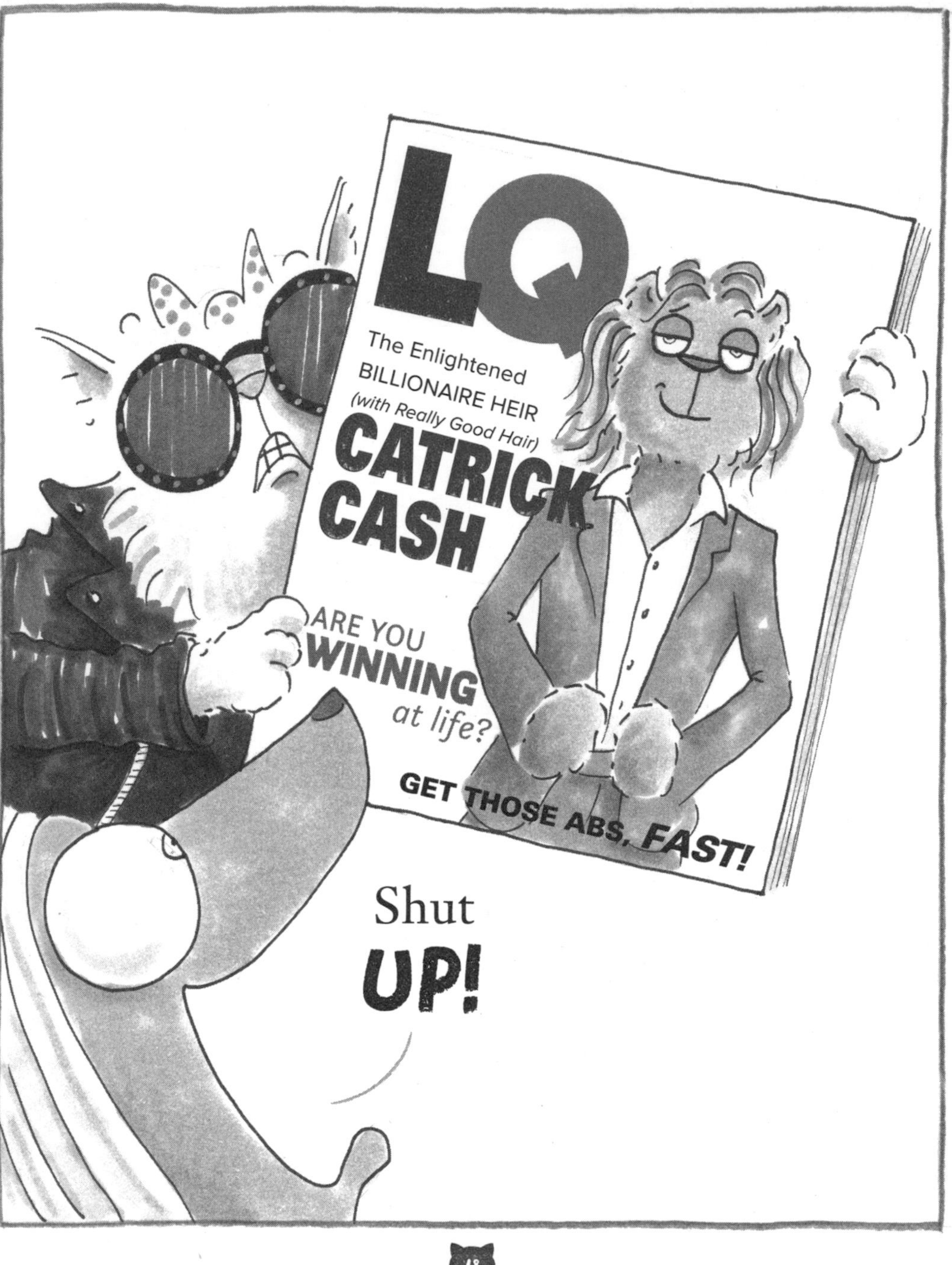
LQ
The Enlightened
BILLIONAIRE HEIR
(with Really Good Hair)
CATRICK CASH
ARE YOU WINNING at life?
GET THOSE ABS, FAST!
Shut UP!

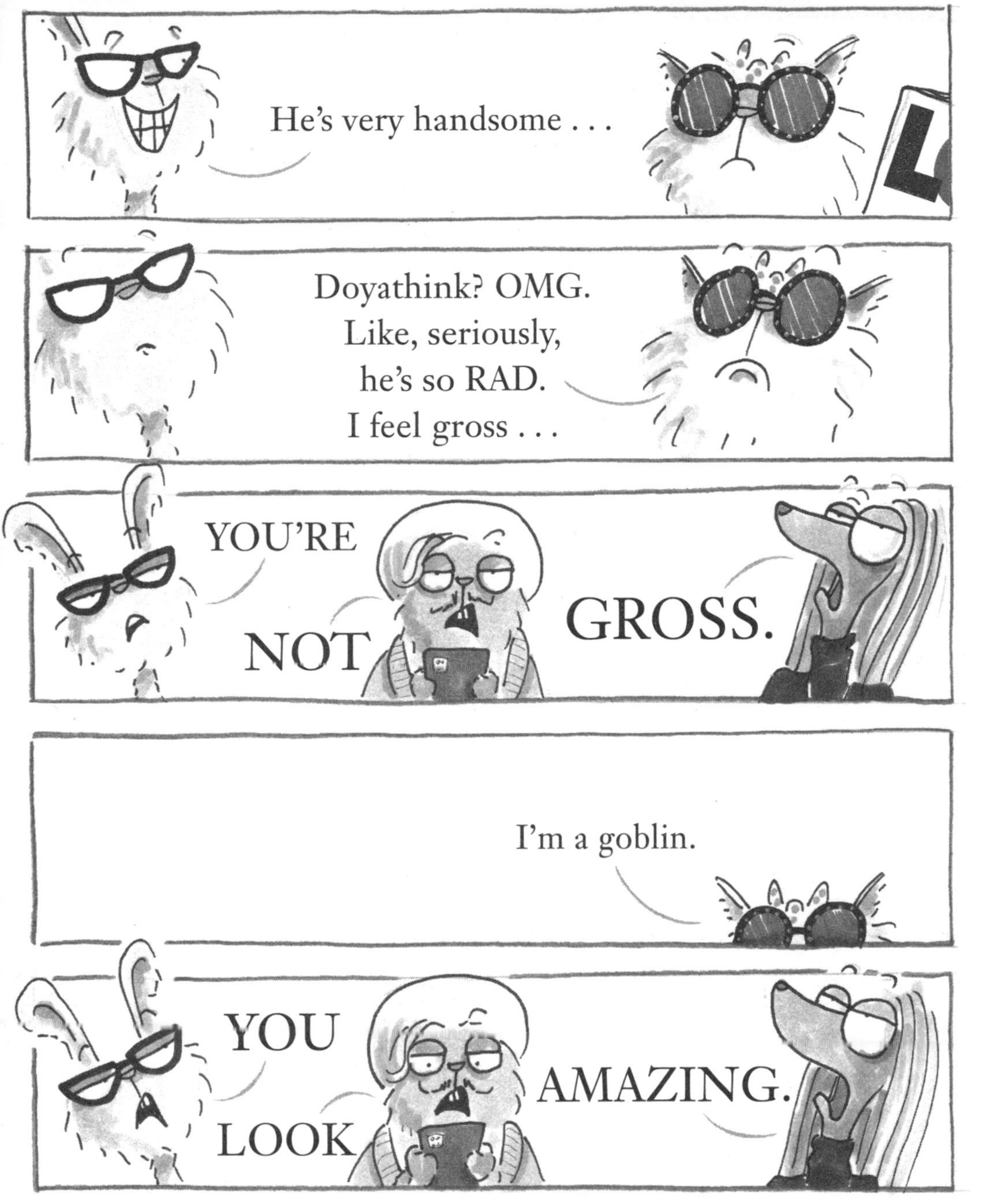
He's very handsome . . .
Doyathink? OMG.
Like, seriously,
he's so RAD.
I feel gross . . .
YOU'RE
NOT
GROSS.
I'm a goblin.
YOU
LOOK
AMAZING.

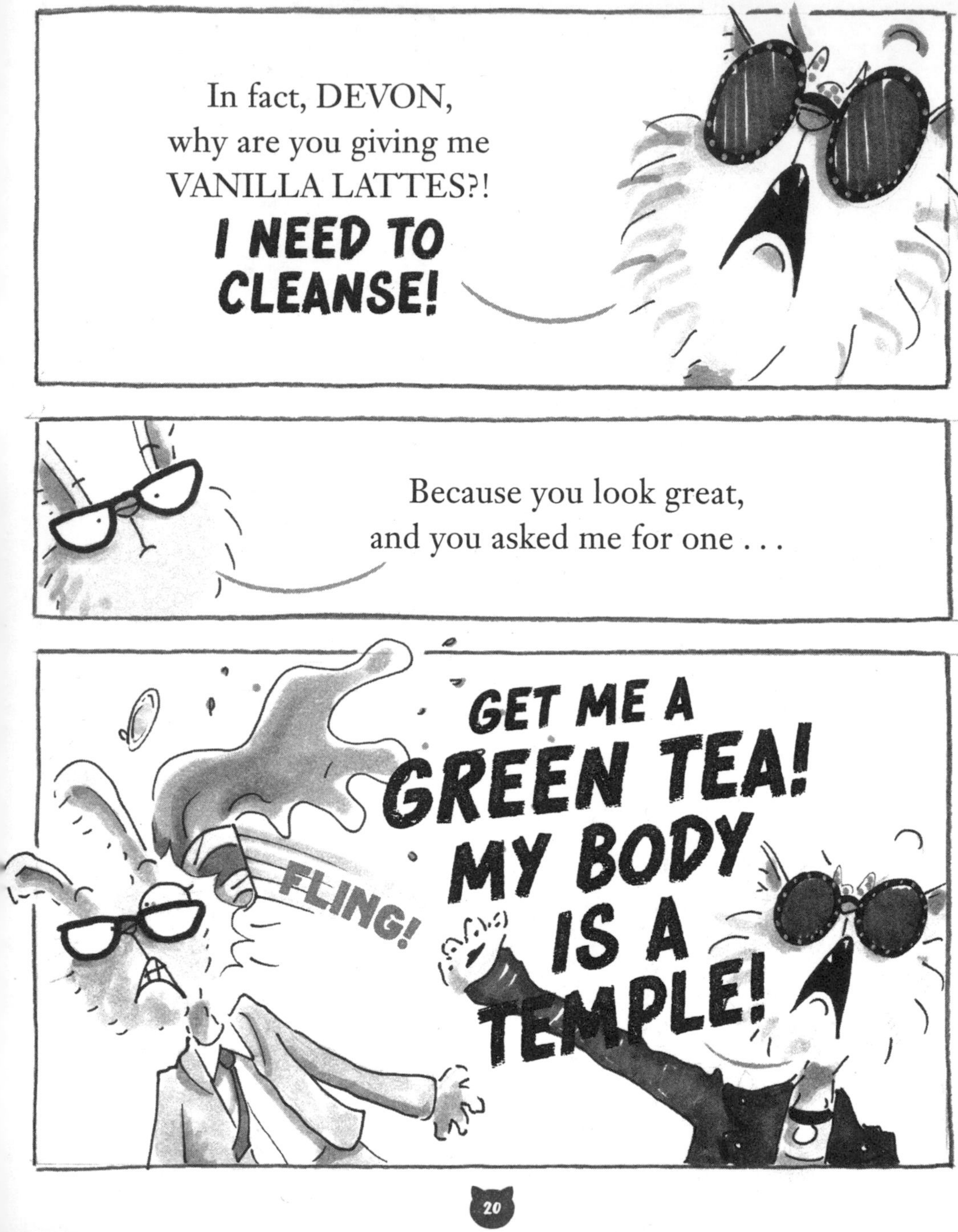

In fact, DEVON, why are you giving me VANILLA LATTES?!
I NEED TO CLEANSE!
Because you look great, and you asked me for one . . .
FLING!
GET ME A GREEN TEA! MY BODY IS A TEMPLE!

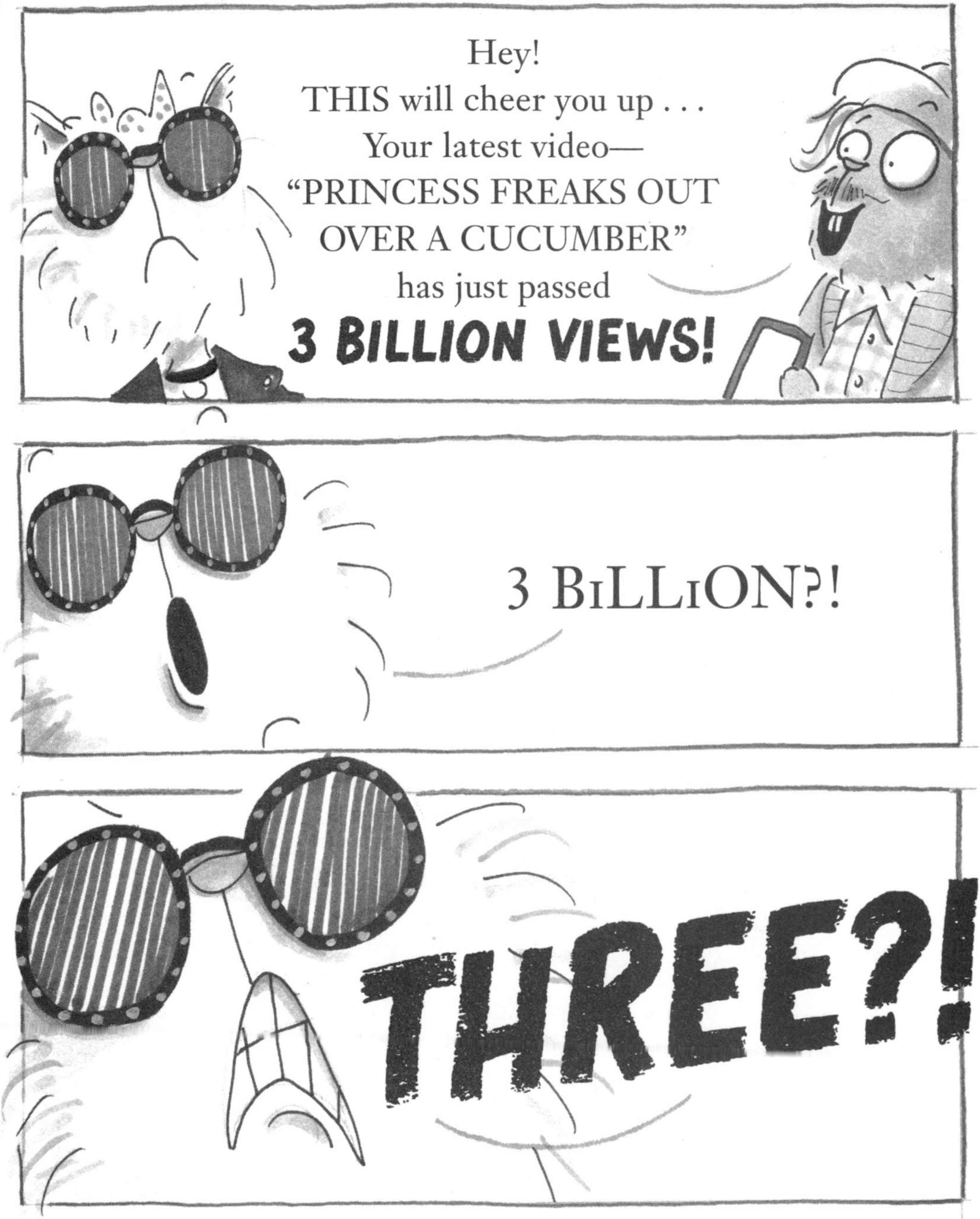
Hey!
THIS will cheer you up . . .
Your latest video—
"PRINCESS FREAKS OUT OVER A CUCUMBER"
has just passed
3 BILLION VIEWS!
3 BiLLiON?!
THREE?!

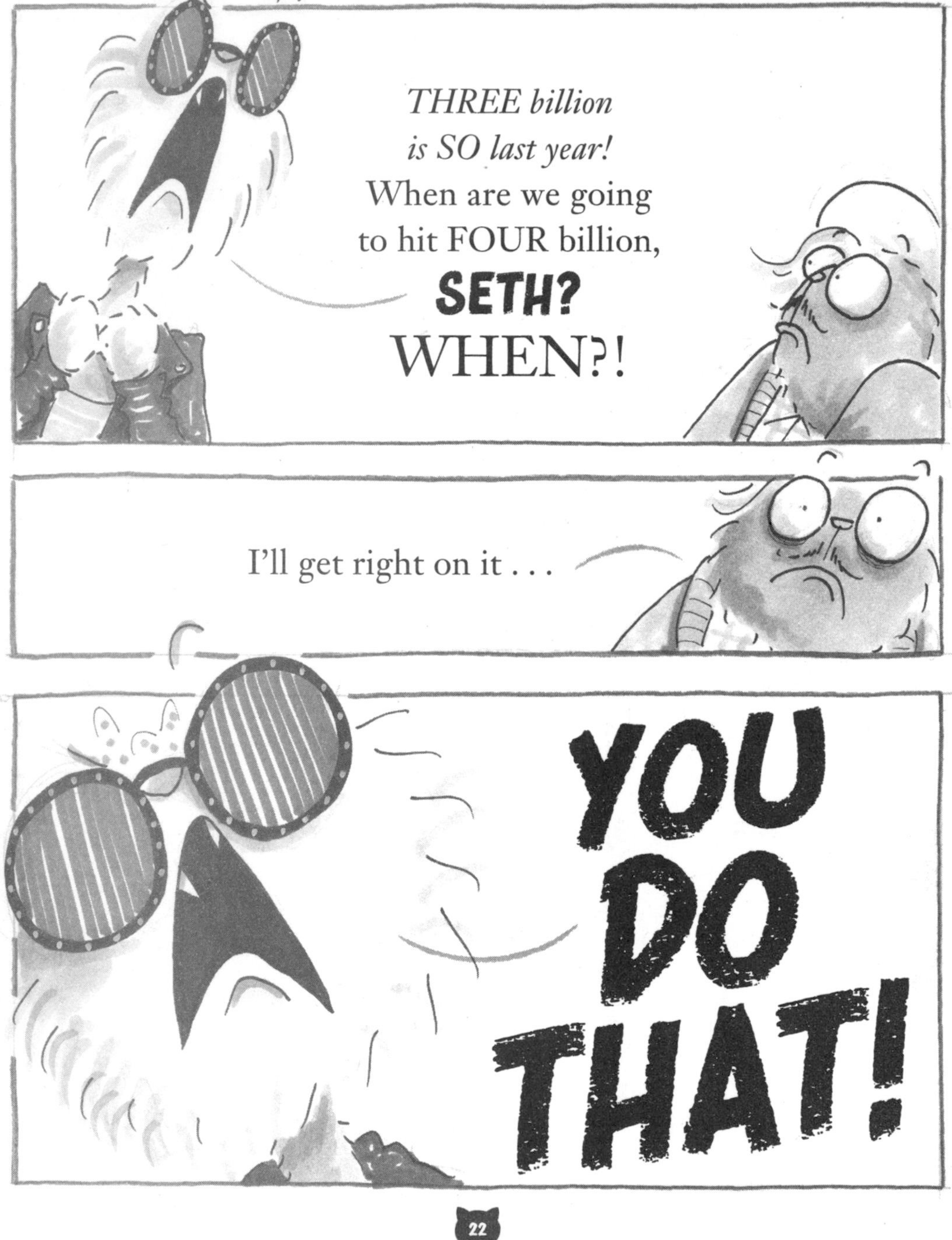
THREE billion is SO last year! When are we going to hit FOUR billion, **SETH?** WHEN?!
I'll get right on it . . .
YOU DO THAT!

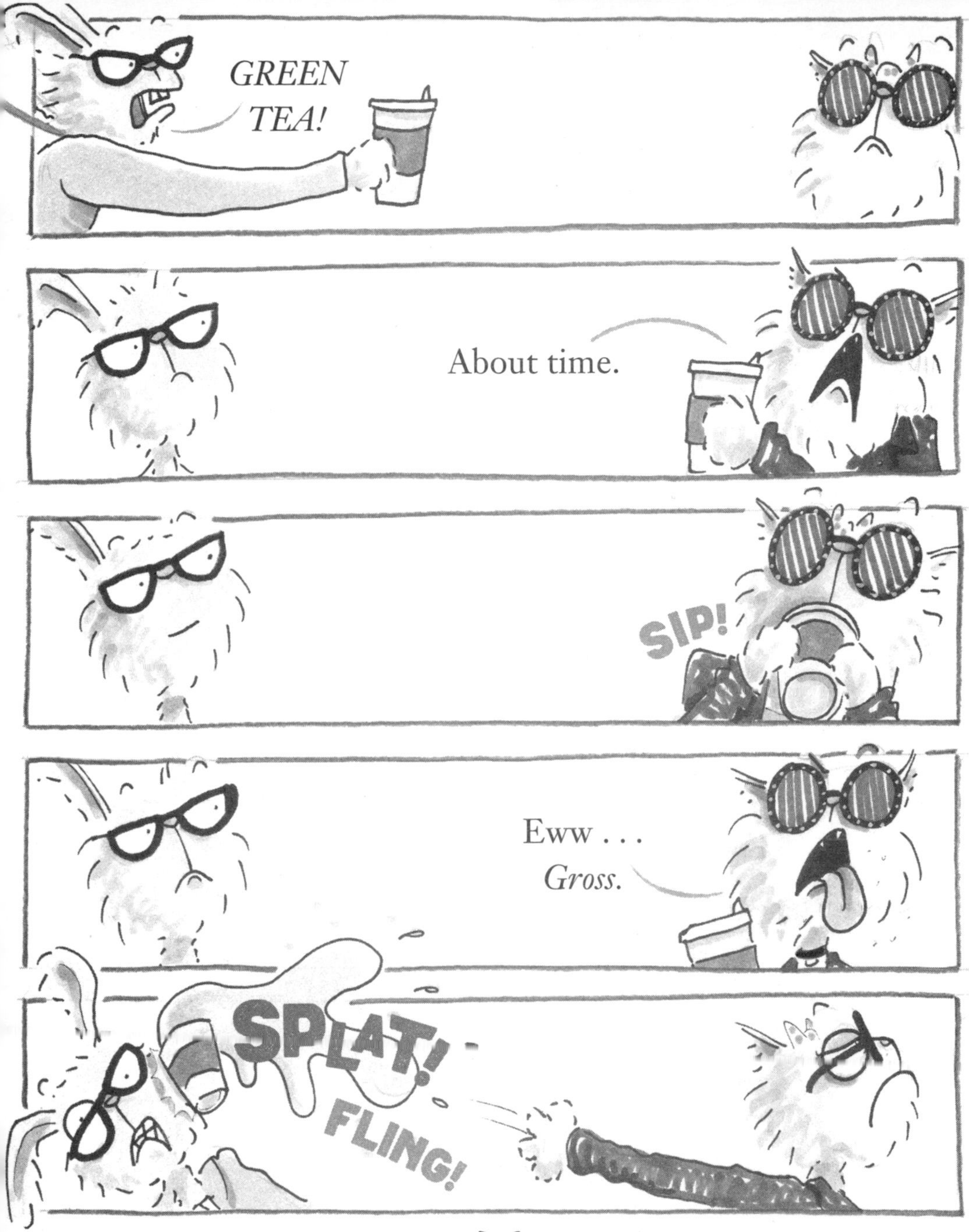
GREEN TEA!
About time.
SIP!
Eww . . .
Gross.
SPLAT!
FLING!

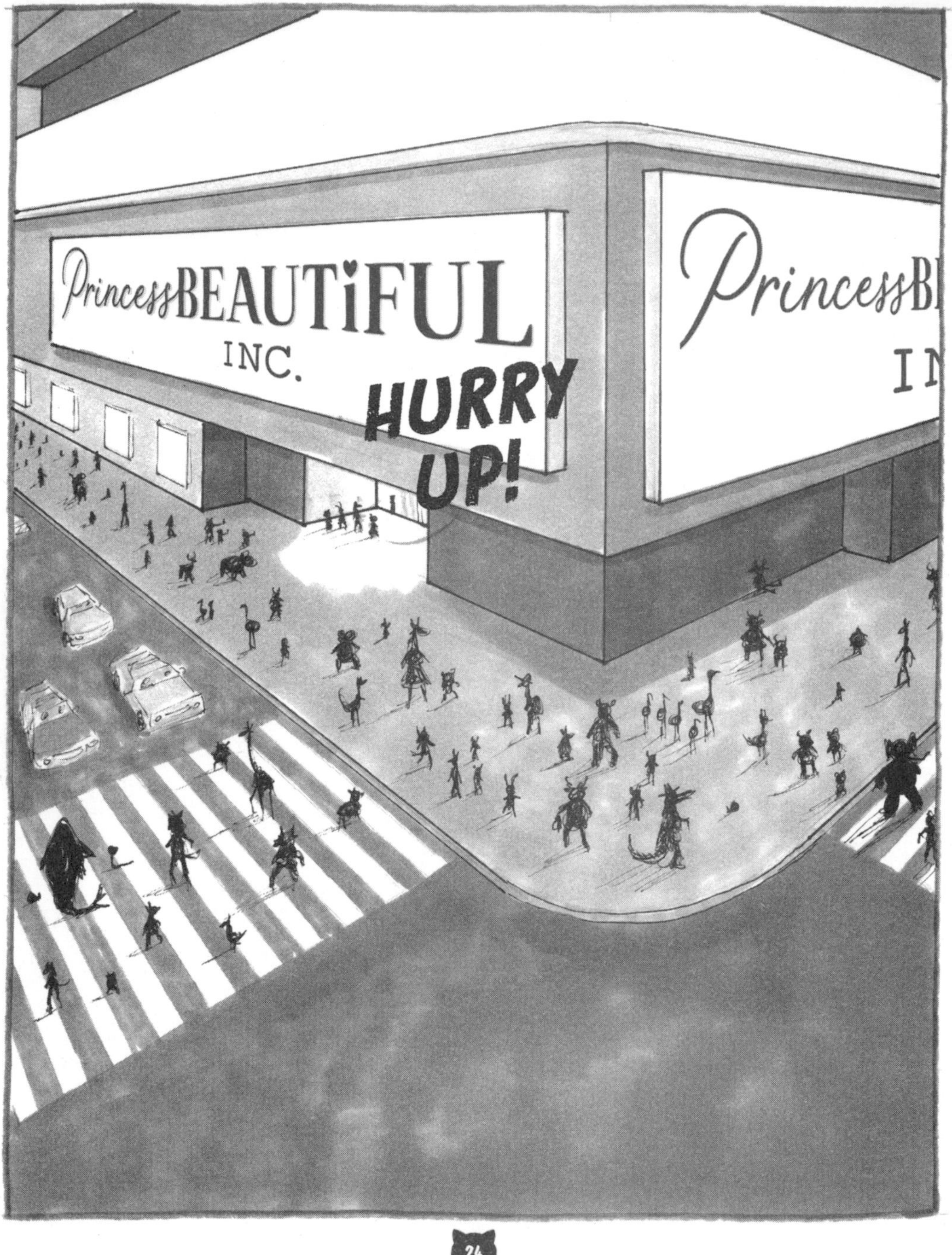
PrincessBEAUTiFUL
INC.
HURRY UP!
PrincessBI
IN

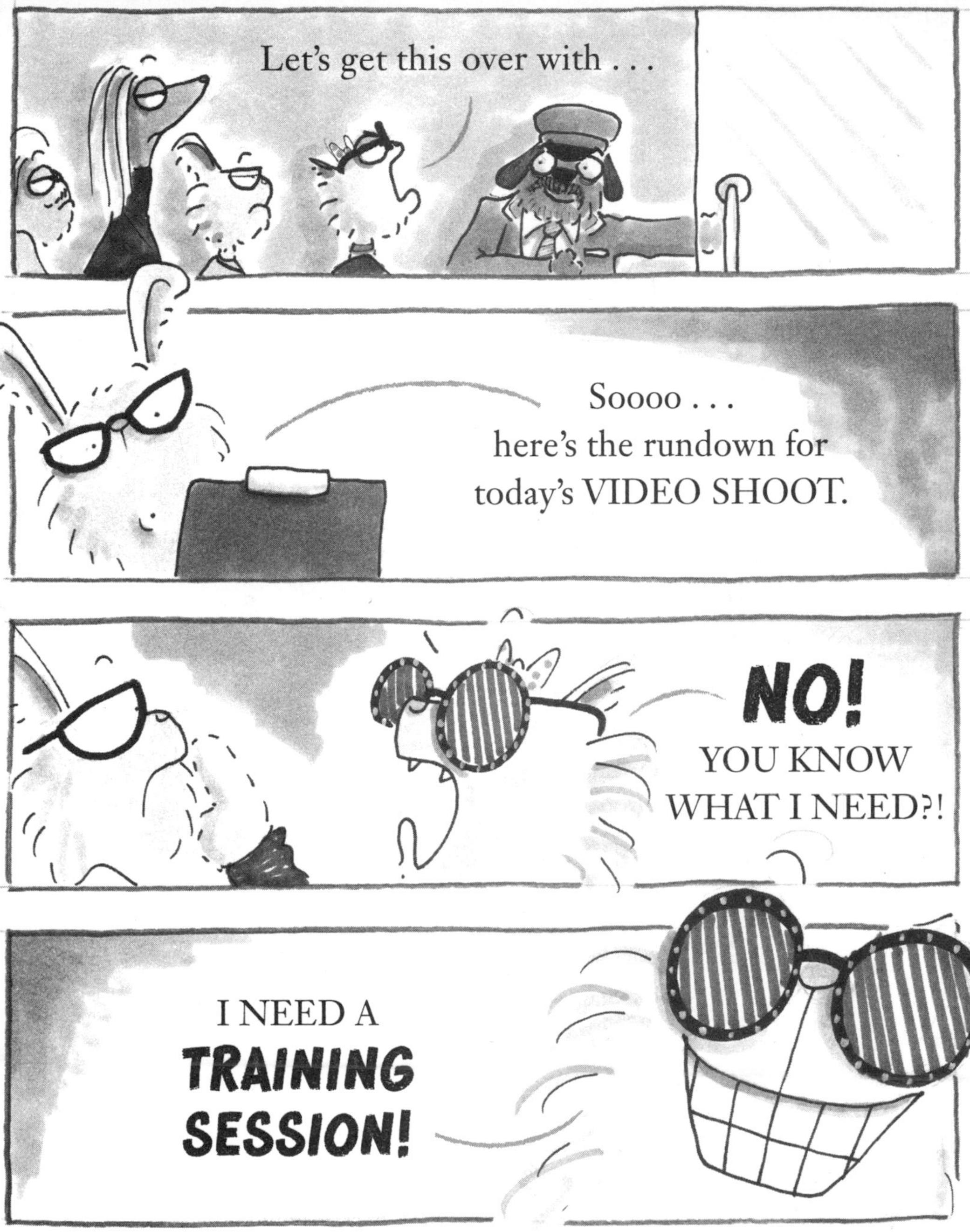
Let's get this over with . . .
Soooo . . . here's the rundown for today's VIDEO SHOOT.
NO! YOU KNOW WHAT I NEED?!
I NEED A TRAINING SESSION!

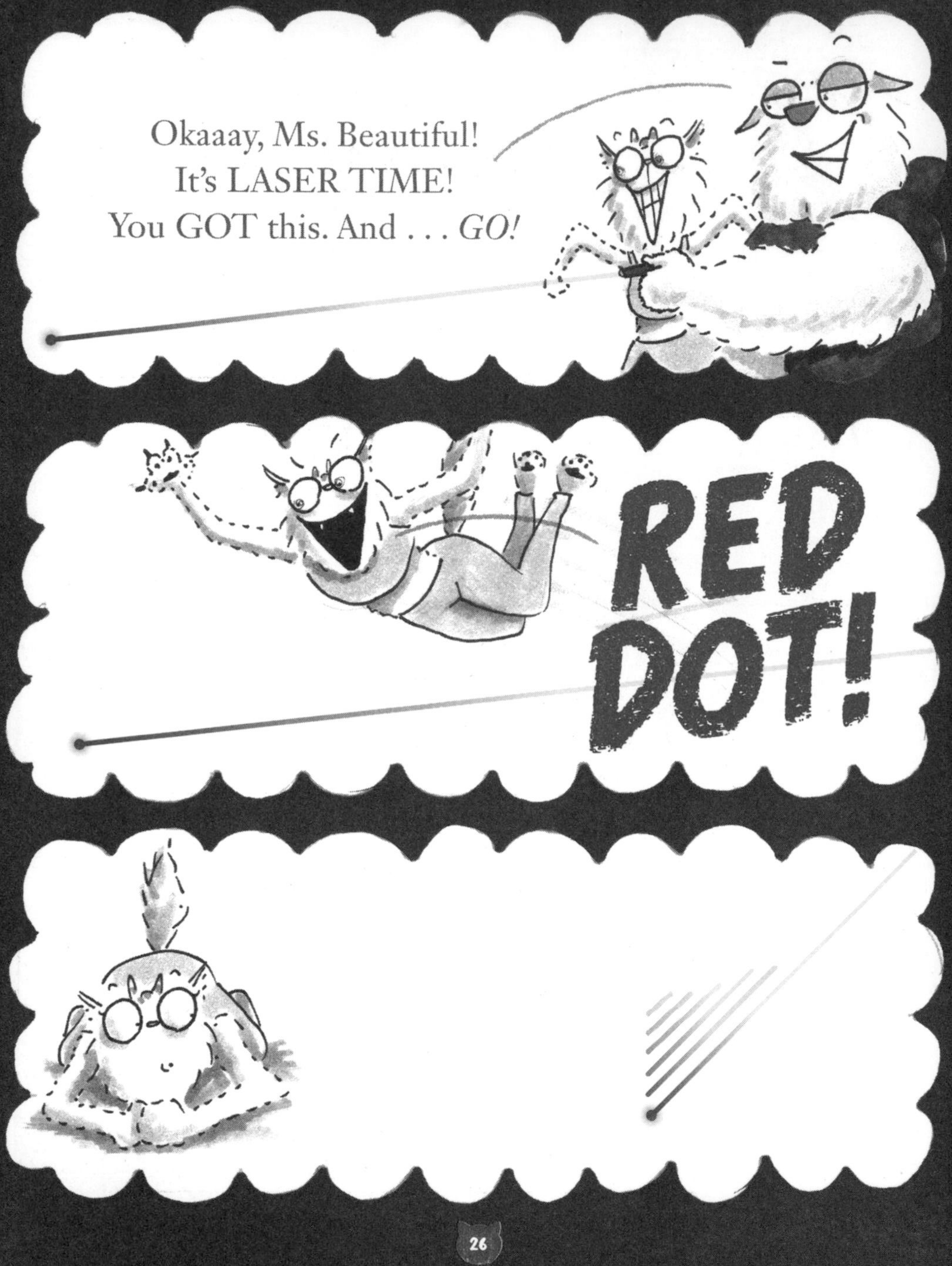
Okaaay, Ms. Beautiful! It's LASER TIME! You GOT this. And . . . *GO!*
RED DOT!

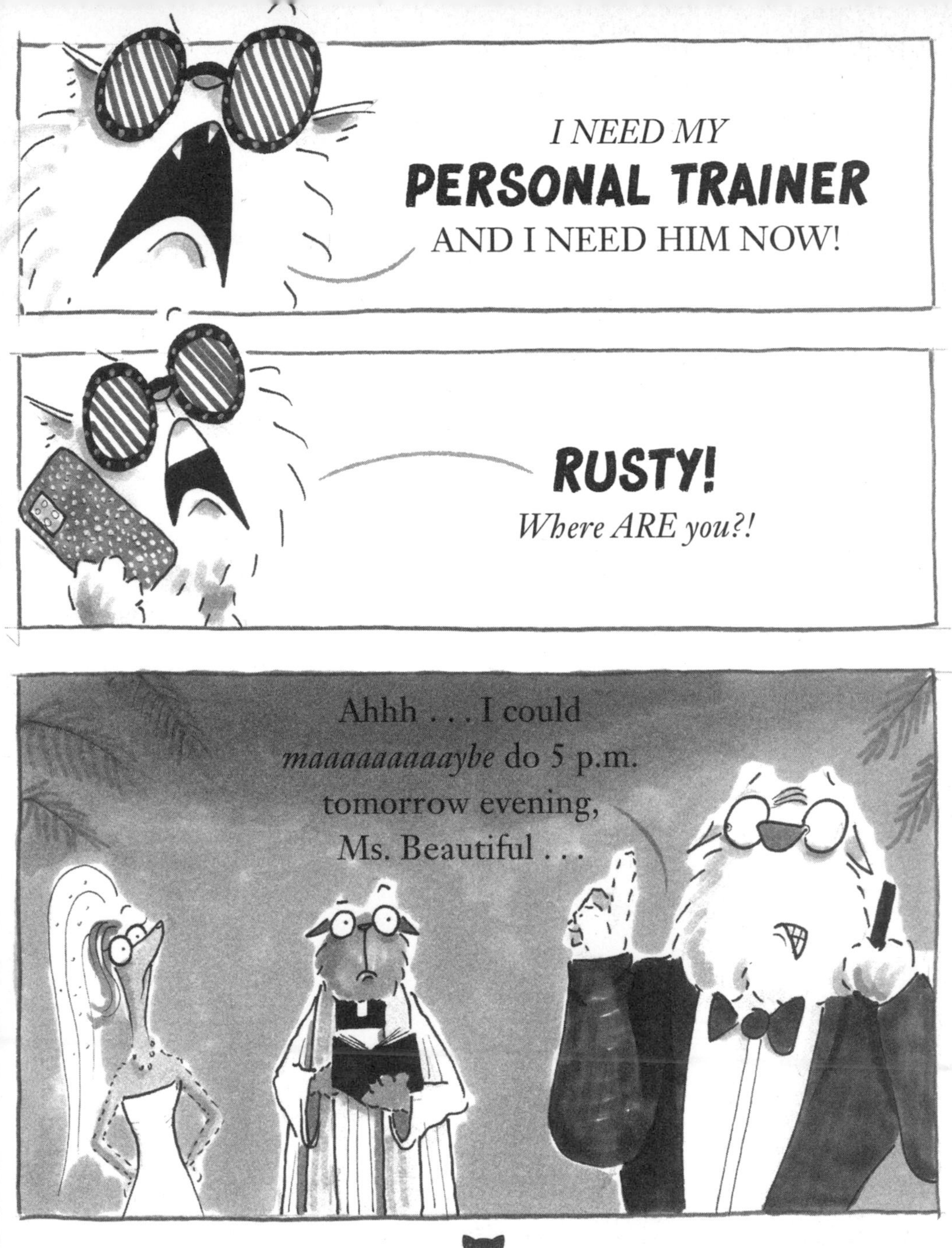
I NEED MY
PERSONAL TRAINER
AND I NEED HIM NOW!
RUSTY!
Where ARE you?!
Ahhh . . . I could *maaaaaaaaaybe* do 5 p.m. tomorrow evening, Ms. Beautiful . . .

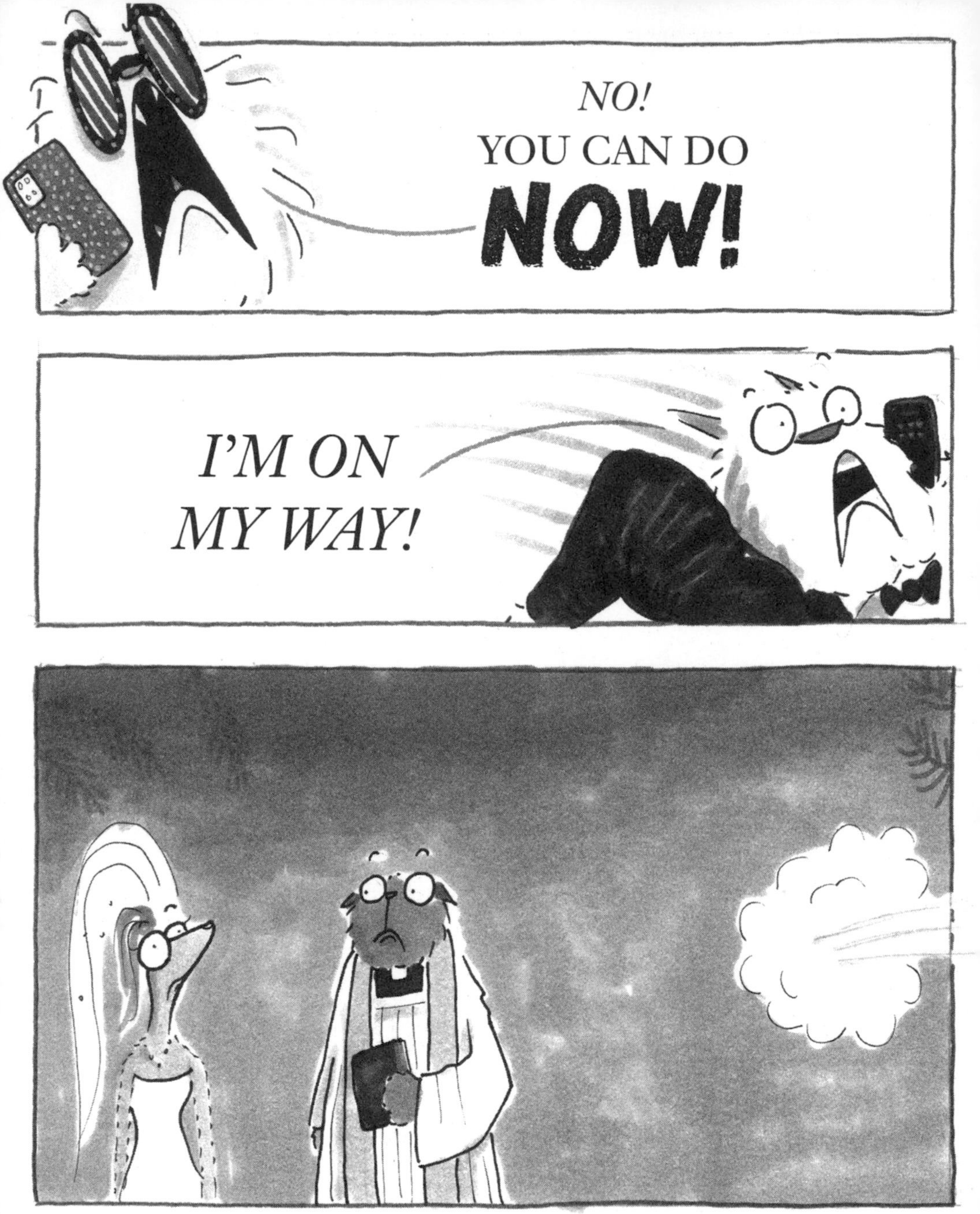
NO!
YOU CAN DO
NOW!
I'M ON
MY WAY!

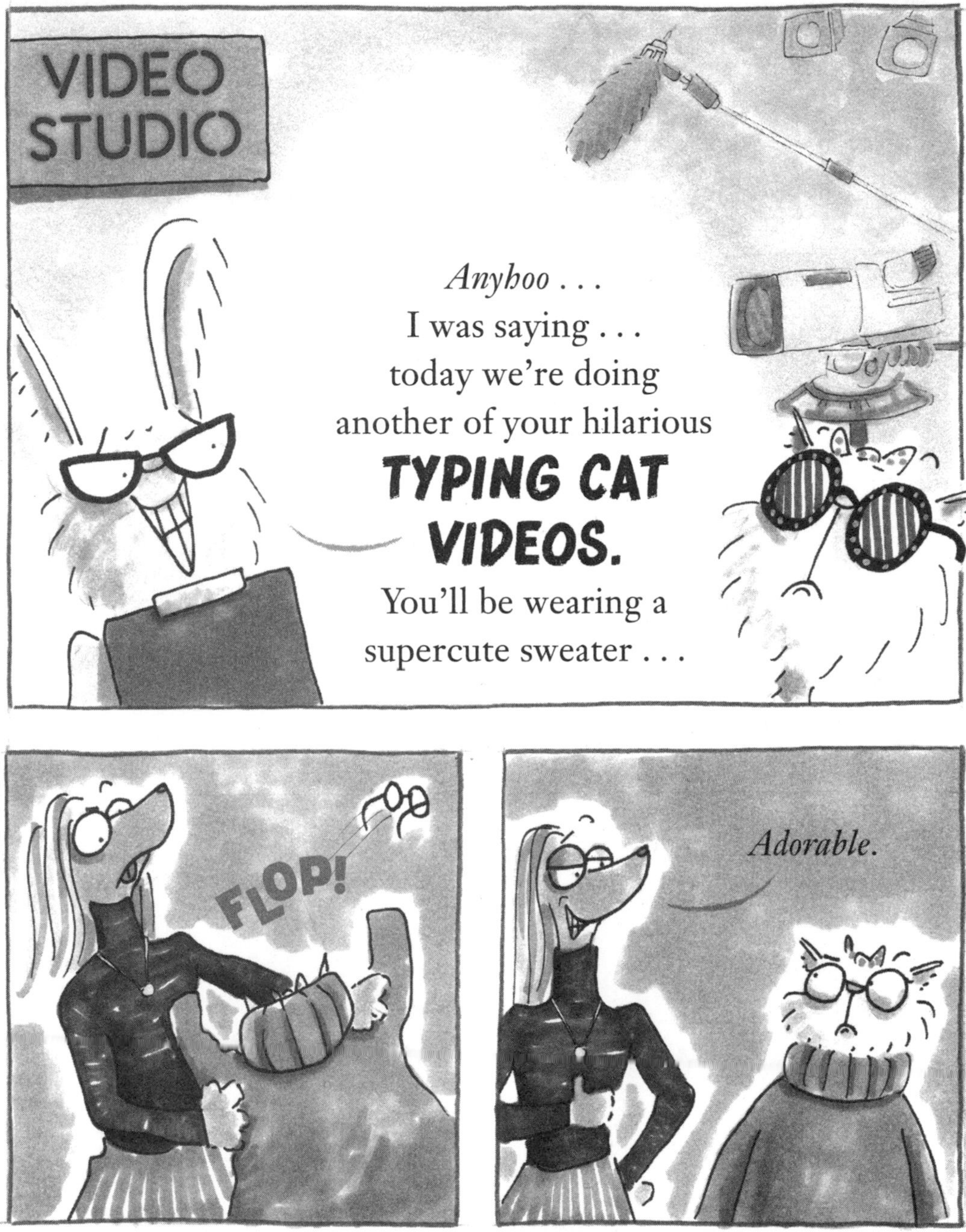
VIDEO STUDIO
Anyhoo . . .
I was saying . . .
today we're doing
another of your hilarious
TYPING CAT VIDEOS.
You'll be wearing a
supercute sweater . . .
FLOP!
Adorable.

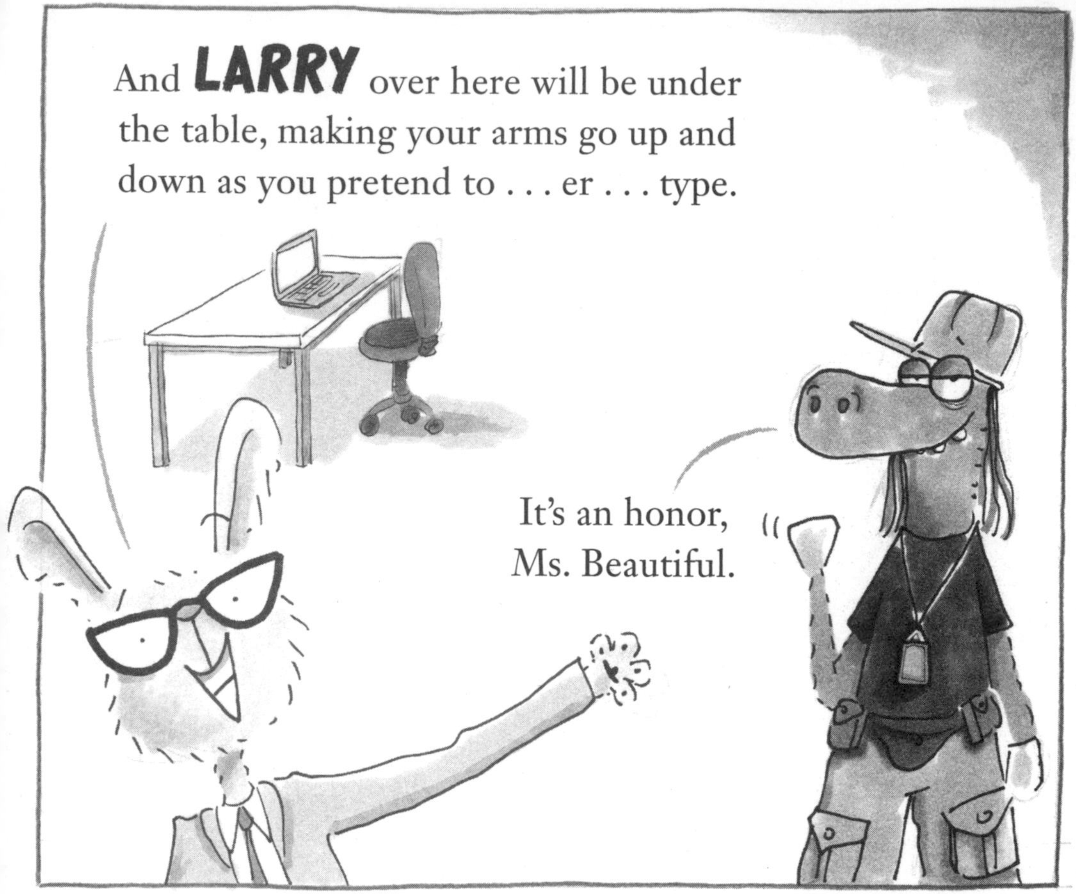
And LARRY over here will be under the table, making your arms go up and down as you pretend to . . . er . . . type.
It's an honor, Ms. Beautiful.

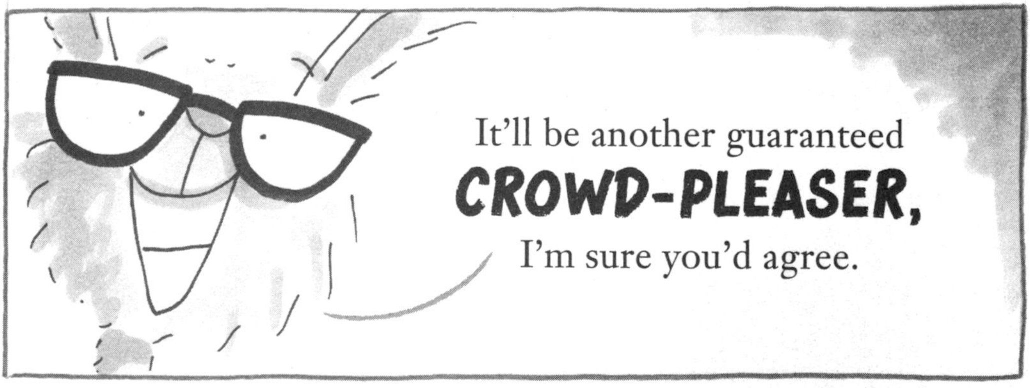
It'll be another guaranteed CROWD-PLEASER, I'm sure you'd agree.

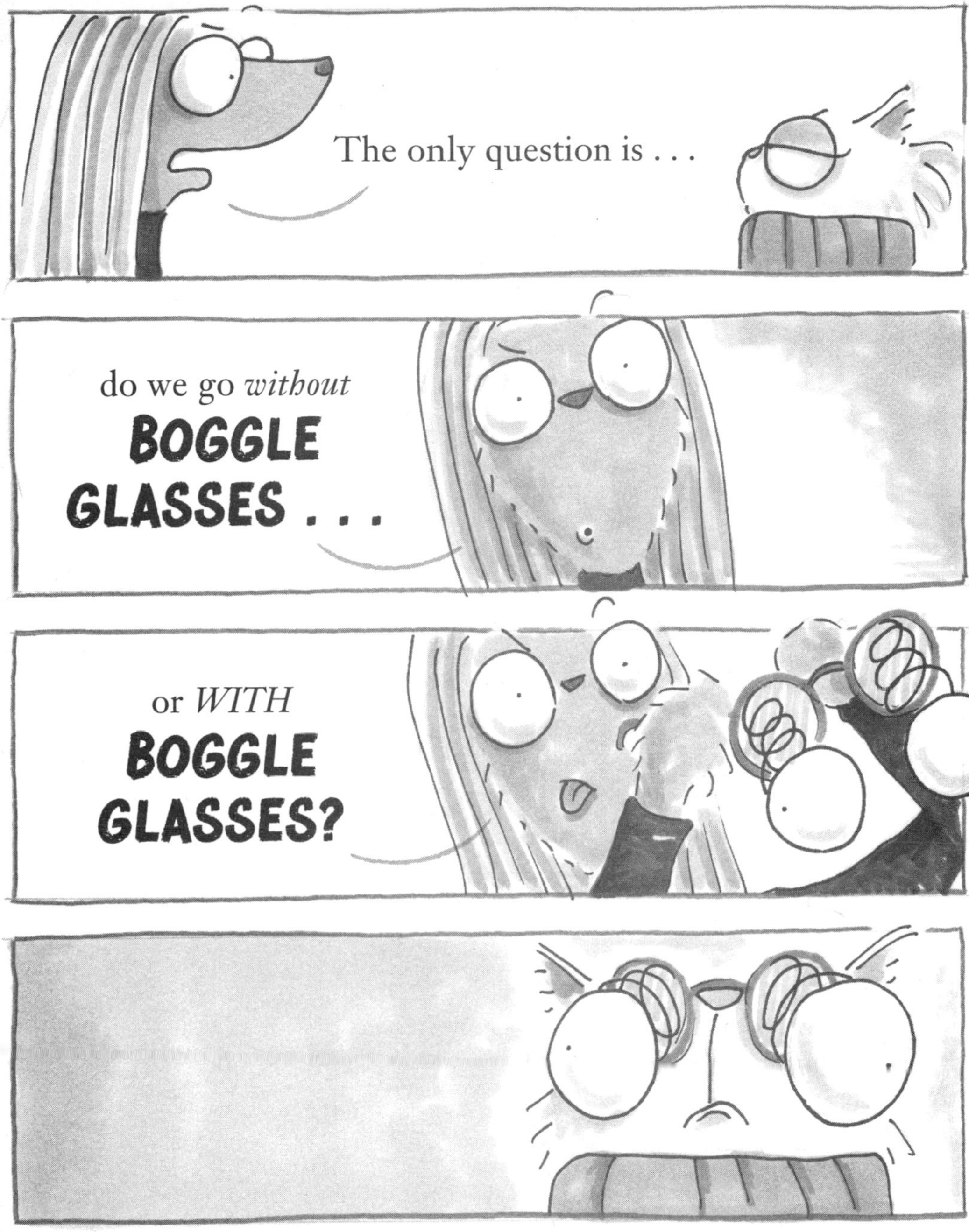

The only question is . . .
do we go *without*
BOGGLE GLASSES . . .
or *WITH*
BOGGLE GLASSES?

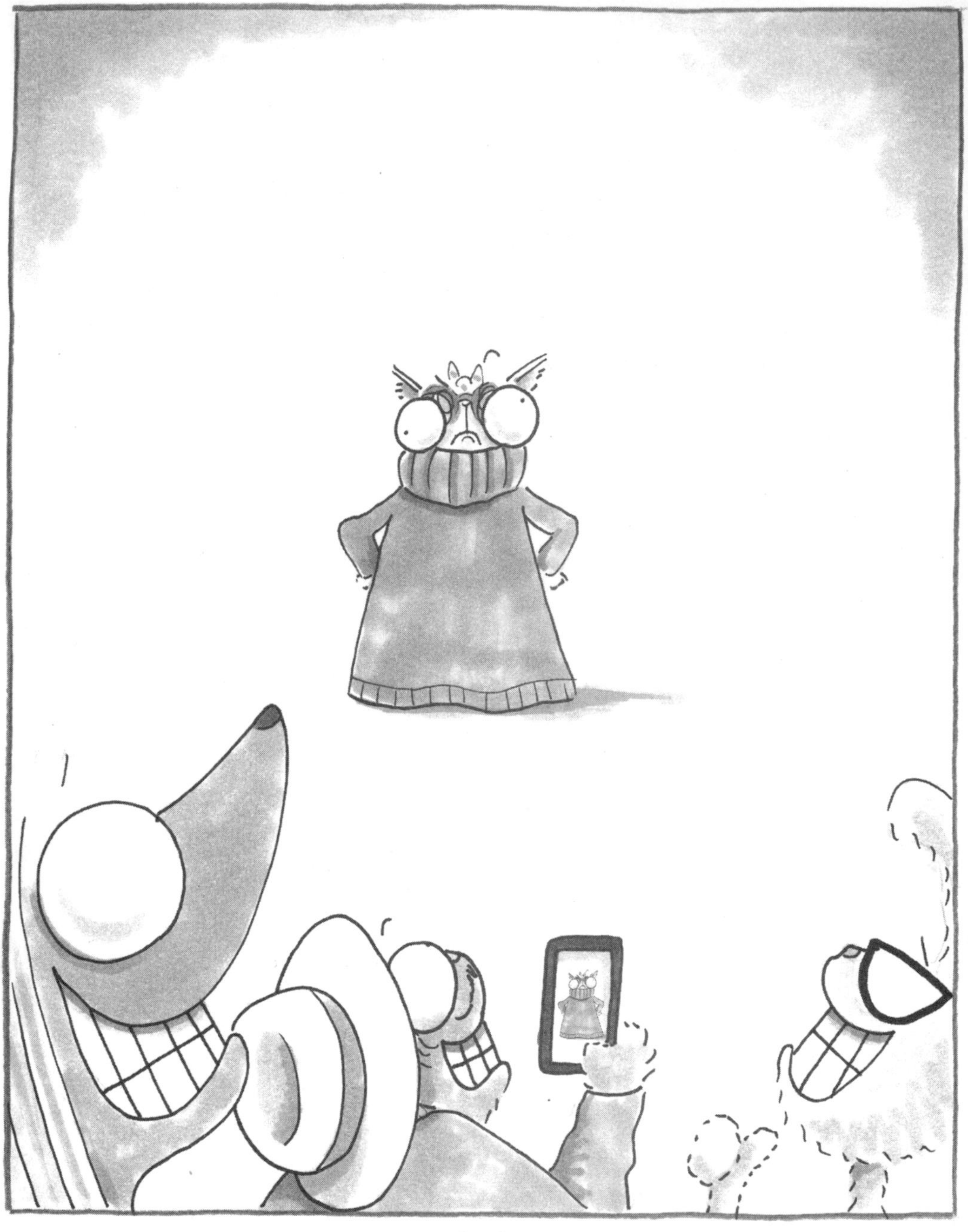

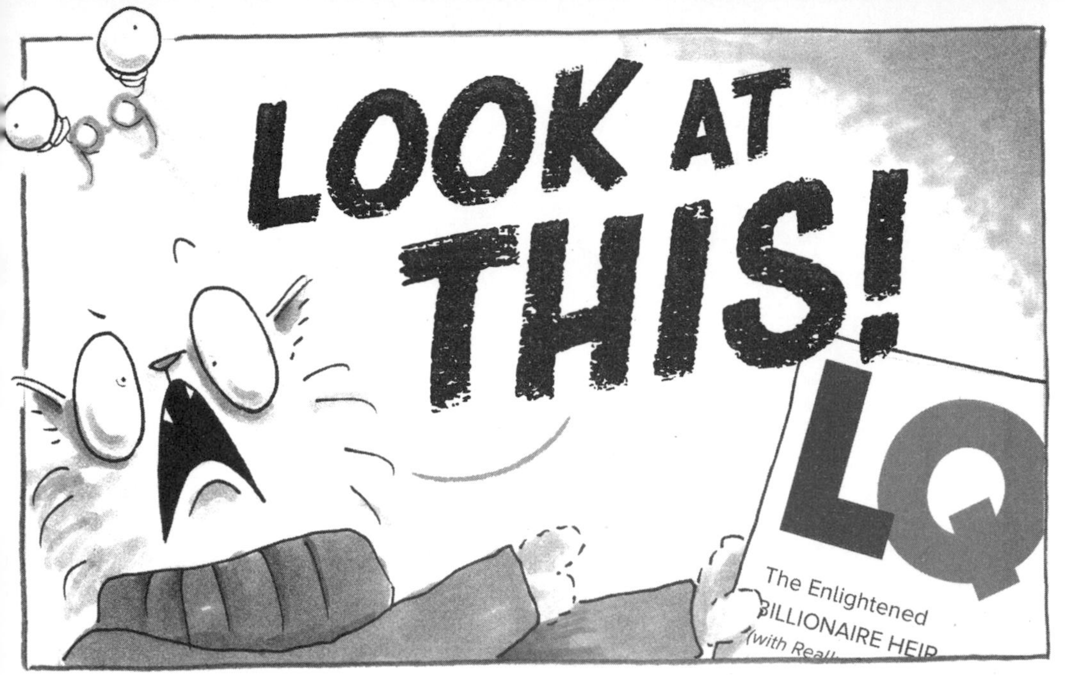
LOOK AT THIS!
LQ
The Enlightened
BILLIONAIRE HEIR
(with Reall

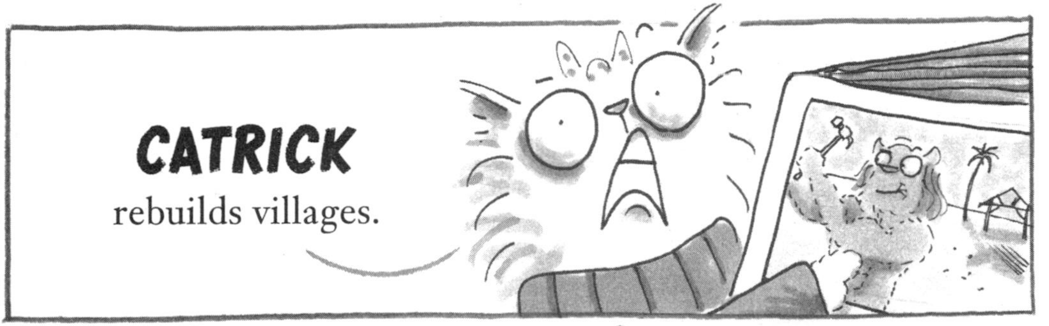
CATRICK
rebuilds villages.

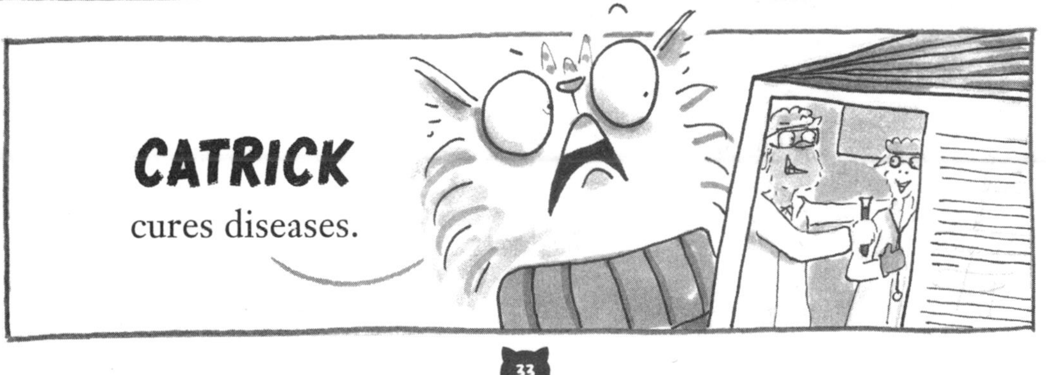
CATRICK
cures diseases.

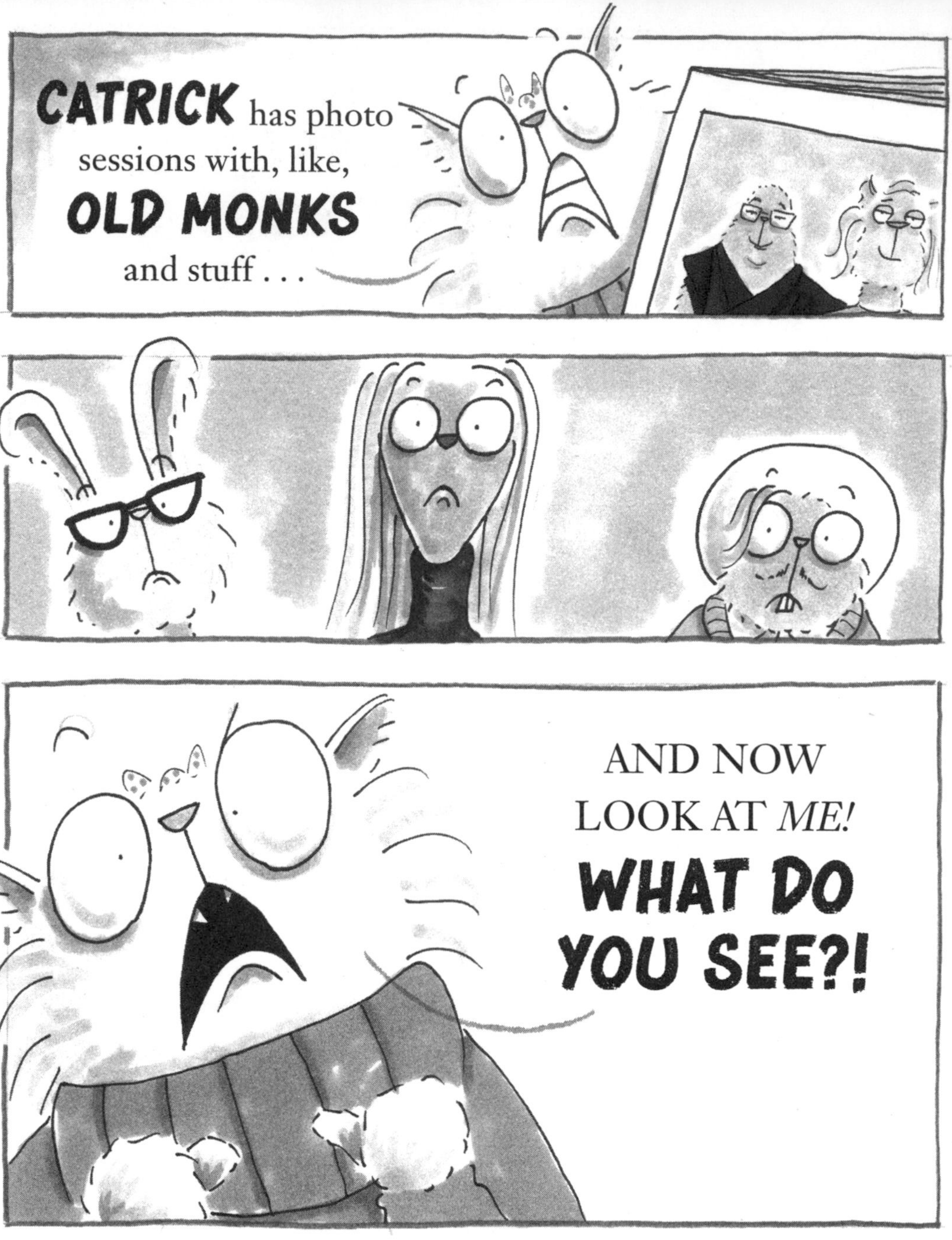
CATRICK has photo sessions with, like, OLD MONKS and stuff . . .
AND NOW LOOK AT *ME!*
WHAT DO YOU SEE?!

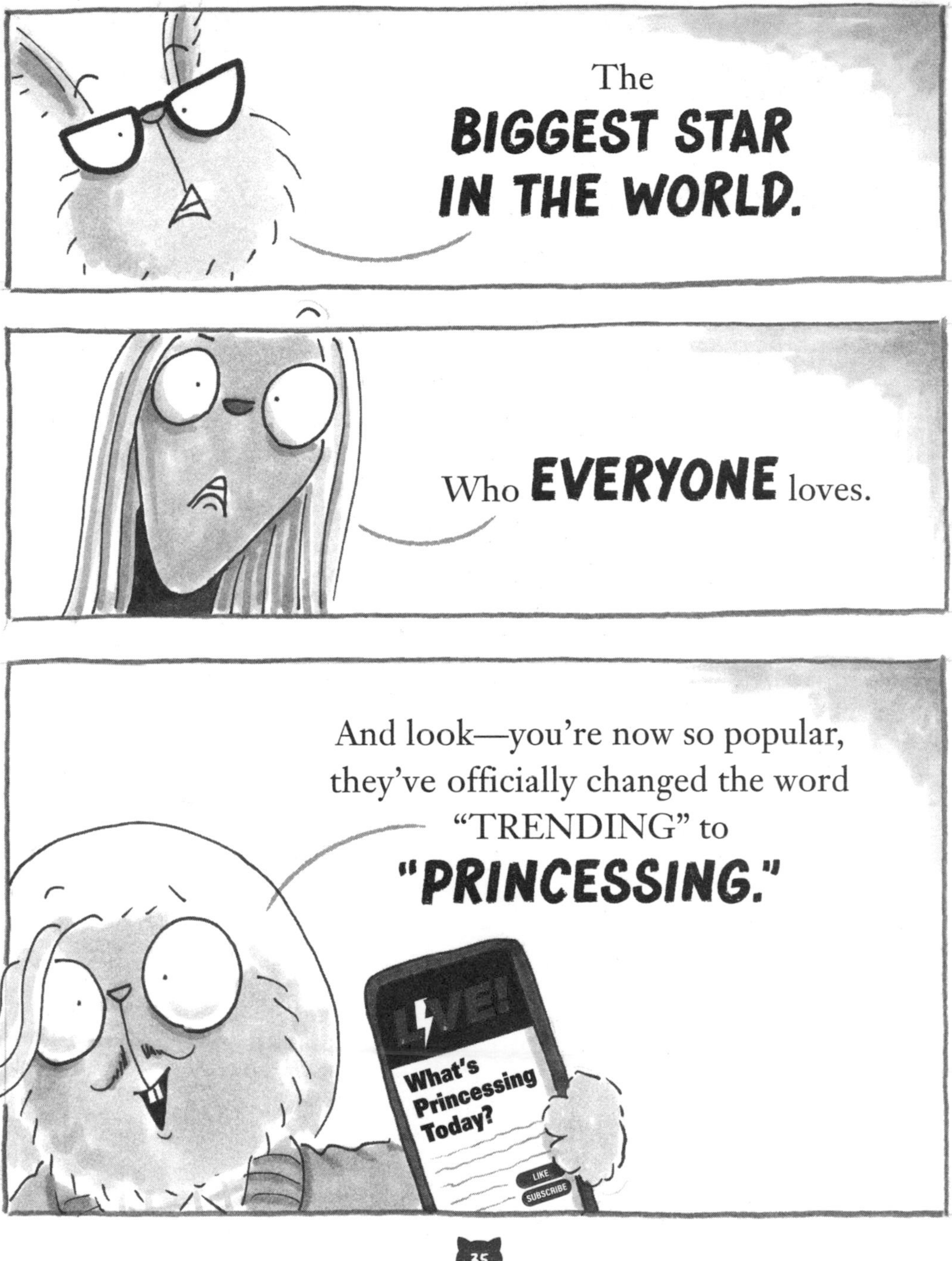
The BIGGEST STAR IN THE WORLD.
Who EVERYONE loves.
And look—you're now so popular, they've officially changed the word "TRENDING" to "PRINCESSING."
LIVE!
What's Princessing Today?
LIKE
SUBSCRIBE

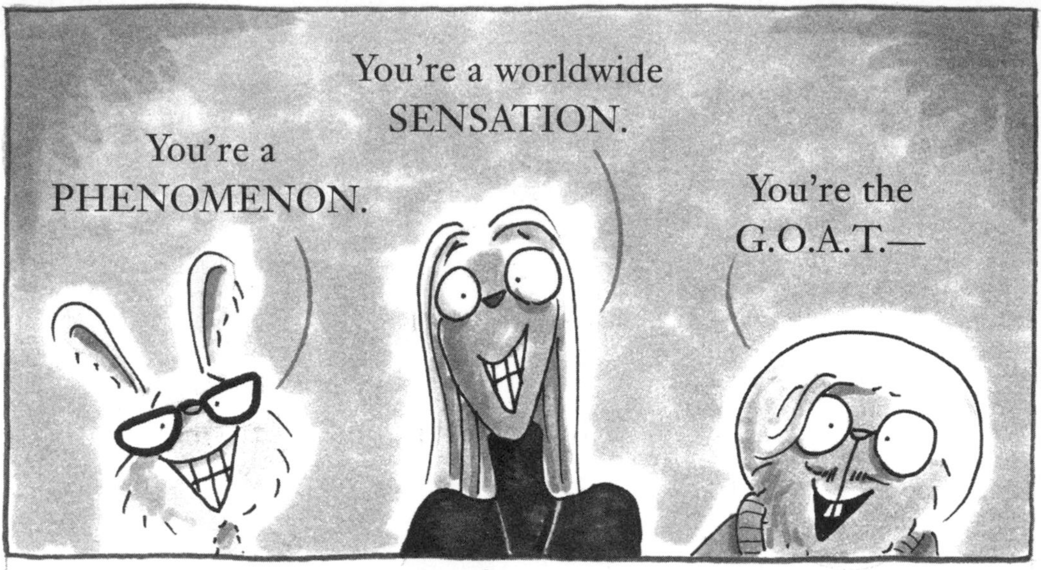
You're a
PHENOMENON.
You're a worldwide
SENSATION.
You're the
G.O.A.T.—

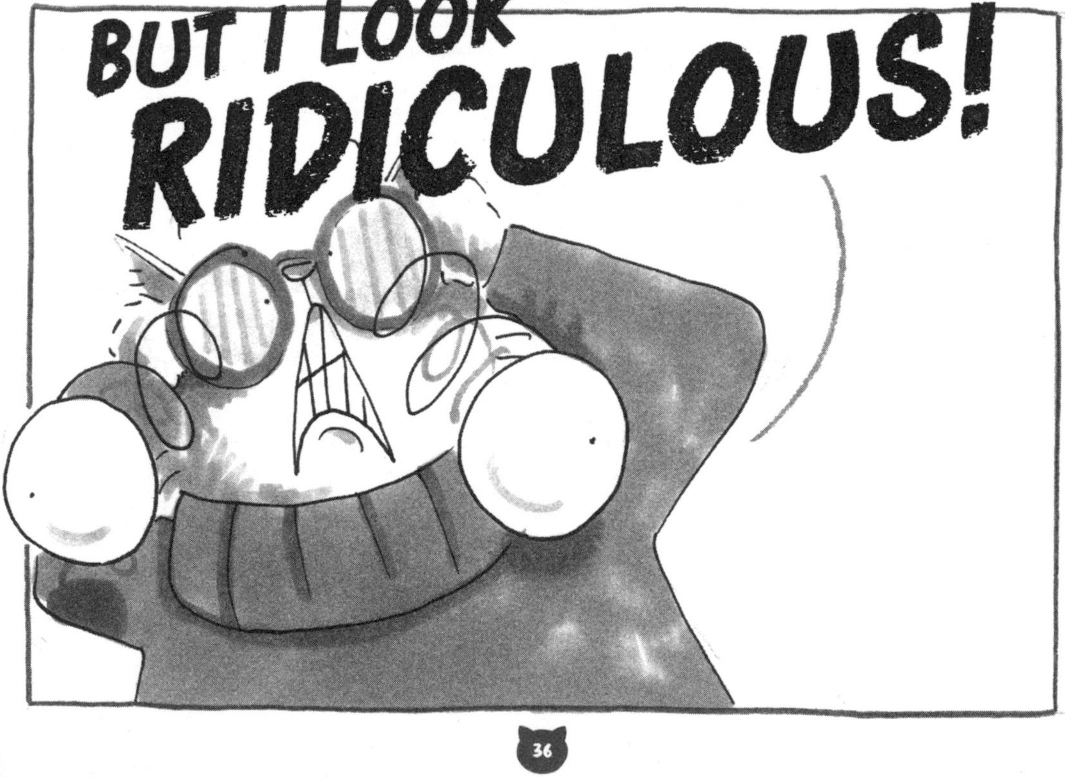
BUT I LOOK
RIDICULOUS!

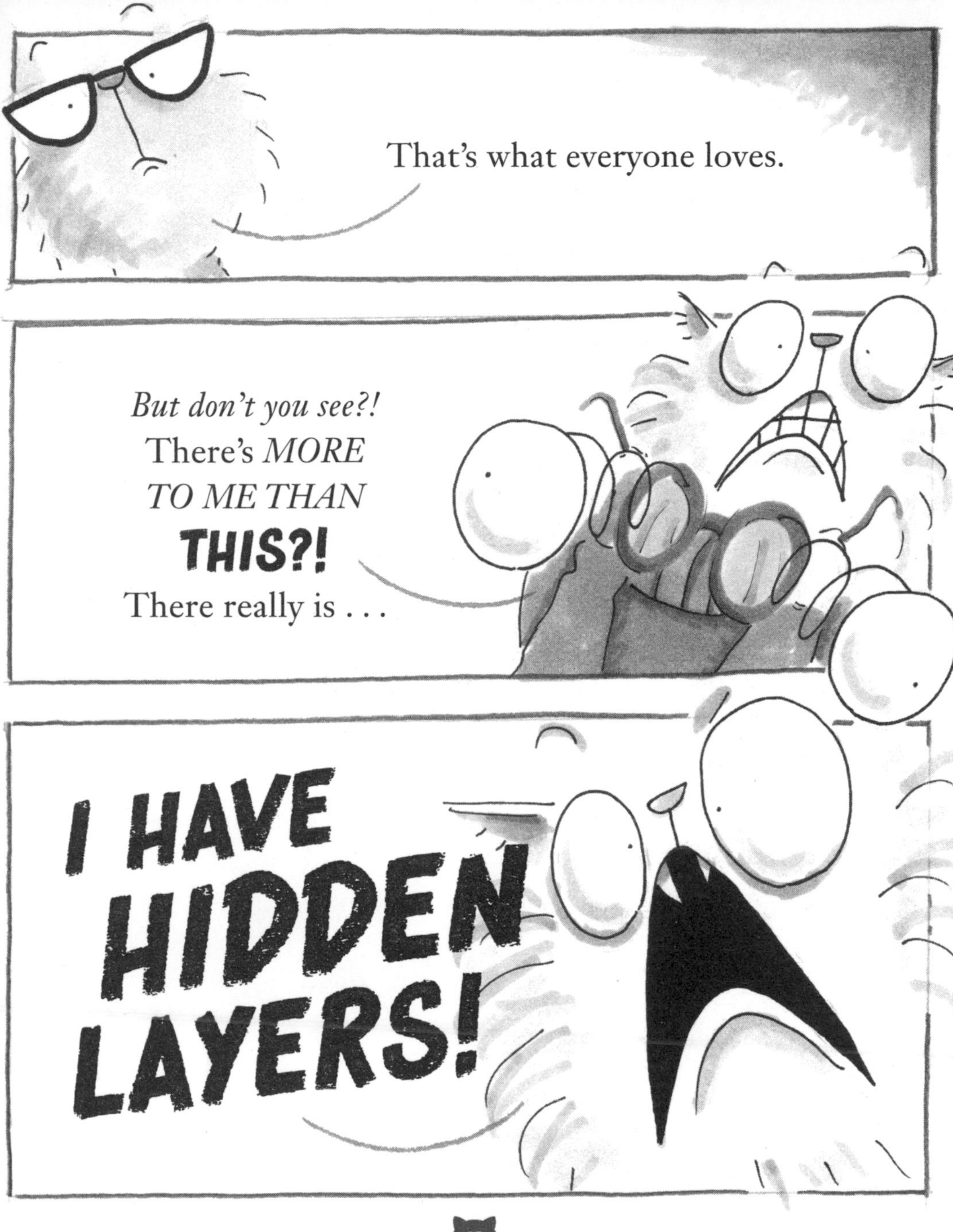
That's what everyone loves.
But don't you see?! There's *MORE TO ME THAN* **THIS?!** There really is . . .
I HAVE HIDDEN LAYERS!

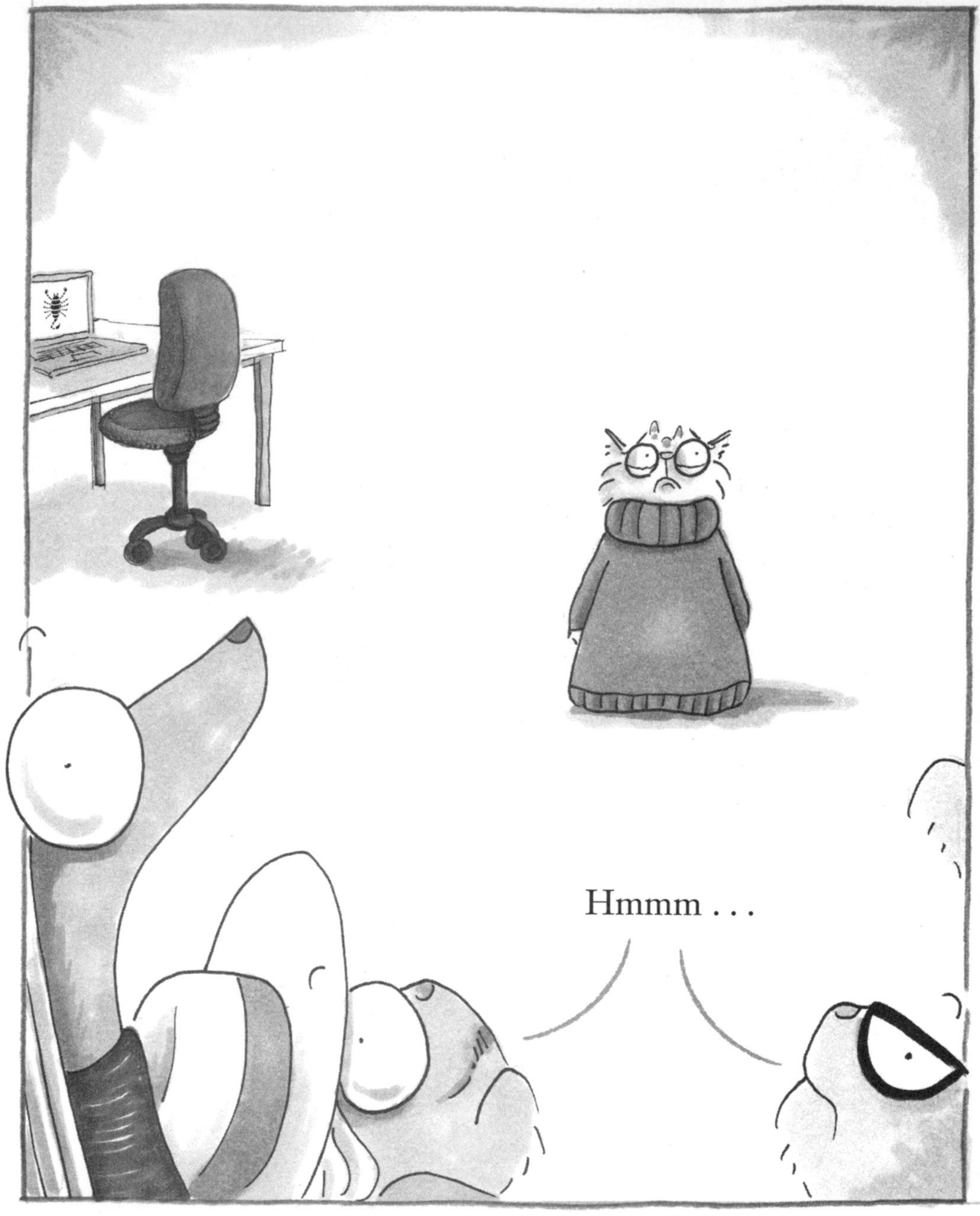
Hmmm . . .

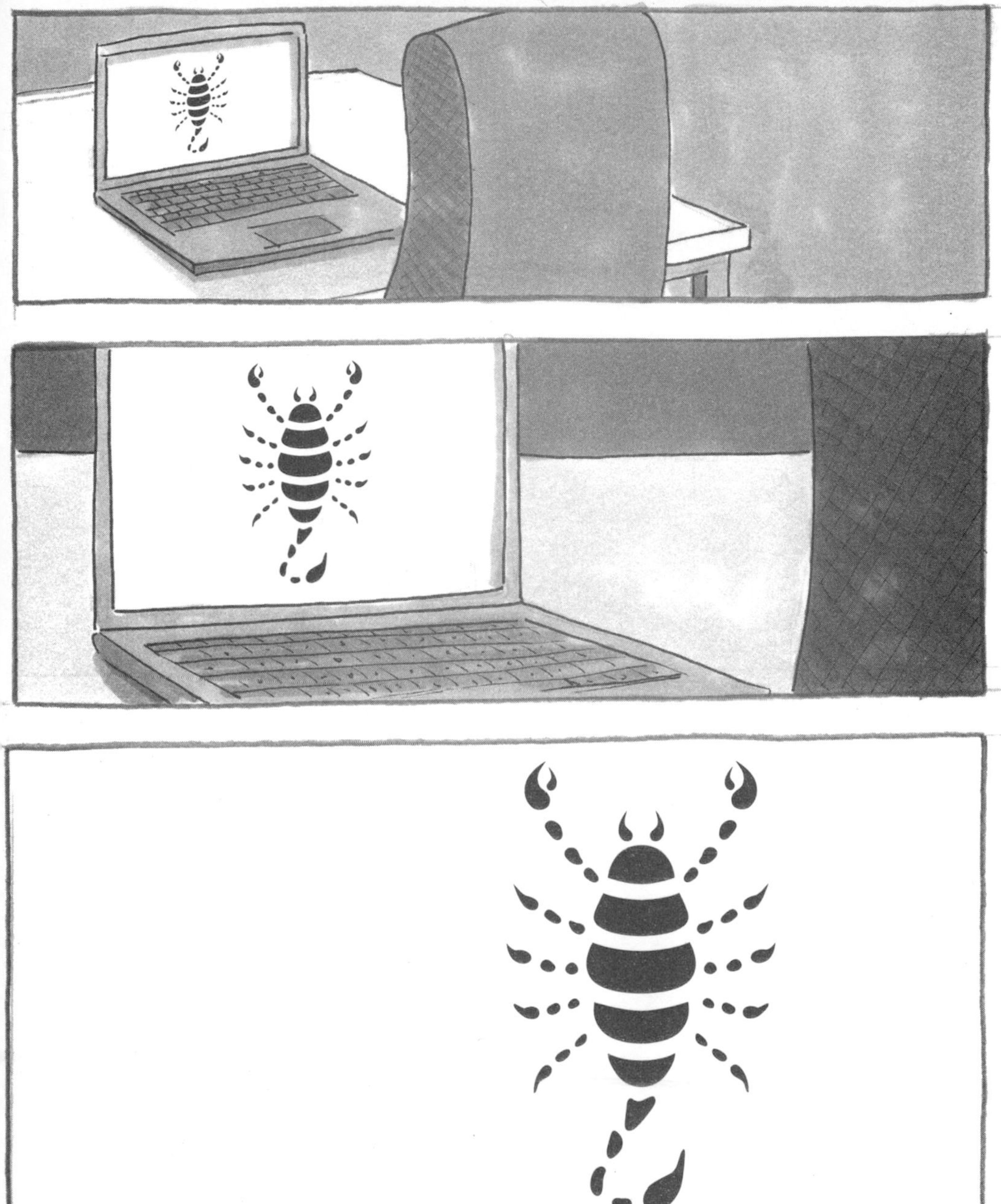

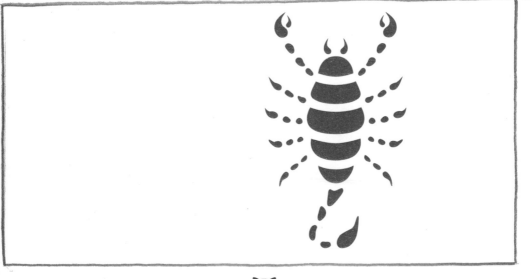

Two

THE FUSE IS LIT

FILMING IN PROGRESS

OK!
QUIET ON SET!
"Hilarious Cat Video #412."
Uh, take #1 . . .
Here we go . . . again.

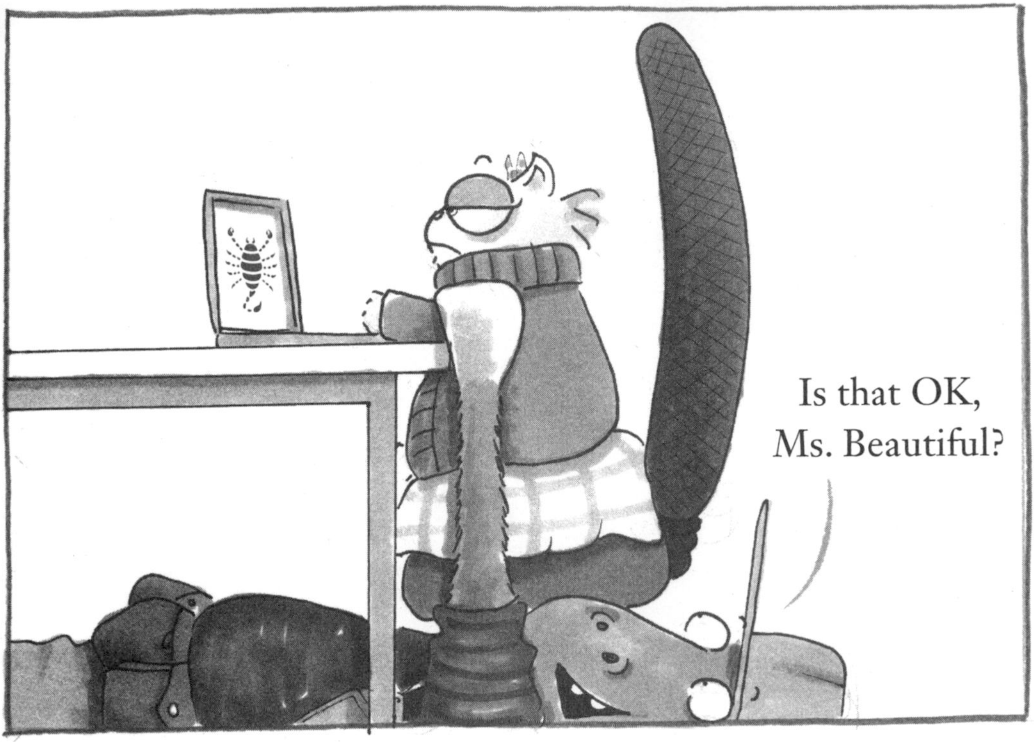
Is that OK,
Ms. Beautiful?

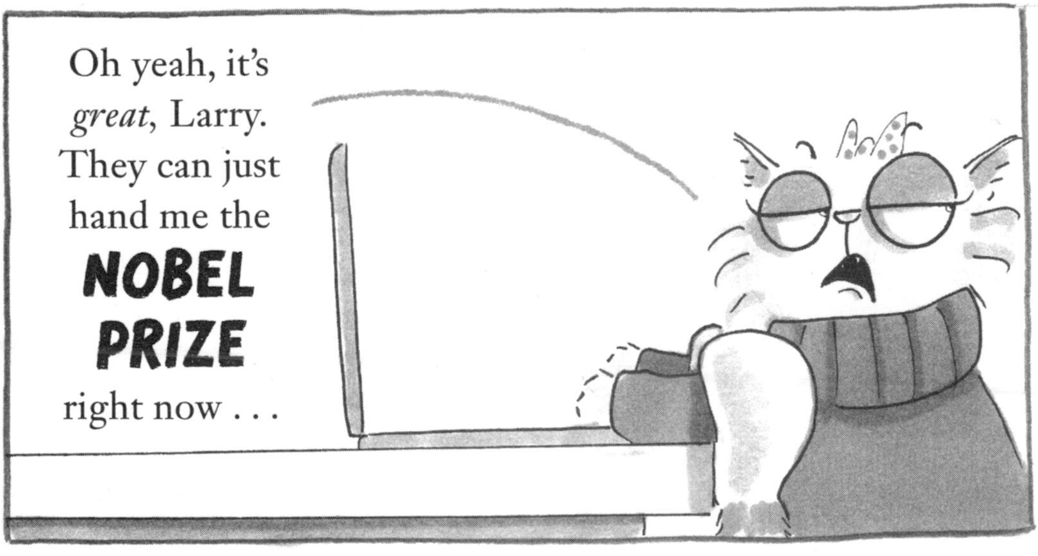
Oh yeah, it's *great*, Larry. They can just hand me the **NOBEL PRIZE** right now . . .

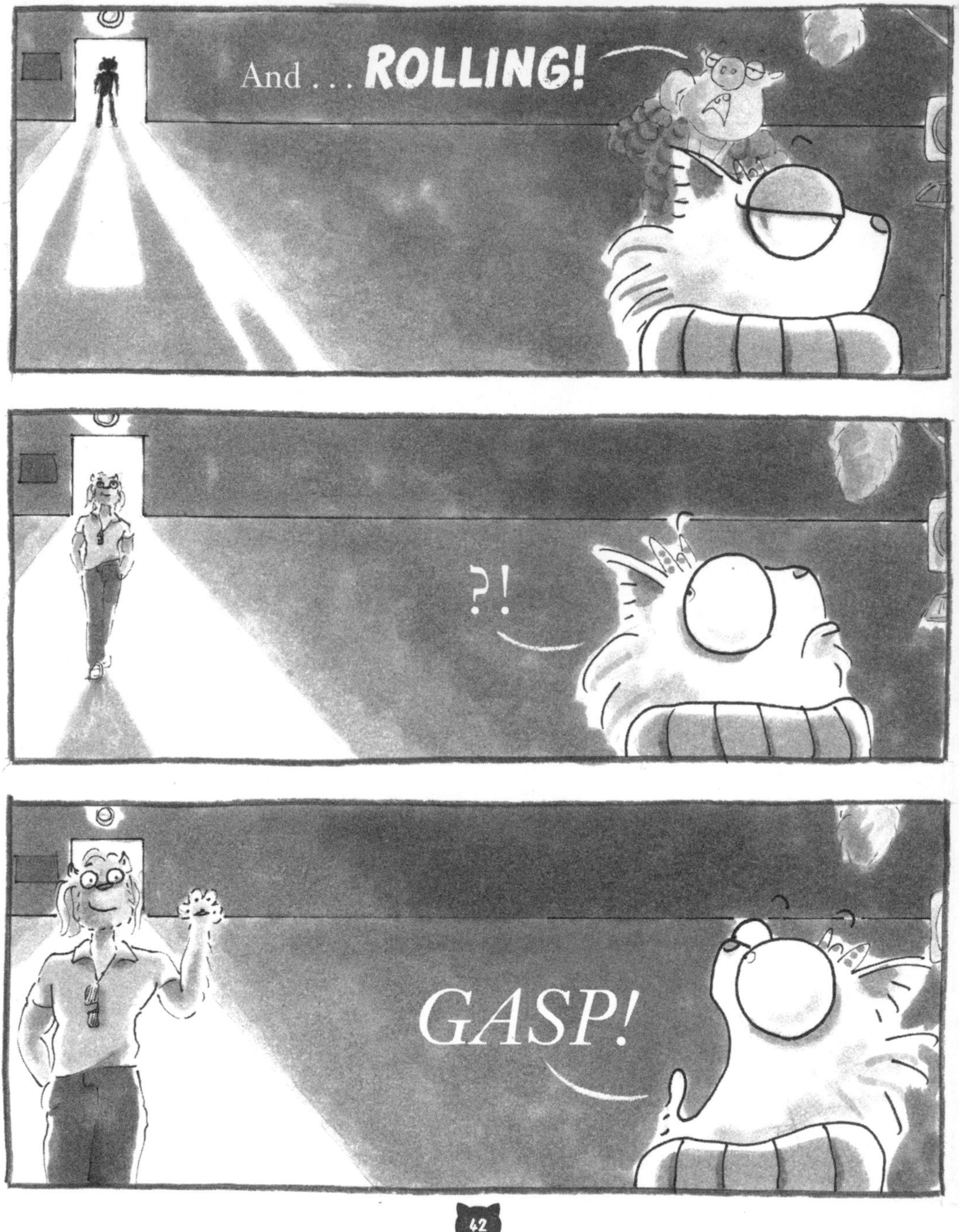
And . . . ROLLING!
?!
GASP!

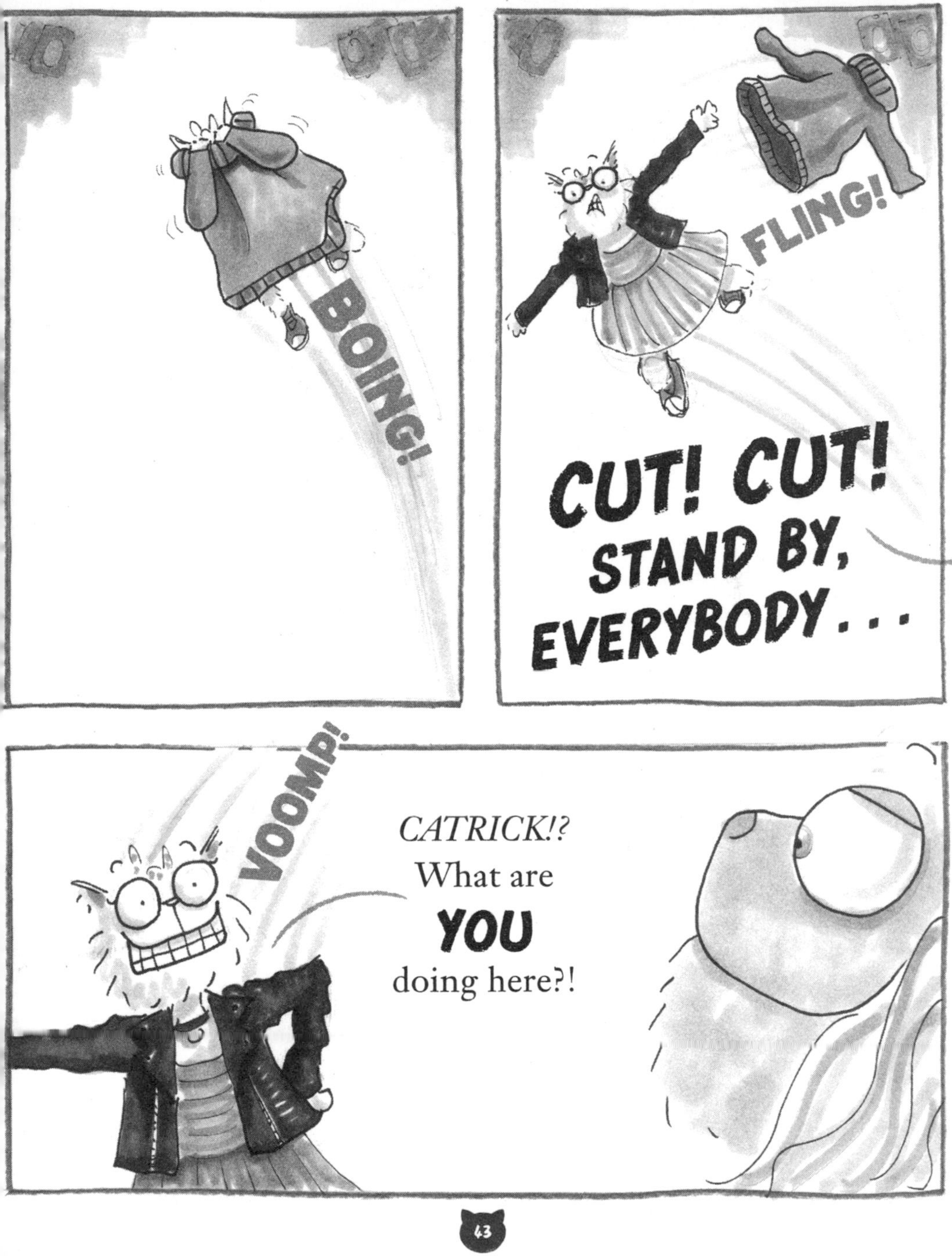
BOING!
FLING!
CUT! CUT! STAND BY, EVERYBODY . . .
VOOMP!
CATRICK!? What are YOU doing here?!

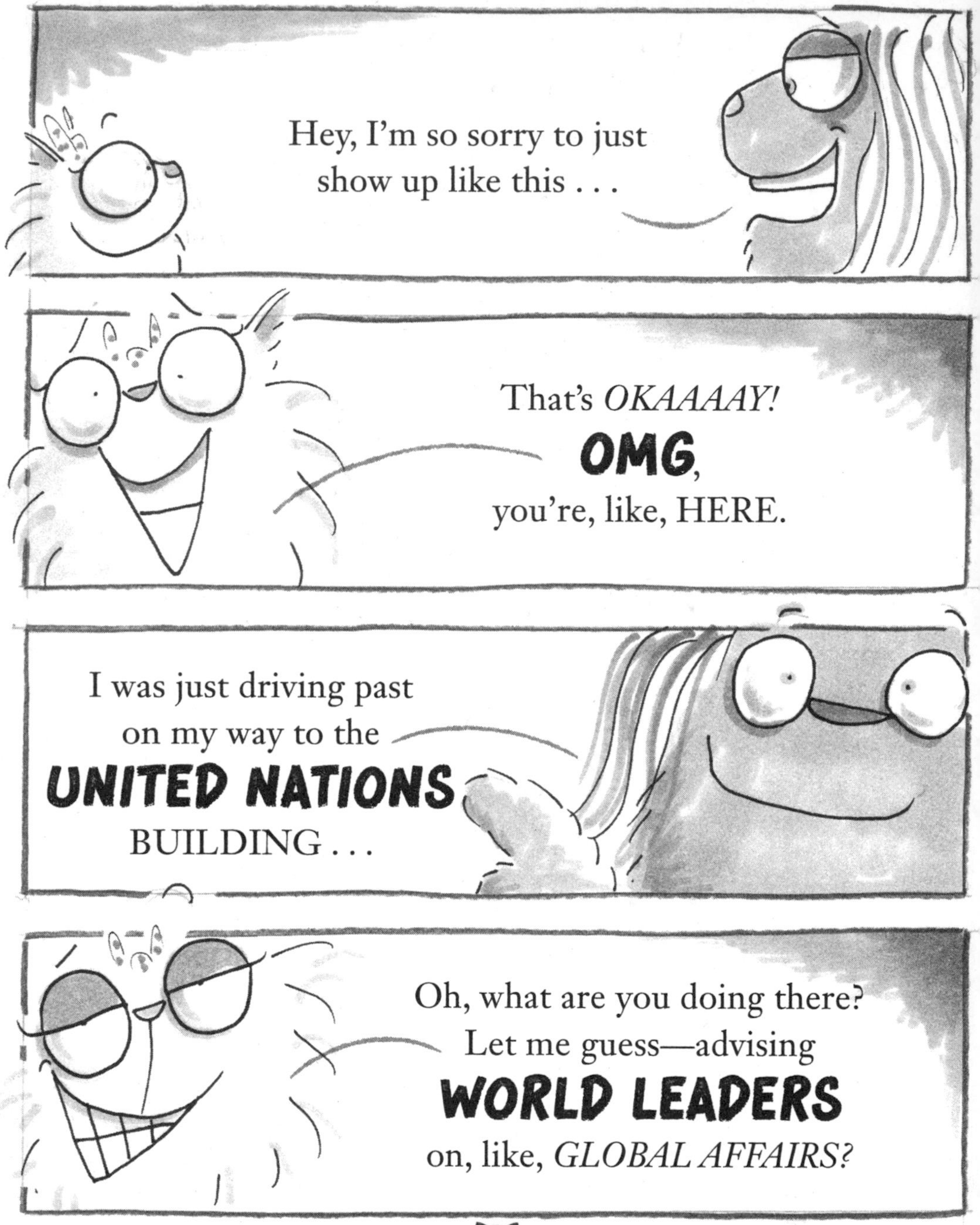
Hey, I'm so sorry to just show up like this . . .
That's *OKAAAAY!* **OMG**, you're, like, HERE.
I was just driving past on my way to the **UNITED NATIONS** BUILDING . . .
Oh, what are you doing there? Let me guess—advising **WORLD LEADERS** on, like, *GLOBAL AFFAIRS?*

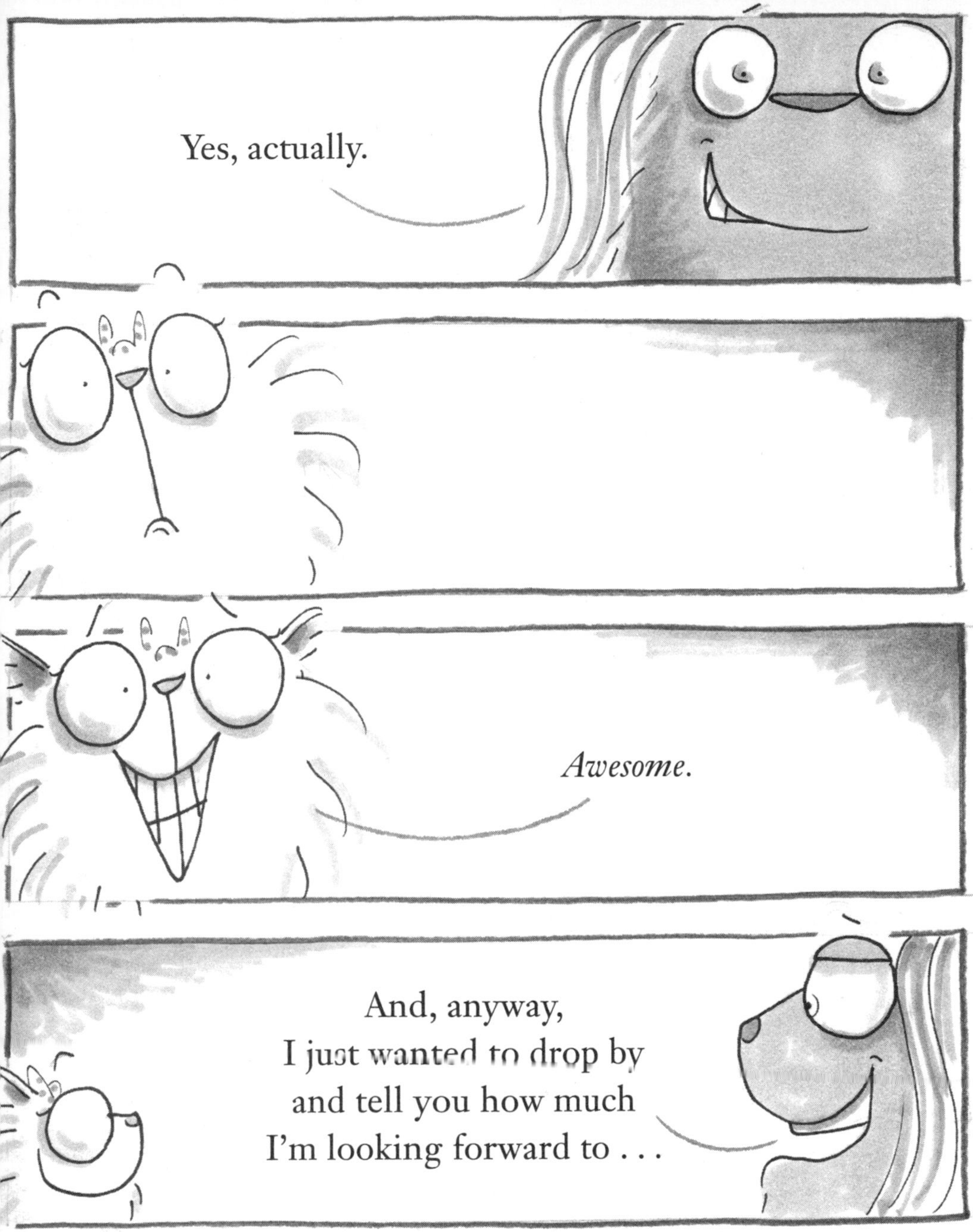
Yes, actually.
Awesome.
And, anyway, I just wanted to drop by and tell you how much I'm looking forward to . . .

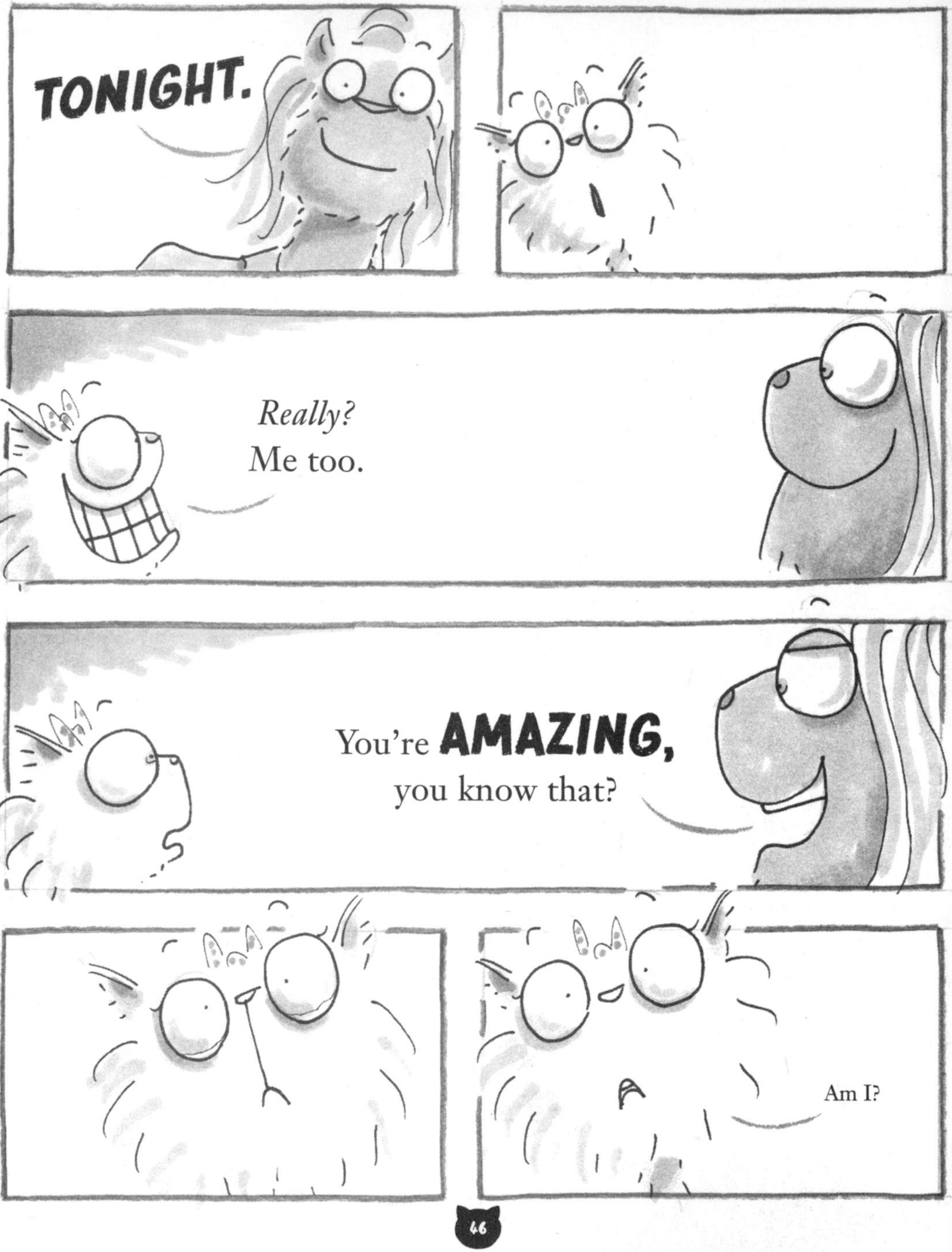
TONIGHT.
Really?
Me too.
You're **AMAZING,**
you know that?
Am I?

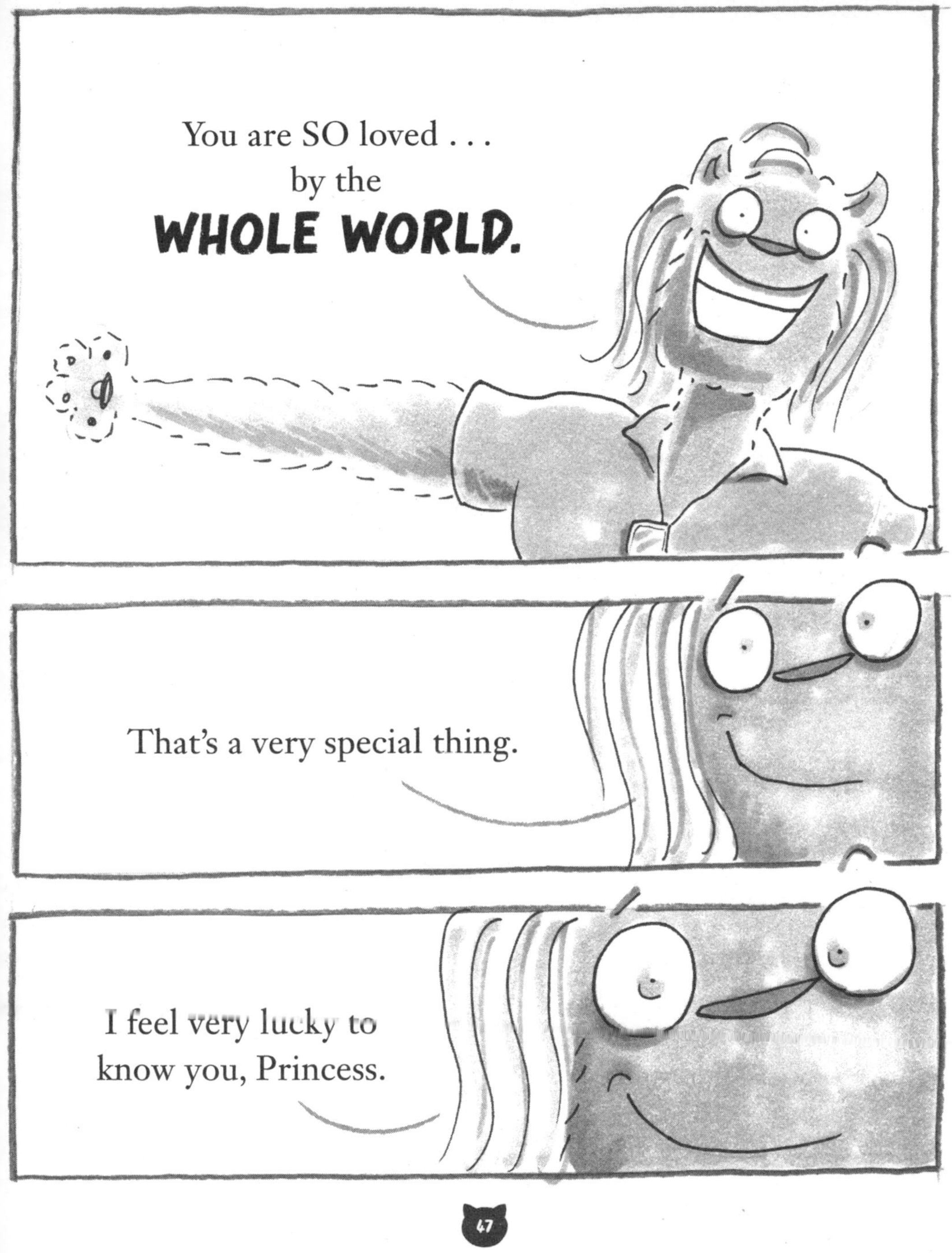
You are SO loved . . .
by the
WHOLE WORLD.
That's a very special thing.
I feel very lucky to
know you, Princess.

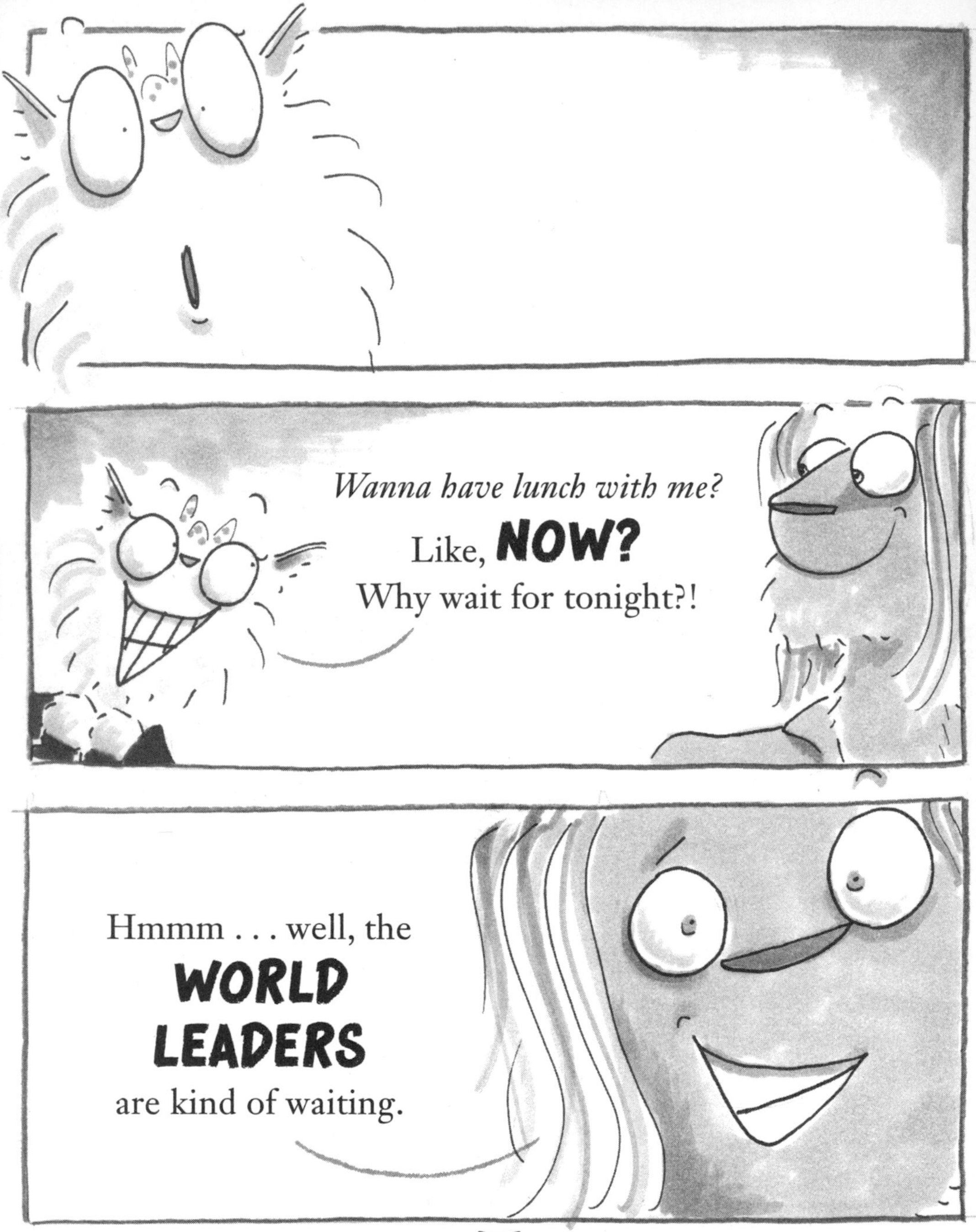

Wanna have lunch with me?
Like, **NOW?**
Why wait for tonight?!
Hmmm . . . well, the
WORLD LEADERS
are kind of waiting.

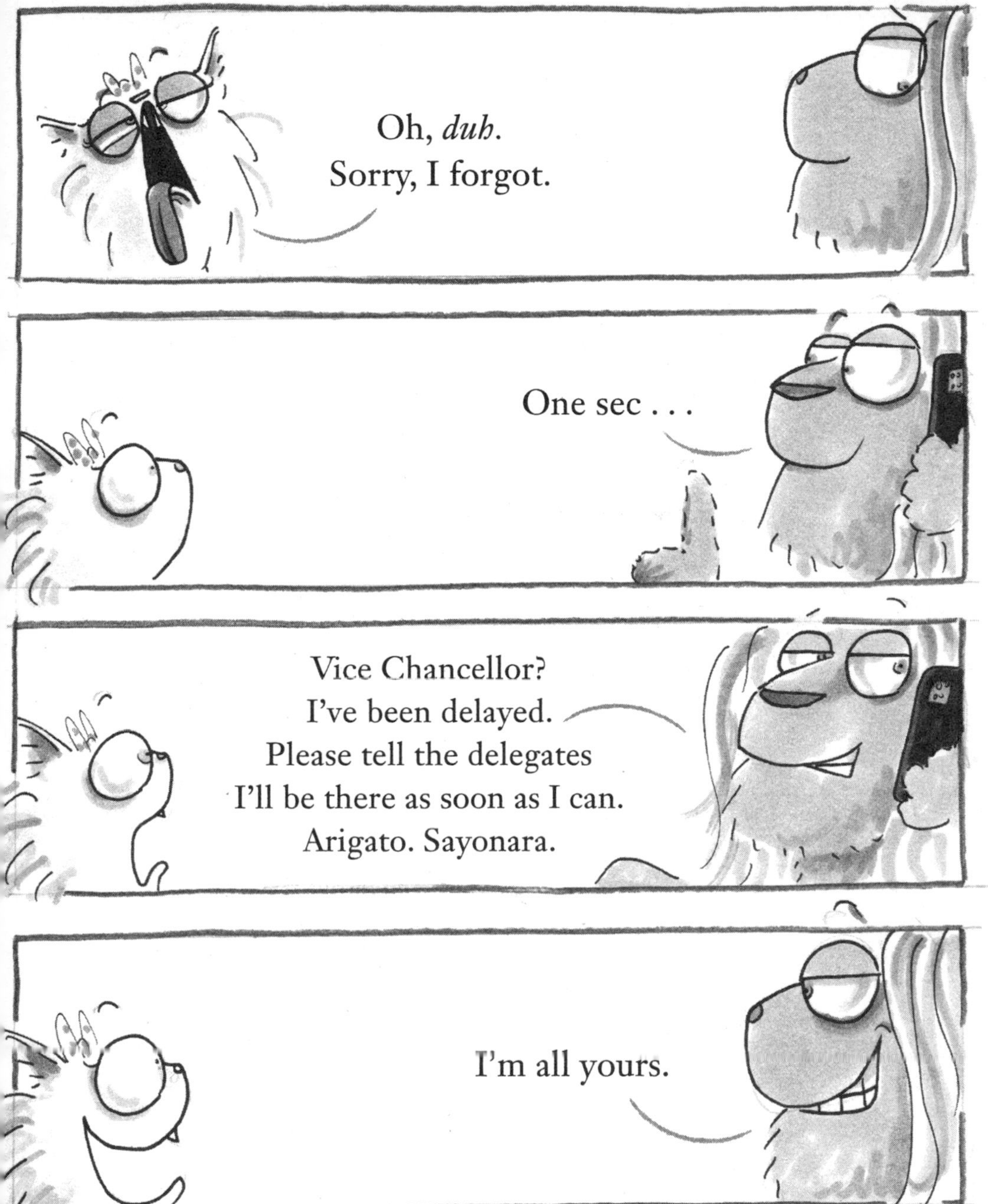
Oh, *duh*.
Sorry, I forgot.
One sec . . .
Vice Chancellor?
I've been delayed.
Please tell the delegates
I'll be there as soon as I can.
Arigato. Sayonara.
I'm all yours.

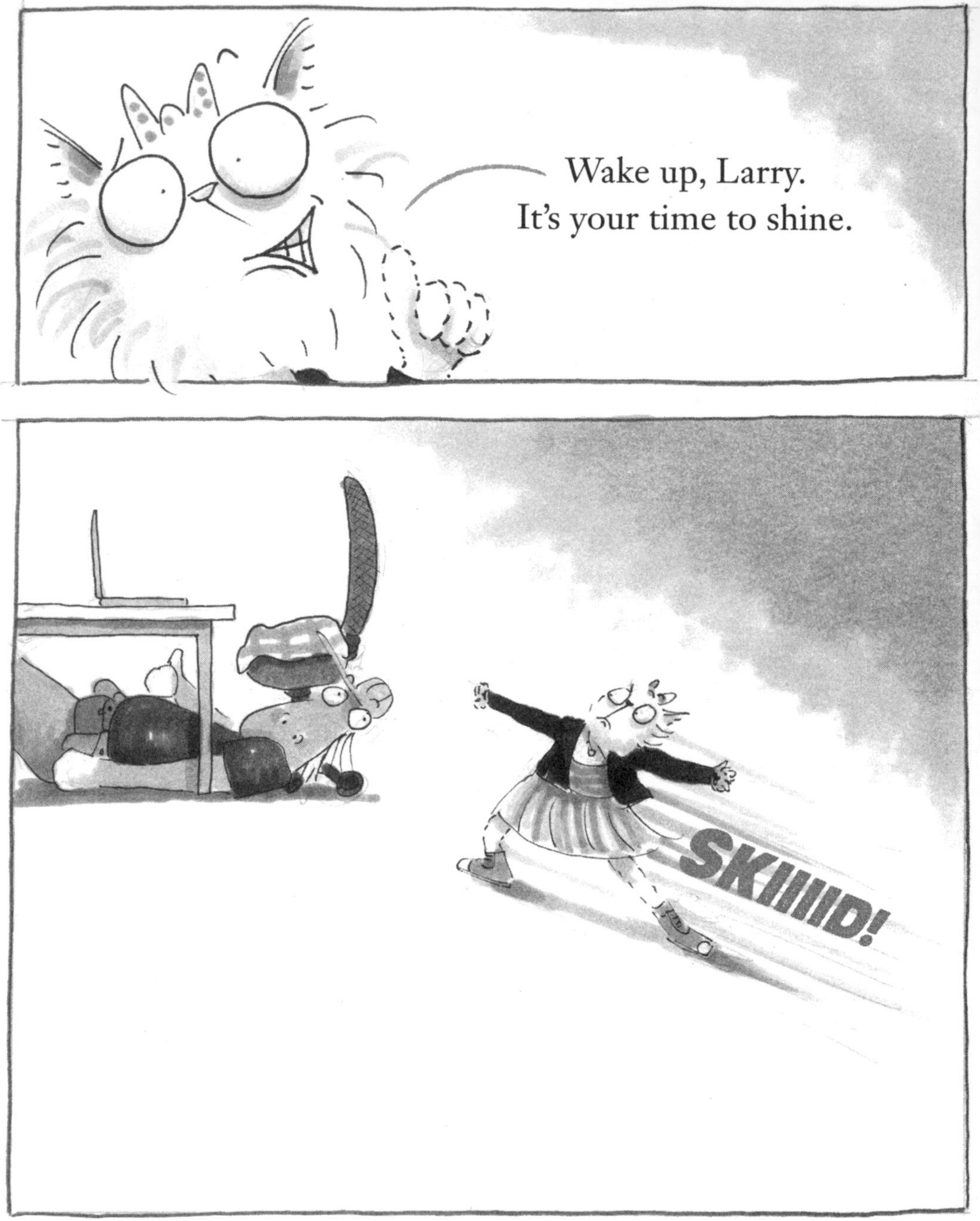
Wake up, Larry.
It's your time to shine.
SKIIIIID!

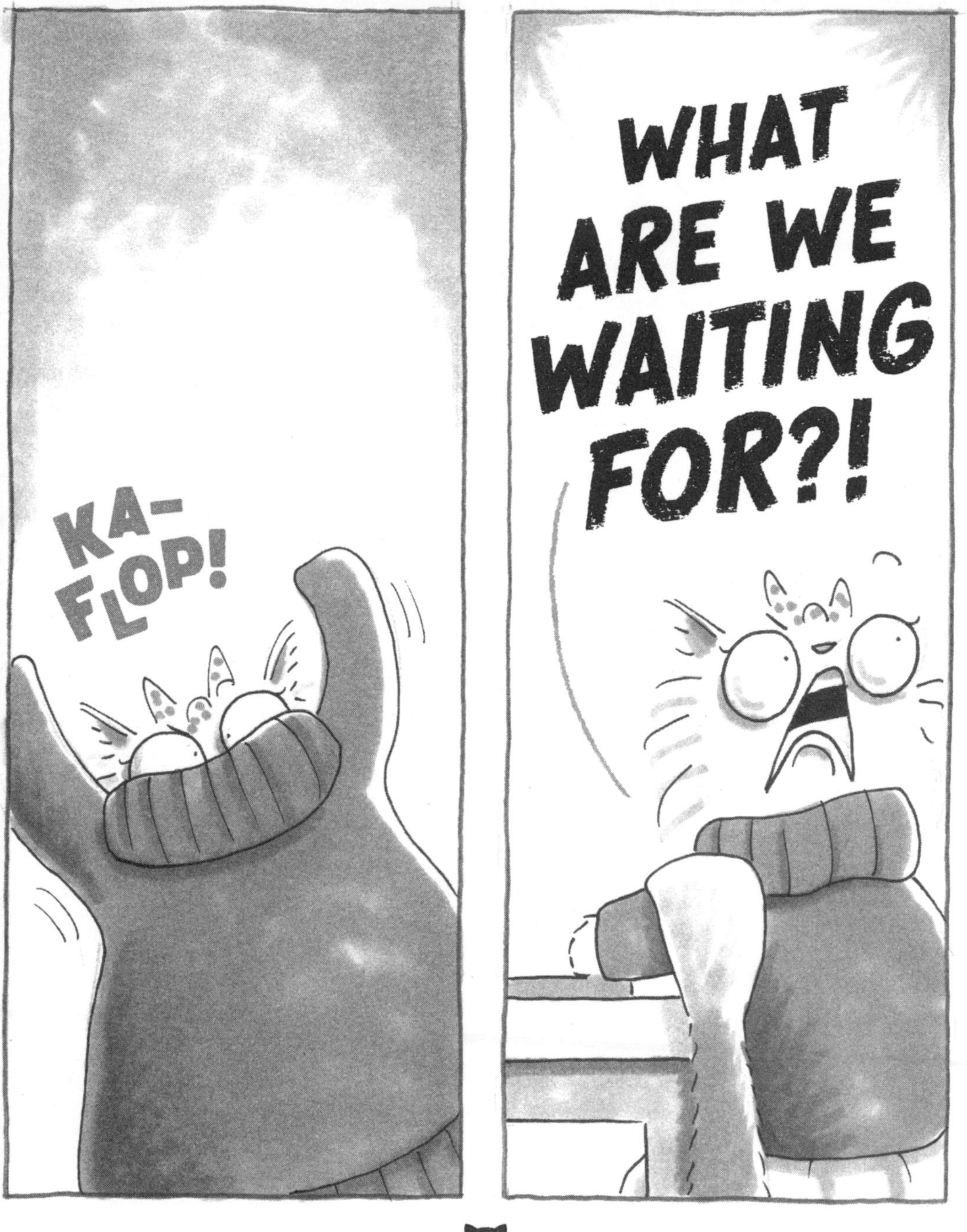
KA-
FLOP!
WHAT
ARE WE
WAITING
FOR?!

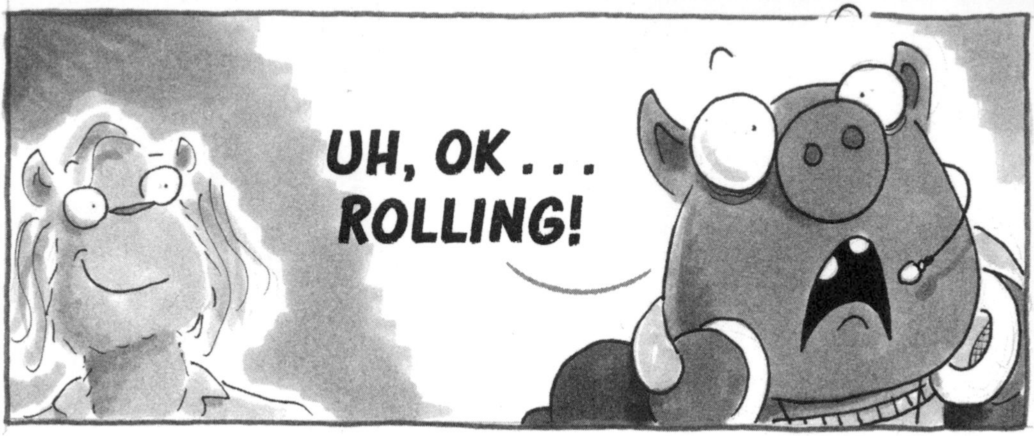
UH, OK . . .
ROLLING!

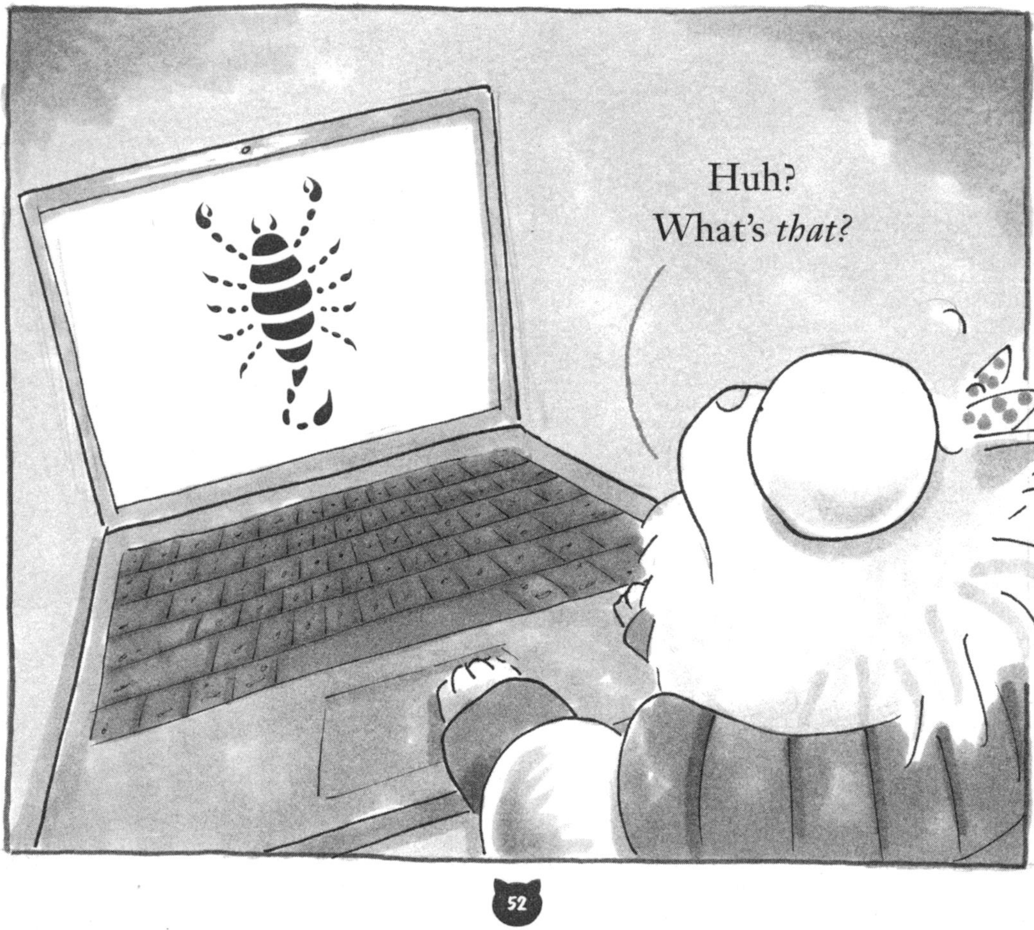
Huh?
What's *that?*

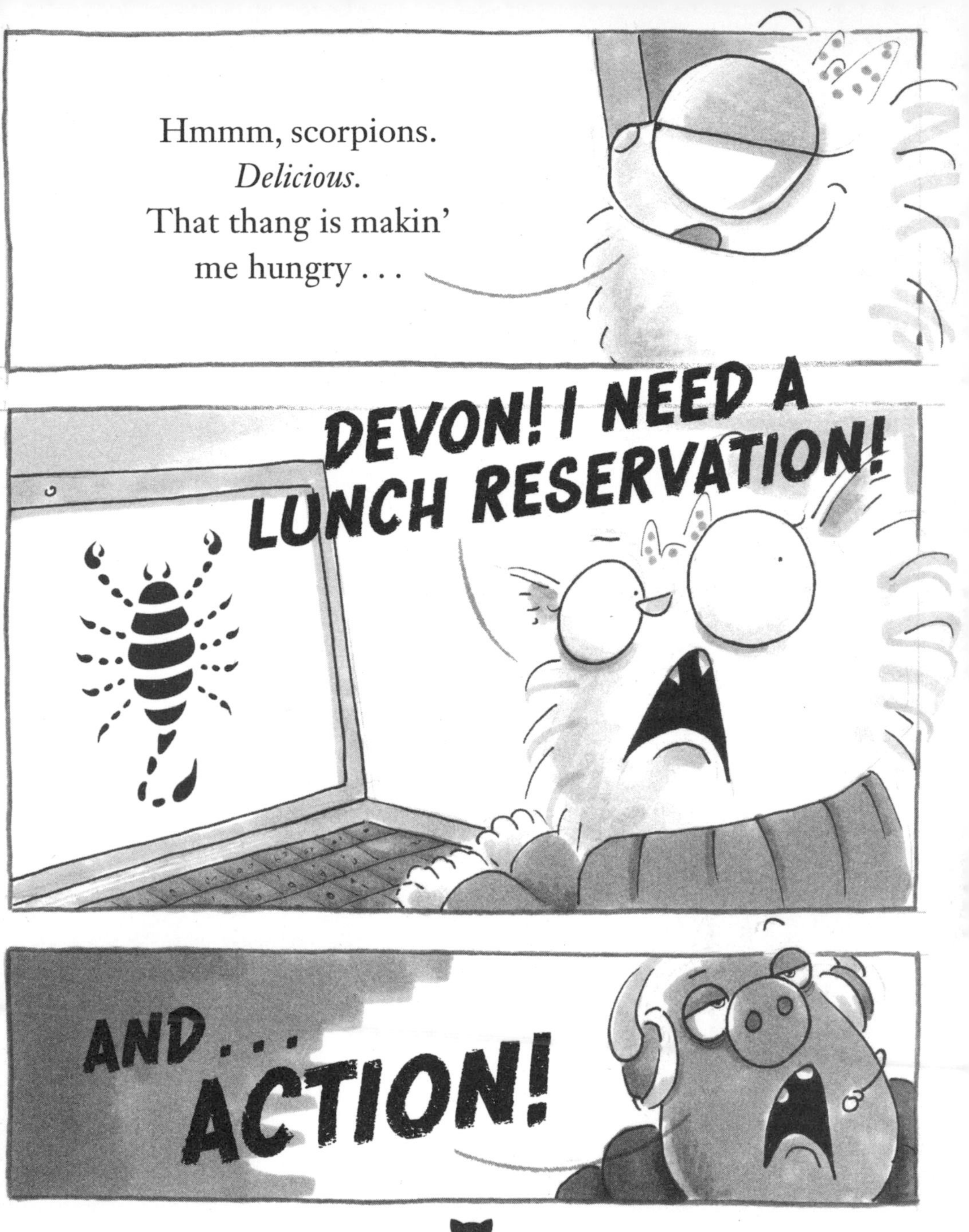
Hmmm, scorpions.
Delicious.
That thang is makin' me hungry . . .
DEVON! I NEED A LUNCH RESERVATION!
AND . . . ACTION!

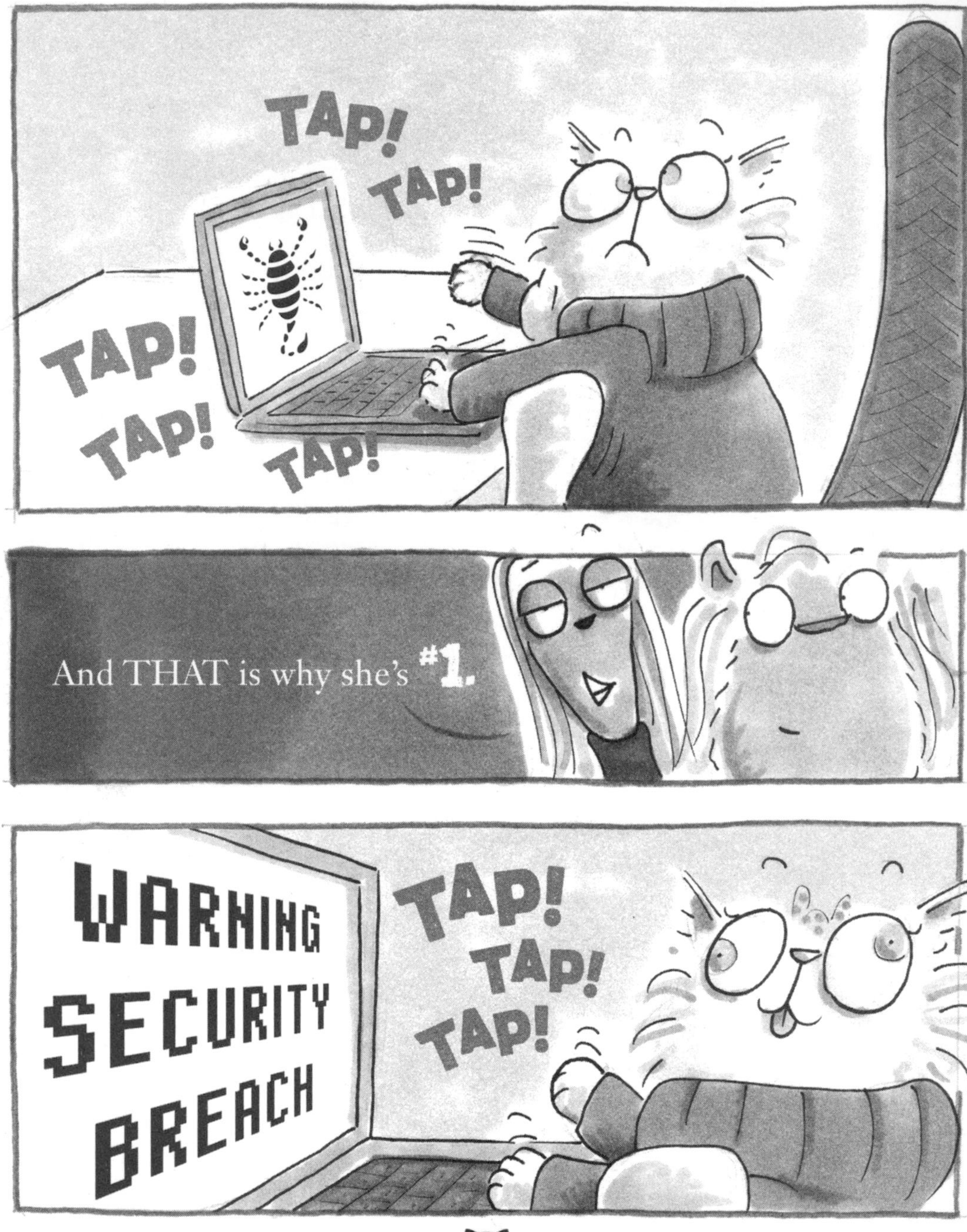
TAP!
TAP!
TAP!
TAP!
TAP!
And THAT is why she's #1.
WARNING
SECURITY
BREACH
TAP!
TAP!
TAP!

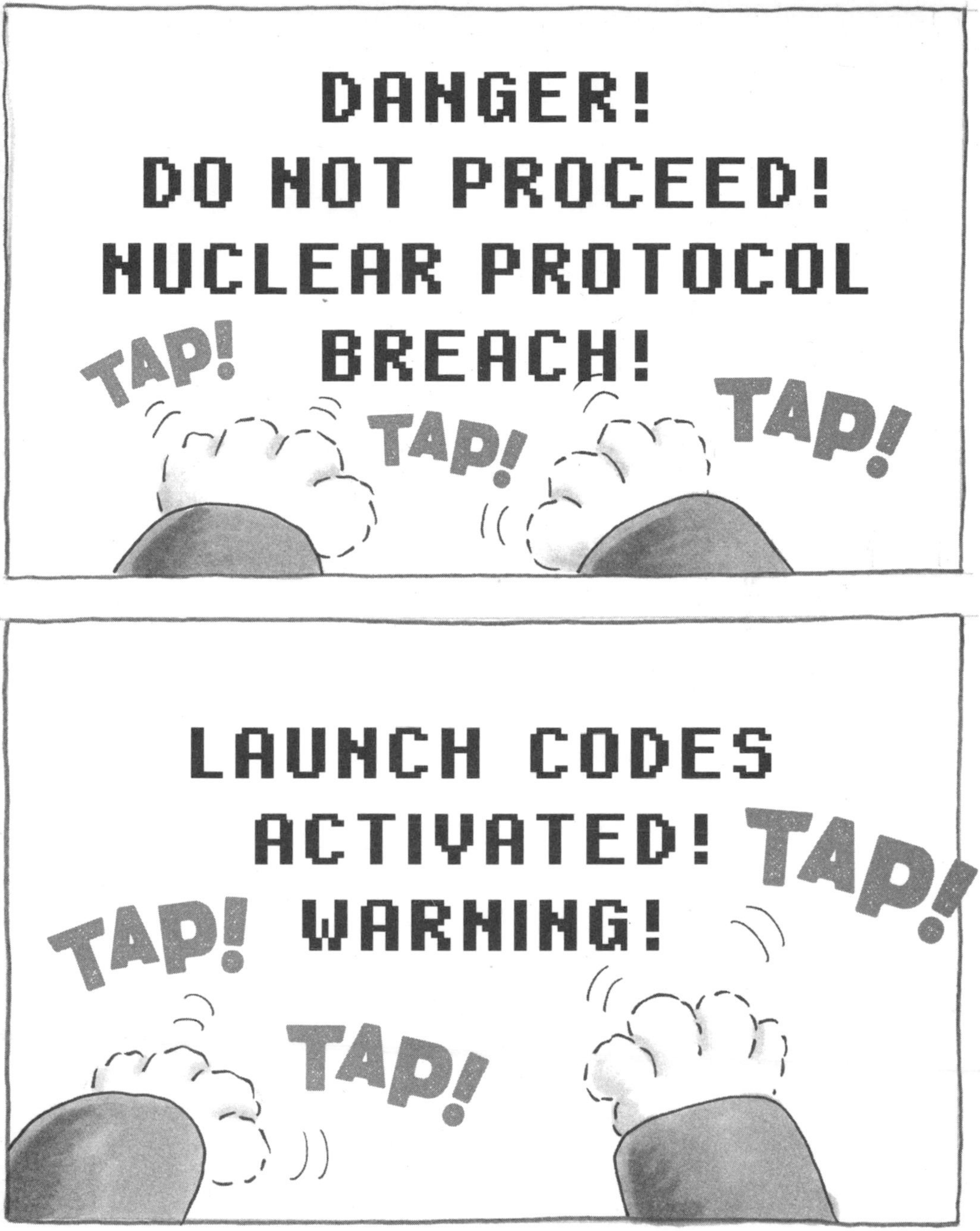
DANGER!
DO NOT PROCEED!
NUCLEAR PROTOCOL
BREACH!
TAP!
TAP!
TAP!
LAUNCH CODES
ACTIVATED!
WARNING!
TAP!
TAP!
TAP!

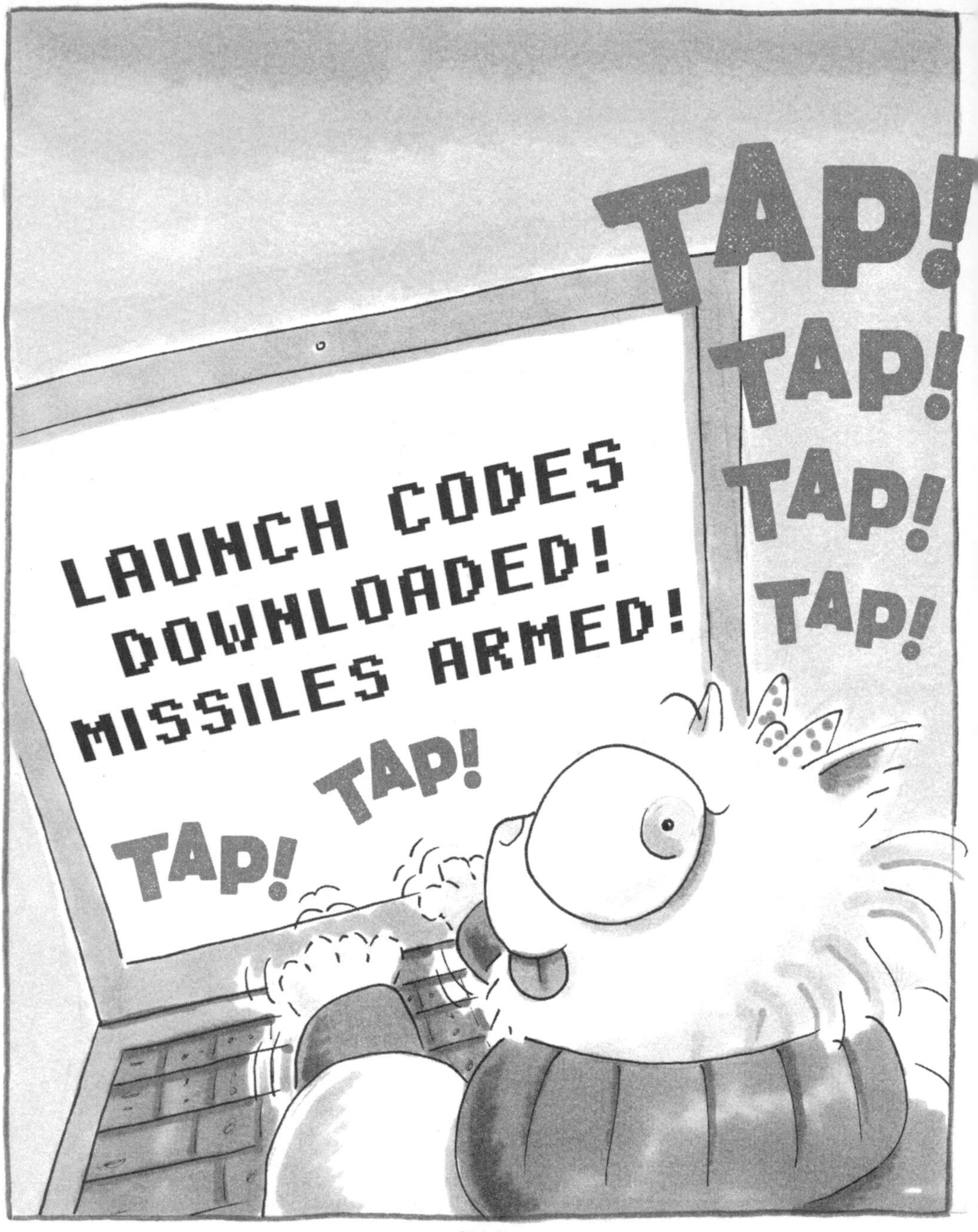
LAUNCH CODES DOWNLOADED! MISSILES ARMED!
TAP!
TAP!
TAP!
TAP!
TAP!
TAP!

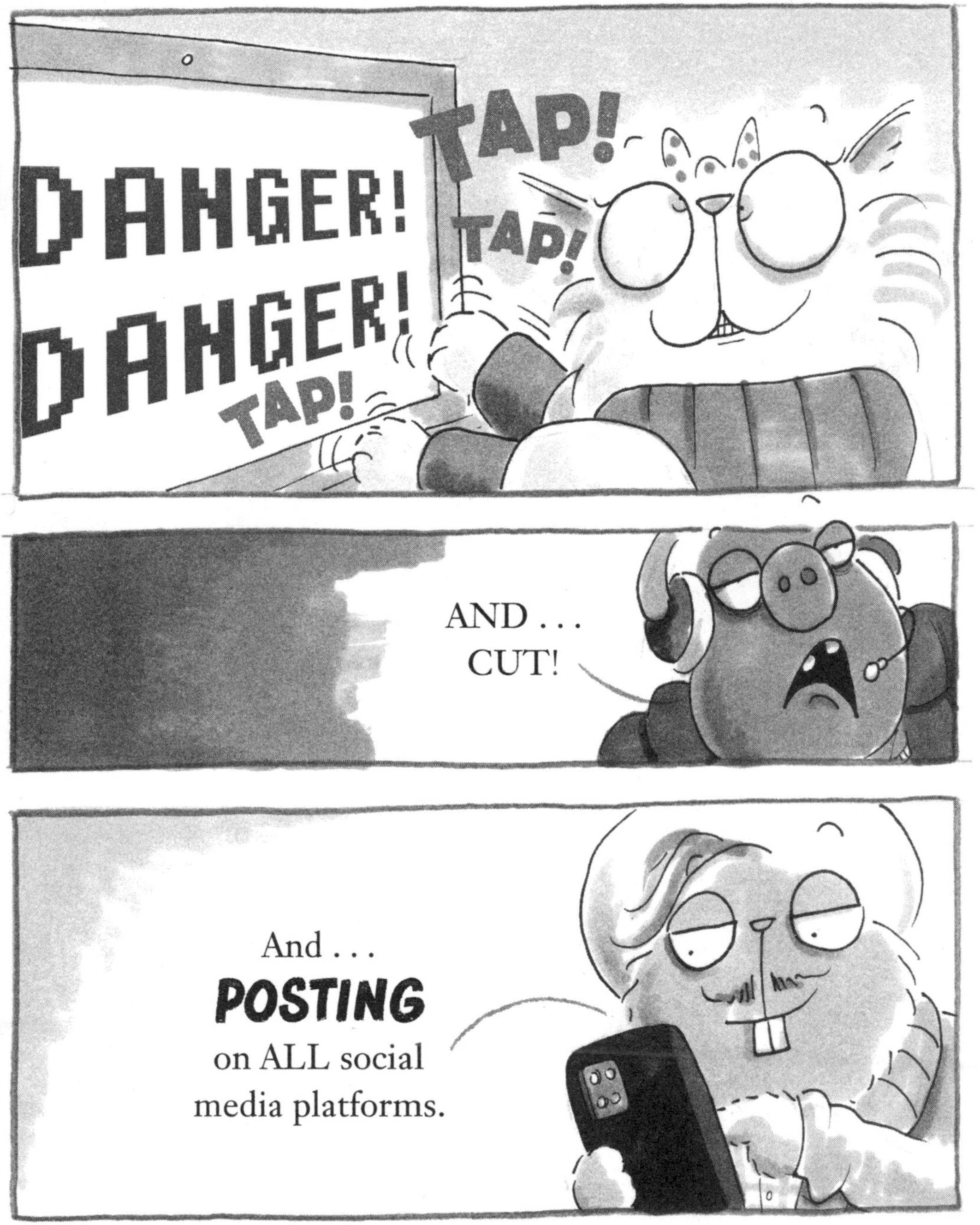
DANGER!
DANGER!
TAP!
TAP!
TAP!
AND . . .
CUT!
And . . .
POSTING
on ALL social
media platforms.

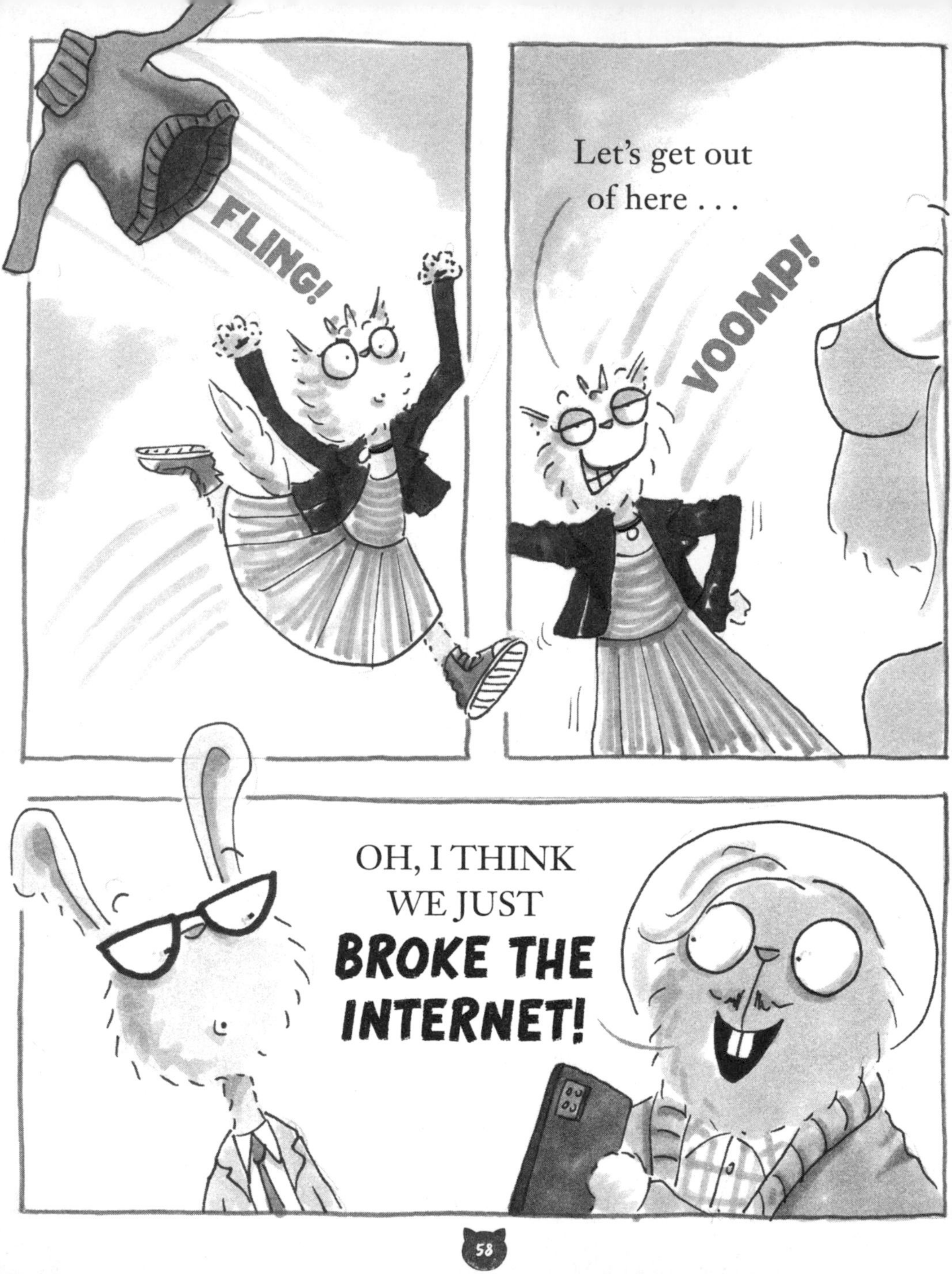
FLING!
Let's get out
of here . . .
VOOMP!
OH, I THINK
WE JUST
BROKE THE
INTERNET!

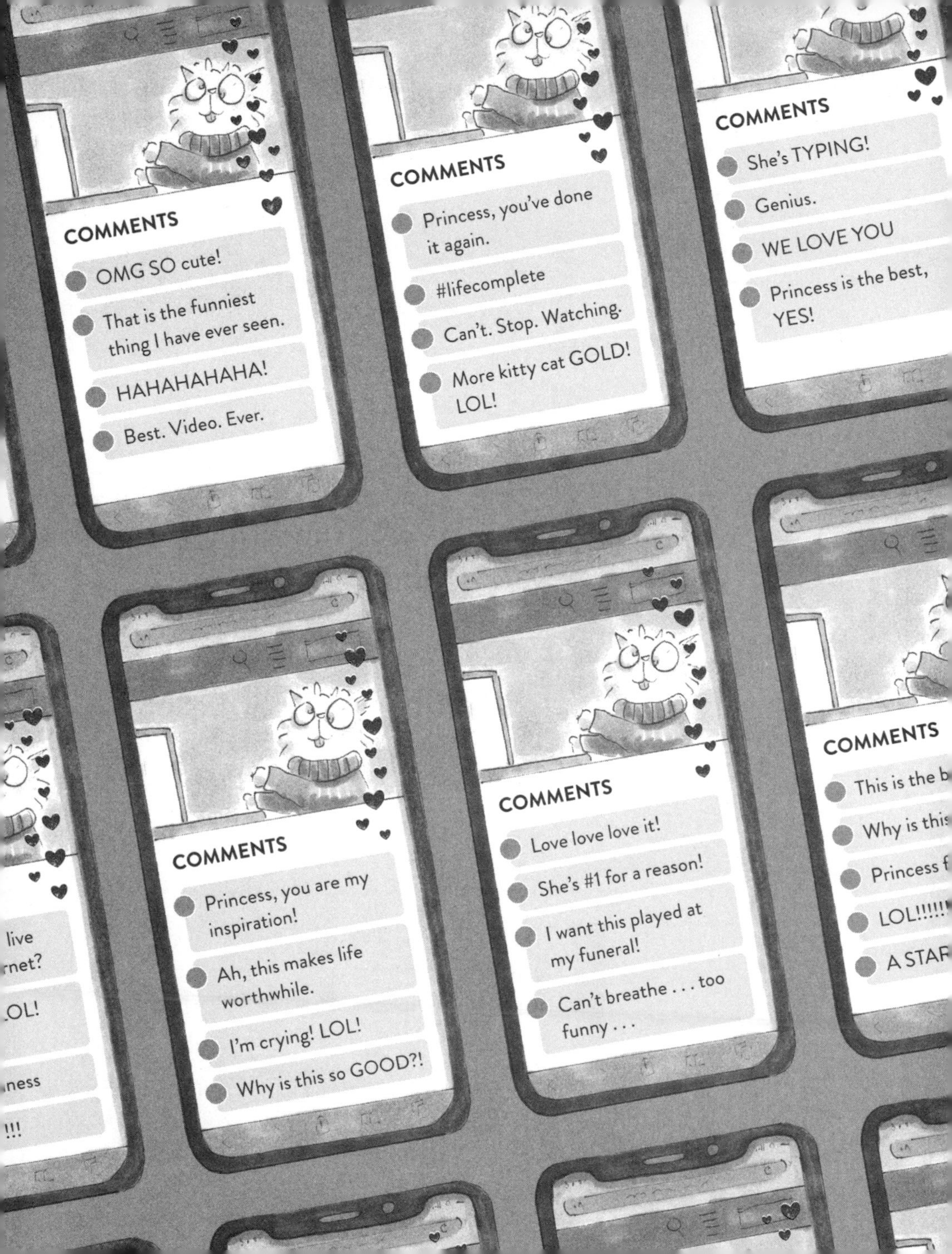
COMMENTS
OMG SO cute!
That is the funniest thing I have ever seen.
HAHAHAHAHA!
Best. Video. Ever.
COMMENTS
Princess, you've done it again.
#lifecomplete
Can't. Stop. Watching.
More kitty cat GOLD! LOL!
COMMENTS
She's TYPING!
Genius.
WE LOVE YOU
Princess is the best, YES!
COMMENTS
Princess, you are my inspiration!
Ah, this makes life worthwhile.
I'm crying! LOL!
Why is this so GOOD?!
COMMENTS
Love love love it!
She's #1 for a reason!
I want this played at my funeral!
Can't breathe . . . too funny . . .
COMMENTS

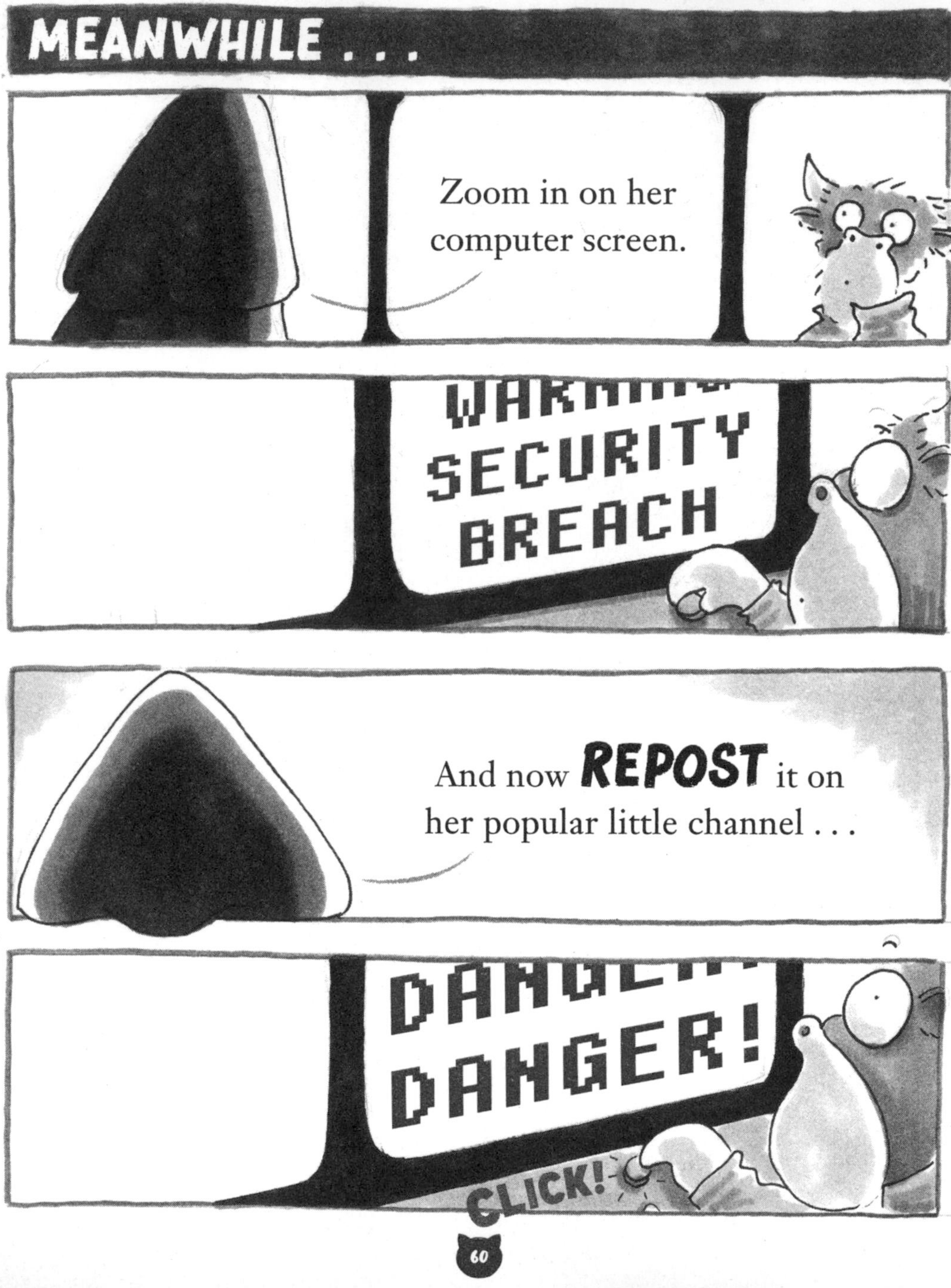
MEANWHILE . . .
Zoom in on her computer screen.
SECURITY BREACH
And now **REPOST** it on her popular little channel . . .
DANGER!
CLICK!

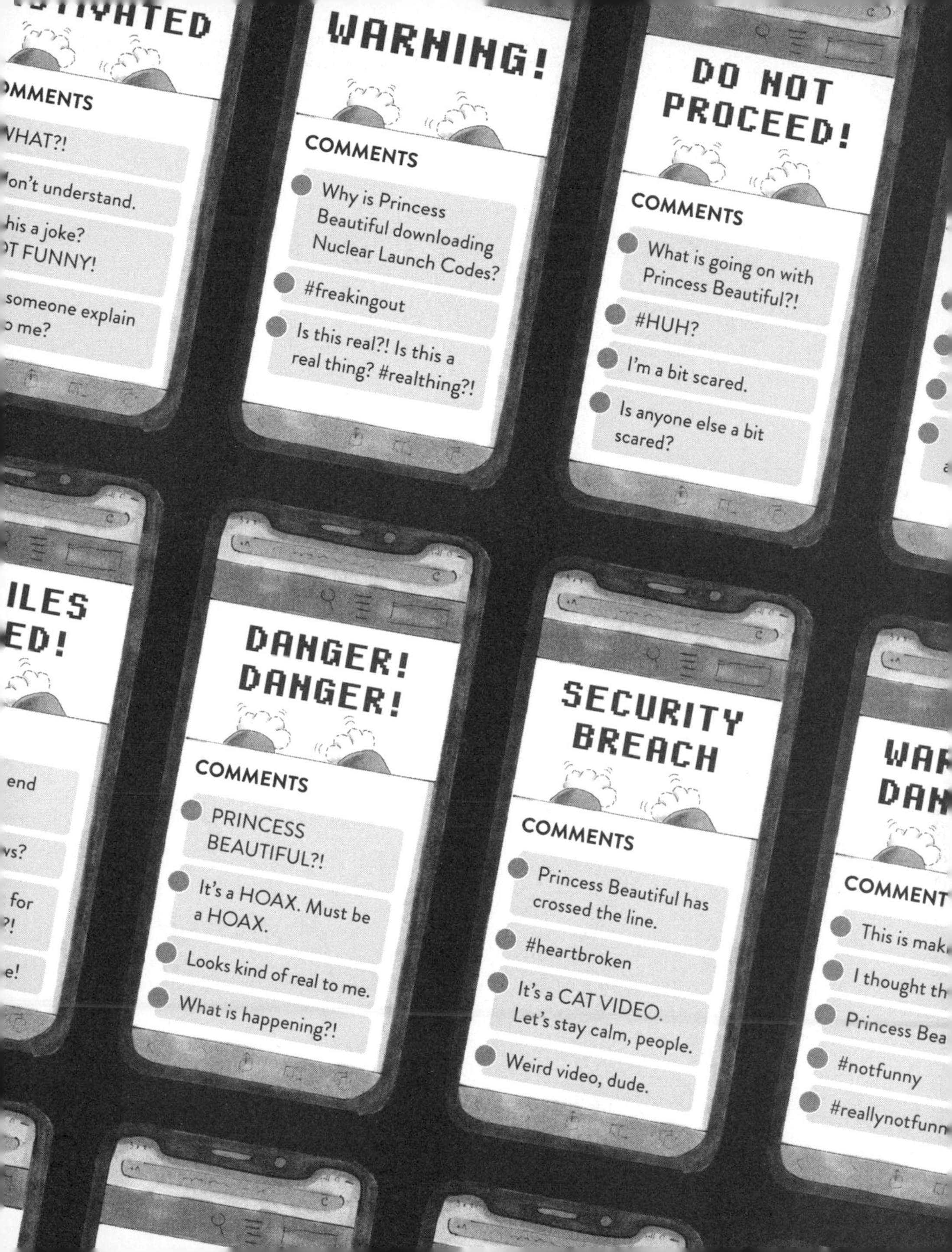

WARNING!
COMMENTS
Why is Princess Beautiful downloading Nuclear Launch Codes?
#freakingout
Is this real?! Is this a real thing? #realthing?!
DO NOT PROCEED!
COMMENTS
What is going on with Princess Beautiful?!
#HUH?
I'm a bit scared.
Is anyone else a bit scared?
DANGER! DANGER!
COMMENTS
PRINCESS BEAUTIFUL?!
It's a HOAX. Must be a HOAX.
Looks kind of real to me.
What is happening?!
SECURITY BREACH
COMMENTS
Princess Beautiful has crossed the line.
#heartbroken
It's a CAT VIDEO. Let's stay calm, people.
Weird video, dude.

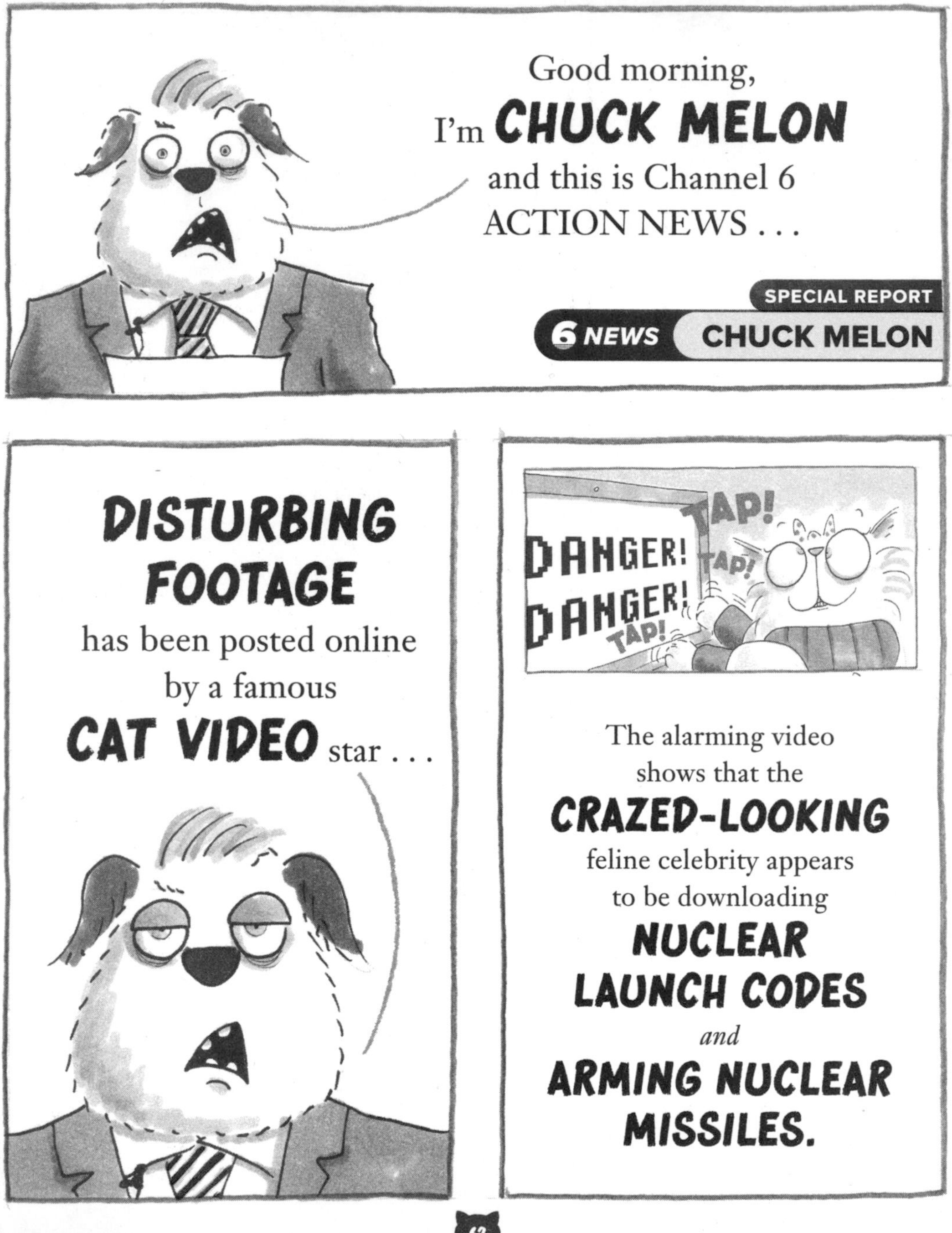
Good morning, I'm CHUCK MELON and this is Channel 6 ACTION NEWS . . .
SPECIAL REPORT
6 NEWS
CHUCK MELON
DISTURBING FOOTAGE has been posted online by a famous CAT VIDEO star . . .
DANGER!
DANGER!
TAP!
TAP!
TAP!
The alarming video shows that the CRAZED-LOOKING feline celebrity appears to be downloading NUCLEAR LAUNCH CODES and ARMING NUCLEAR MISSILES.

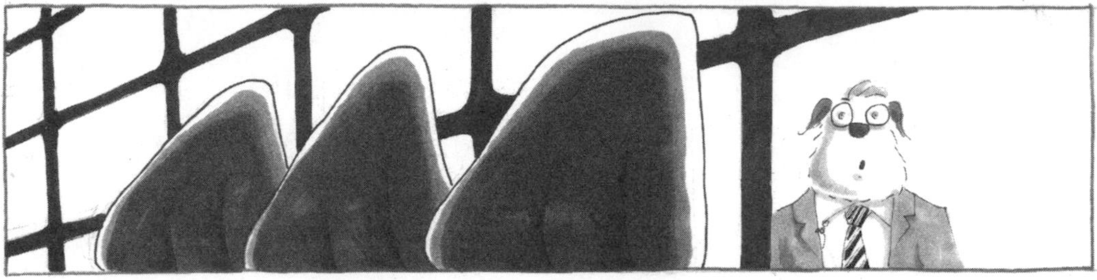

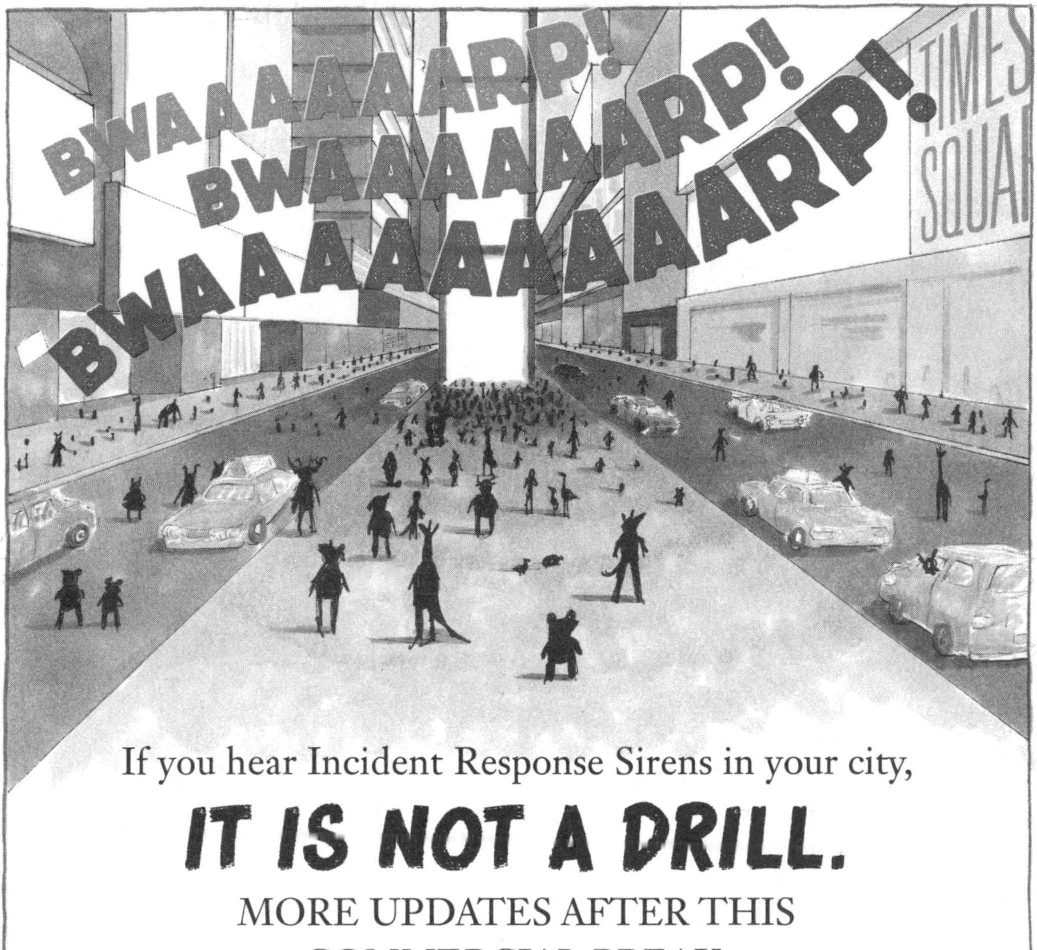
BWAAAAARP!
BWAAAAAARP!
BWAAAAAAAAARP!
TIMES
If you hear Incident Response Sirens in your city,
IT IS NOT A DRILL.
MORE UPDATES AFTER THIS COMMERCIAL BREAK.

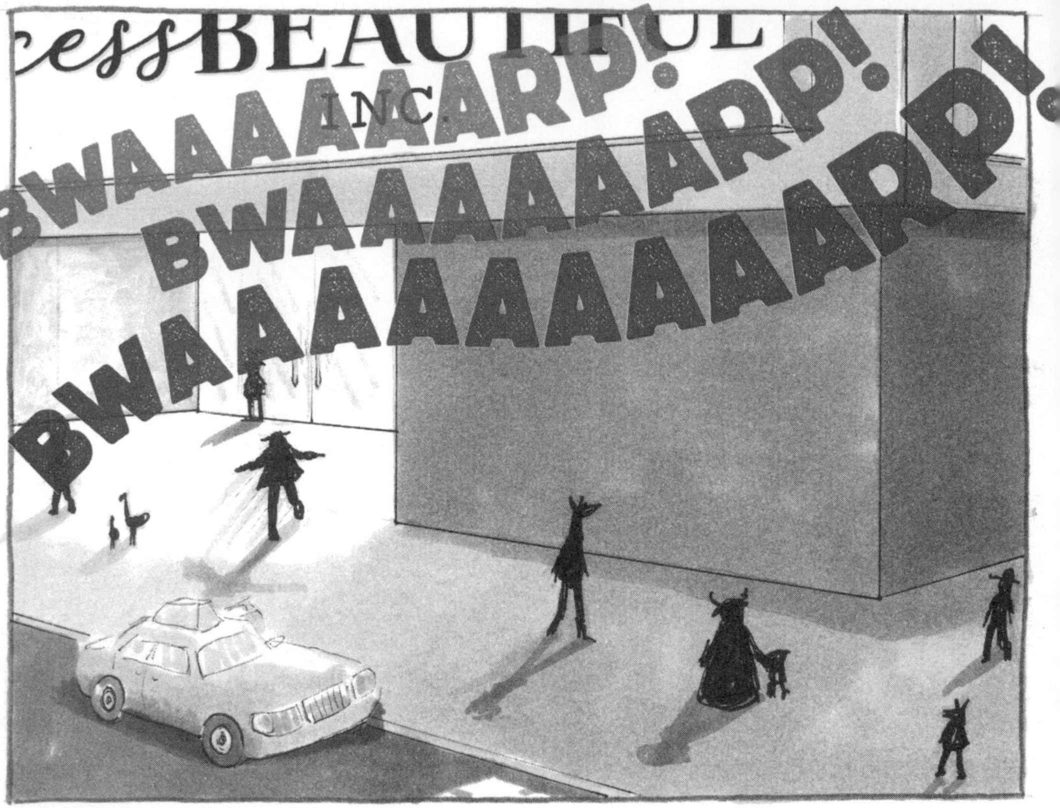
cessBEAUTIFUL
INC.
BWAAAAARP!
BWAAAAAARP!
BWAAAAAAAAARP!

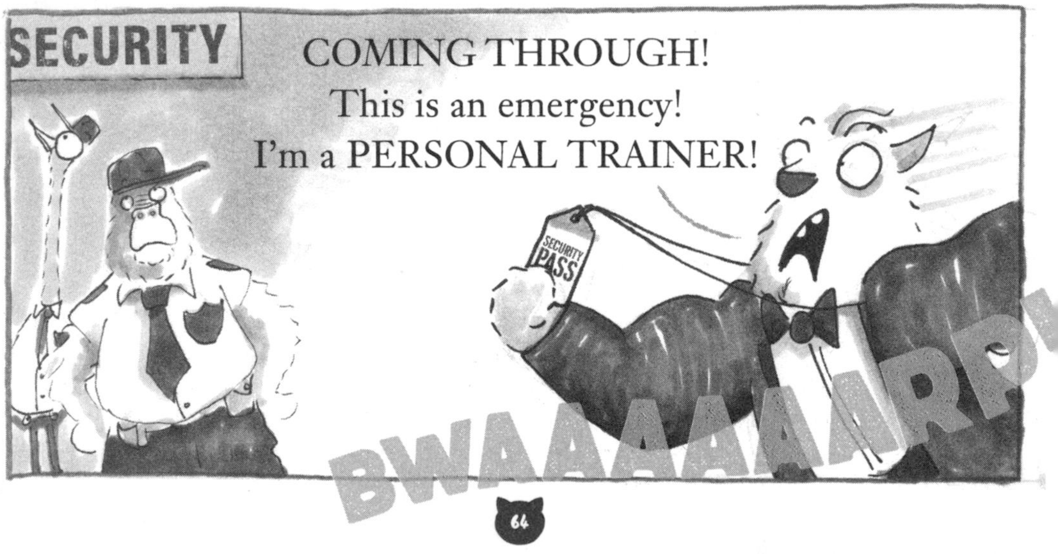
SECURITY
COMING THROUGH!
This is an emergency!
I'm a PERSONAL TRAINER!
SECURITY PASS

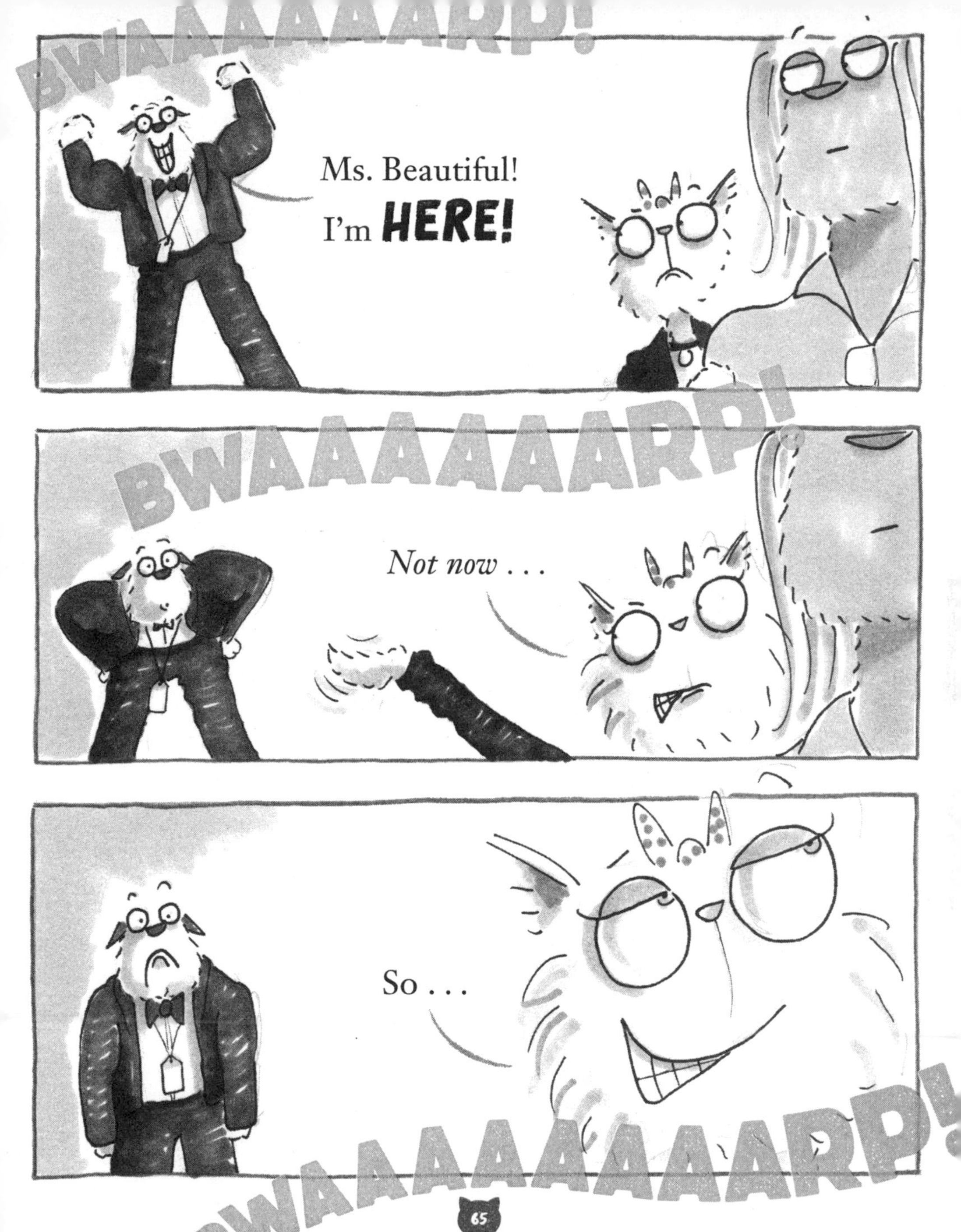
BWAAAAAARP!
Ms. Beautiful! I'm HERE!
BWAAAAAAARP!
Not now . . .
So . . .
BWAAAAAAAARP!

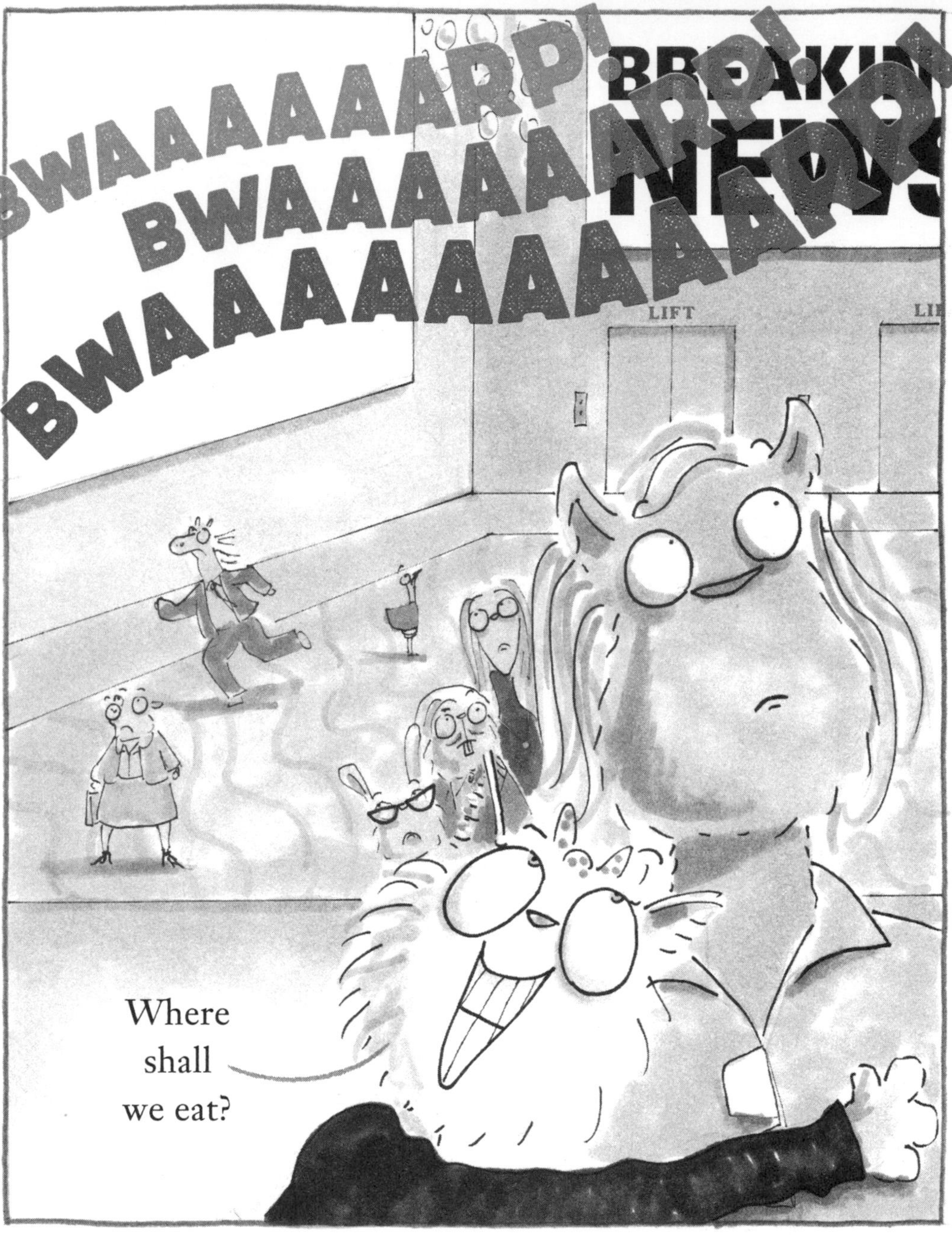
BWAAAAAAARP!
BWAAAAAAARP!
BWAAAAAAAAARP!
LIFT
Where shall we eat?

Three
WILD FIRE

THE **END** OF THE **WORLD?!**

A **6** NEWS SPECIAL REPORT

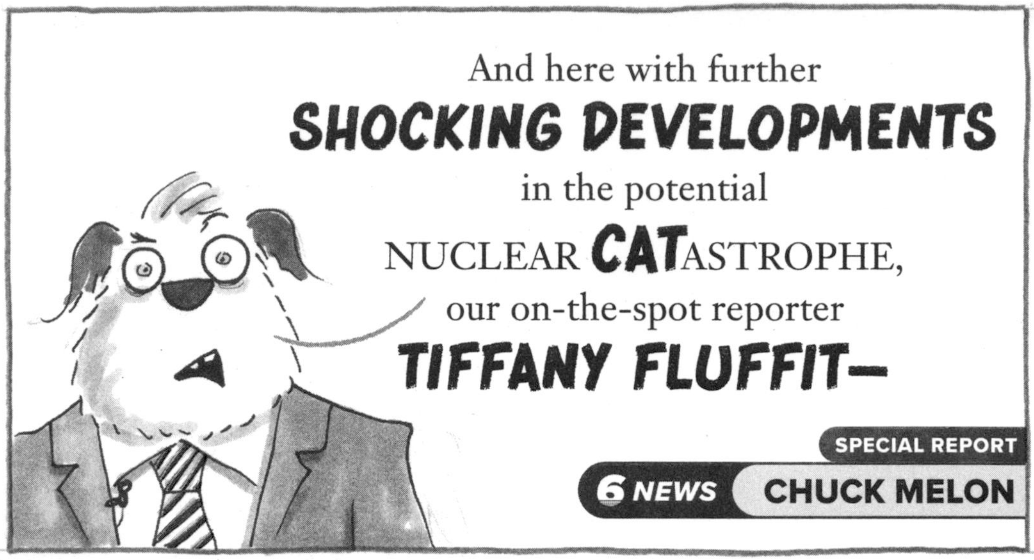
And here with further
SHOCKING DEVELOPMENTS
in the potential
NUCLEAR CATASTROPHE,
our on-the-spot reporter
TIFFANY FLUFFIT—
SPECIAL REPORT
6 NEWS
CHUCK MELON

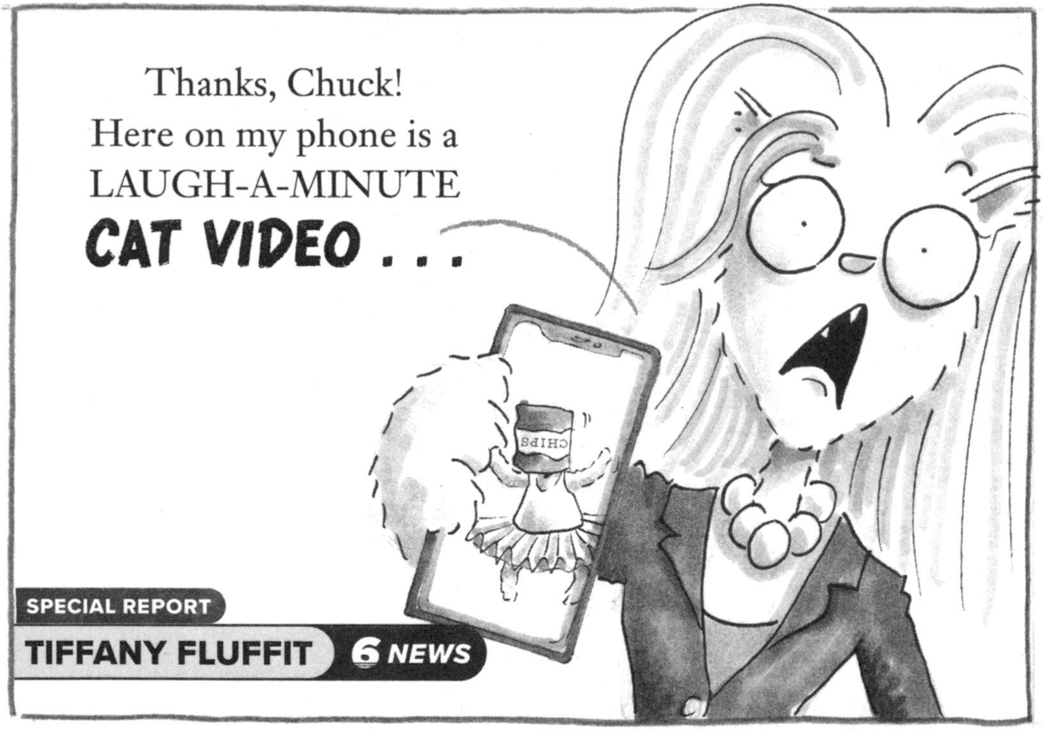
Thanks, Chuck!
Here on my phone is a
LAUGH-A-MINUTE
CAT VIDEO . . .
CHIPS
SPECIAL REPORT
TIFFANY FLUFFIT
6 NEWS

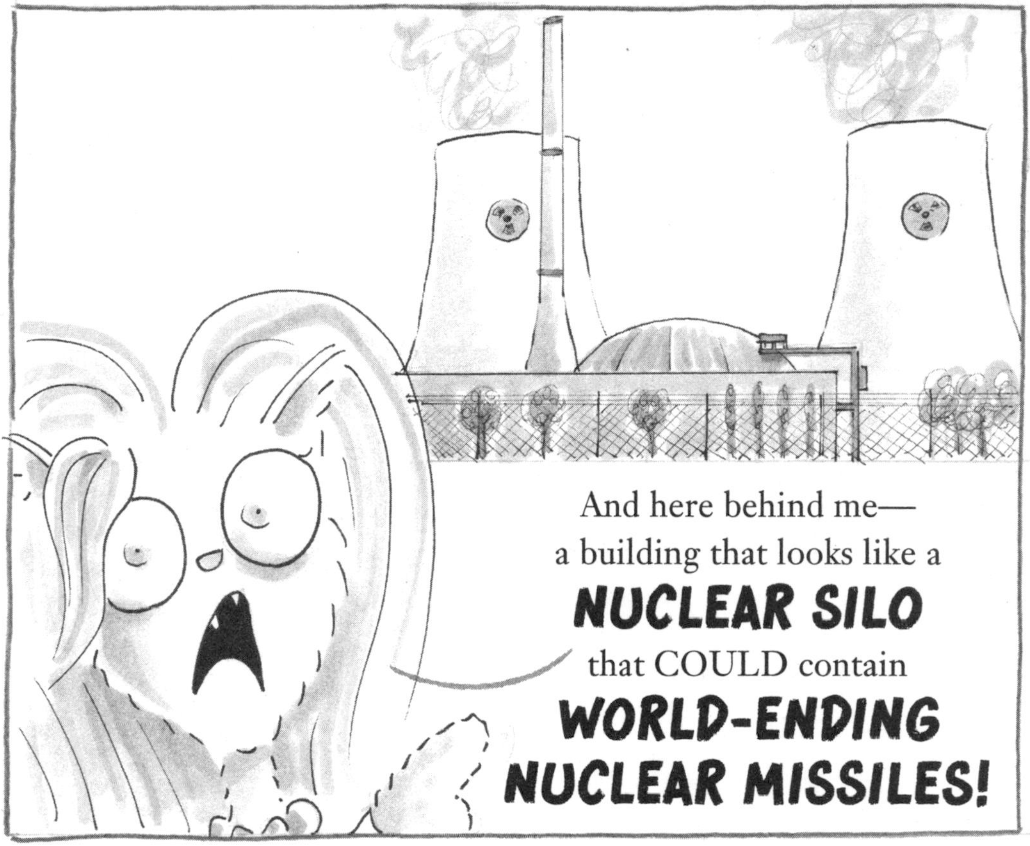
And here behind me—
a building that looks like a
NUCLEAR SILO
that COULD contain
WORLD-ENDING
NUCLEAR MISSILES!

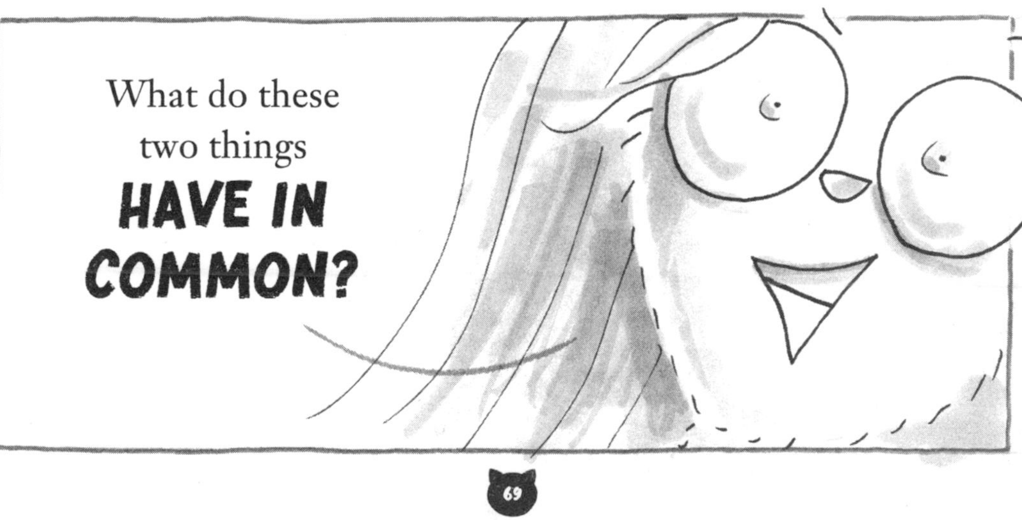
What do these
two things
HAVE IN
COMMON?

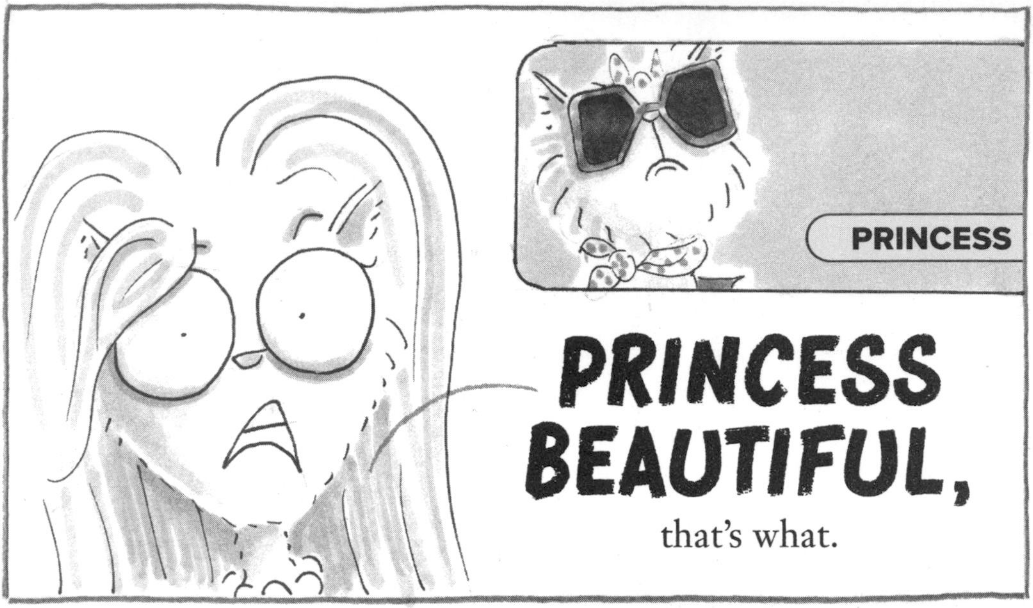
PRINCESS
PRINCESS BEAUTIFUL,
that's what.

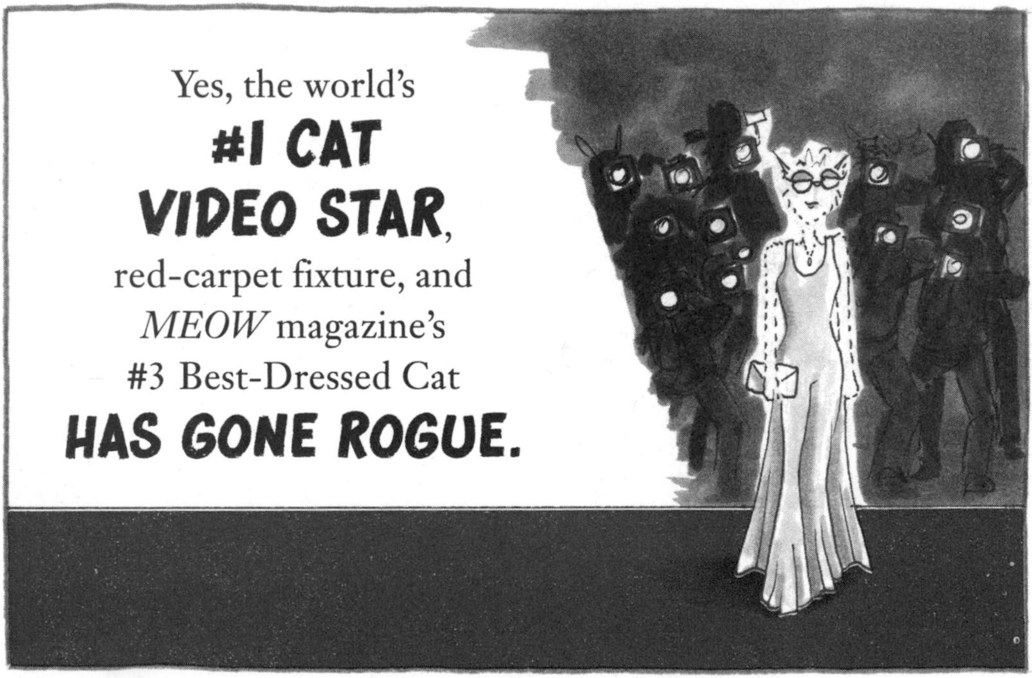
Yes, the world's
#1 CAT VIDEO STAR,
red-carpet fixture, and
MEOW magazine's
#3 Best-Dressed Cat
HAS GONE ROGUE.

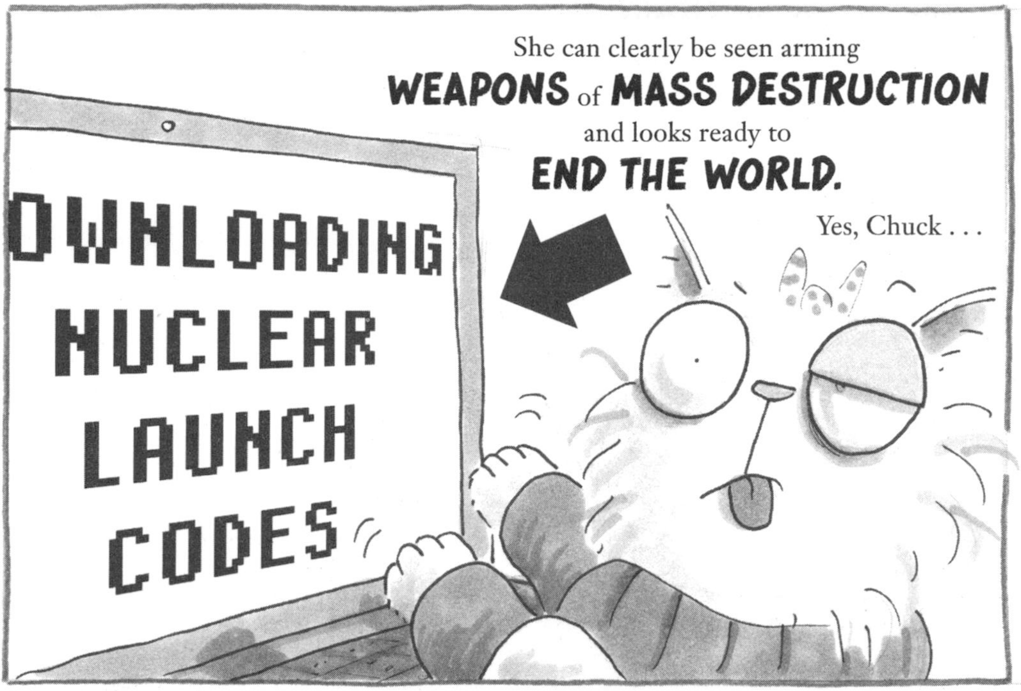
She can clearly be seen arming
WEAPONS of MASS DESTRUCTION
and looks ready to
END THE WORLD.
Yes, Chuck . . .
OWNLOADING
NUCLEAR
LAUNCH
CODES

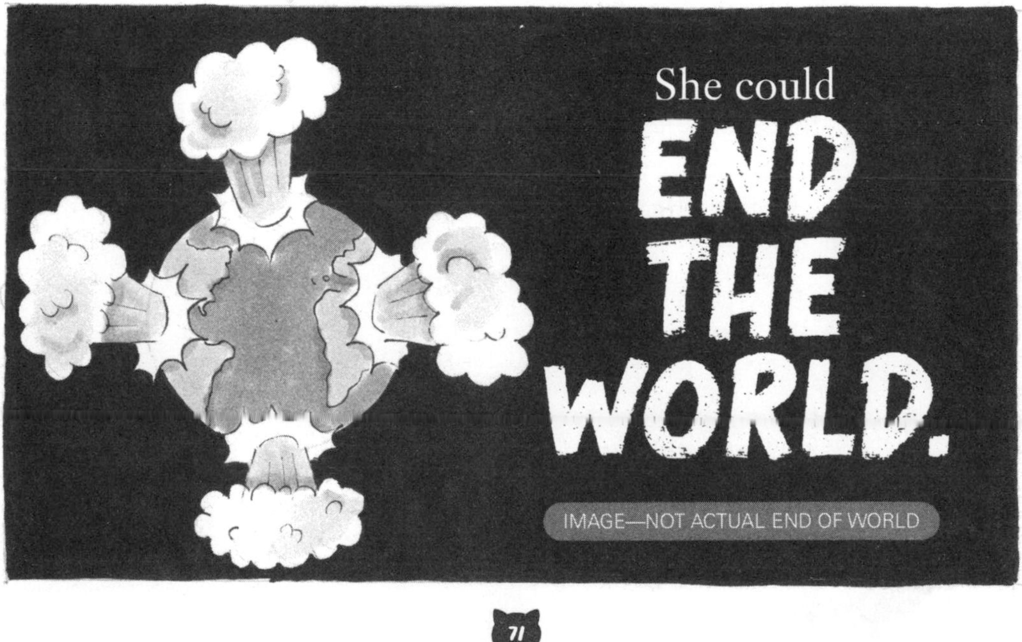
She could
END
THE
WORLD.
IMAGE—NOT ACTUAL END OF WORLD

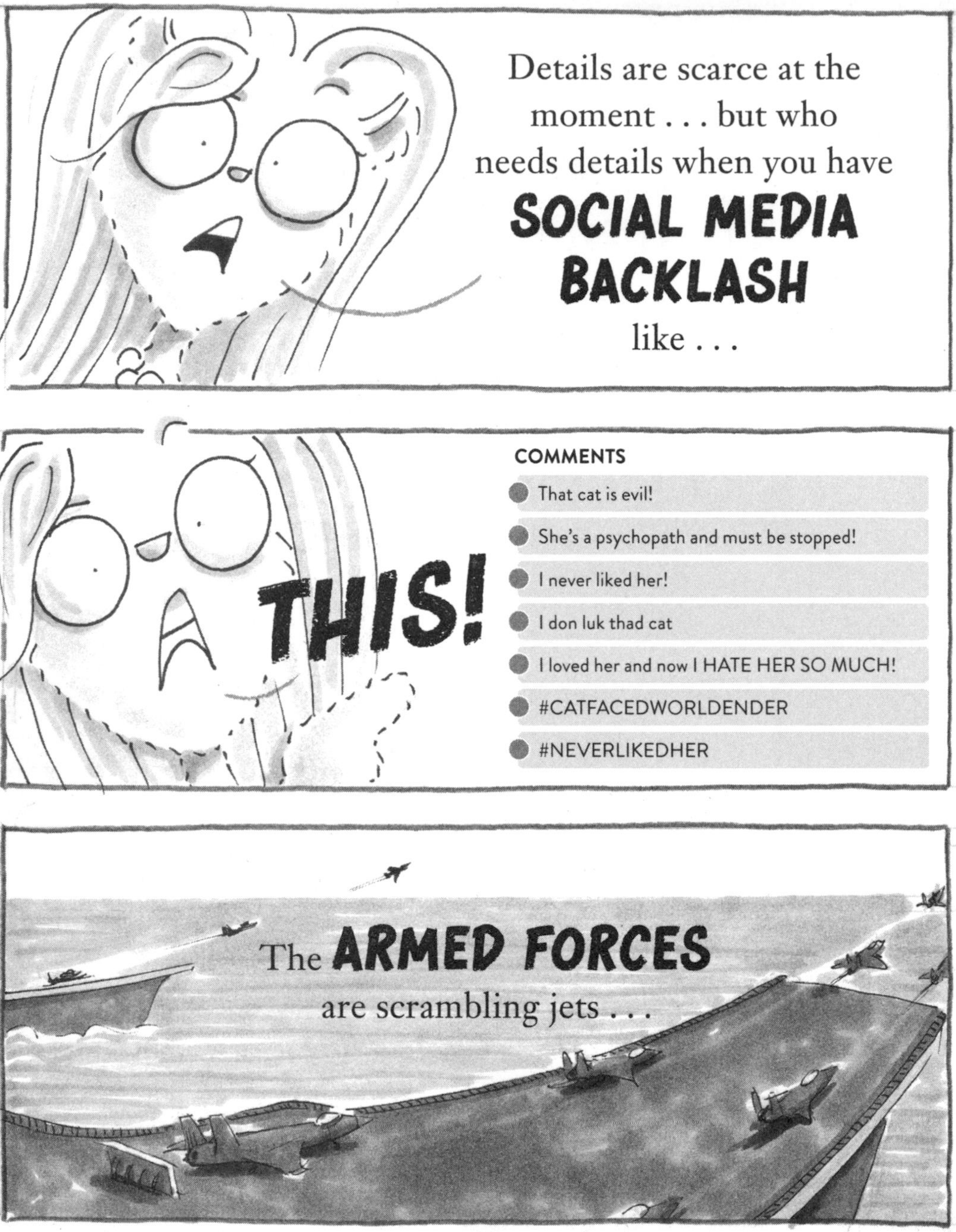
Details are scarce at the moment . . . but who needs details when you have
SOCIAL MEDIA BACKLASH
like . . .
THIS!
COMMENTS
That cat is evil!
She's a psychopath and must be stopped!
I never liked her!
I don luk thad cat
I loved her and now I HATE HER SO MUCH!
#CATFACEDWORLDENDER
#NEVERLIKEDHER
The ARMED FORCES
are scrambling jets . . .

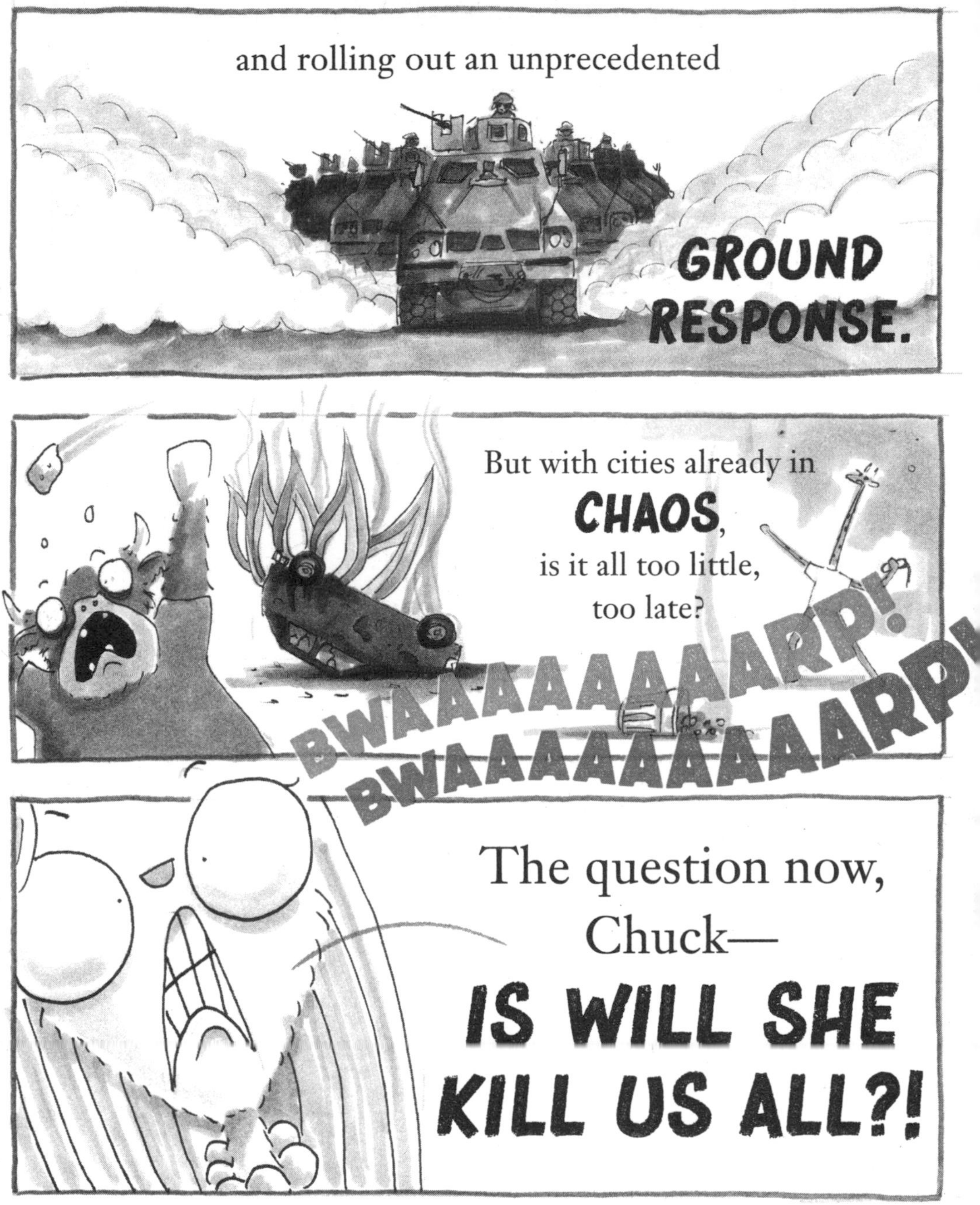
and rolling out an unprecedented
GROUND RESPONSE.
But with cities already in CHAOS, is it all too little, too late?
BWAAAAAAAARP!
BWAAAAAAAAARP!
The question now, Chuck—
IS WILL SHE KILL US ALL?!

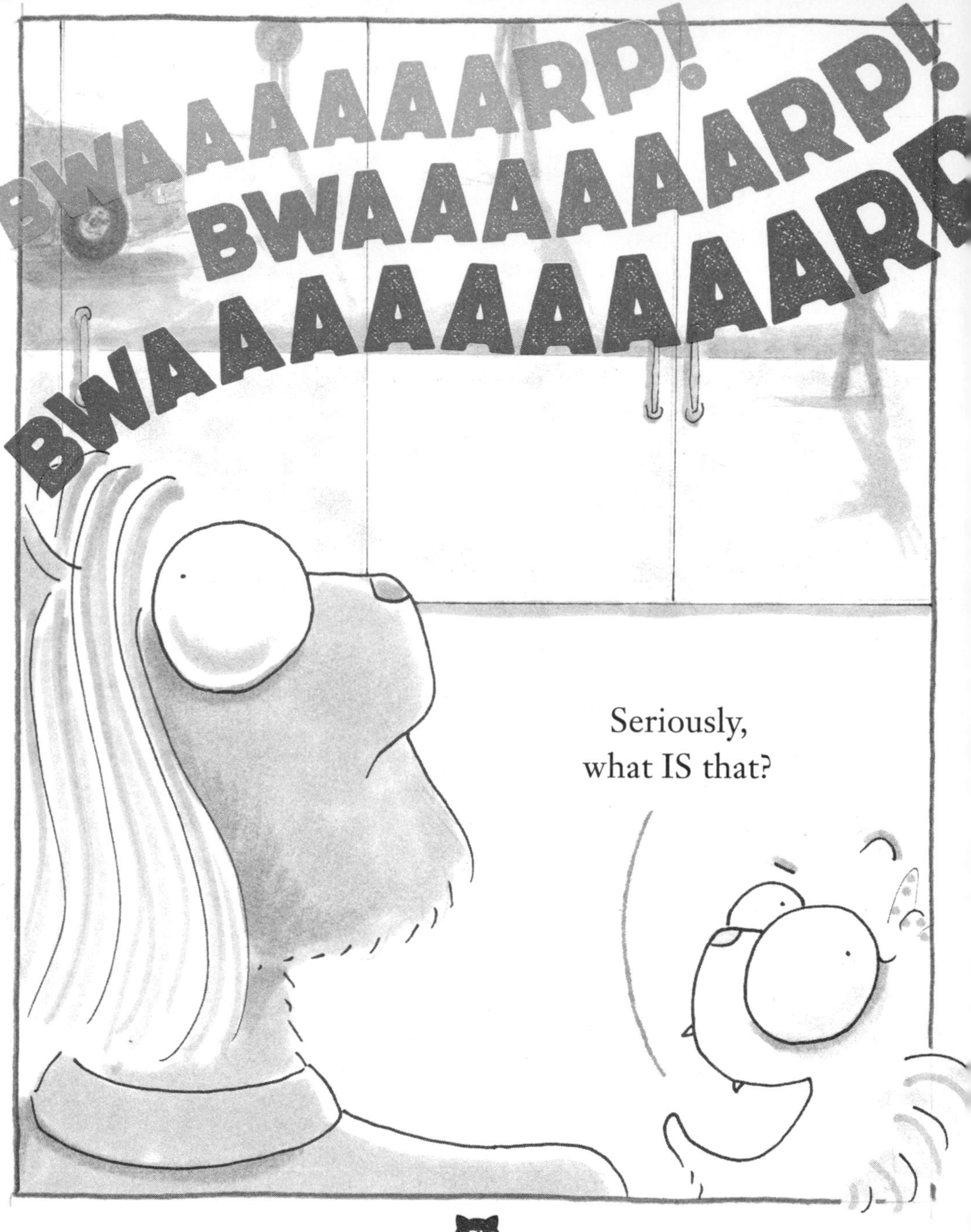
BWAAAAAARP!
BWAAAAAAARP!
BWAAAAAAAAARP
Seriously, what IS that?

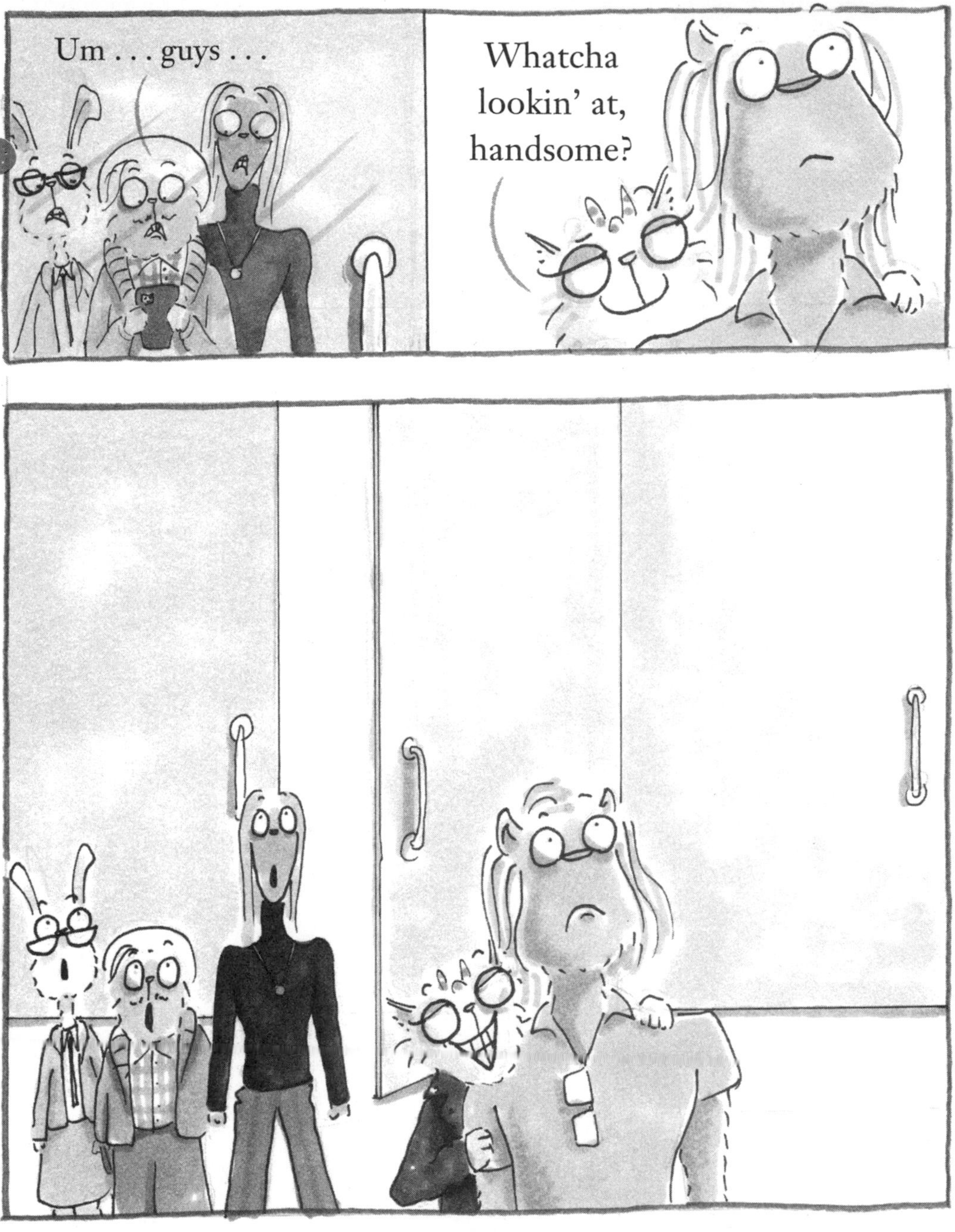
Um . . . guys . . .
Whatcha lookin' at, handsome?

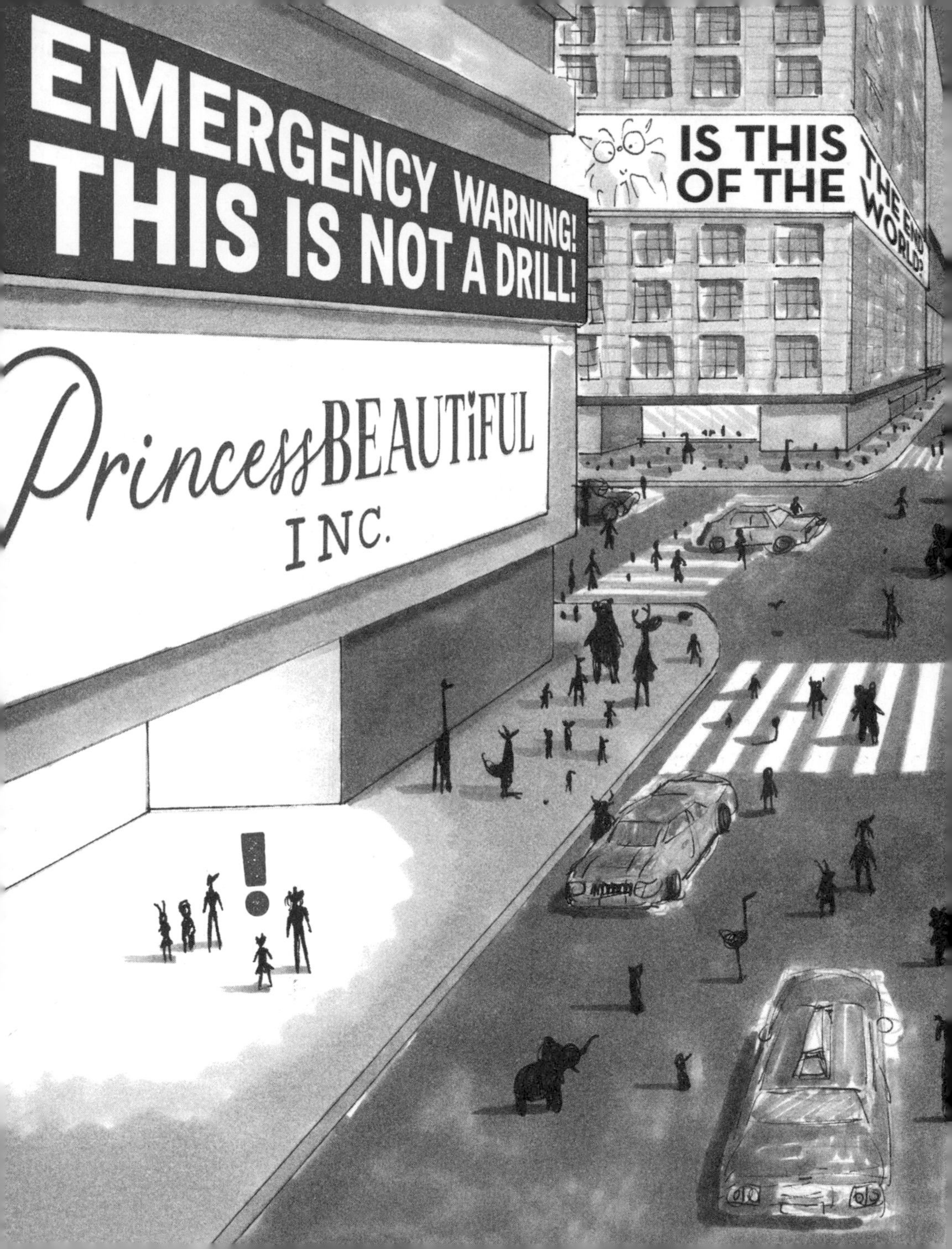
EMERGENCY WARNING!
THIS IS NOT A DRILL!
IS THIS THE END
OF THE WORLD?
PrincessBEAUTiFUL
INC.
!

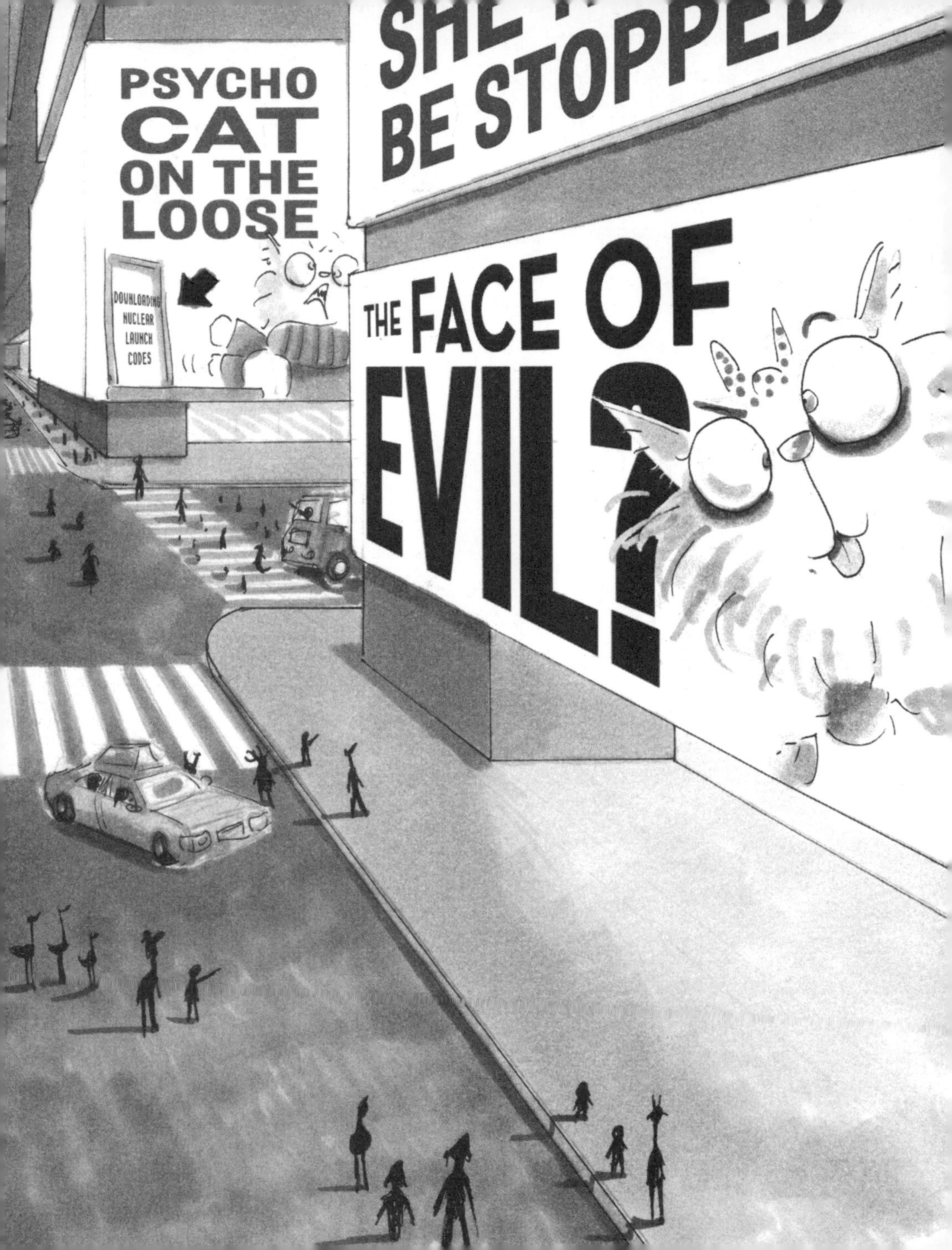

PSYCHO CAT ON THE LOOSE
DOWNLOADING NUCLEAR LAUNCH CODES
BE STOPPED
THE FACE OF EVIL?

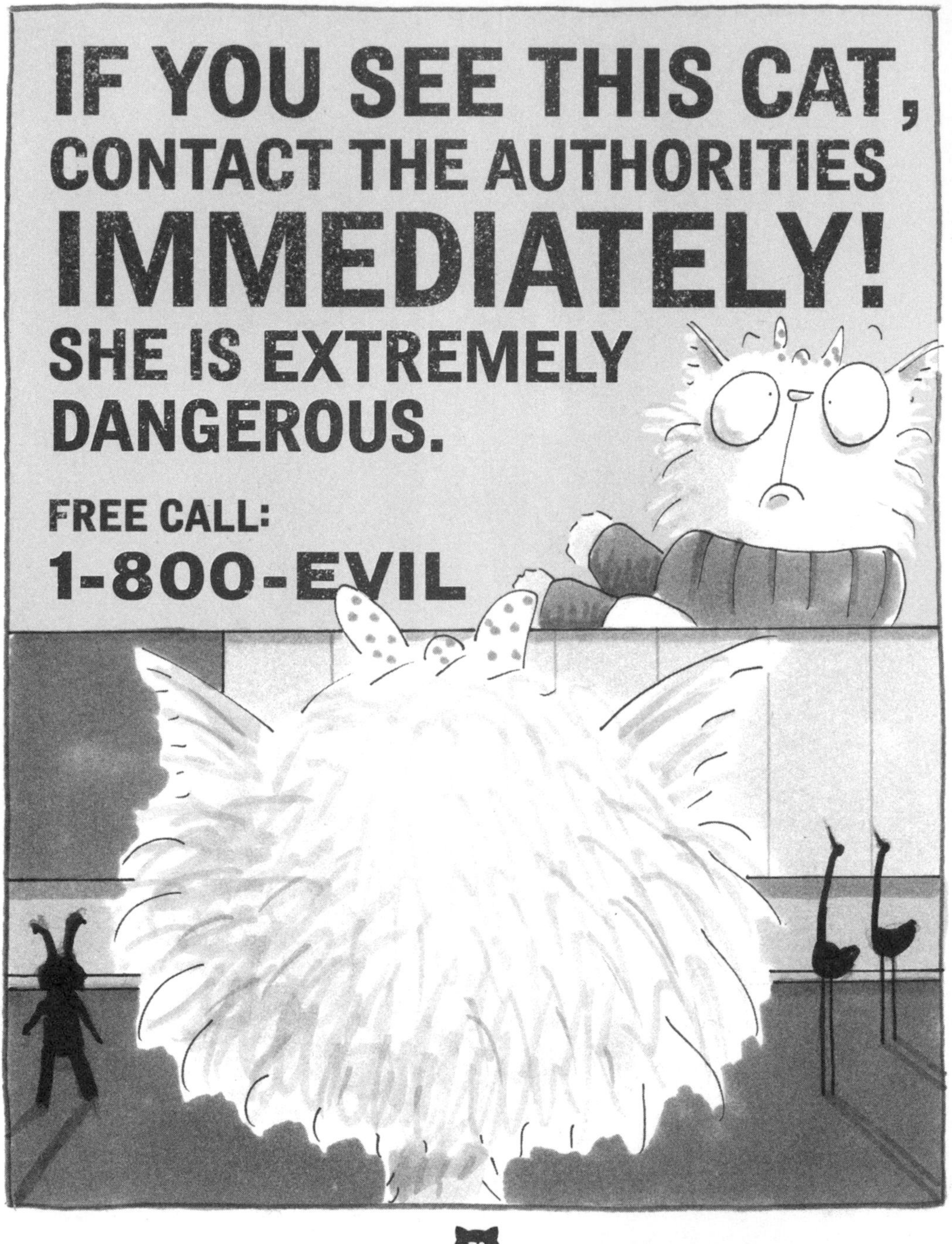
IF YOU SEE THIS CAT,
CONTACT THE AUTHORITIES
IMMEDIATELY!
SHE IS EXTREMELY
DANGEROUS.
FREE CALL:
1-800-EVIL

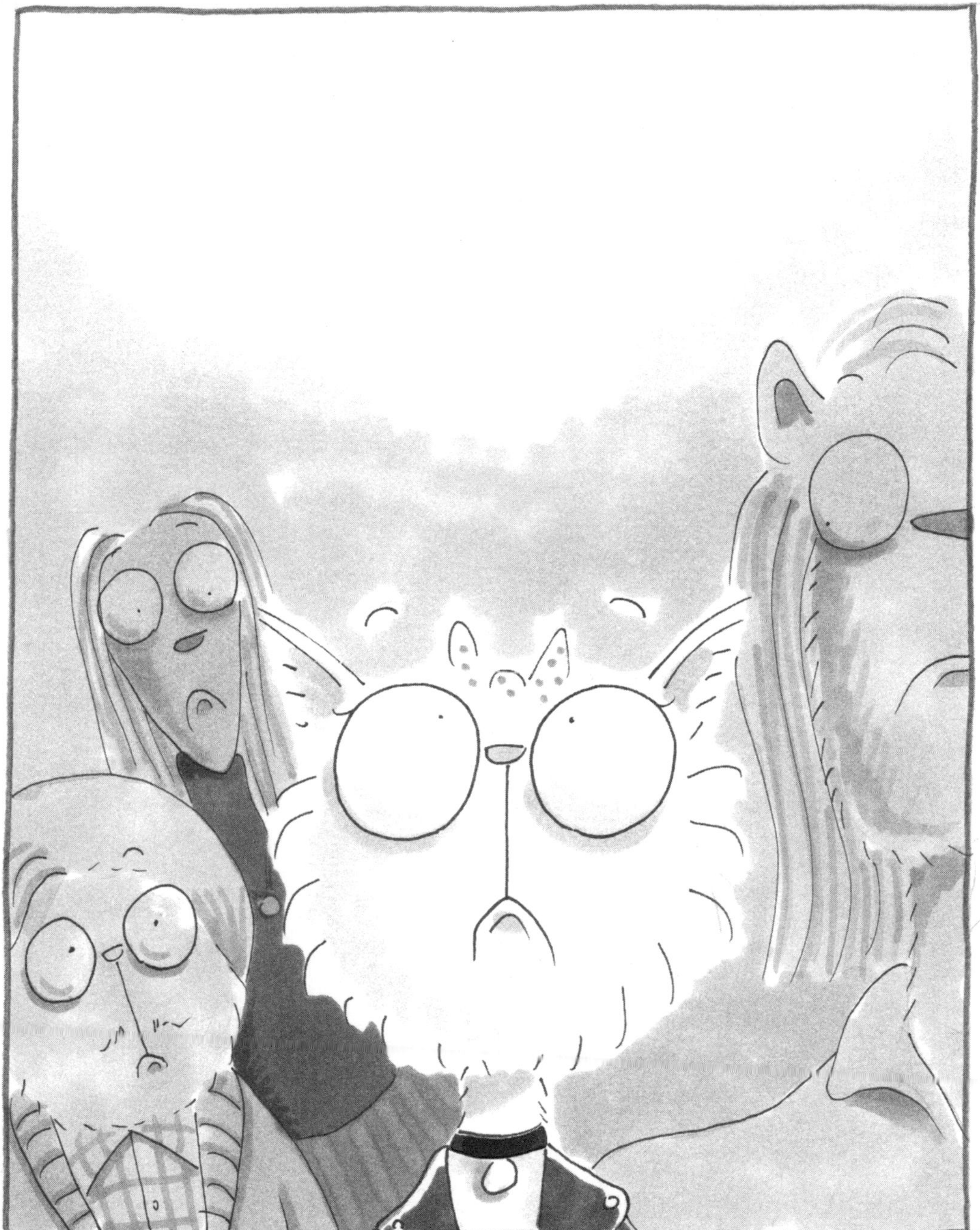

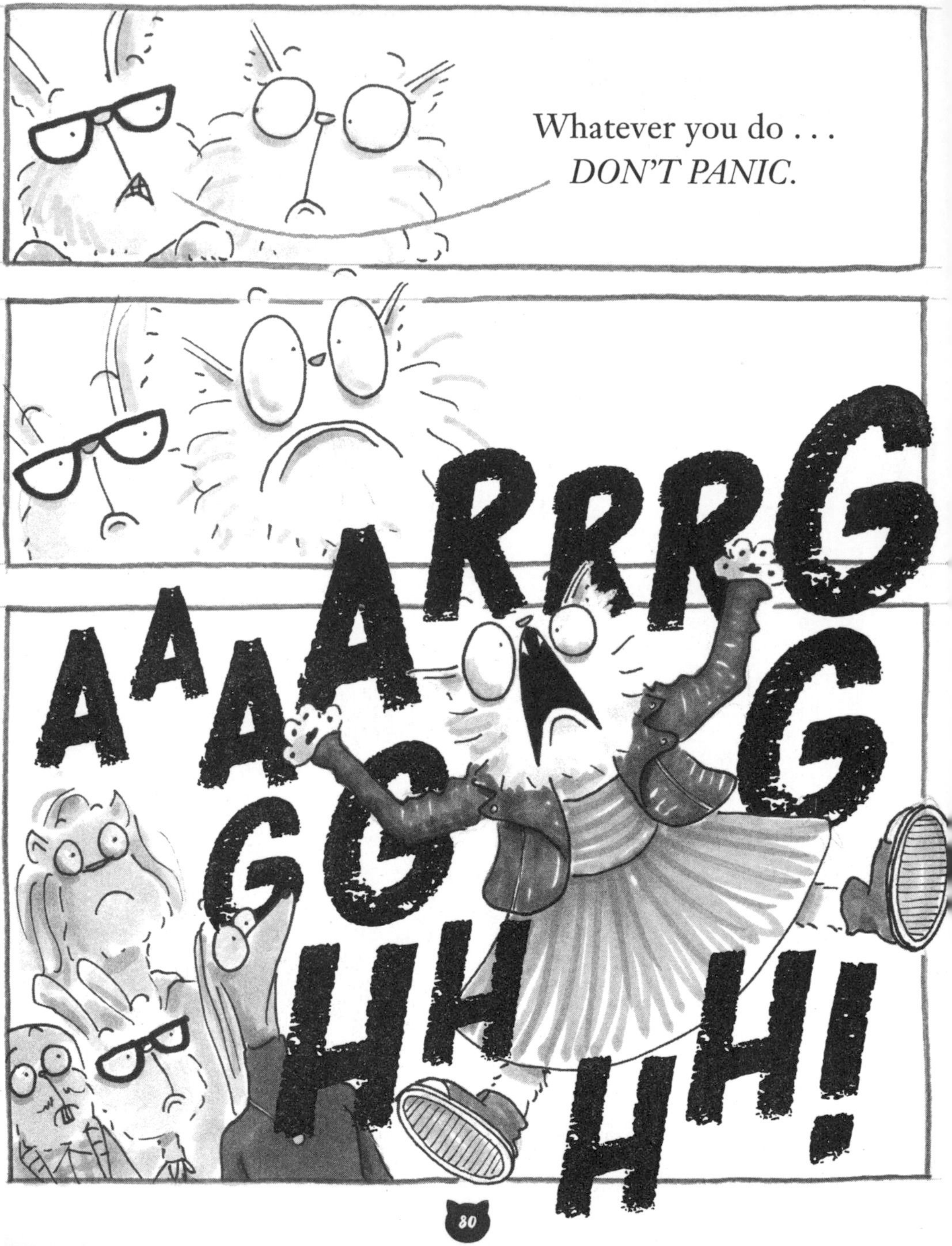
Whatever you do . . .
DON'T PANIC.
AAAAARRRGGGGHHHHH!

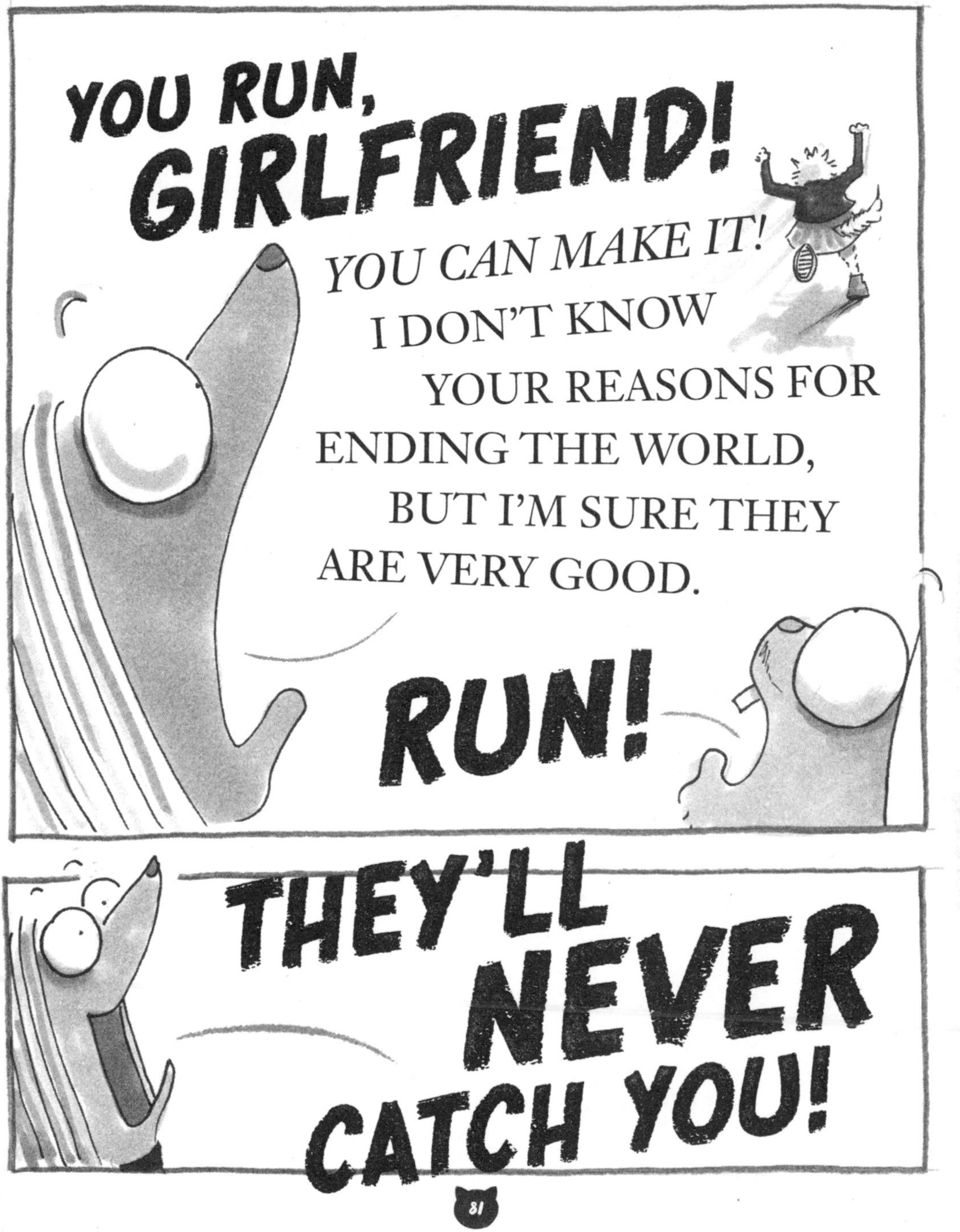
YOU RUN, GIRLFRIEND!
YOU CAN MAKE IT! I DON'T KNOW YOUR REASONS FOR ENDING THE WORLD, BUT I'M SURE THEY ARE VERY GOOD.
RUN!
THEY'LL NEVER CATCH YOU!

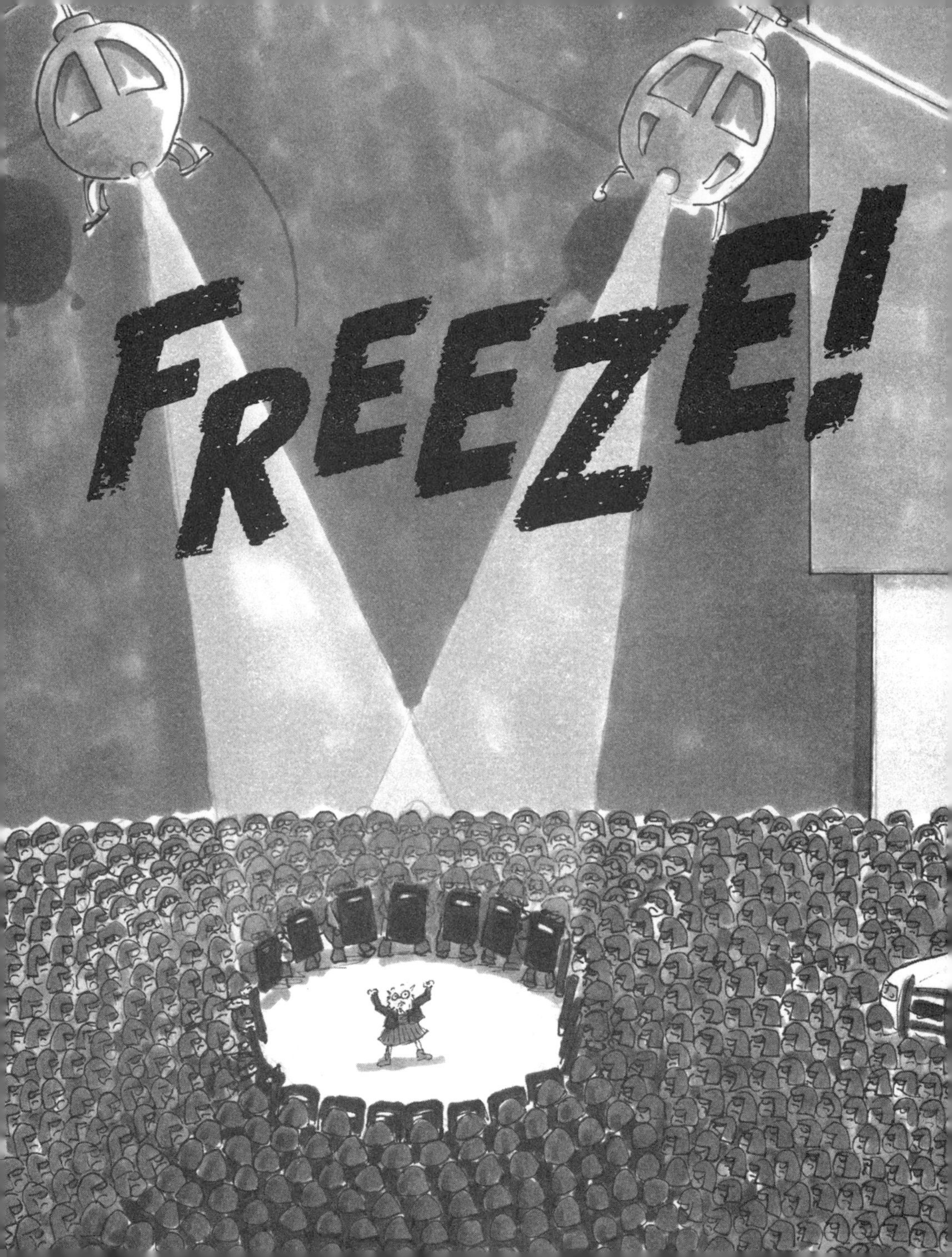
FREEZE!

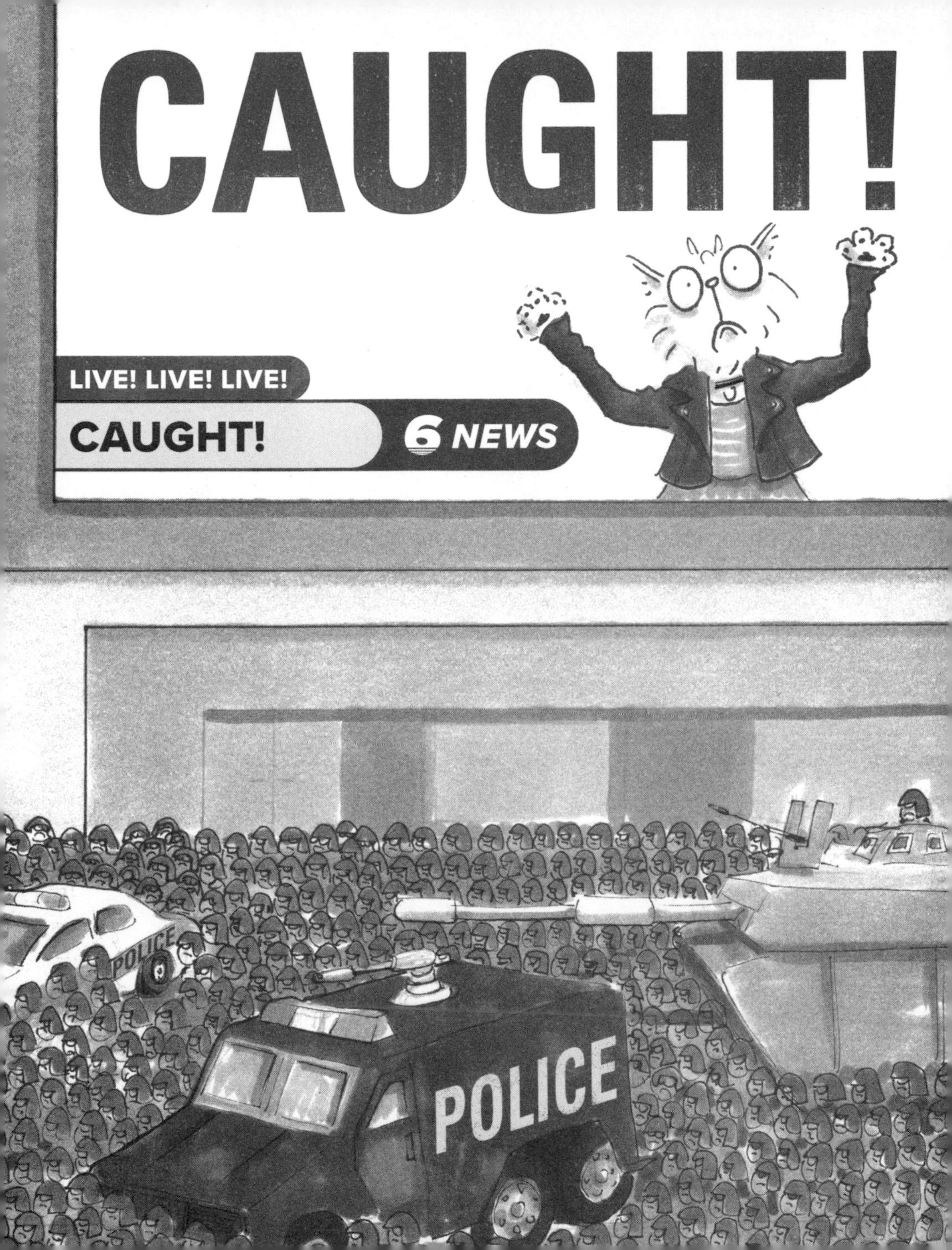
CAUGHT!
LIVE! LIVE! LIVE!
CAUGHT!
6 NEWS
POLICE
POLICE

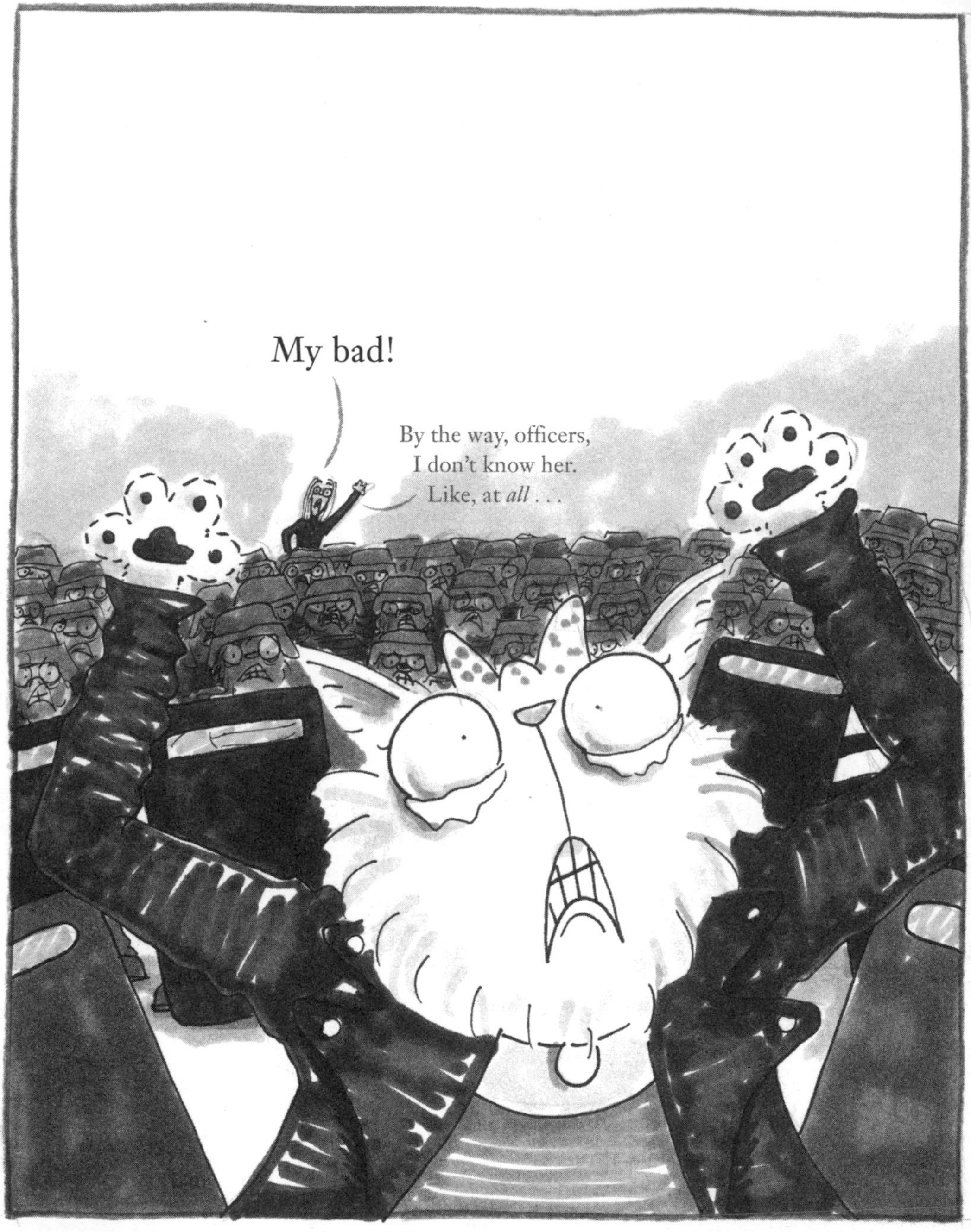
My bad!
By the way, officers, I don't know her. Like, at *all* . . .

Four

TRIAL BY INTERNET...

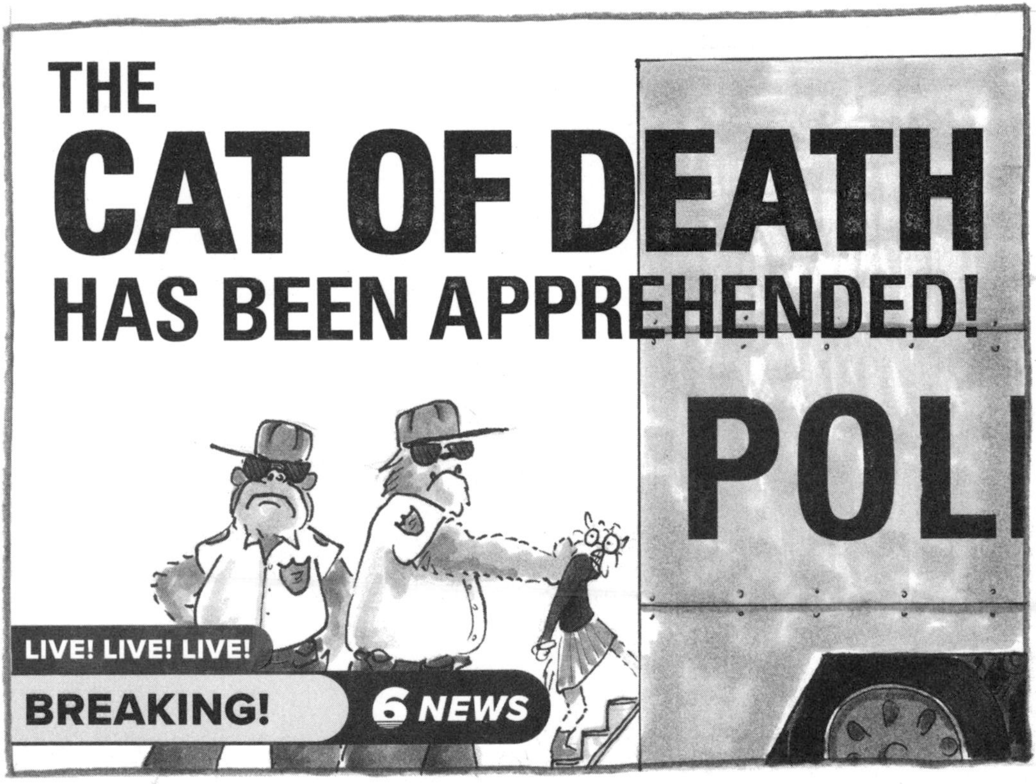
THE
CAT OF DEATH
HAS BEEN APPREHENDED!
POLI
LIVE! LIVE! LIVE!
BREAKING!
6 NEWS

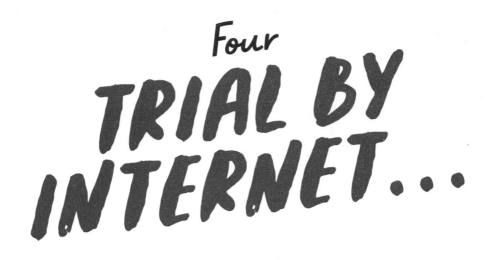

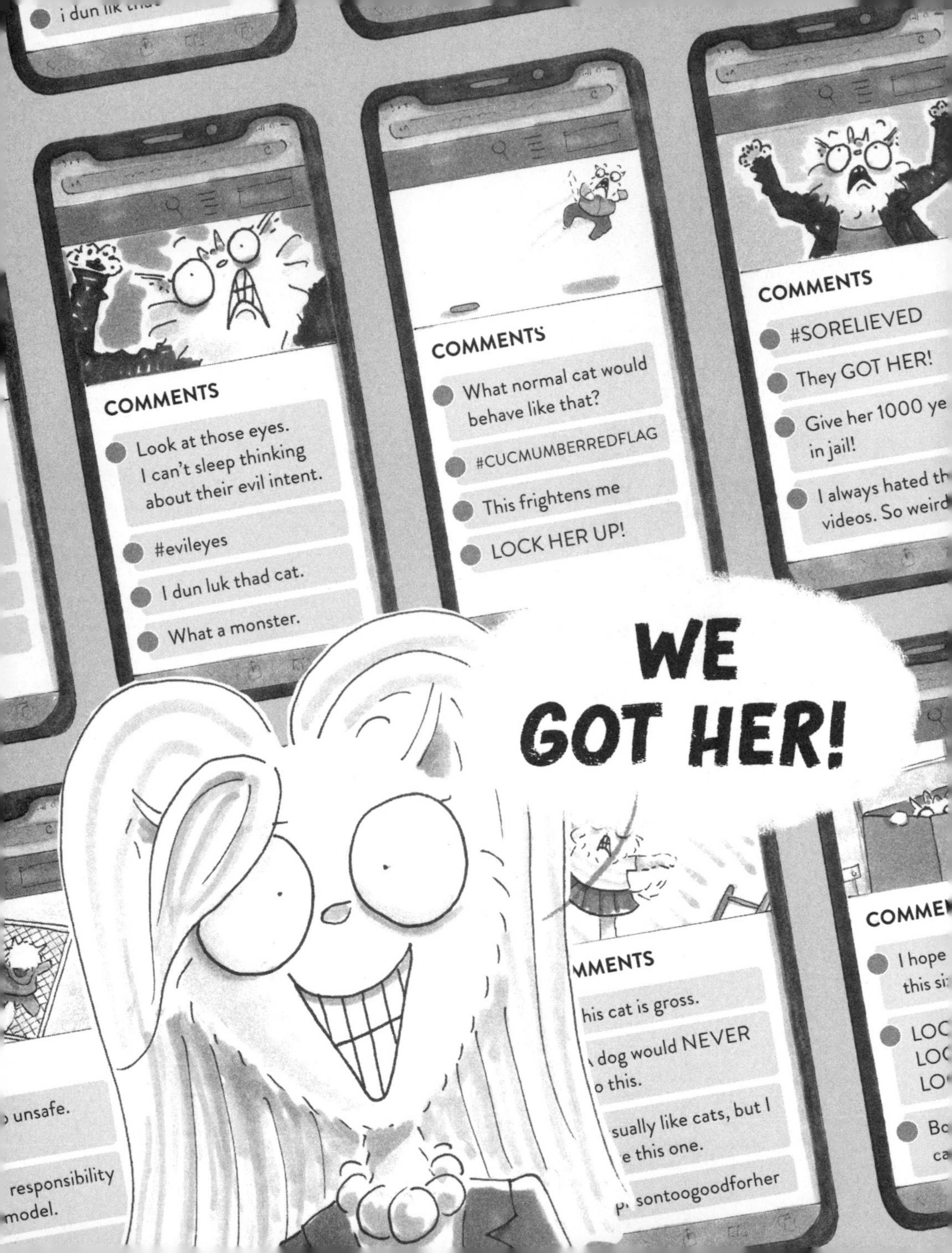

i dun lik tha
COMMENTS
Look at those eyes. I can't sleep thinking about their evil intent.
#evileyes
I dun luk thad cat.
What a monster.
COMMENTS
What normal cat would behave like that?
#CUCMUMBERREDFLAG
This frightens me
LOCK HER UP!
COMMENTS
#SORELIEVED
They GOT HER!
Give her 1000 ye in jail!
I always hated th videos. So weird
WE GOT HER!
unsafe.
responsibility model.
MMENTS
his cat is gross.
dog would NEVER o this.
sually like cats, but I e this one.
sontoogoodforher
COMME
I hope this si
LOC LOC LO
Bo ca

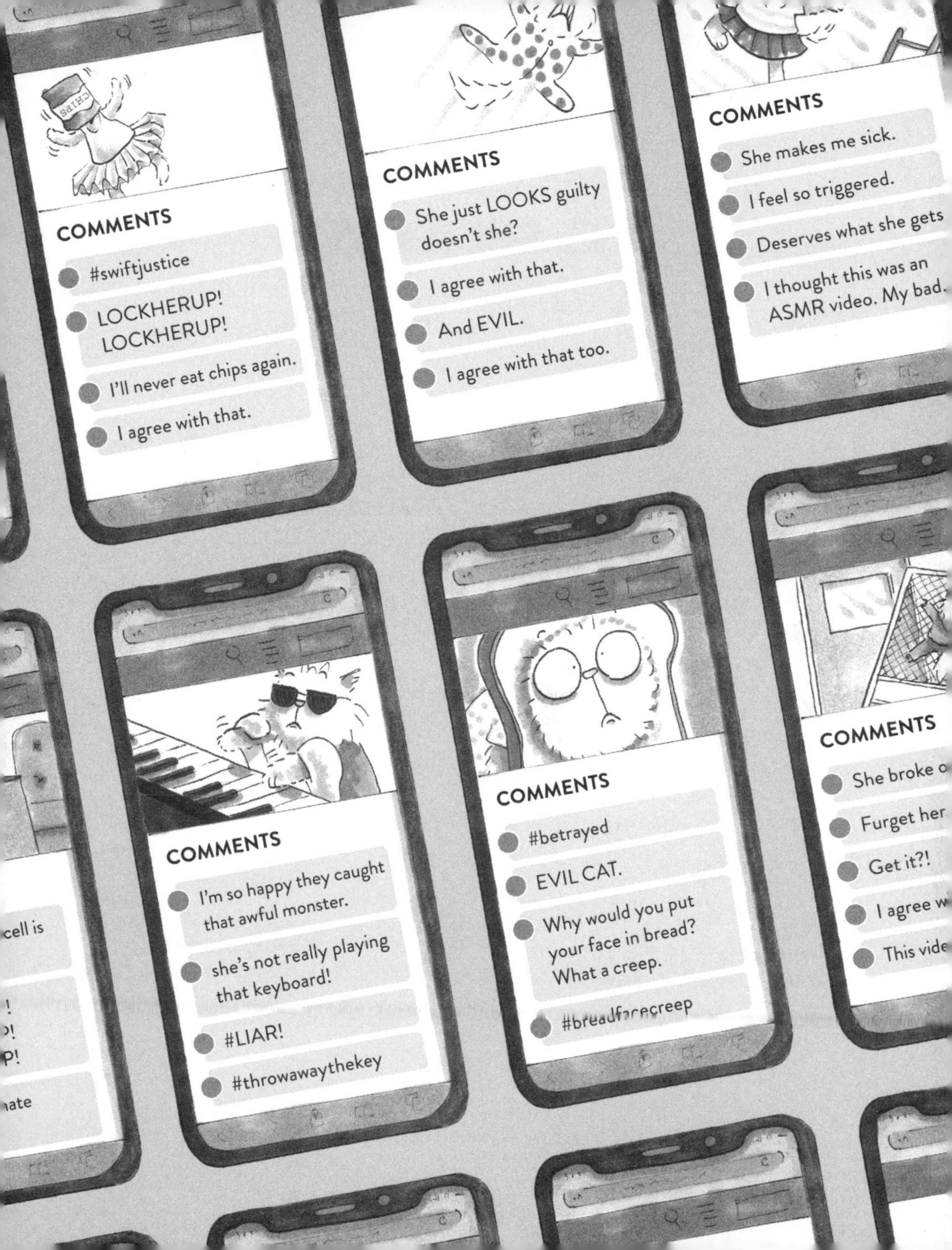

CHIPS
COMMENTS
#swiftjustice
LOCKHERUP! LOCKHERUP!
I'll never eat chips again.
I agree with that.
COMMENTS
She just LOOKS guilty doesn't she?
I agree with that.
And EVIL.
I agree with that too.
COMMENTS
She makes me sick.
I feel so triggered.
Deserves what she gets
I thought this was an ASMR video. My bad.
cell is
COMMENTS
I'm so happy they caught that awful monster.
she's not really playing that keyboard!
#LIAR!
#throwawaythekey
COMMENTS
#betrayed
EVIL CAT.
Why would you put your face in bread? What a creep.
#breadfacecreep
COMMENTS
She broke
Furget her
Get it?!
I agree
This

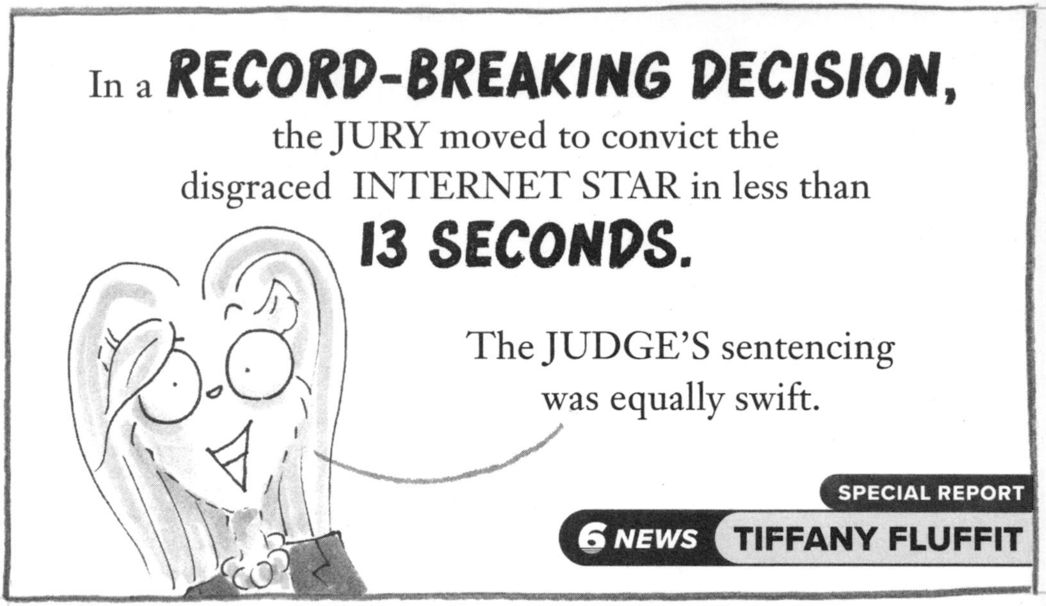
In a RECORD-BREAKING DECISION,
the JURY moved to convict the disgraced INTERNET STAR in less than
13 SECONDS.
The JUDGE'S sentencing was equally swift.
SPECIAL REPORT
6 NEWS
TIFFANY FLUFFIT

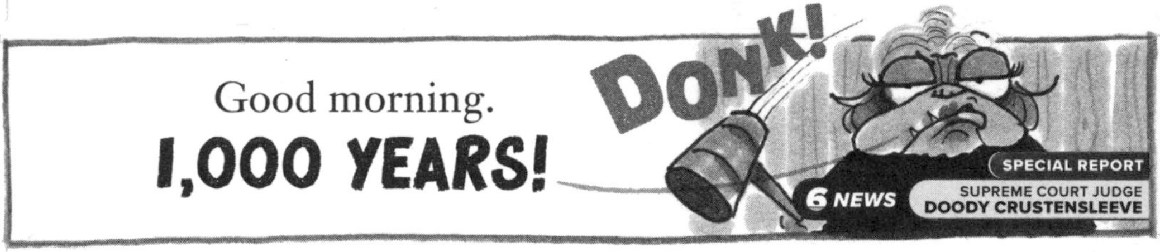
Good morning.
1,000 YEARS!
DONK!
SPECIAL REPORT
6 NEWS
SUPREME COURT JUDGE
DOODY CRUSTENSLEEVE

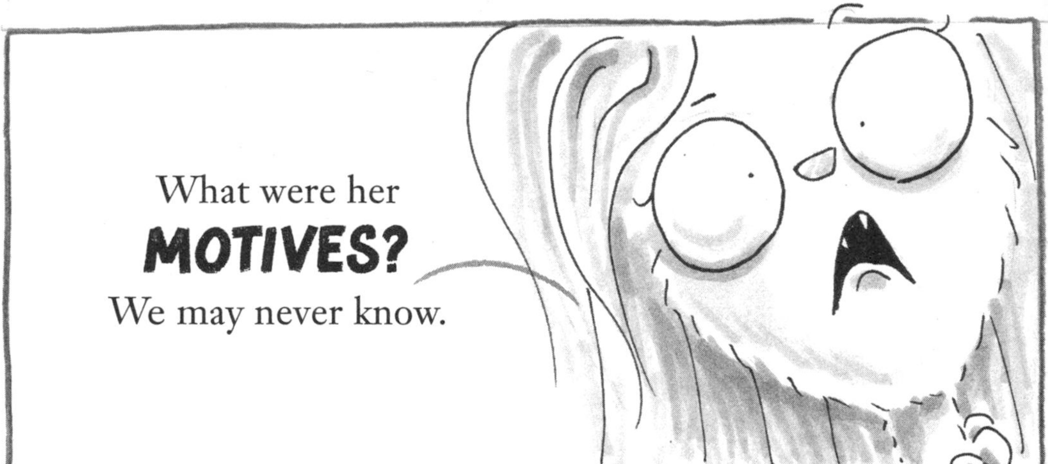
What were her MOTIVES? We may never know.

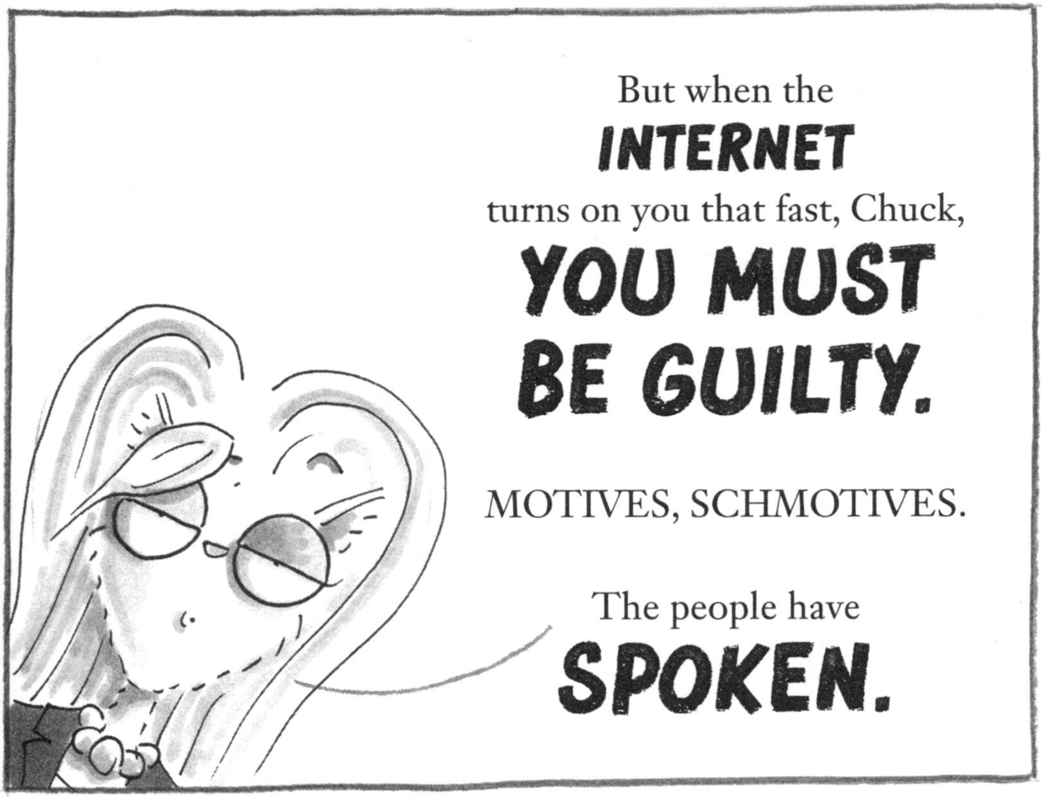
But when the INTERNET turns on you that fast, Chuck, YOU MUST BE GUILTY.
MOTIVES, SCHMOTIVES.
The people have SPOKEN.

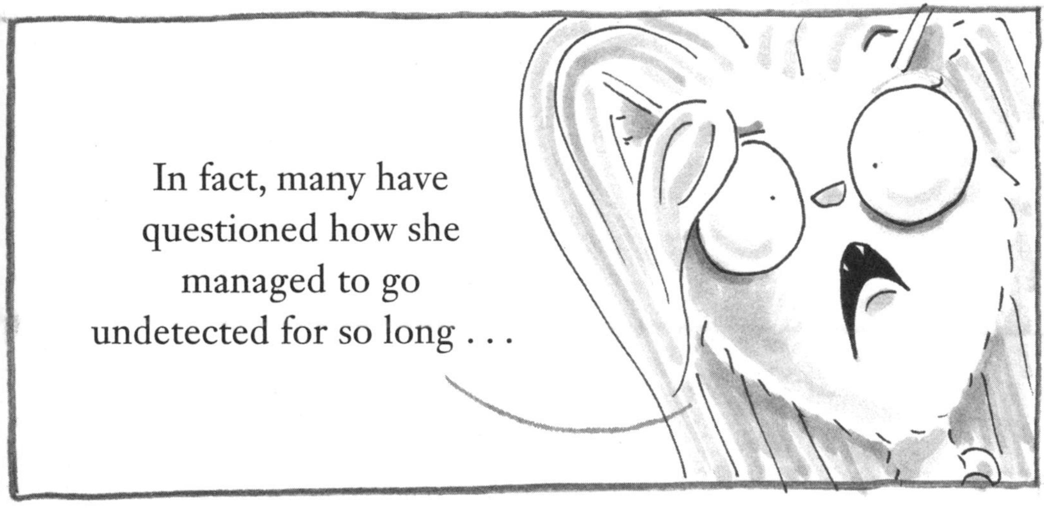
In fact, many have questioned how she managed to go undetected for so long . . .

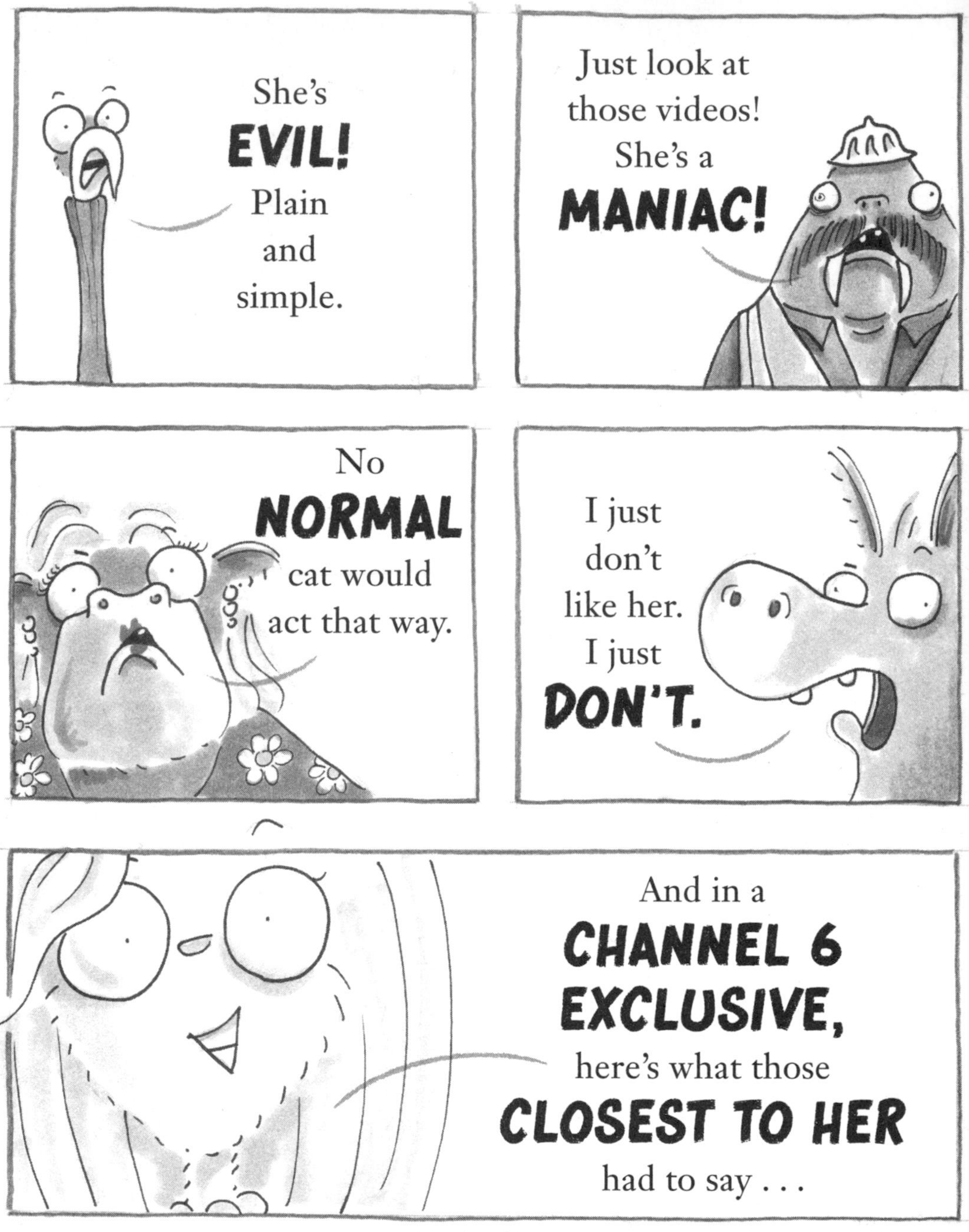
She's EVIL! Plain and simple.
Just look at those videos! She's a MANIAC!
No NORMAL cat would act that way.
I just don't like her. I just DON'T.
And in a CHANNEL 6 EXCLUSIVE, here's what those CLOSEST TO HER had to say . . .

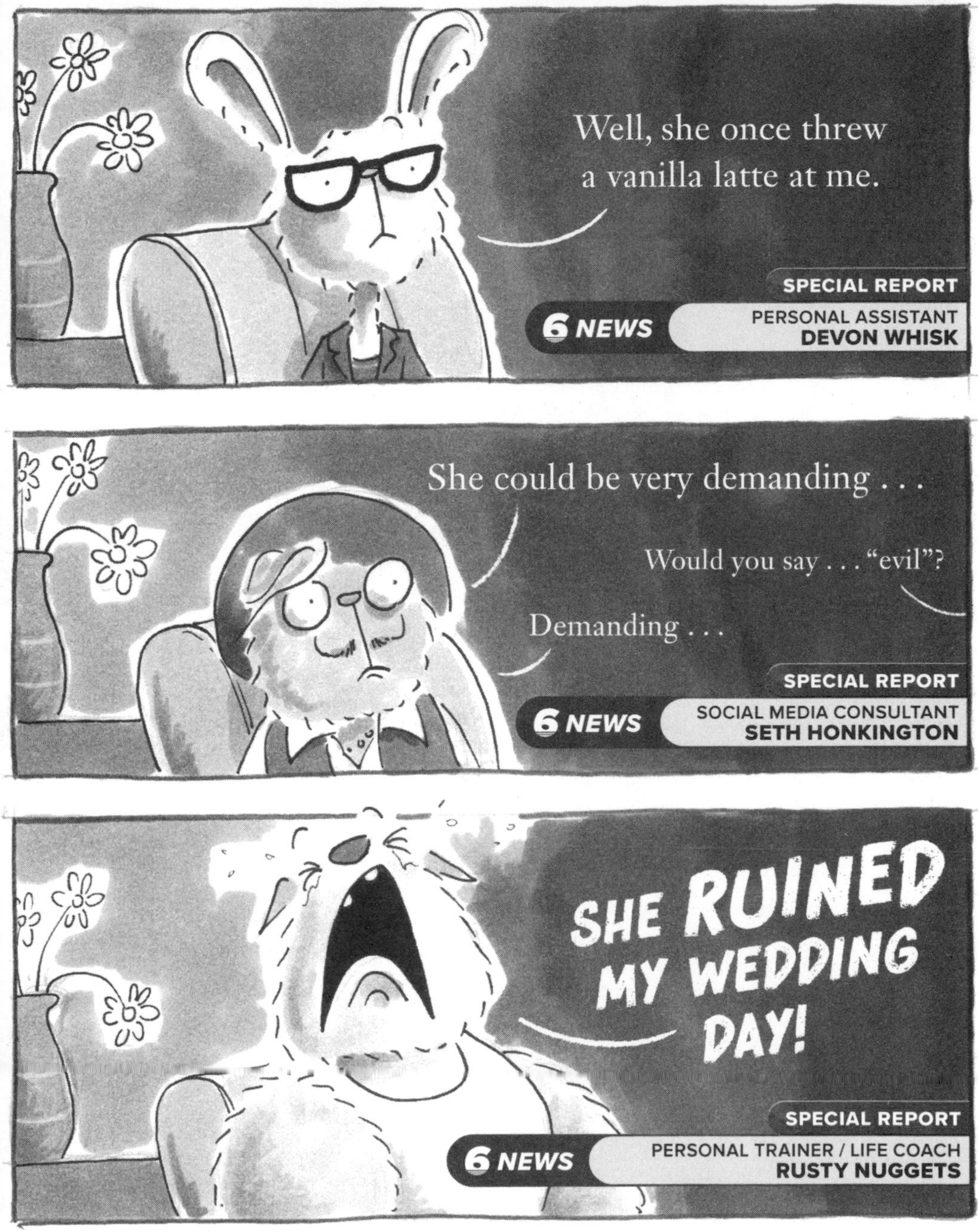
Well, she once threw a vanilla latte at me.
SPECIAL REPORT
6 NEWS
PERSONAL ASSISTANT
DEVON WHISK
She could be very demanding . . .
Would you say . . . "evil"?
Demanding . . .
SPECIAL REPORT
6 NEWS
SOCIAL MEDIA CONSULTANT
SETH HONKINGTON
SHE RUINED MY WEDDING DAY!
SPECIAL REPORT
6 NEWS
PERSONAL TRAINER / LIFE COACH
RUSTY NUGGETS

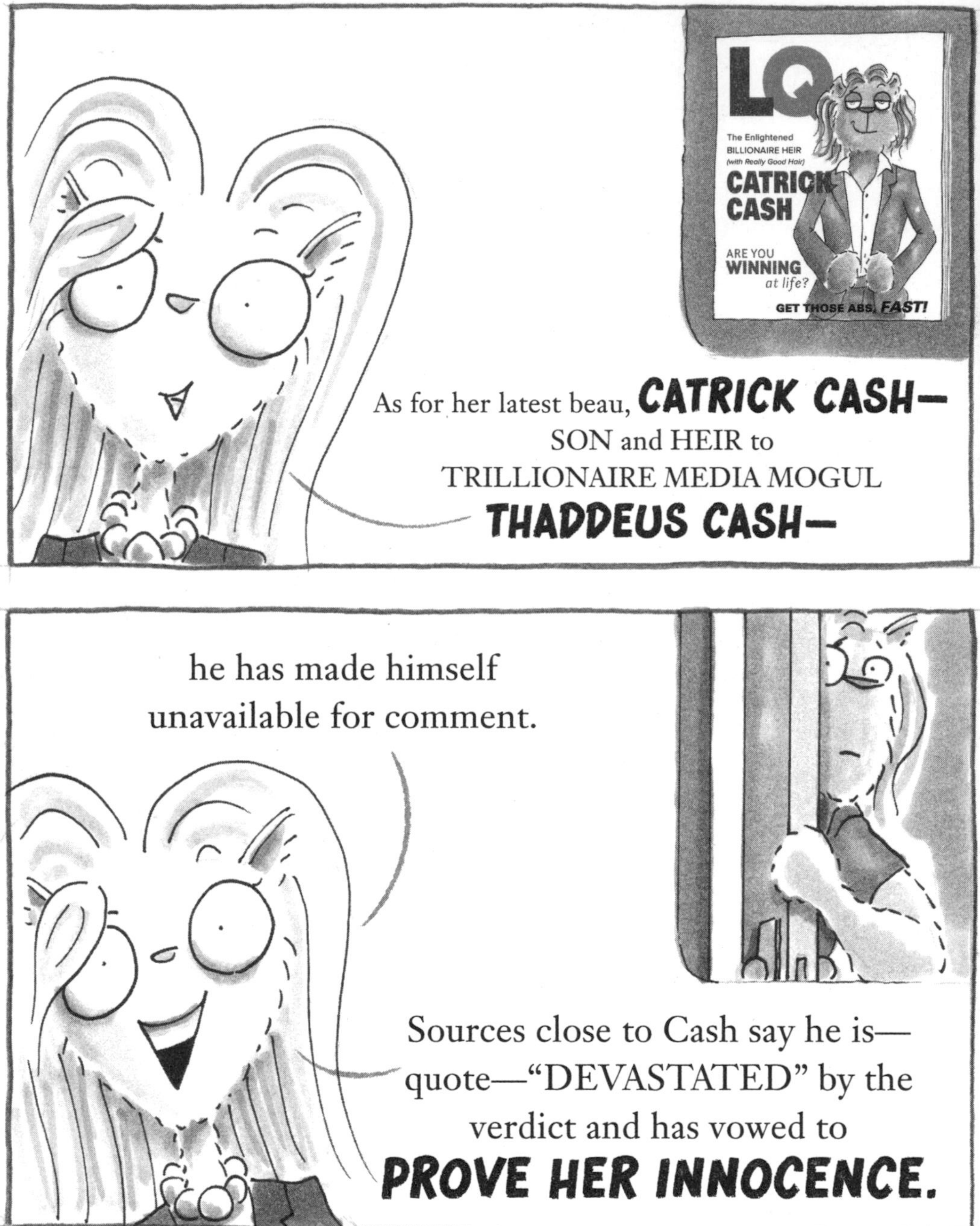
LQ
The Enlightened
BILLIONAIRE HEIR
(with Really Good Hair)
CATRICK
CASH
ARE YOU
WINNING
at life?
GET THOSE ABS, FAST!
As for her latest beau, CATRICK CASH—
SON and HEIR to
TRILLIONAIRE MEDIA MOGUL
THADDEUS CASH—
he has made himself
unavailable for comment.
Sources close to Cash say he is—
quote—"DEVASTATED" by the
verdict and has vowed to
PROVE HER INNOCENCE.

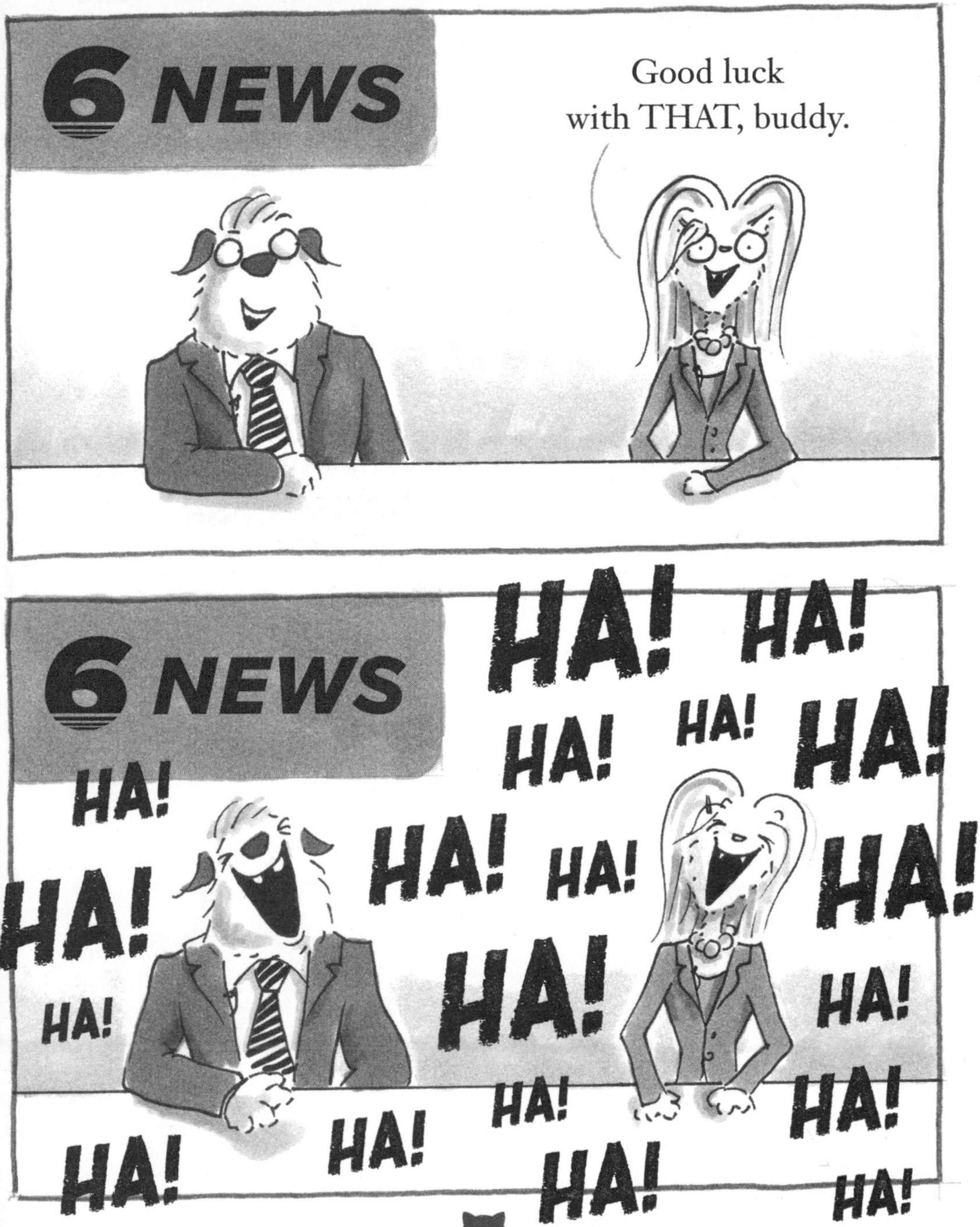
6 NEWS
Good luck with THAT, buddy.
6 NEWS
HA!
HA!
HA!
HA!
HA!
HA!
HA!
HA!
HA!
HA!
HA!
HA!
HA!
HA!
HA!
HA!
HA!
HA!
HA!

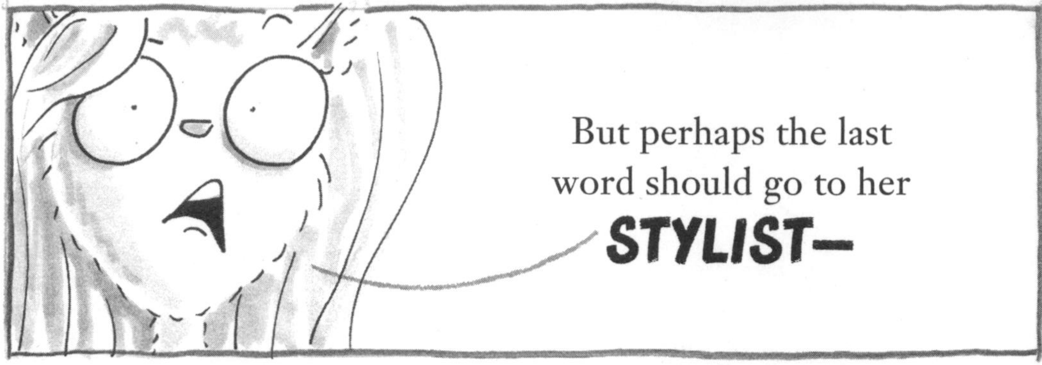
But perhaps the last word should go to her
STYLIST—

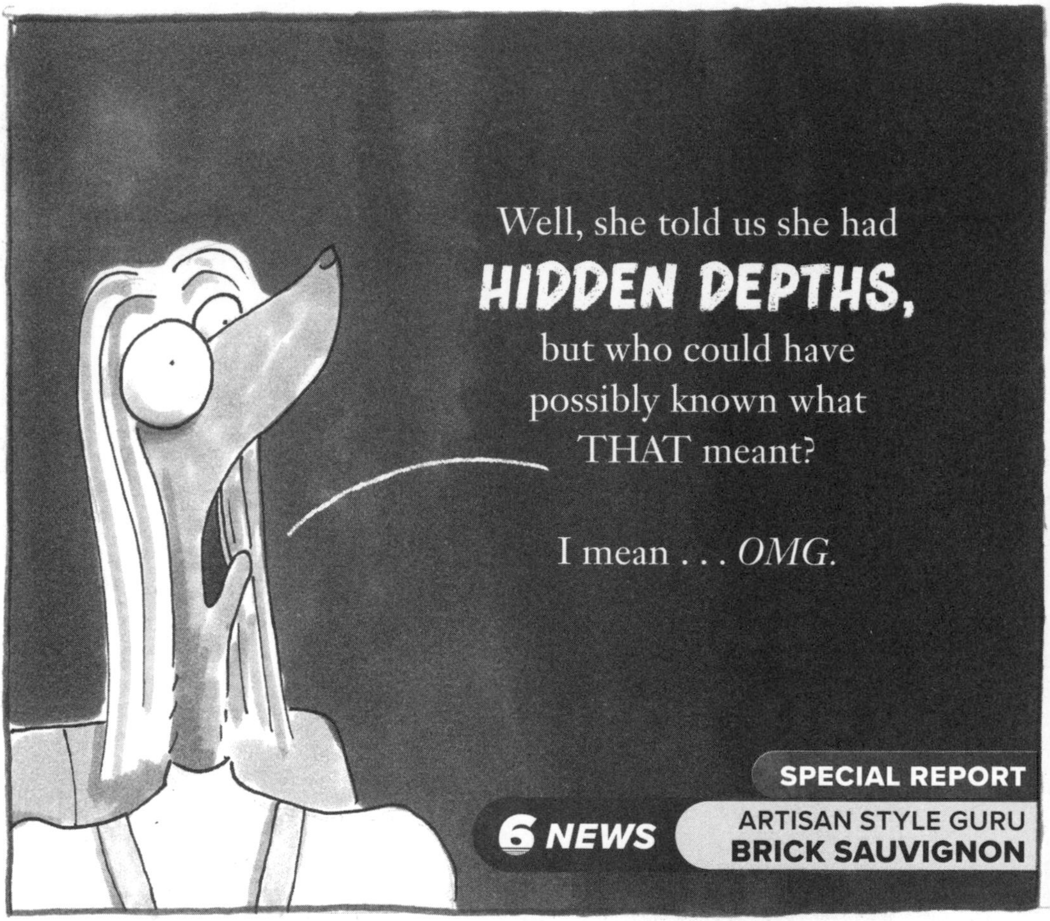
Well, she told us she had
HIDDEN DEPTHS,
but who could have possibly known what THAT meant?
I mean . . . *OMG.*
SPECIAL REPORT
6 NEWS
ARTISAN STYLE GURU
BRICK SAUVIGNON

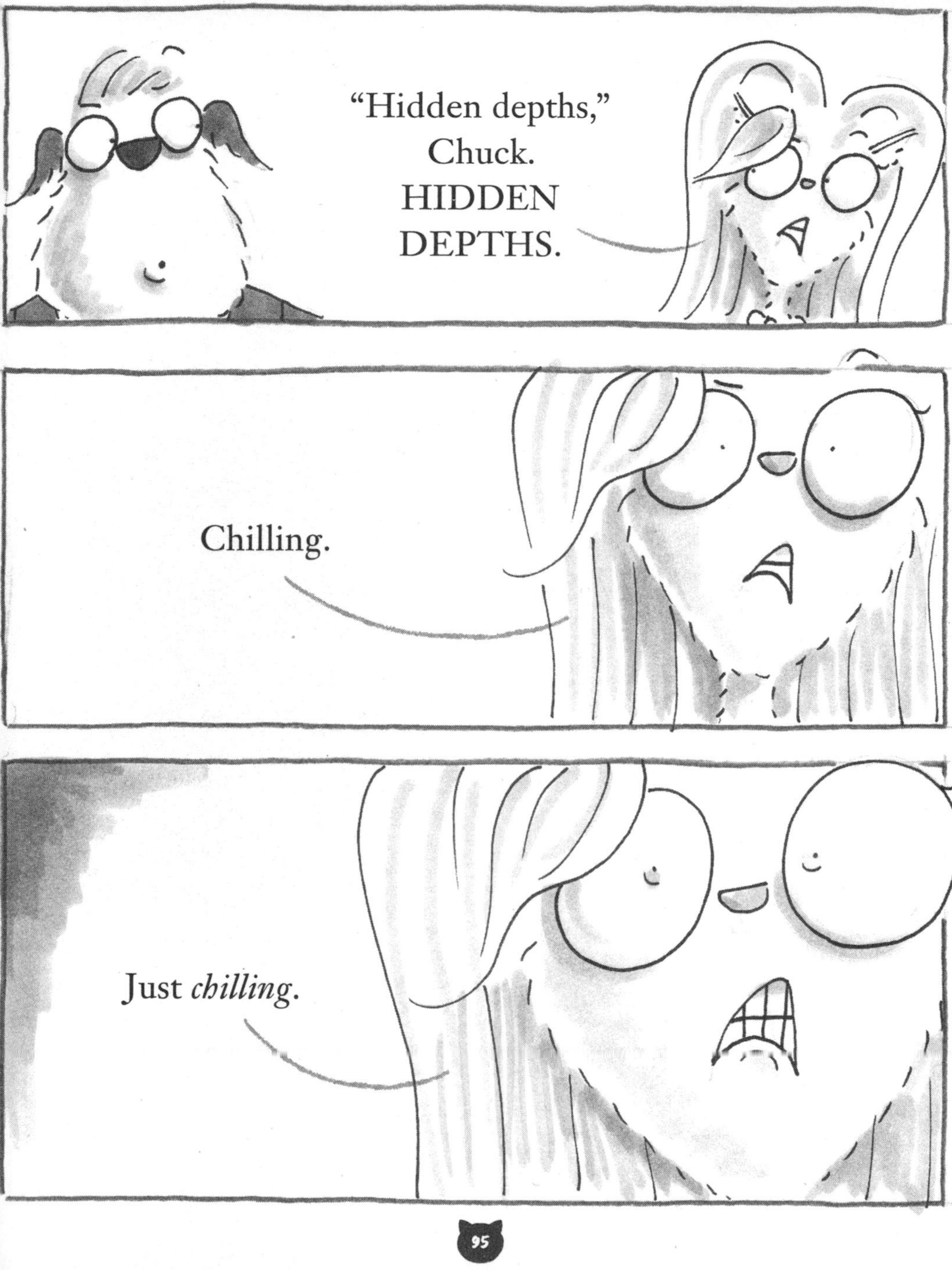
"Hidden depths," Chuck. HIDDEN DEPTHS.
Chilling.
Just *chilling*.

Five

OFF TO THE BIG HOUSE

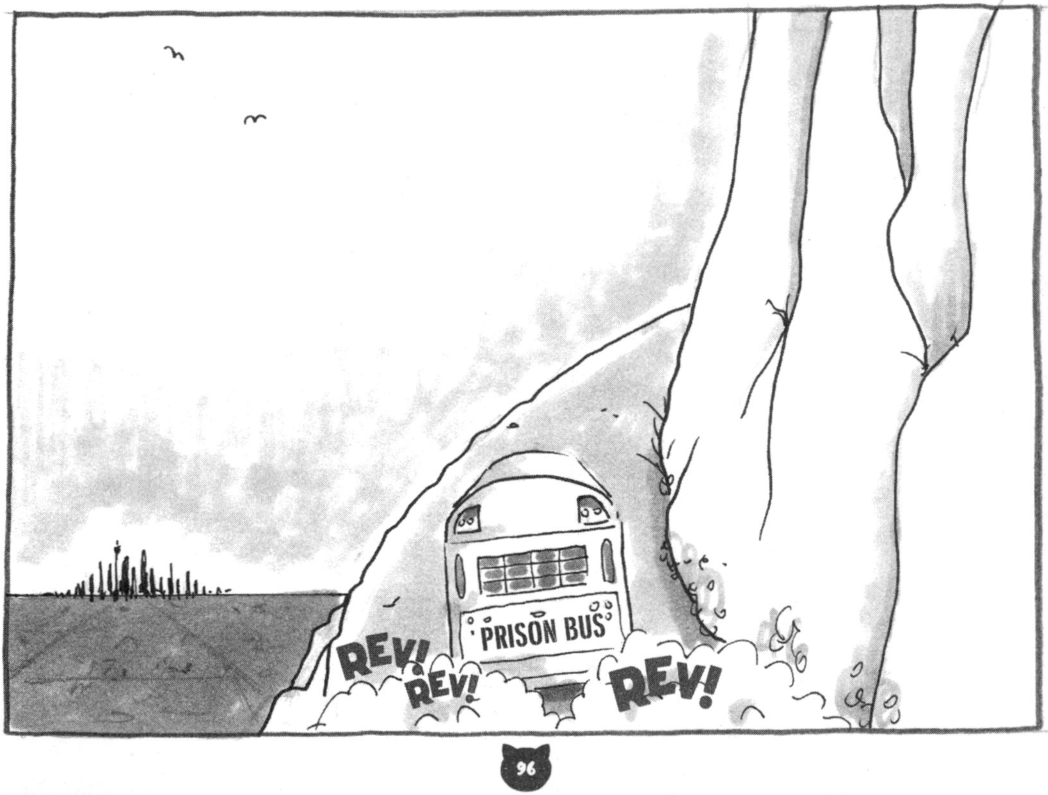
PRISON BUS
REV!
REV!
REV!

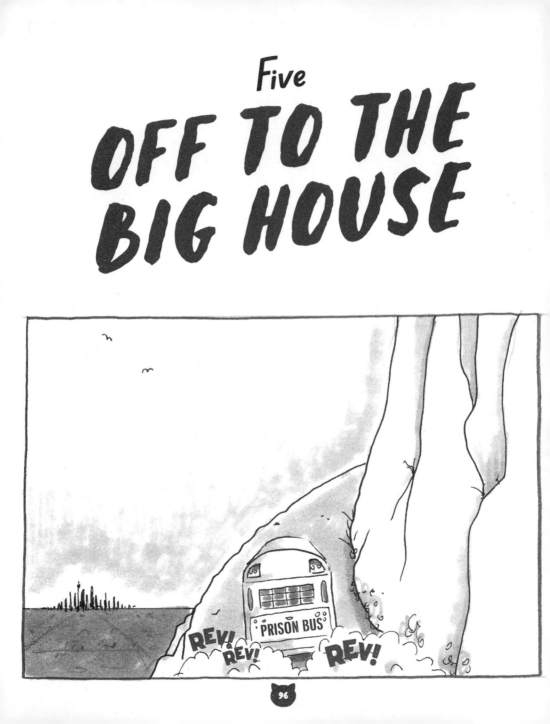

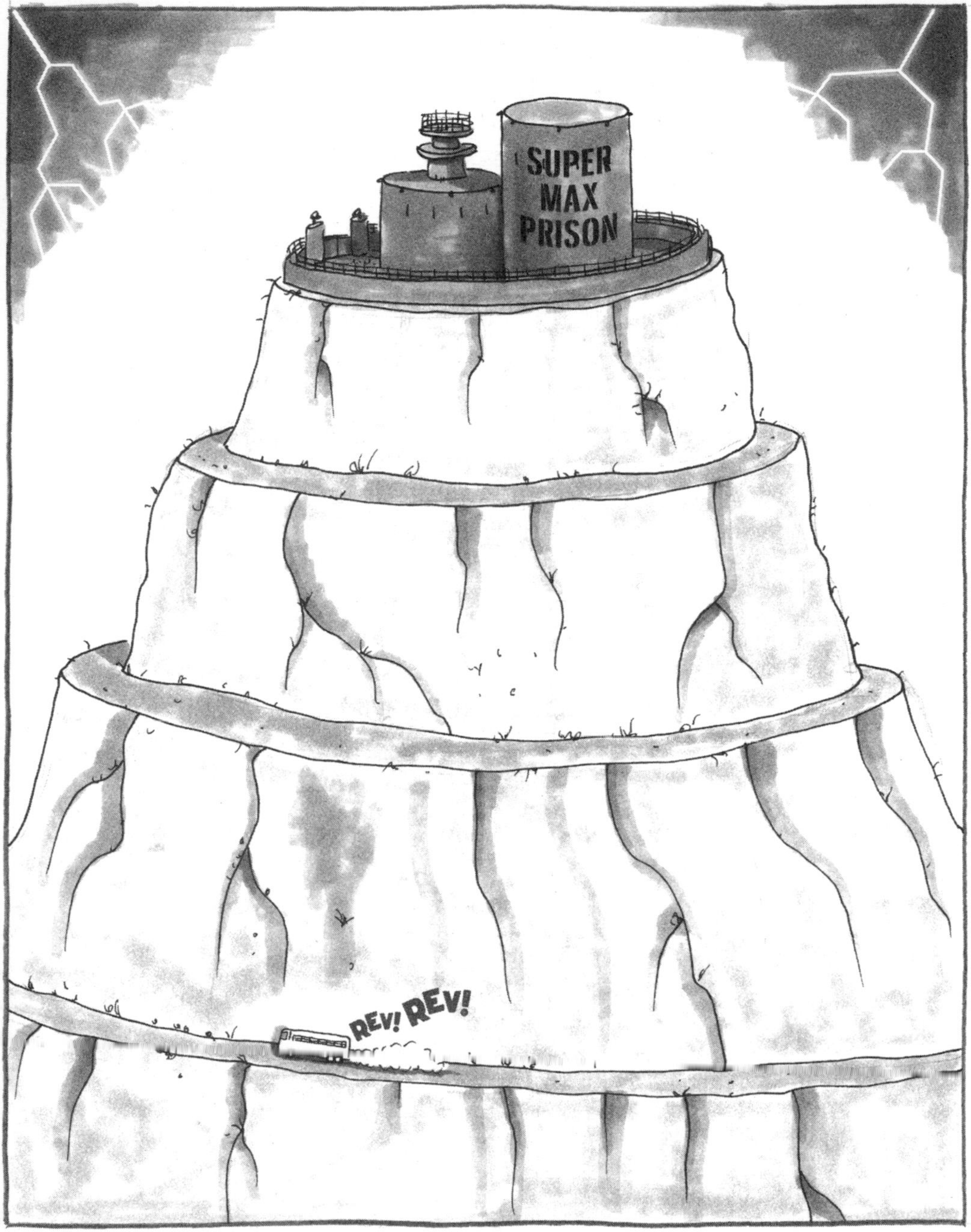
SUPER
MAX
PRISON
REV! REV!

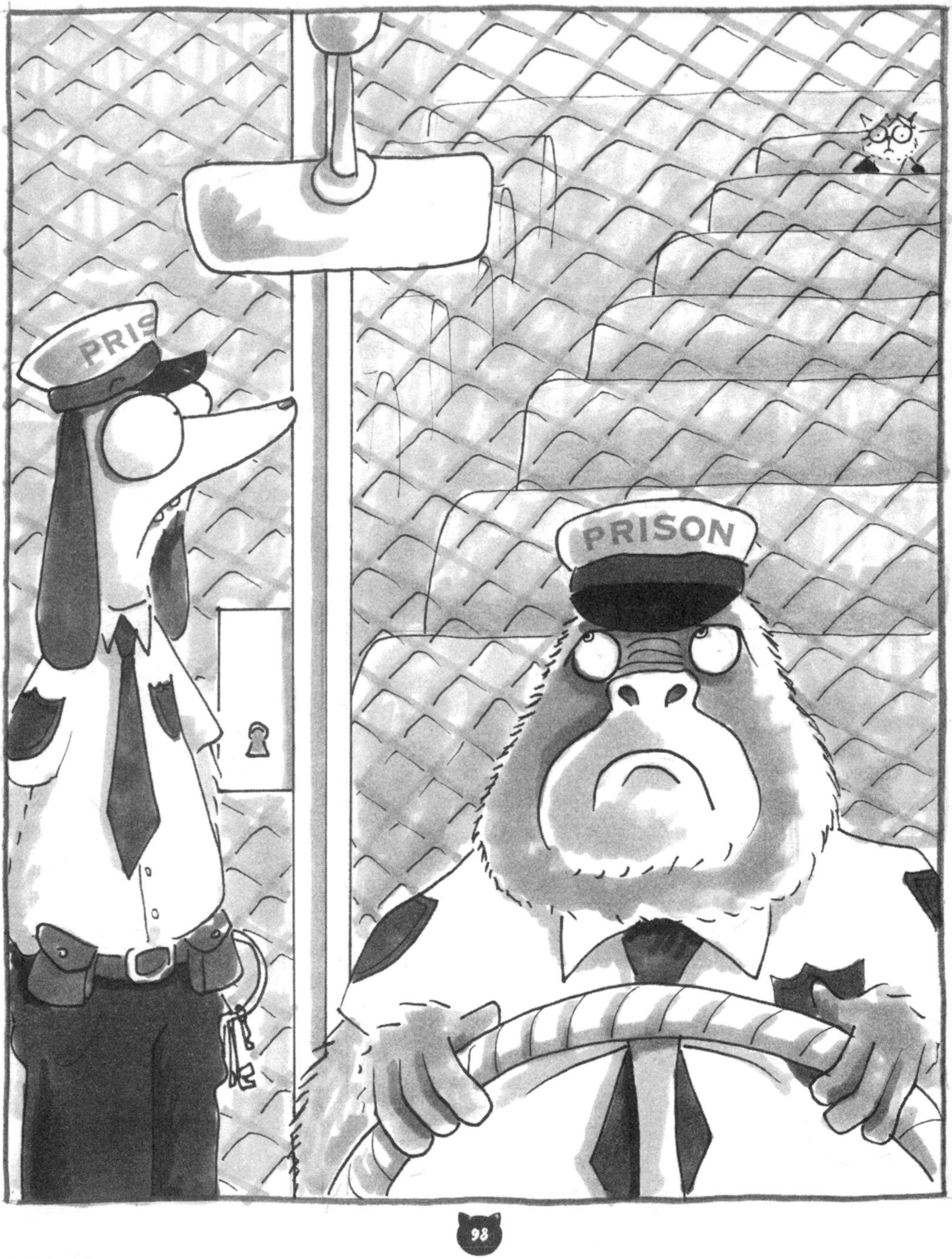
PRIS
PRISON

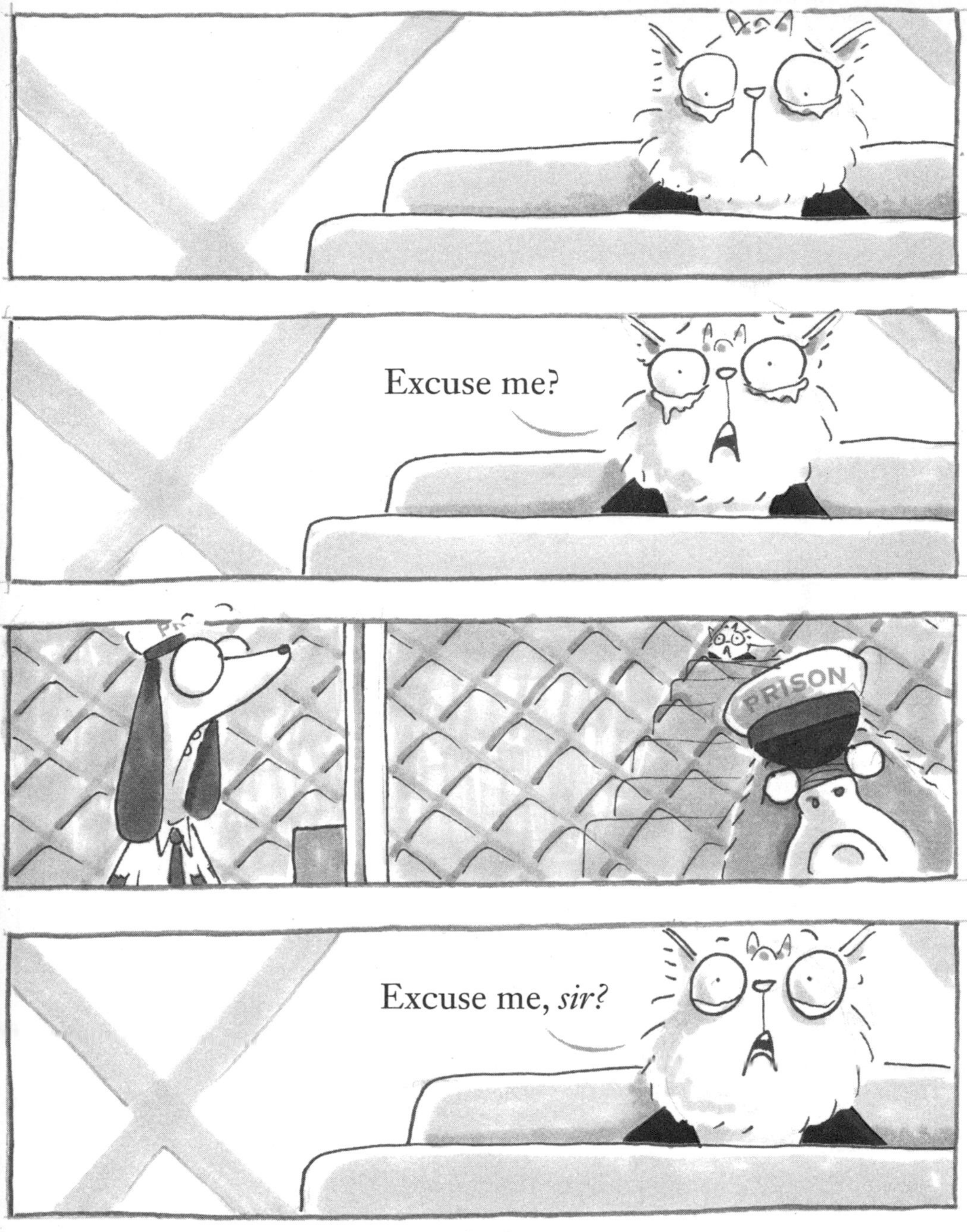

Excuse me?
PRISON
Excuse me, *sir?*

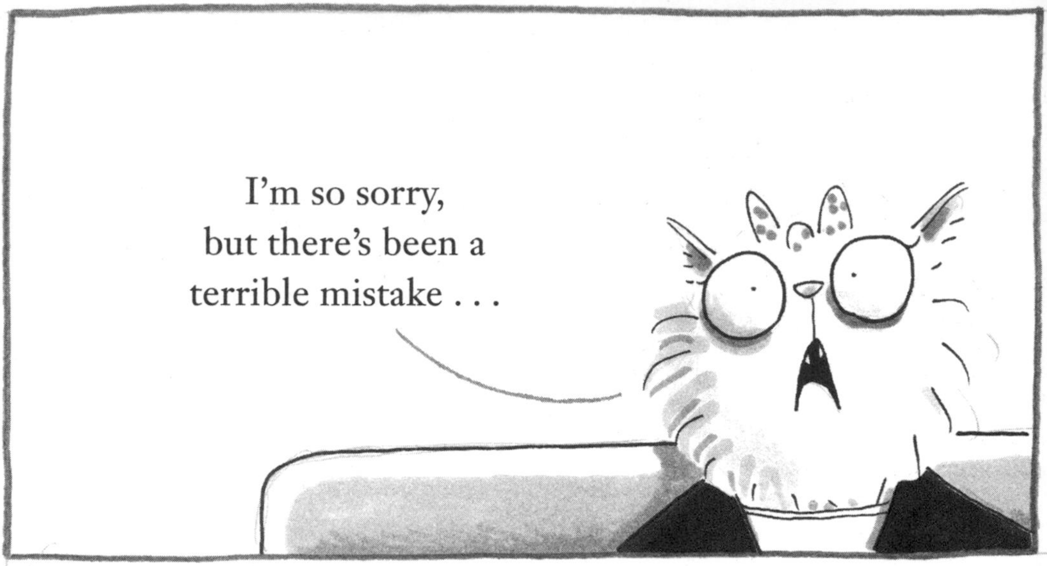
I'm so sorry, but there's been a terrible mistake . . .

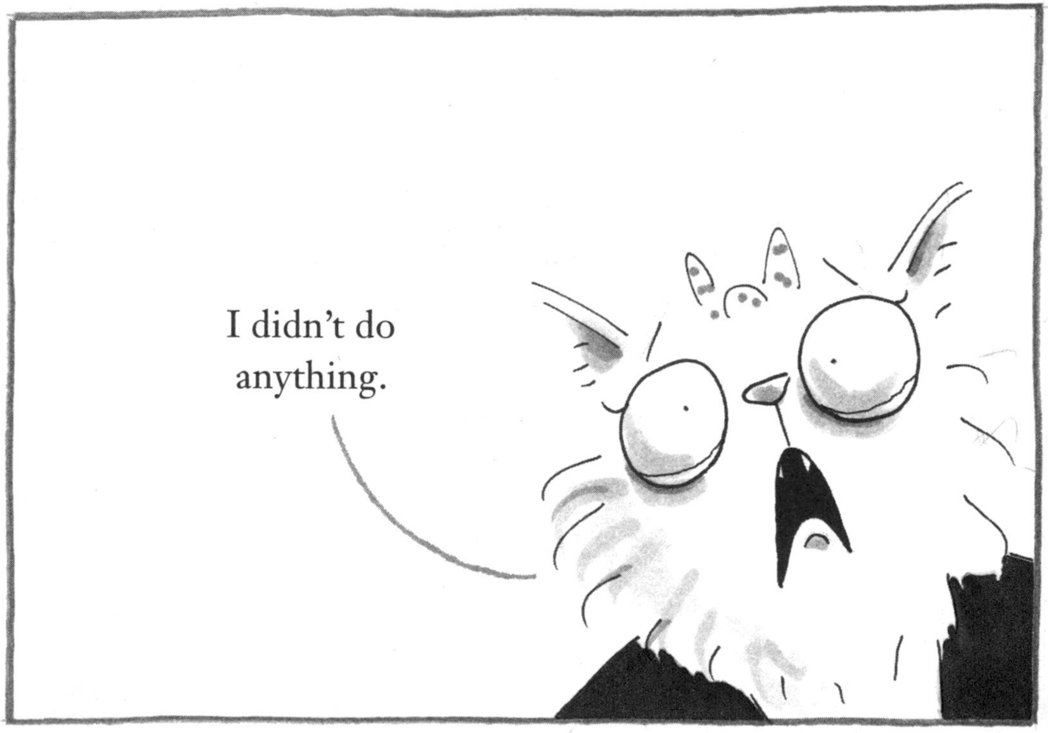
I didn't do anything.

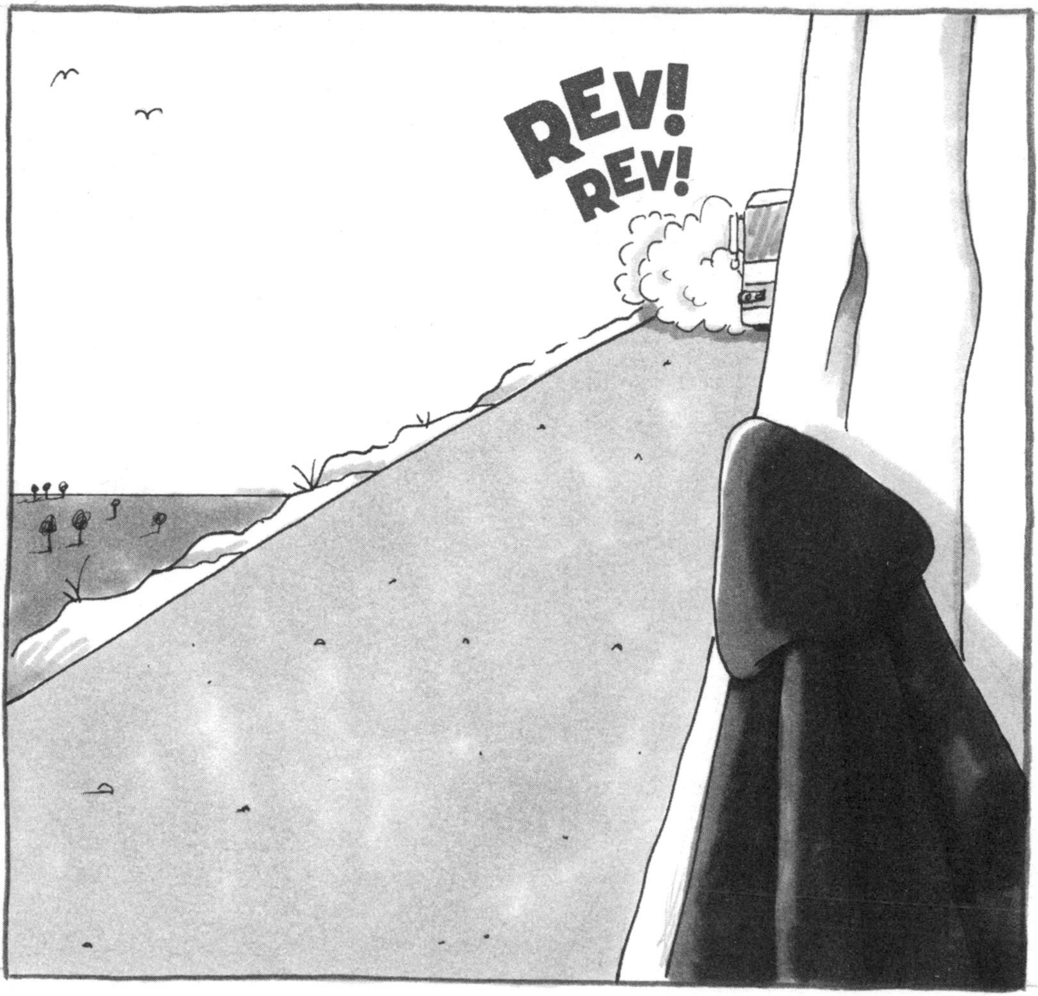
REV!
REV!

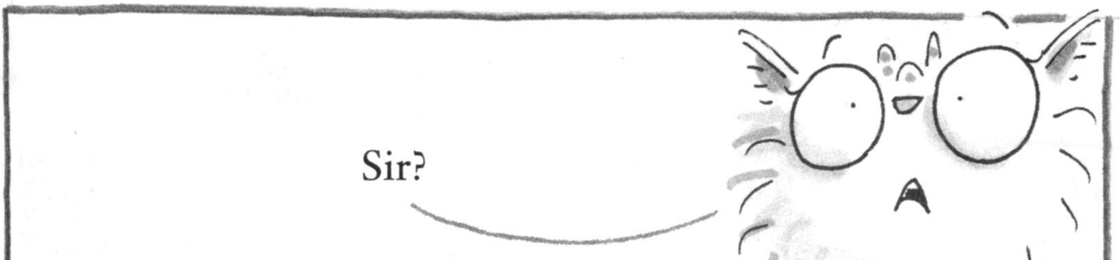
Sir?

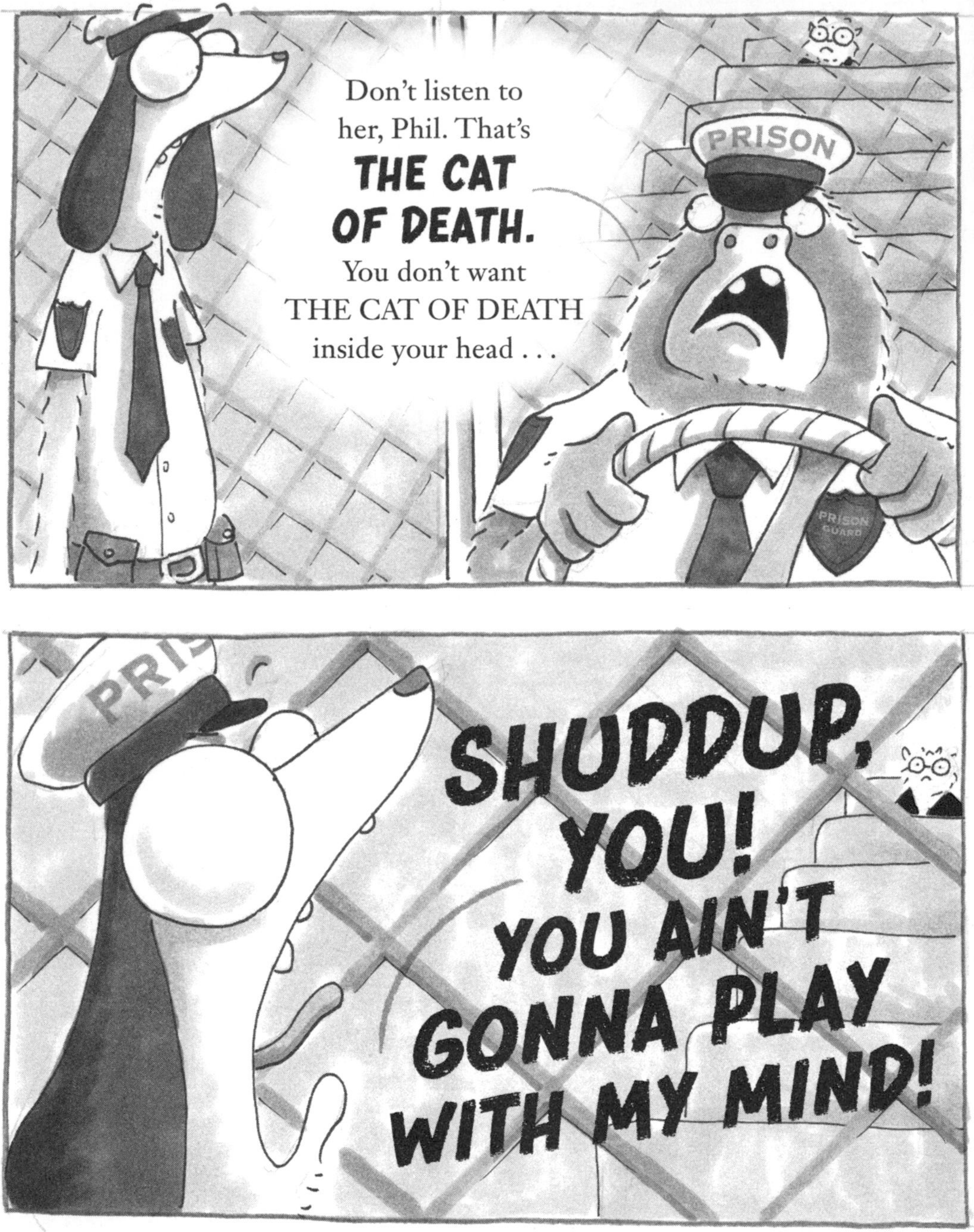
Don't listen to her, Phil. That's THE CAT OF DEATH. You don't want THE CAT OF DEATH inside your head . . .
PRISON
PRISON GUARD
PRI
SHUDDUP, YOU! YOU AIN'T GONNA PLAY WITH MY MIND!

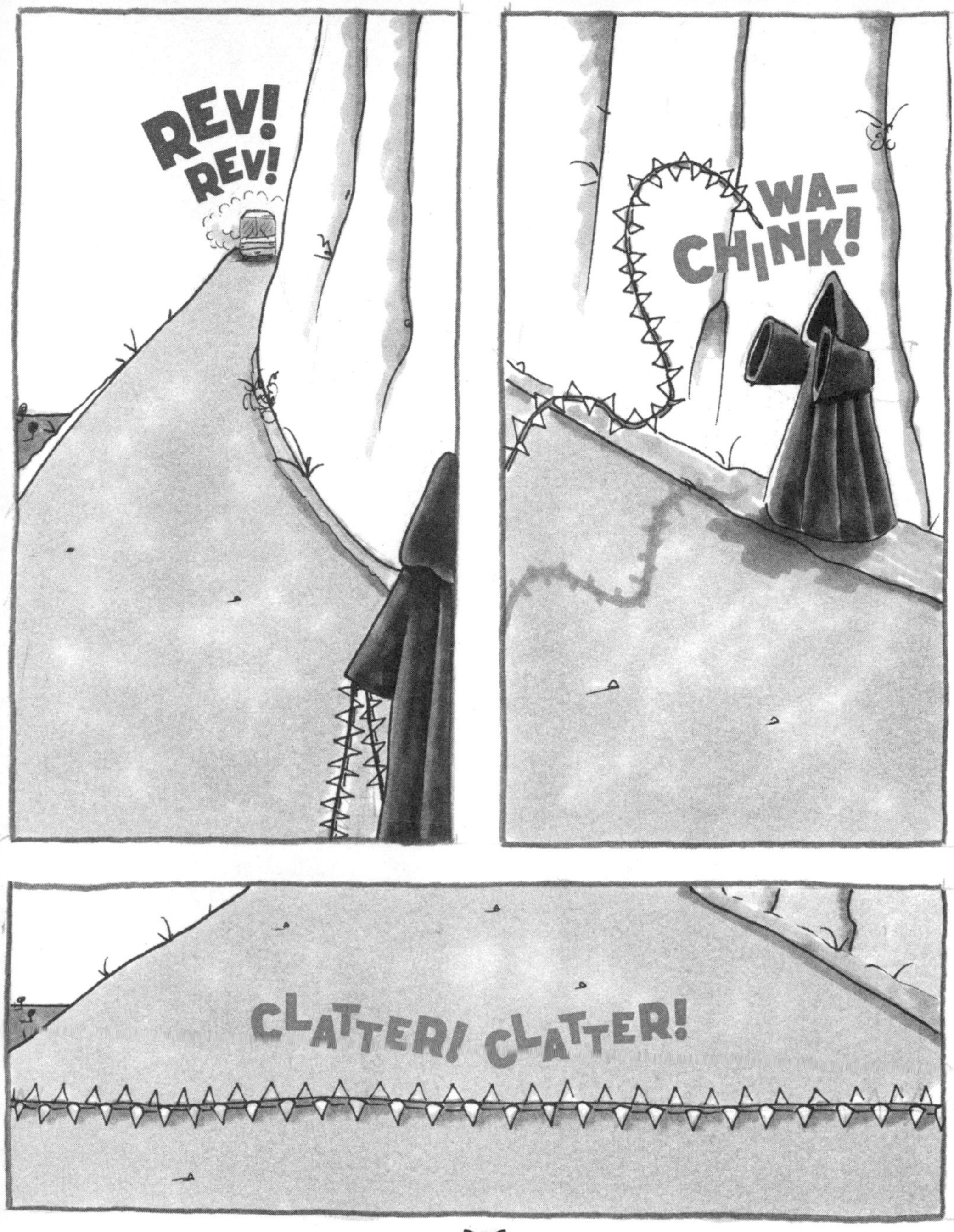
REV! REV!
WA-CHINK!
CLATTER! CLATTER!

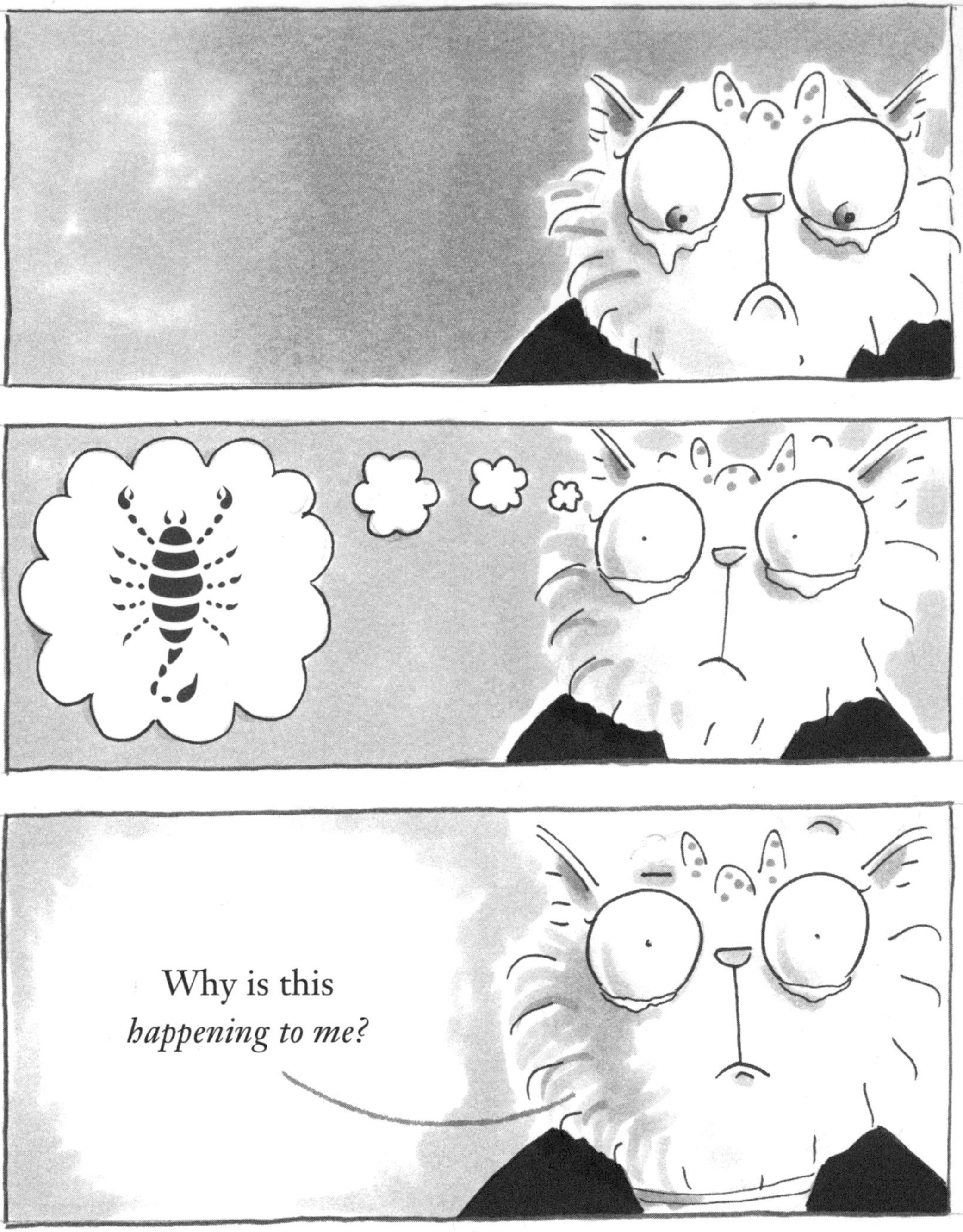
Why is this *happening to me?*

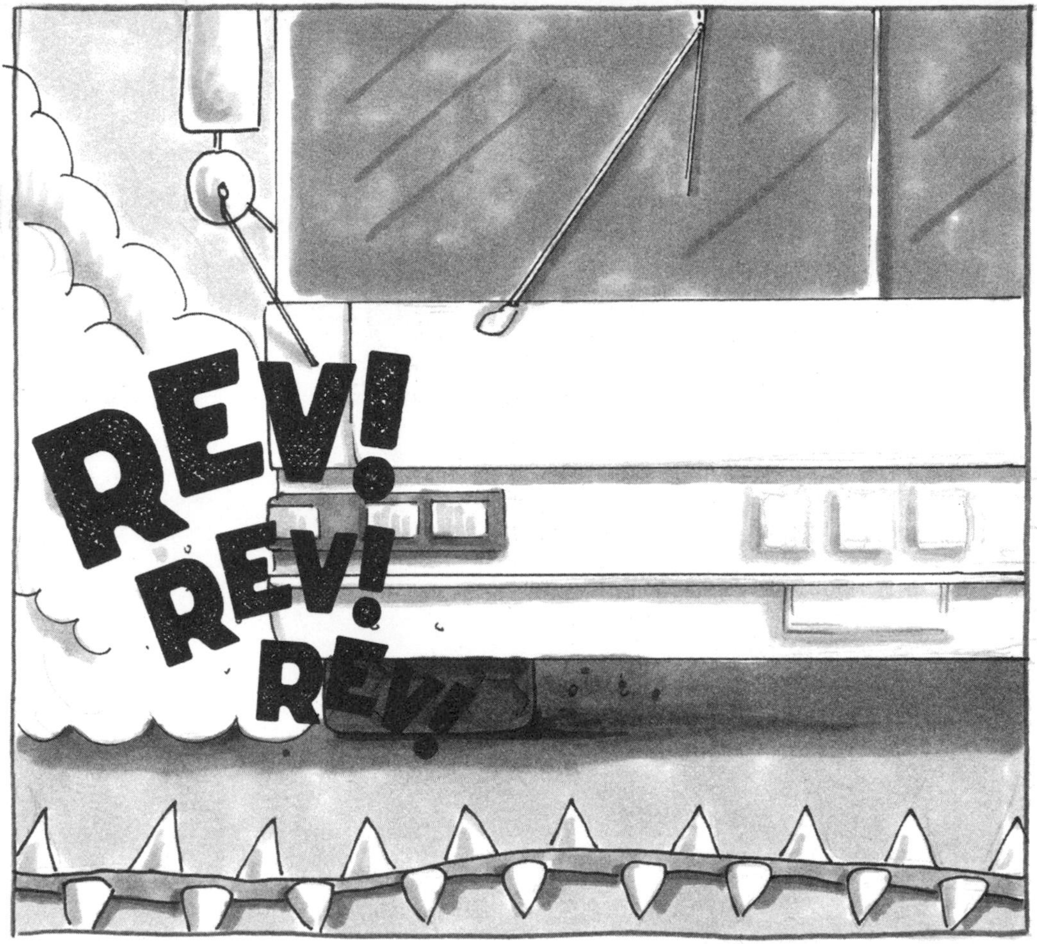
REV!
REV!
REV!

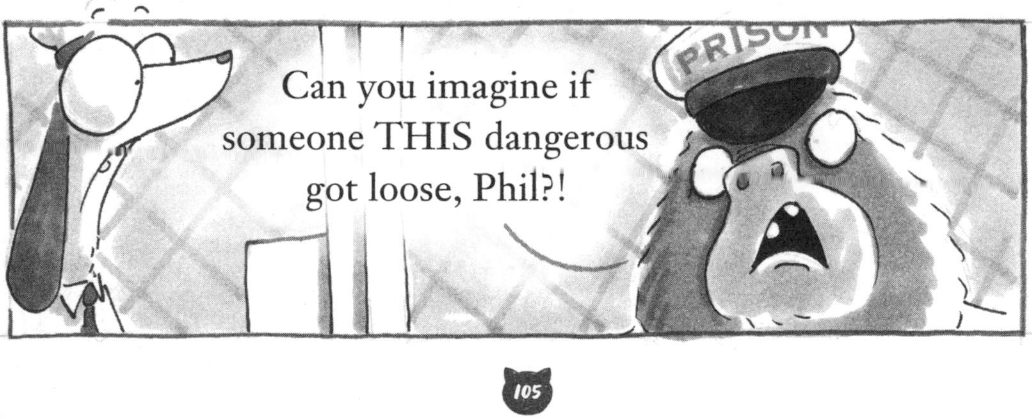
PRISON
Can you imagine if someone THIS dangerous got loose, Phil?!

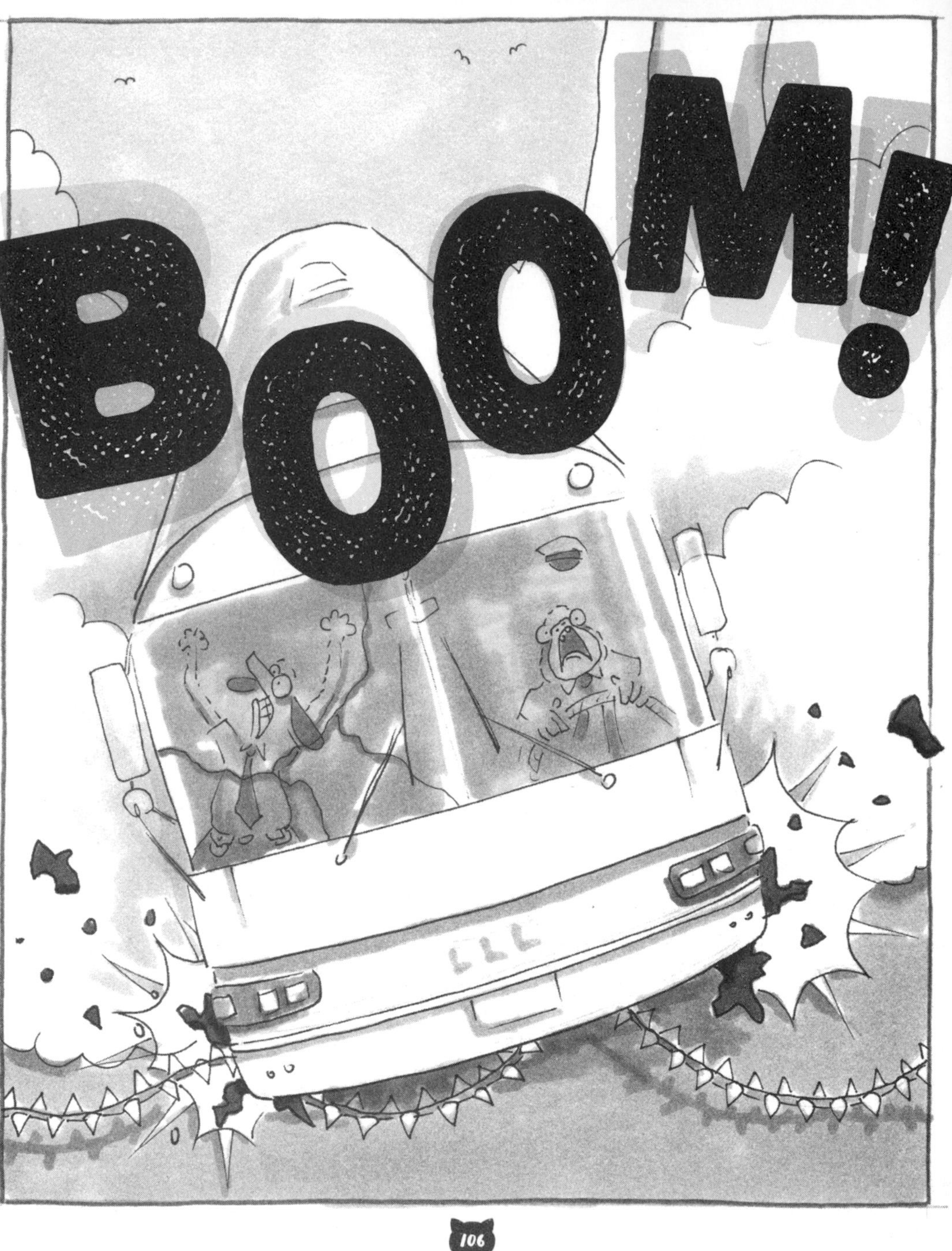
BOOOM!

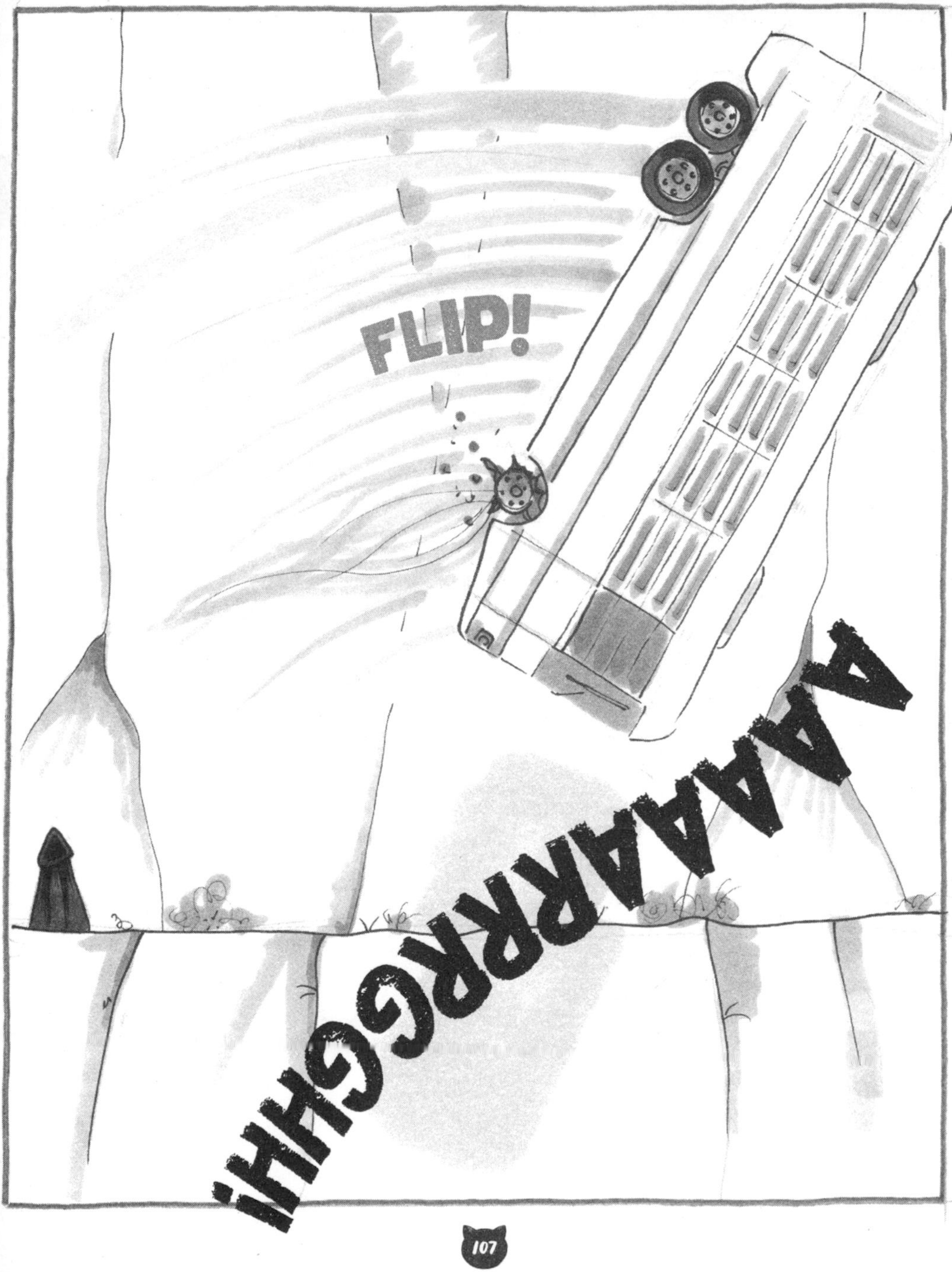
FLIP!
AAAAARRRGGH!

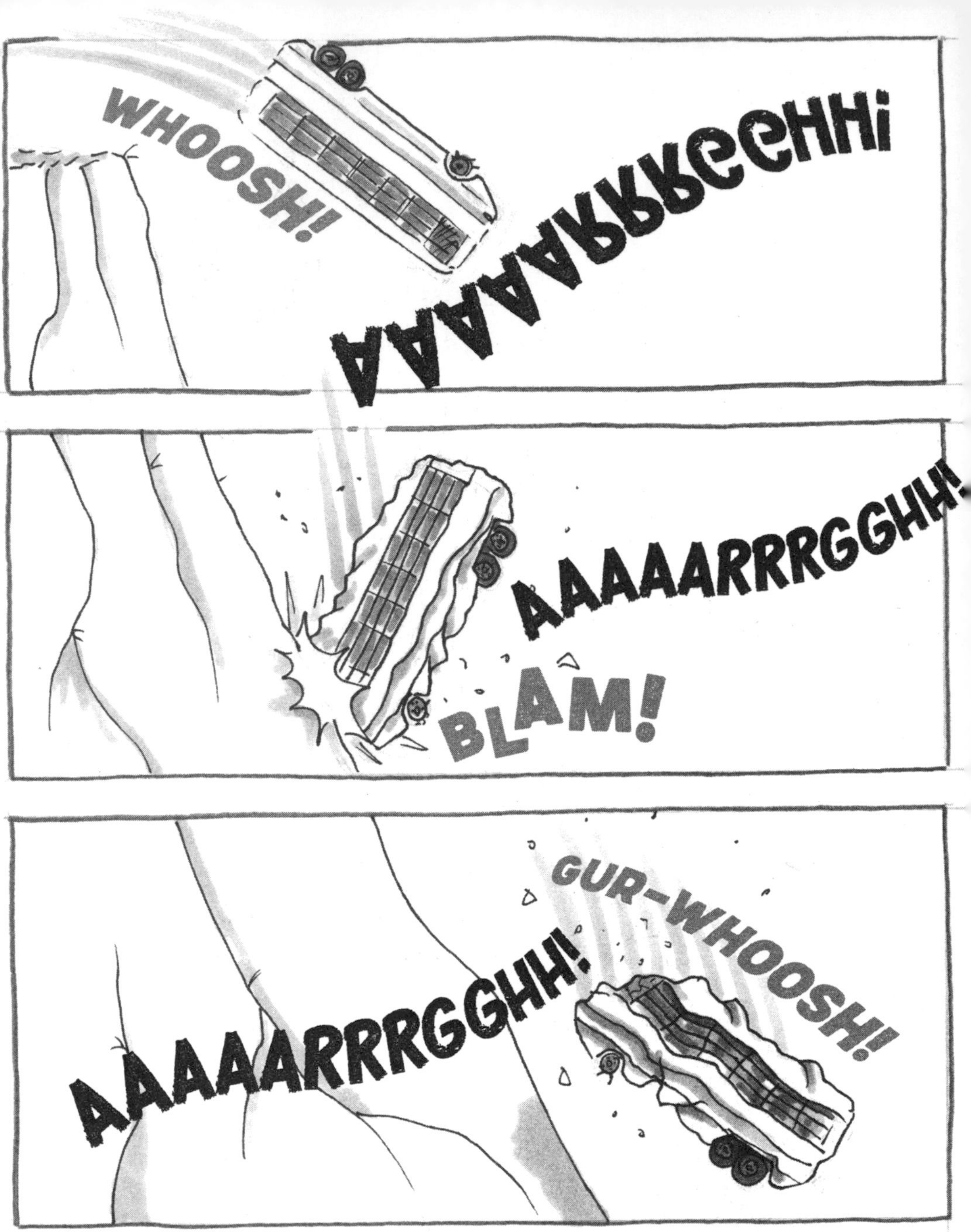
WHOOSH!
AAAAARRRGGHH!
AAAAARRRGGHH!
BLAM!
GUR-WHOOSH!
AAAAARRRGGHH!

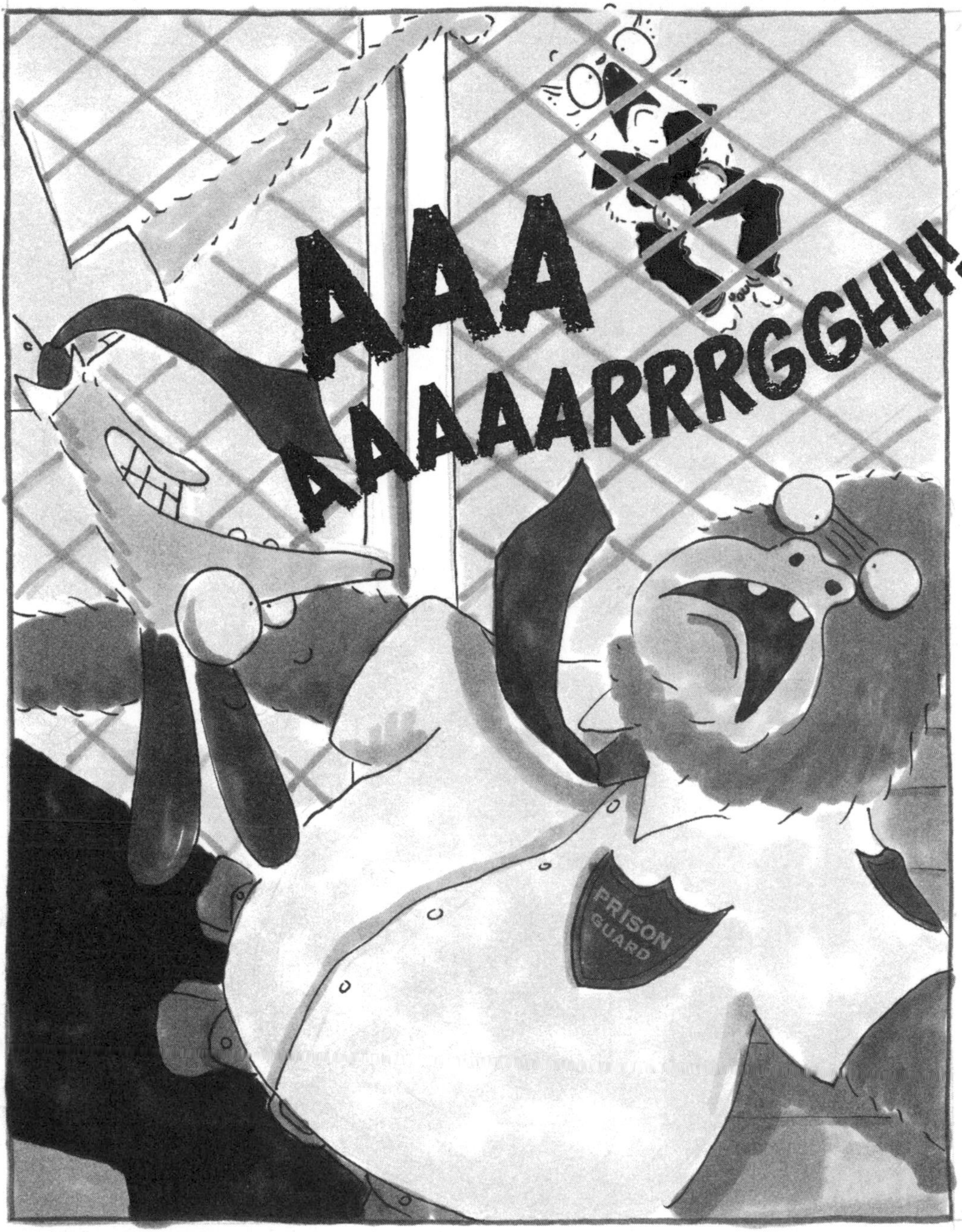
AAA
AAAAARRRRGGHH!
PRISON GUARD

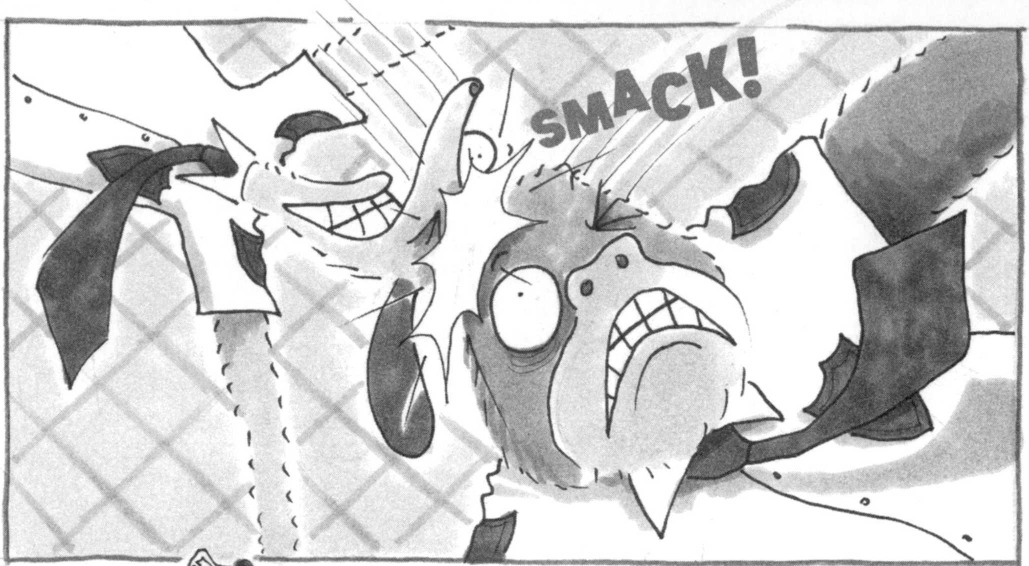
SMACK!

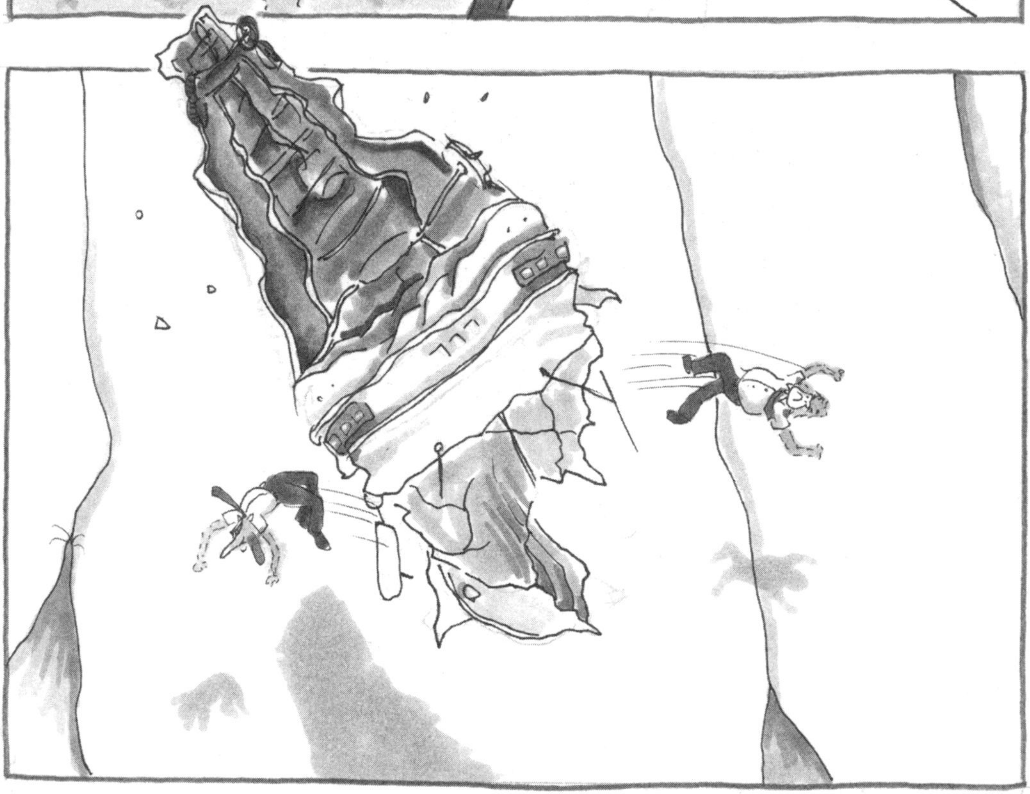

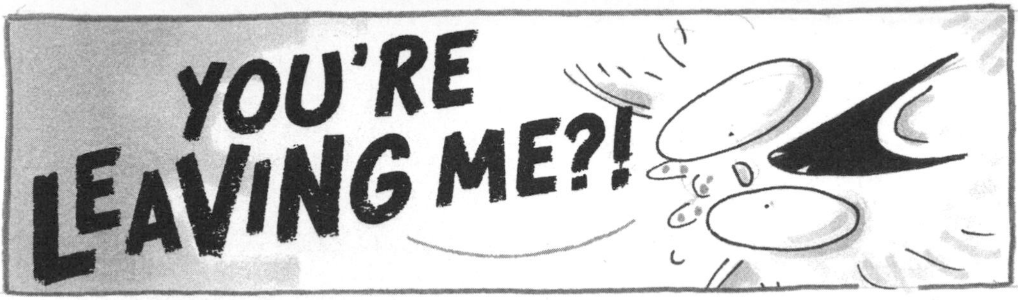
YOU'RE LEAVING ME?!

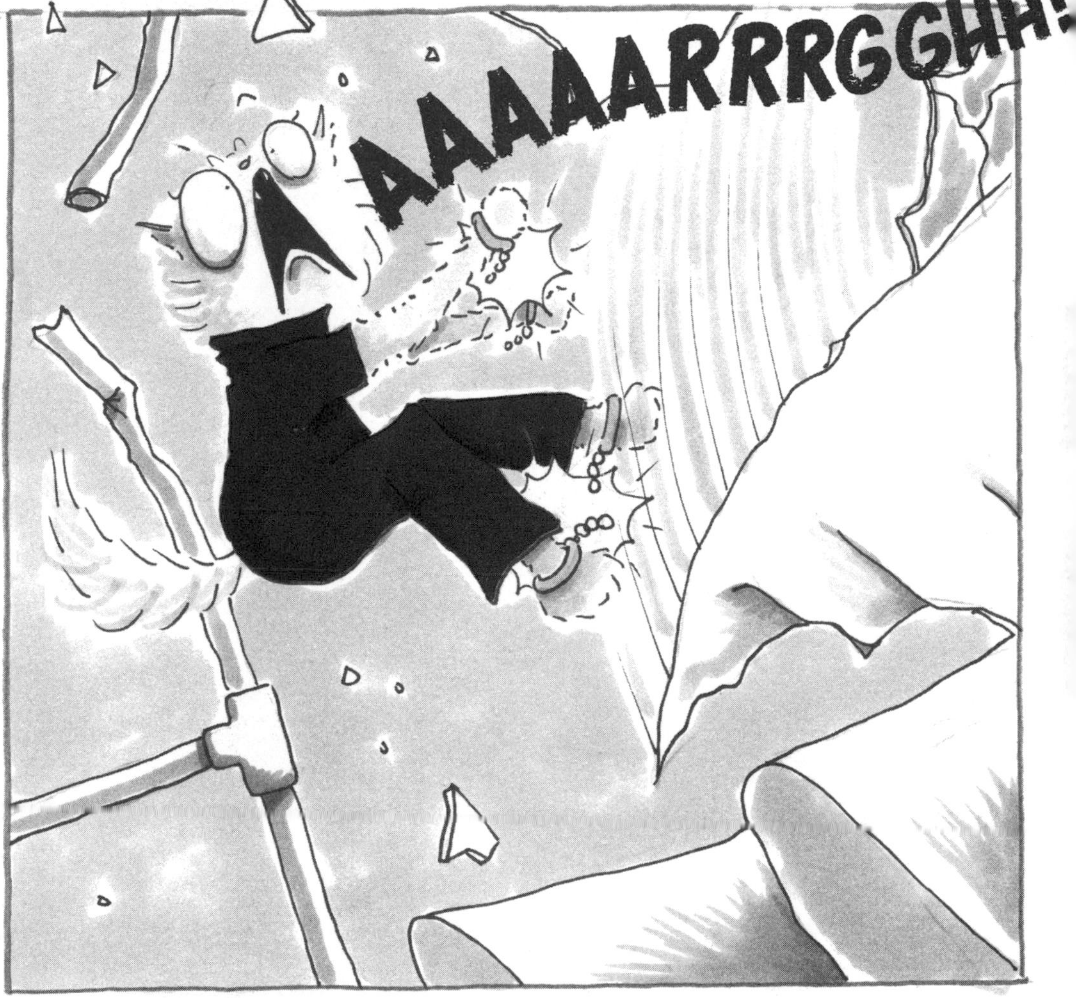
AAAAAARRRRGGHH!

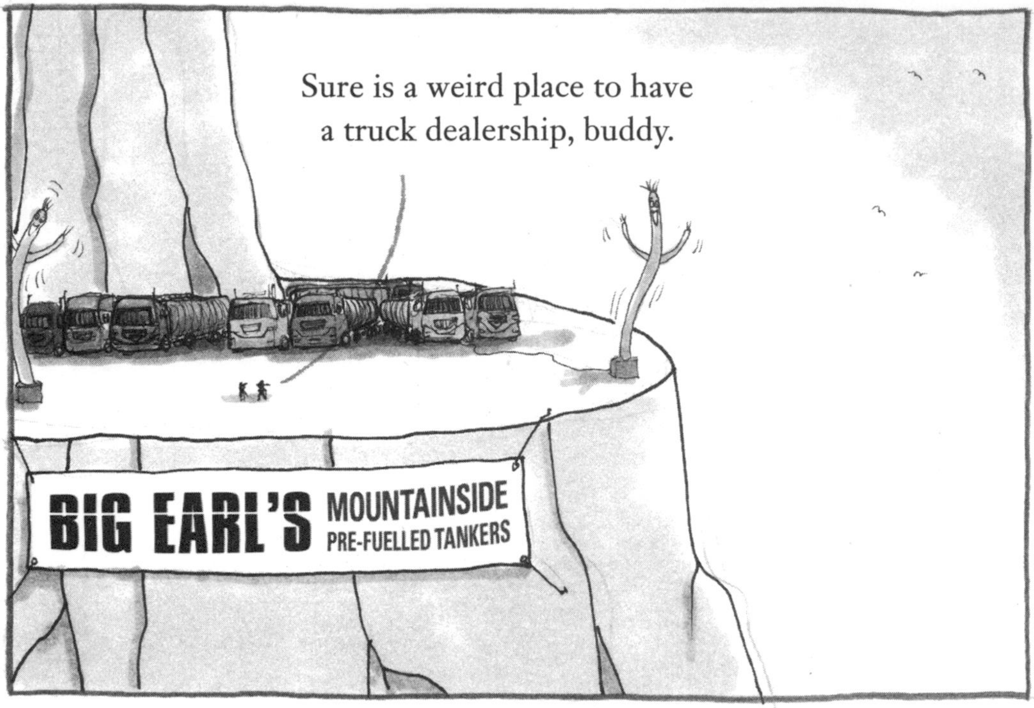
Sure is a weird place to have a truck dealership, buddy.
BIG EARL'S MOUNTAINSIDE PRE-FUELLED TANKERS

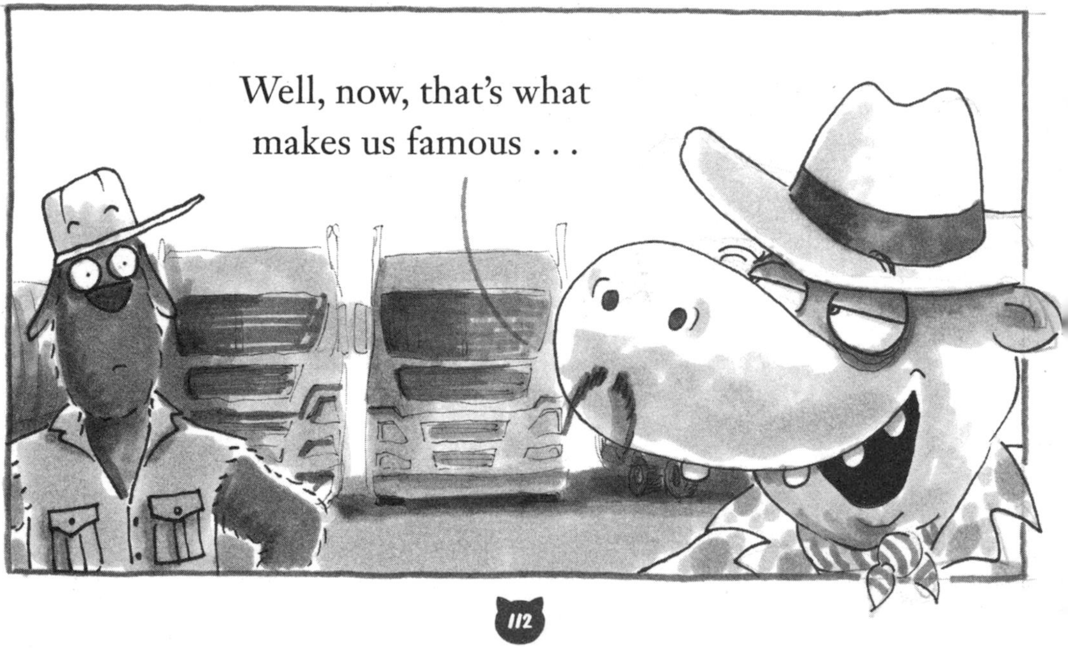
Well, now, that's what makes us famous . . .

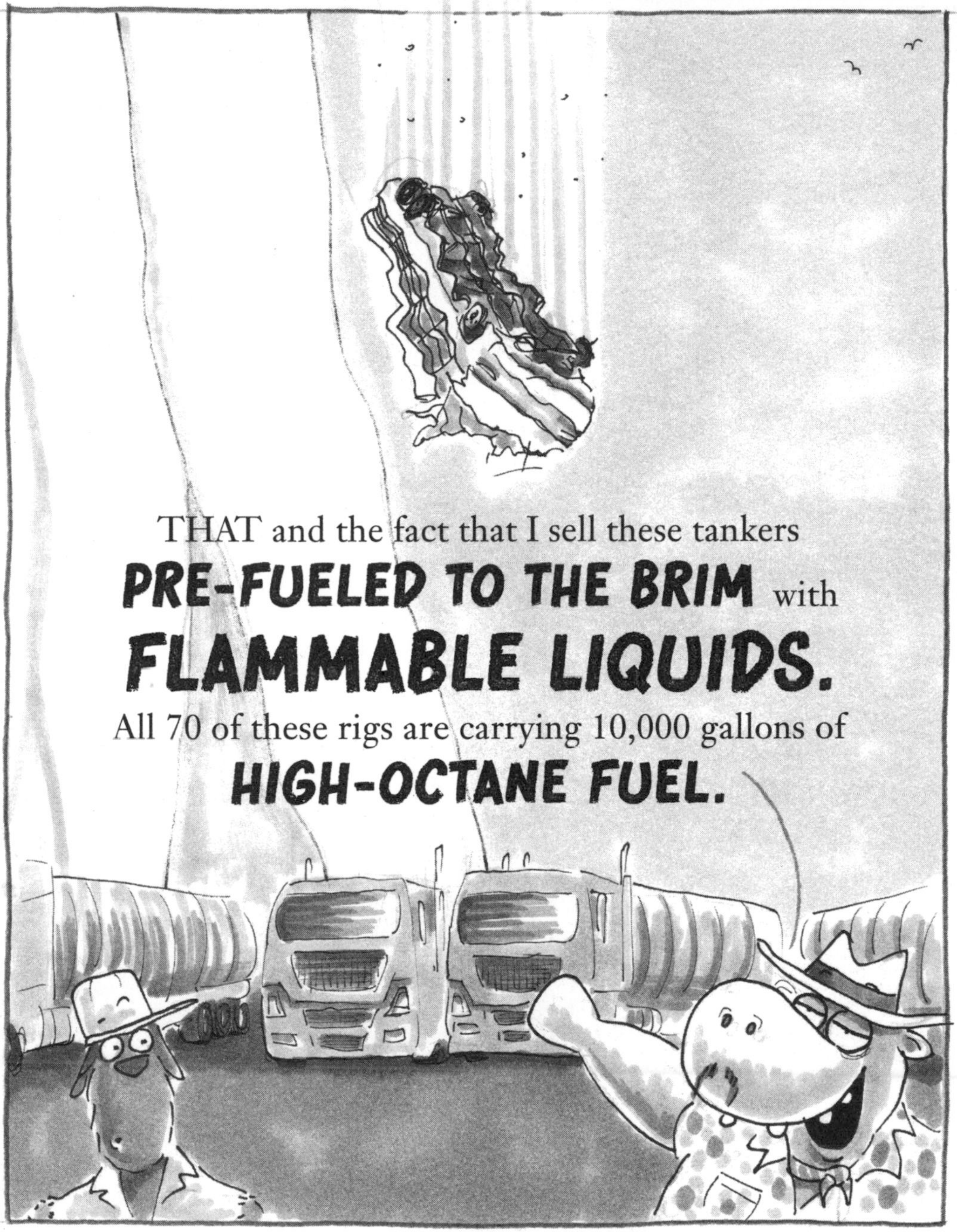
THAT and the fact that I sell these tankers
PRE-FUELED TO THE BRIM with
FLAMMABLE LIQUIDS.
All 70 of these rigs are carrying 10,000 gallons of
HIGH-OCTANE FUEL.

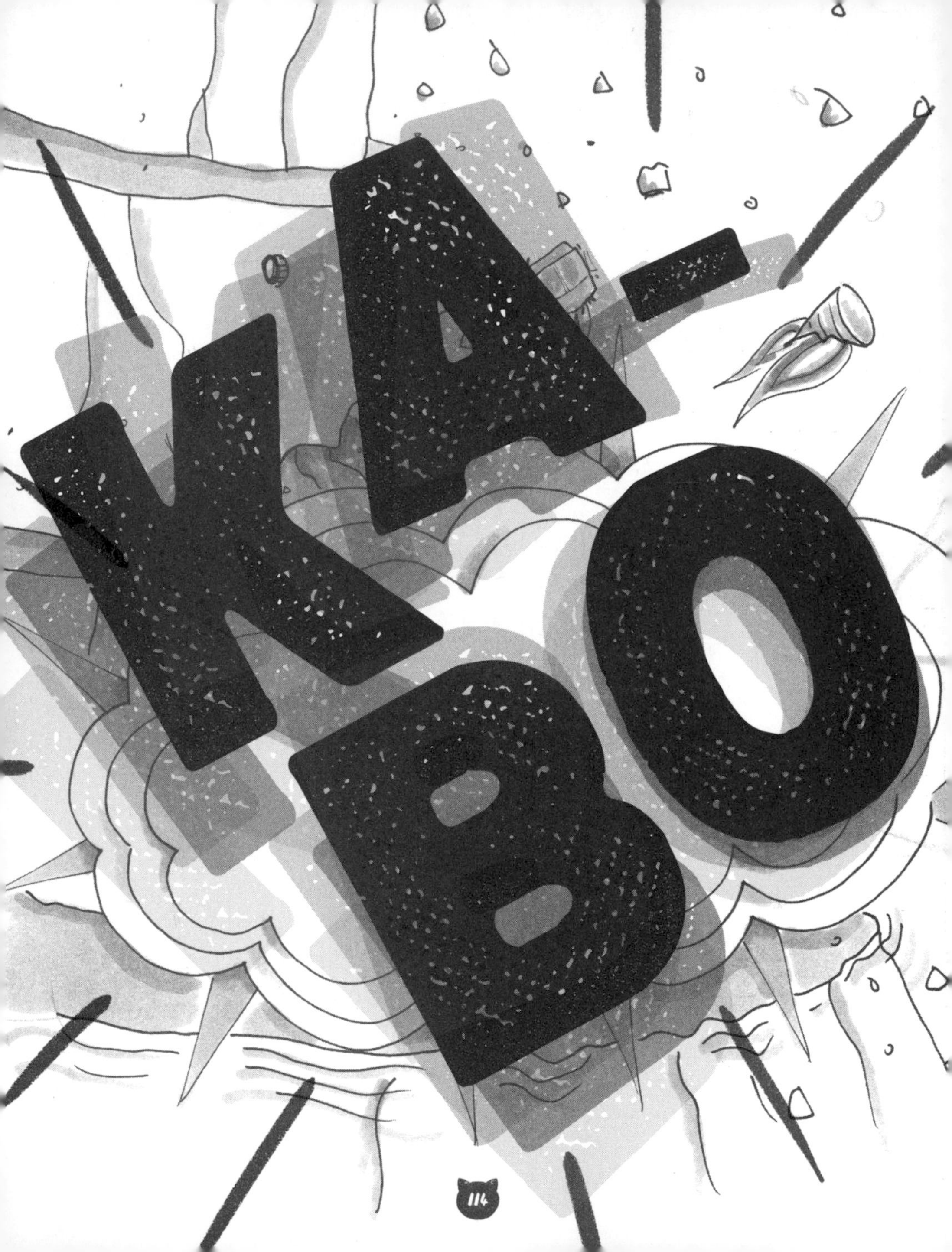
KA-
BO

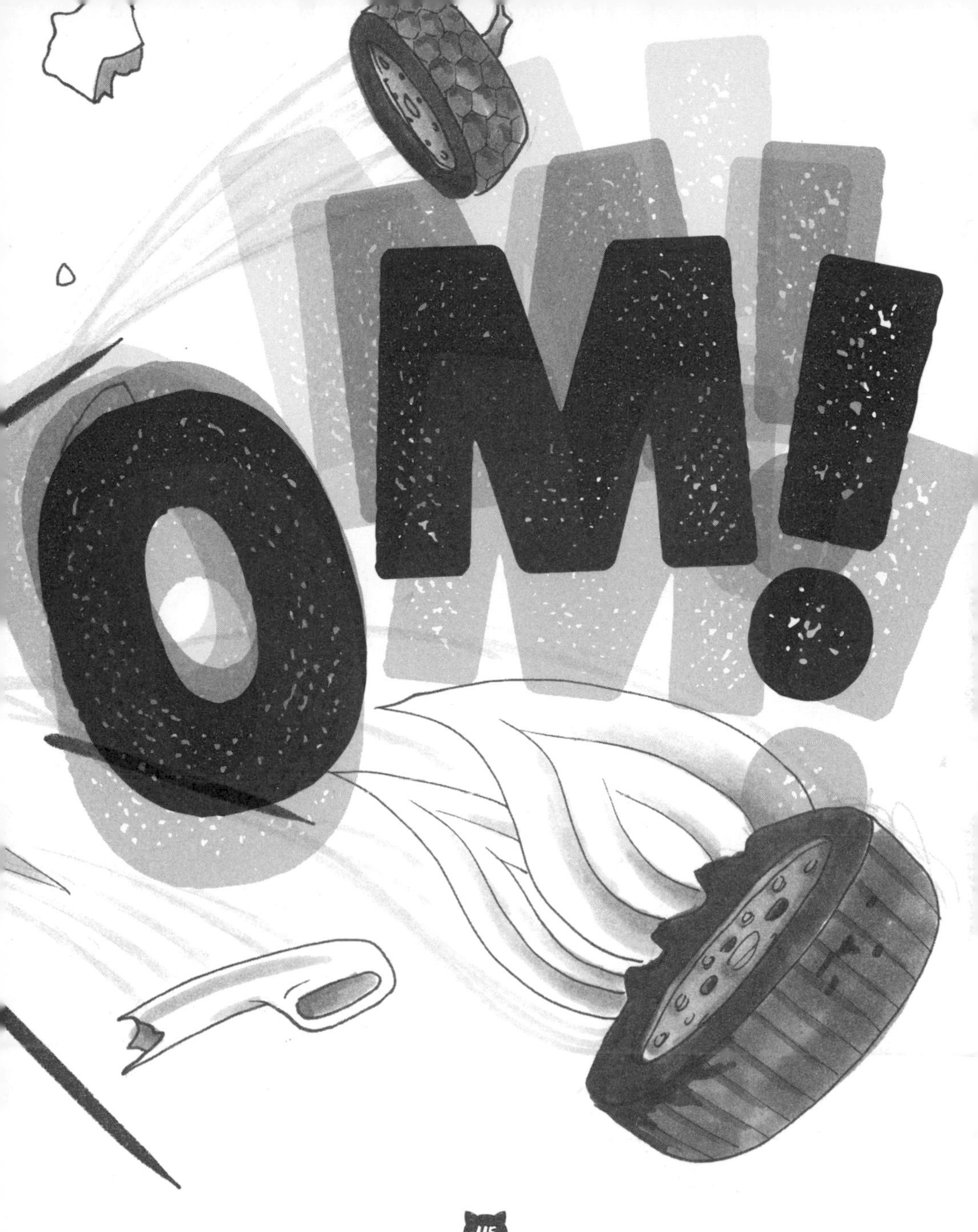
OM!

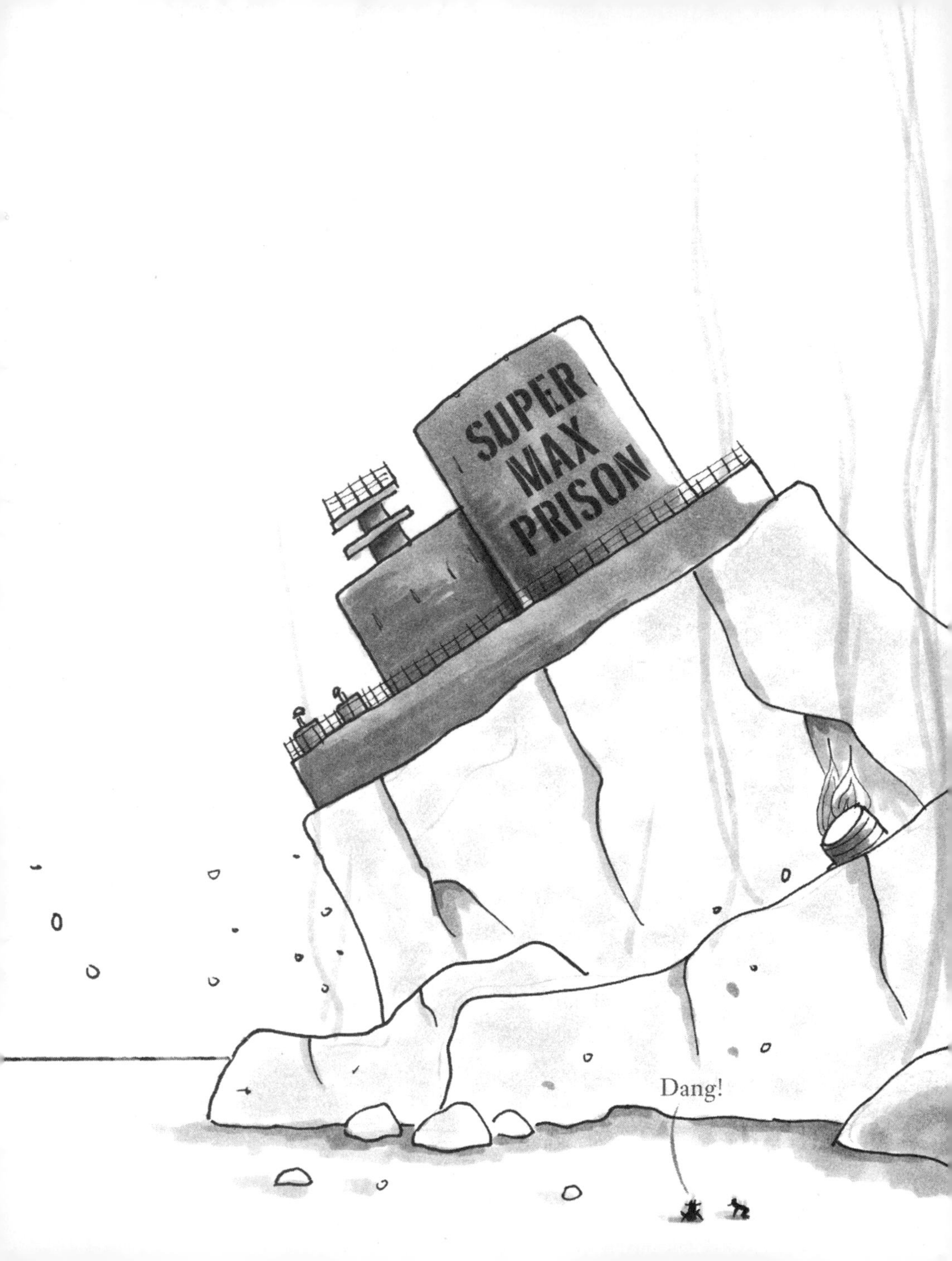
SUPER MAX PRISON
Dang!

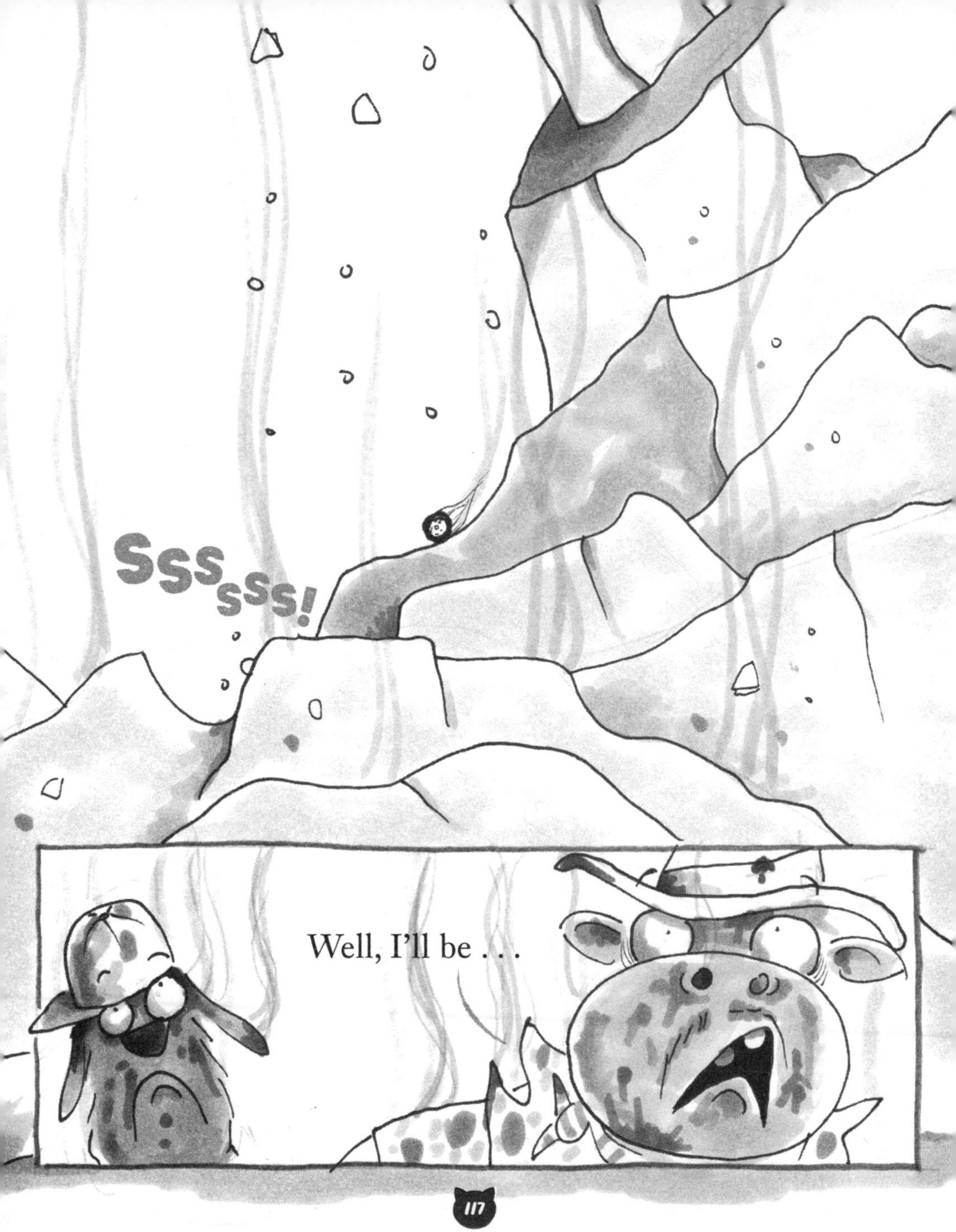
Sssssss!
Well, I'll be . . .

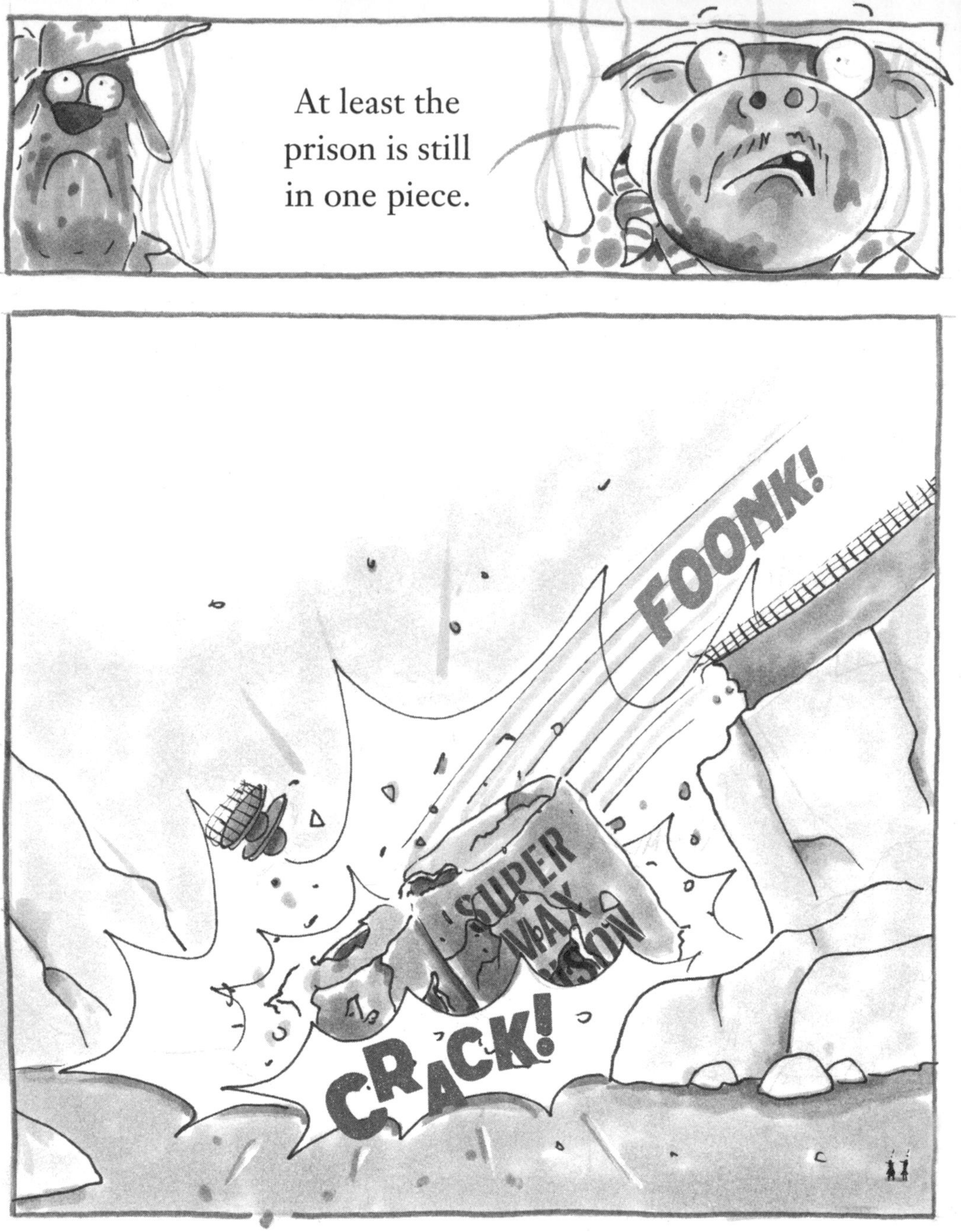
At least the prison is still in one piece.
FOONK!
SUPER MAX
CRACK!

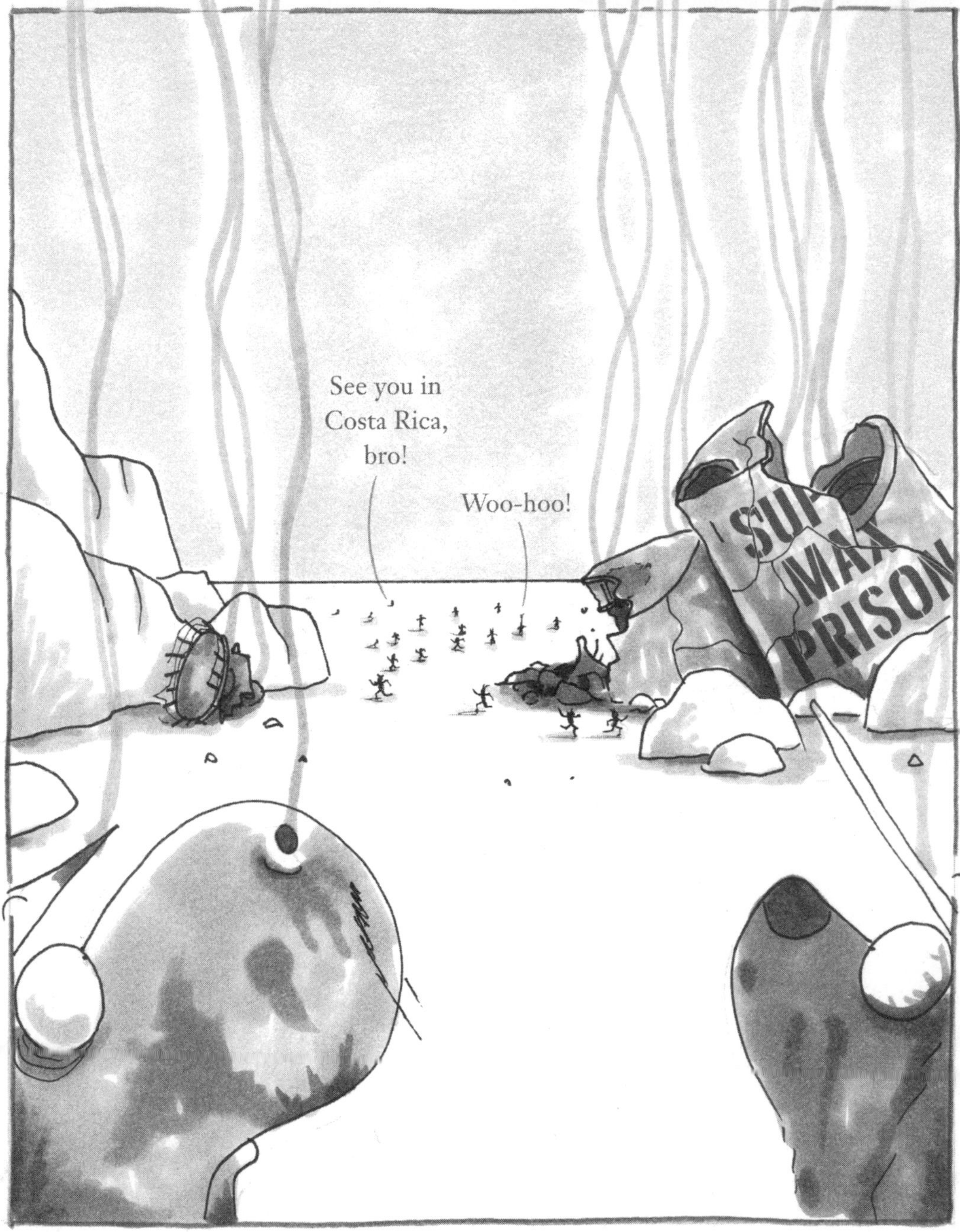
See you in Costa Rica, bro!
Woo-hoo!
SUPER MAX PRISON

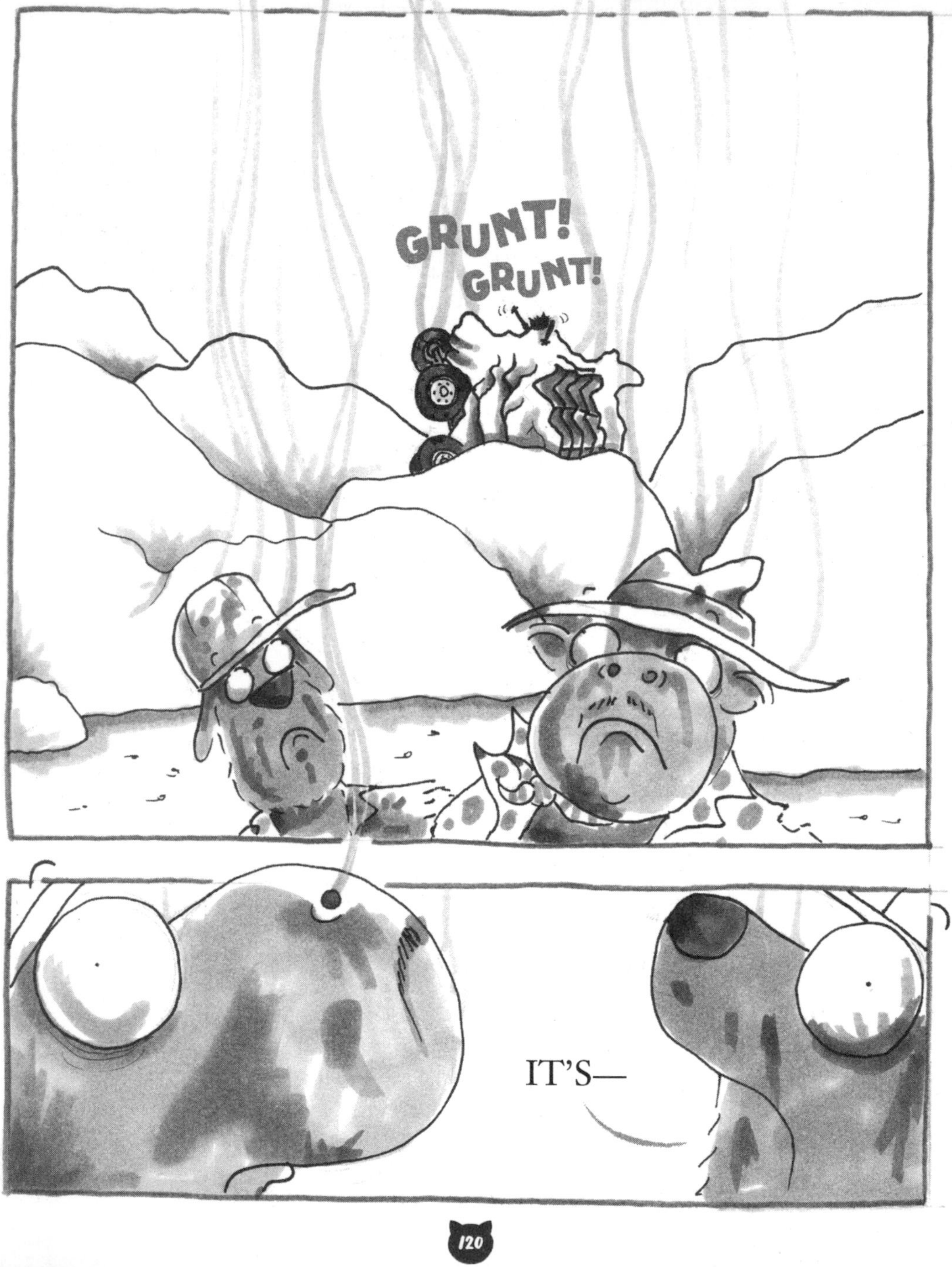
GRUNT!
GRUNT!
IT'S—

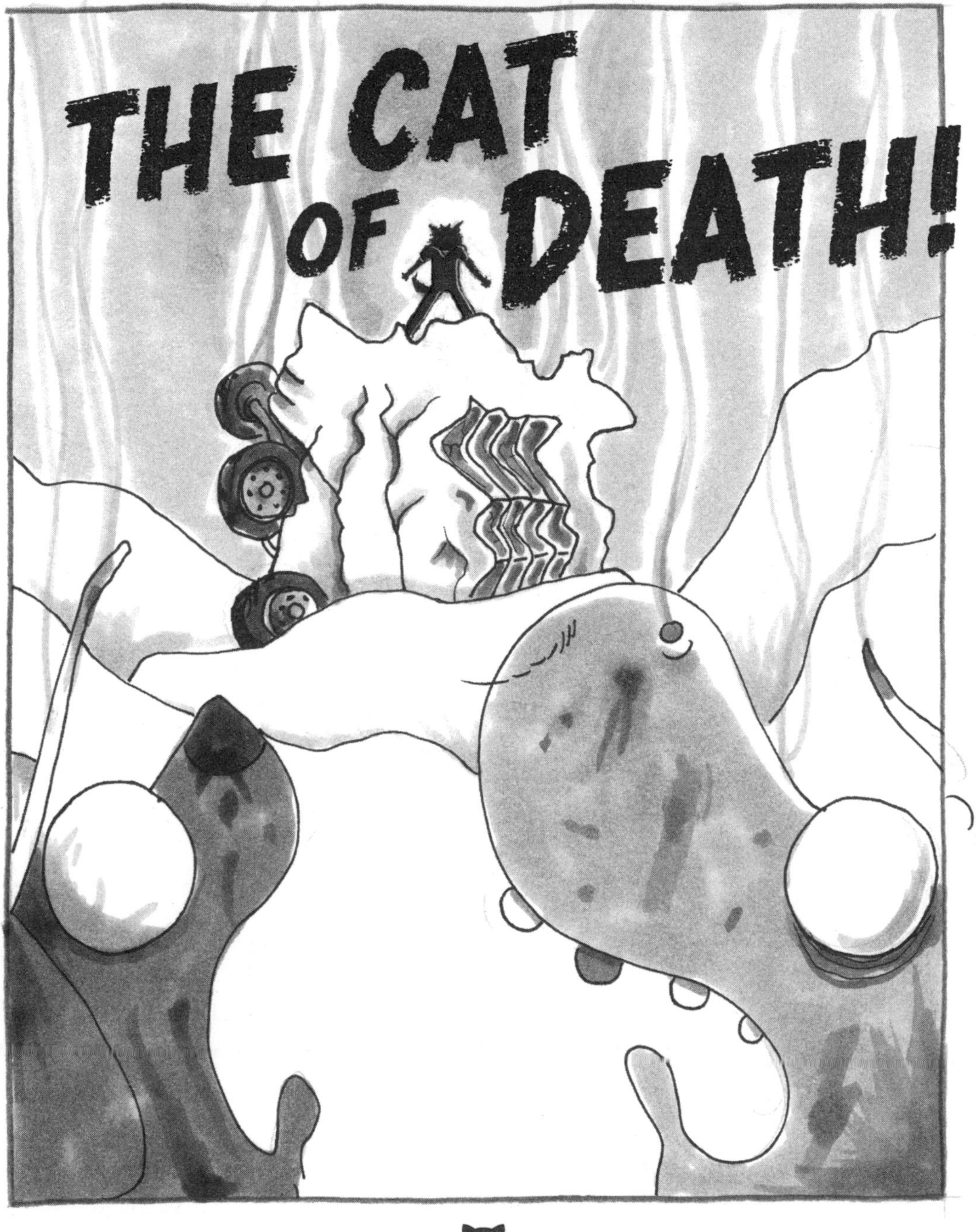
THE CAT OF DEATH!

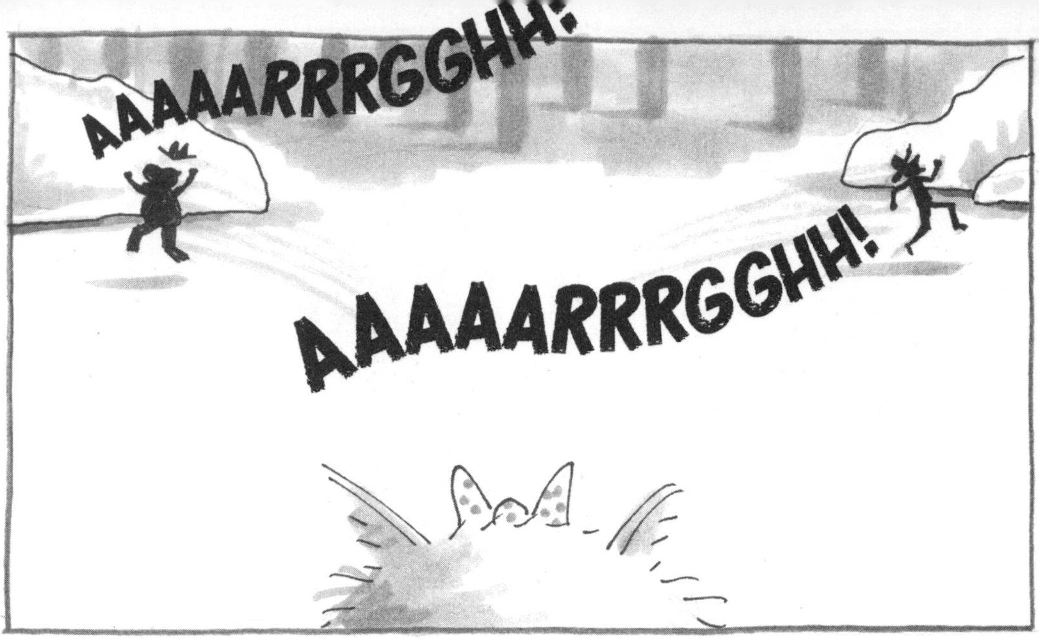
AAAAARRRGGHH!
AAAAARRRGGHH!

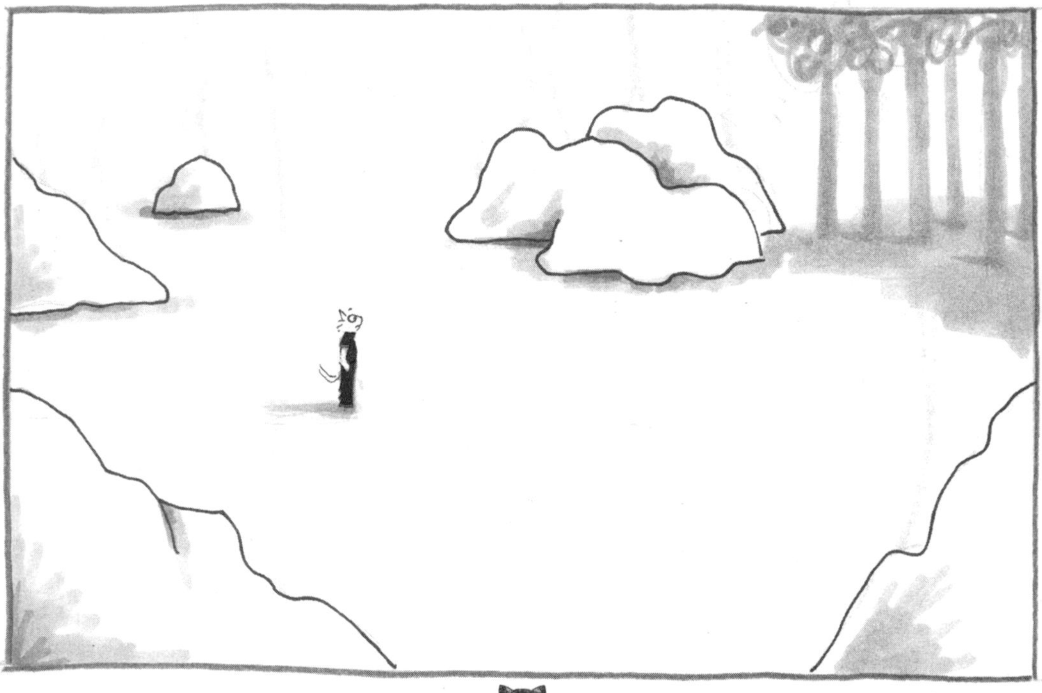

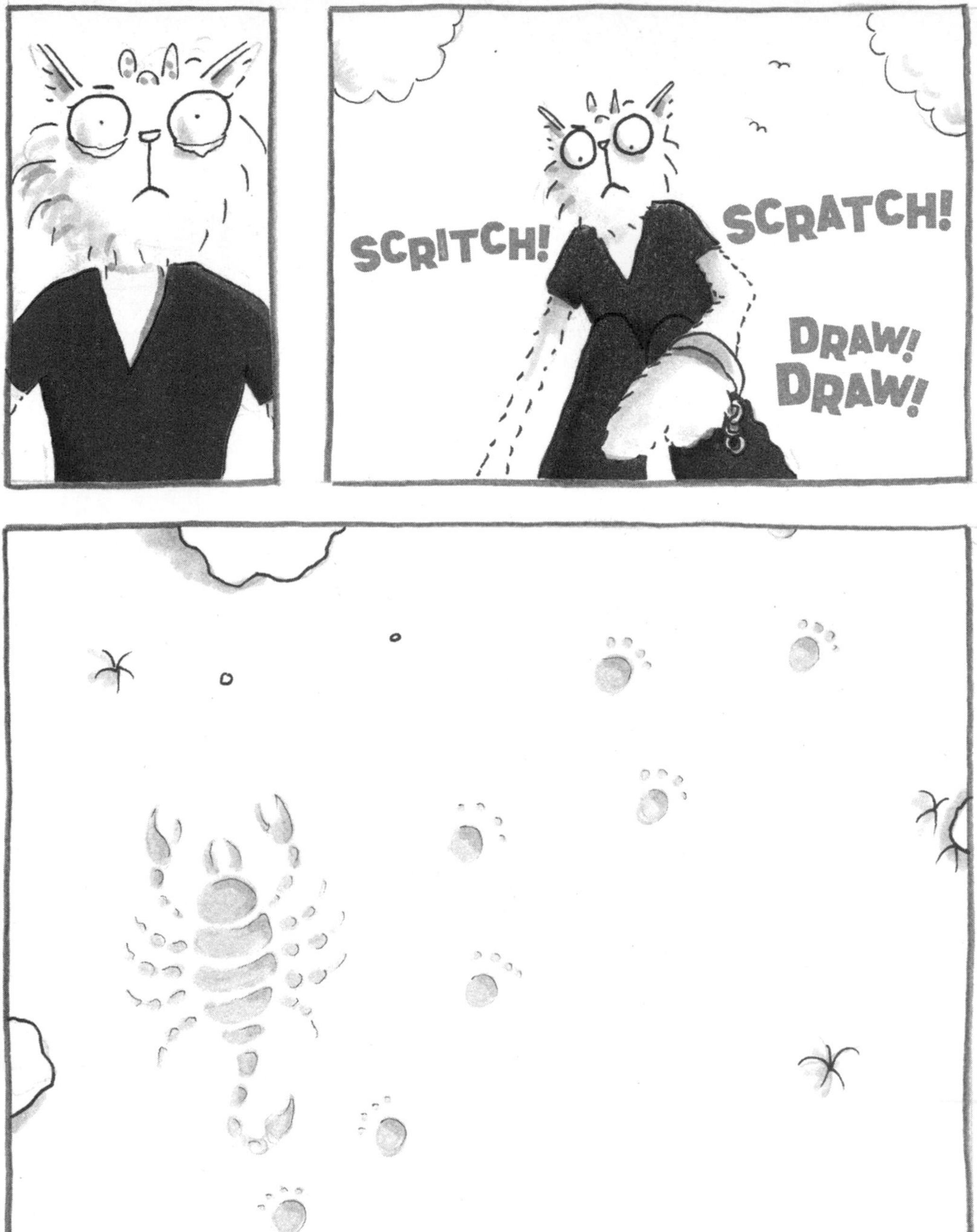
SCRITCH!
SCRATCH!
DRAW! DRAW!

Six
THE CHEESEMAN COMETH

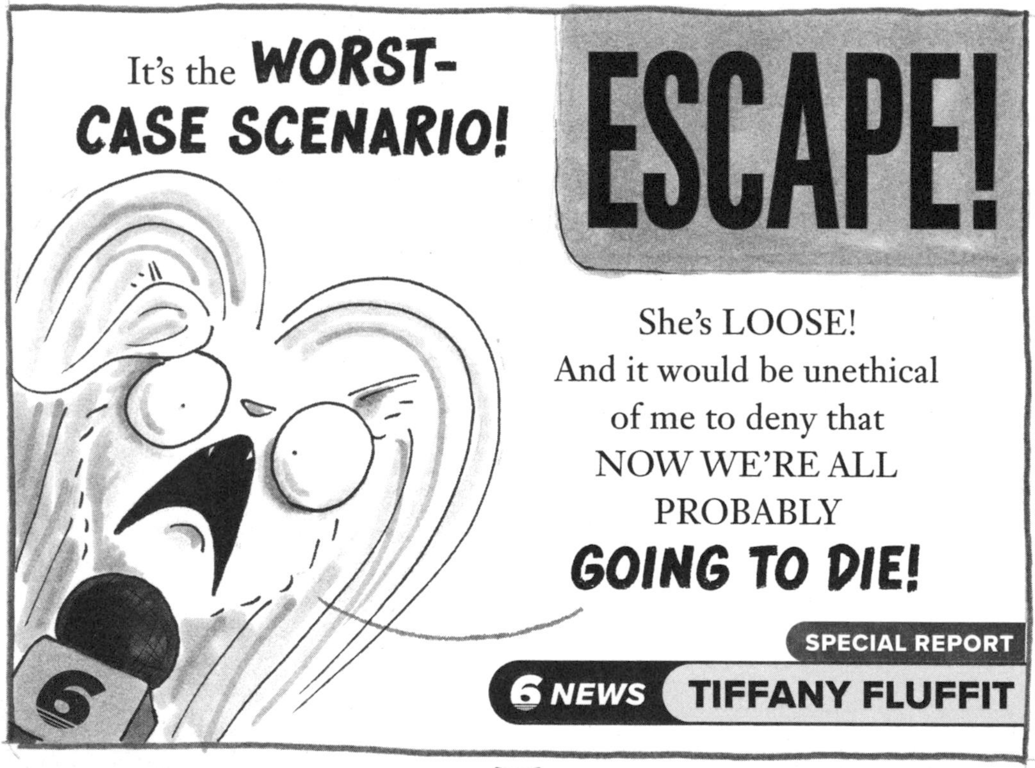

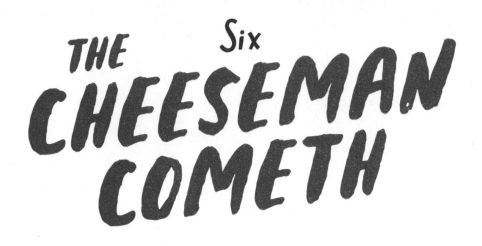

It's the WORST-CASE SCENARIO!
ESCAPE!
She's LOOSE! And it would be unethical of me to deny that NOW WE'RE ALL PROBABLY GOING TO DIE!
SPECIAL REPORT
6 NEWS TIFFANY FLUFFIT

Unsurprisingly, the internet is **ABLAZE.**

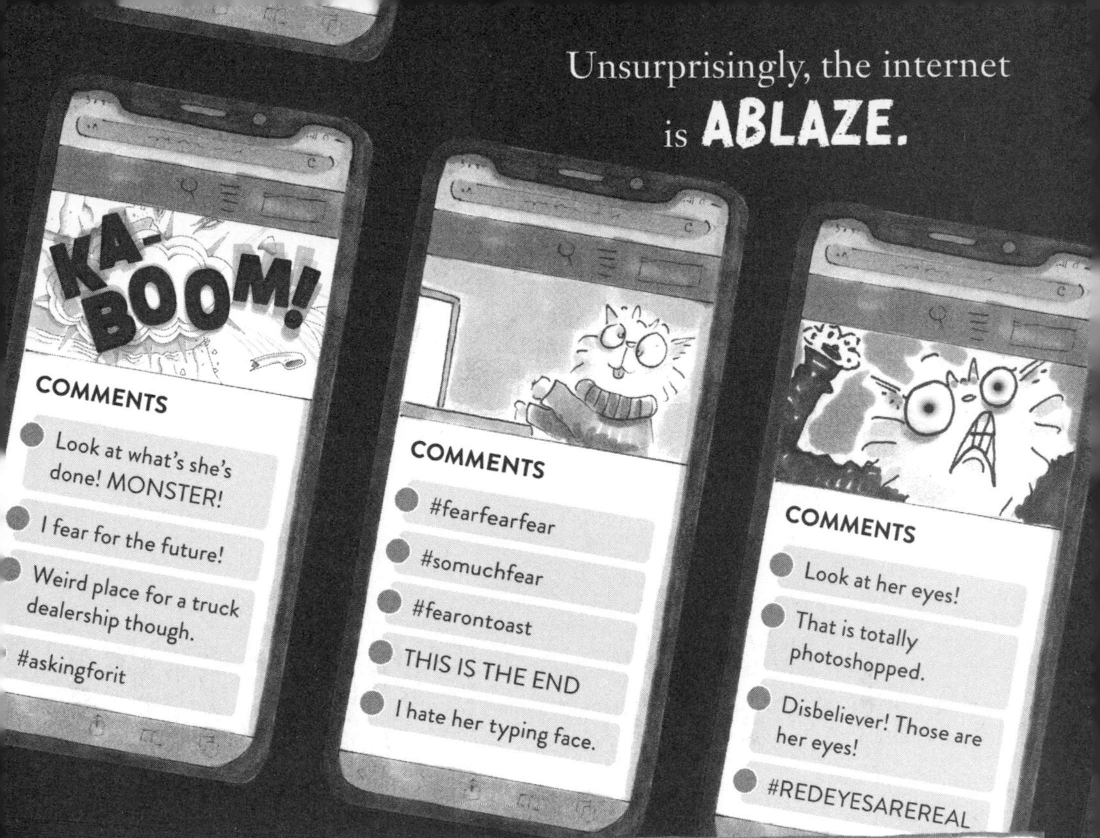
KA-BOOM!
COMMENTS
Look at what's she's done! MONSTER!
I fear for the future!
Weird place for a truck dealership though.
#askingforit
COMMENTS
#fearfearfear
#somuchfear
#fearontoast
THIS IS THE END
I hate her typing face.
COMMENTS
Look at her eyes!
That is totally photoshopped.
Disbeliever! Those are her eyes!
#REDEYESAREREAL

Here are the lucky few who **MIRACULOUSLY** escaped with their lives . . .

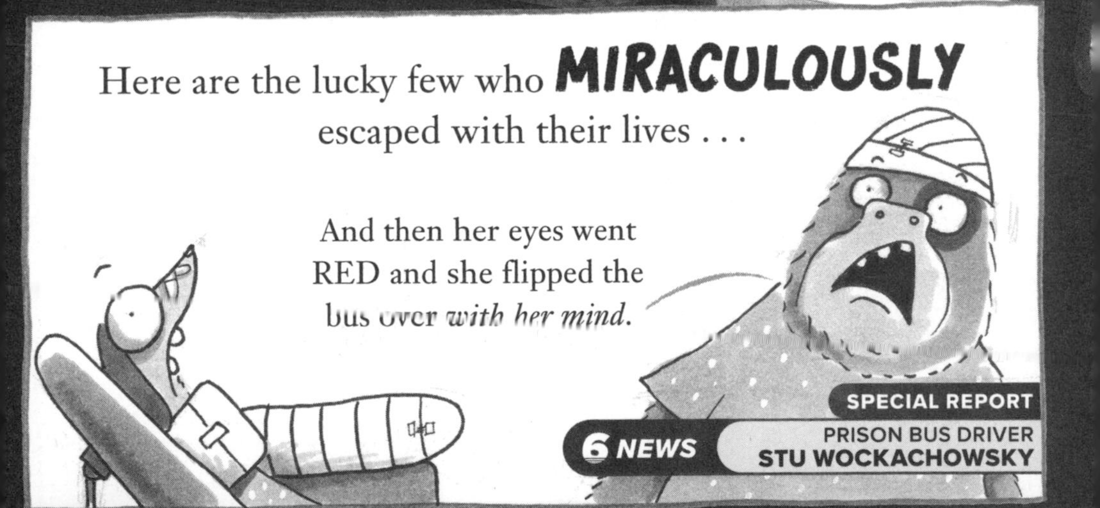
And then her eyes went RED and she flipped the bus over *with her mind*.
SPECIAL REPORT
6 NEWS
PRISON BUS DRIVER
STU WOCKACHOWSKY

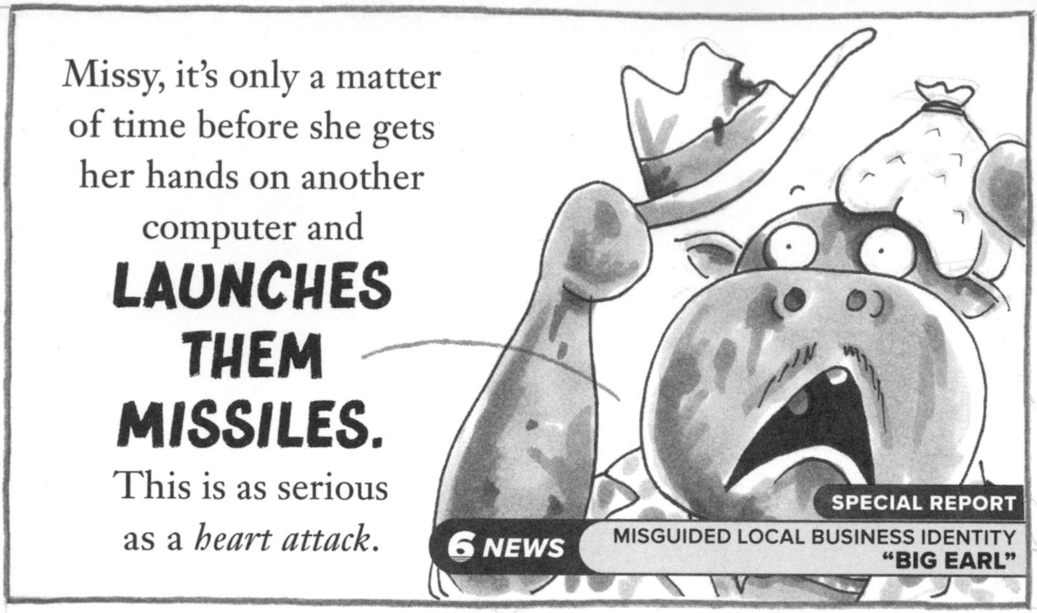
Missy, it's only a matter of time before she gets her hands on another computer and **LAUNCHES THEM MISSILES.** This is as serious as a *heart attack*.
SPECIAL REPORT
6 NEWS
MISGUIDED LOCAL BUSINESS IDENTITY
"BIG EARL"

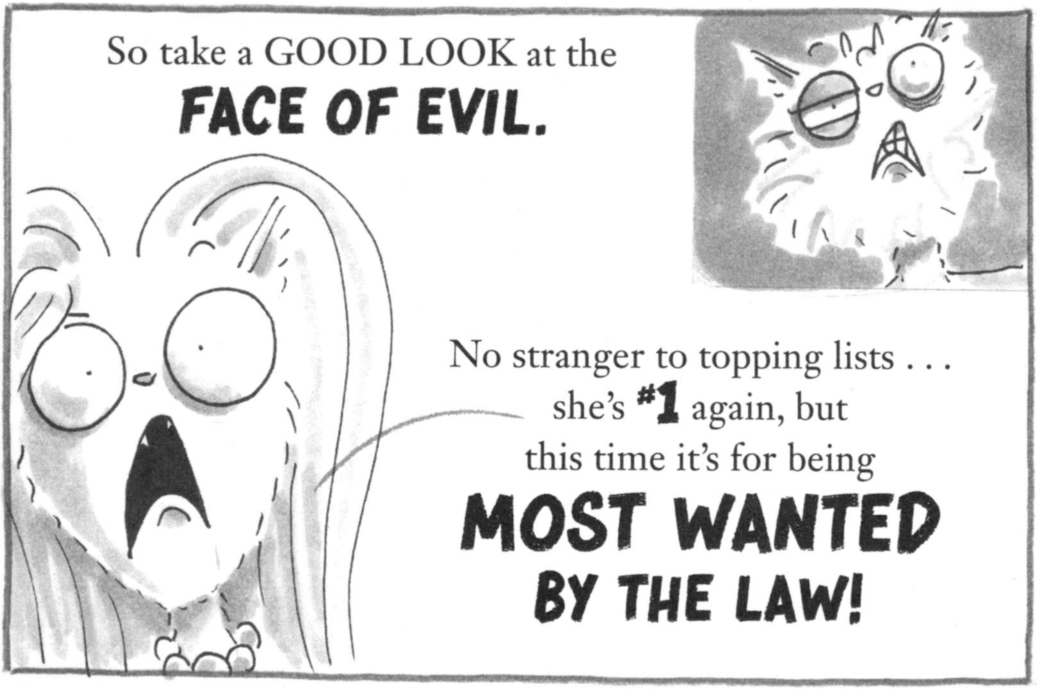
So take a GOOD LOOK at the **FACE OF EVIL.**
No stranger to topping lists . . . she's #1 again, but this time it's for being **MOST WANTED BY THE LAW!**

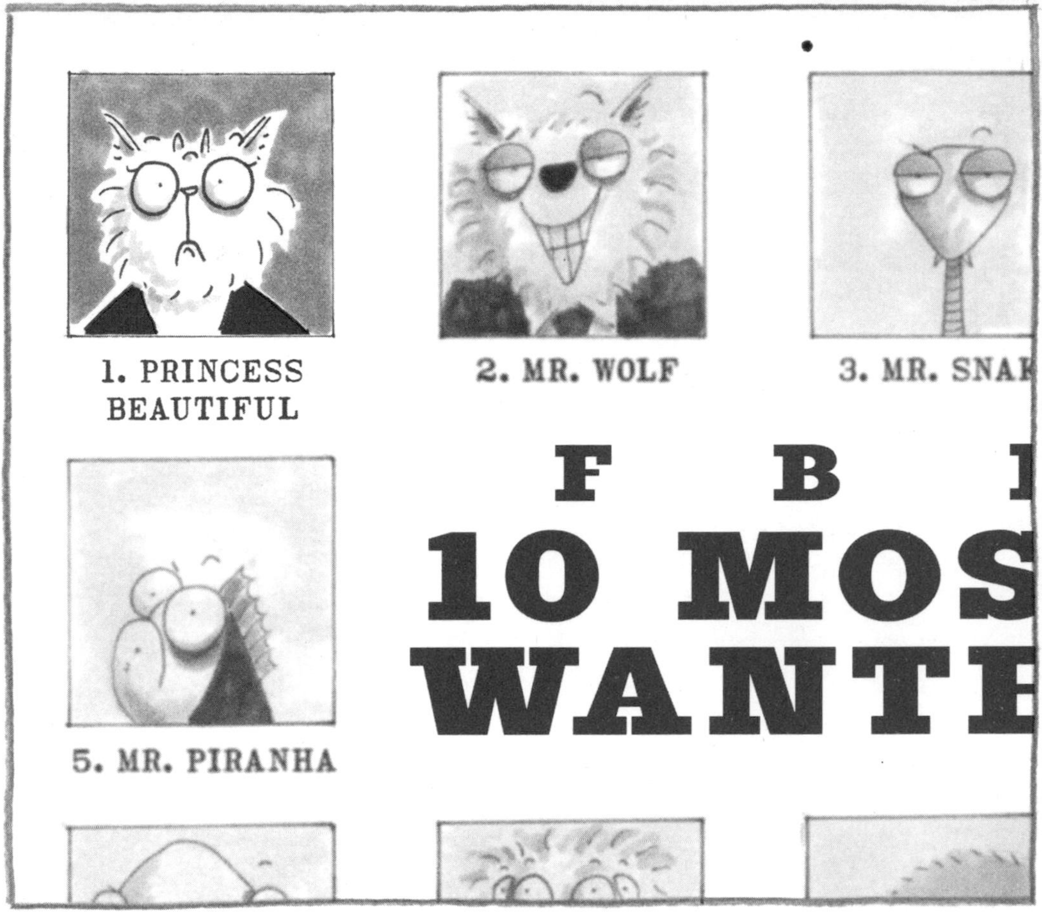
1. PRINCESS BEAUTIFUL
2. MR. WOLF
3. MR. SNAK
F B I
10 MOS
WANTE
5. MR. PIRANHA

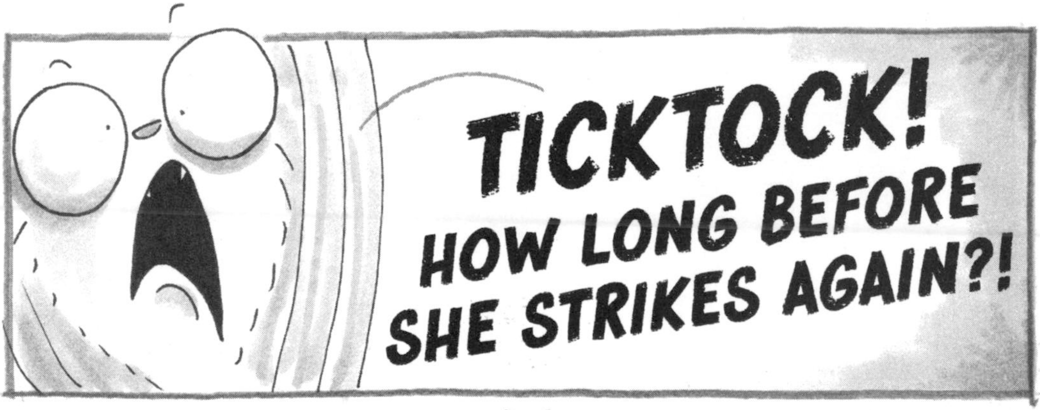
TICKTOCK!
HOW LONG BEFORE SHE STRIKES AGAIN?!

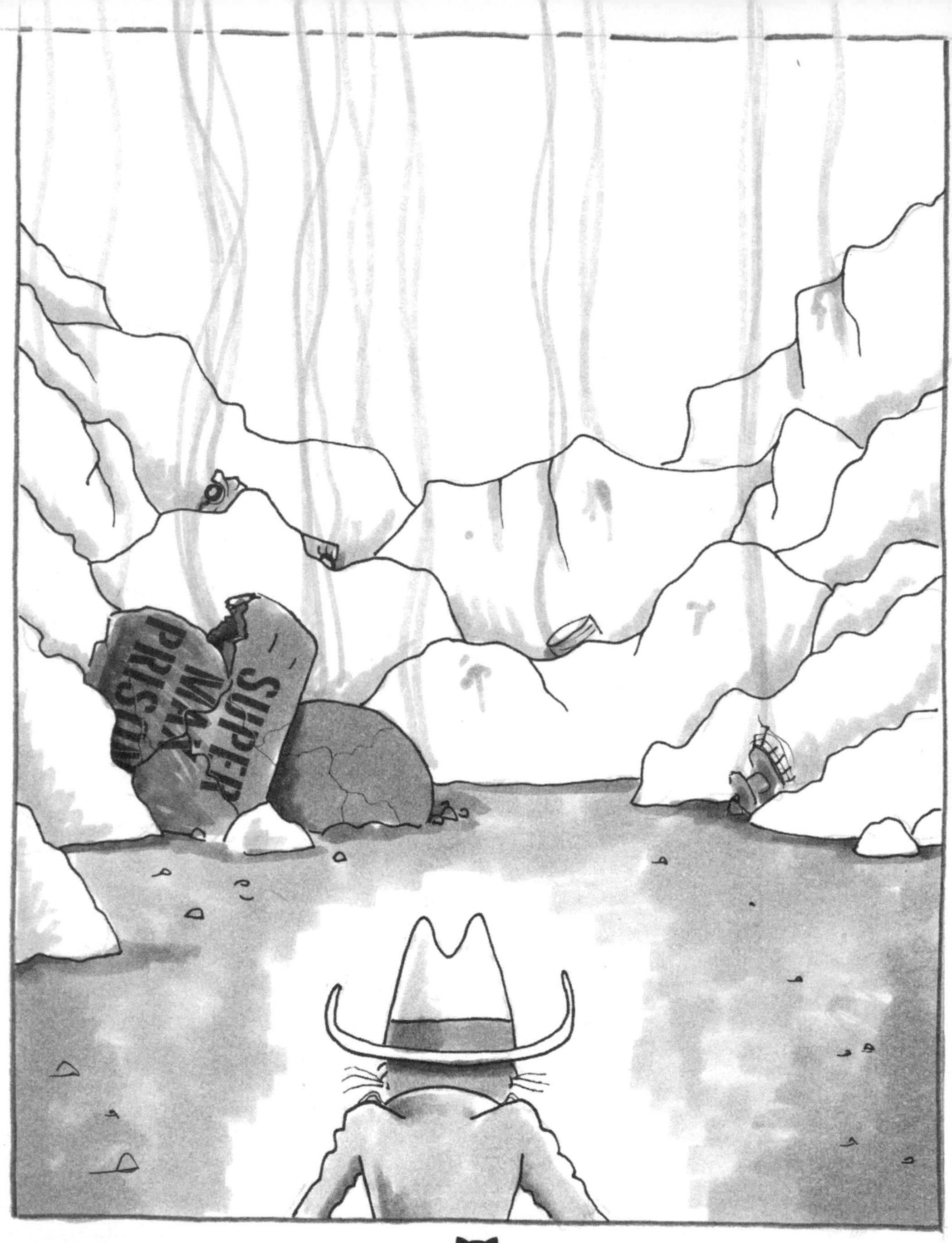
SUPER MAX PRISON

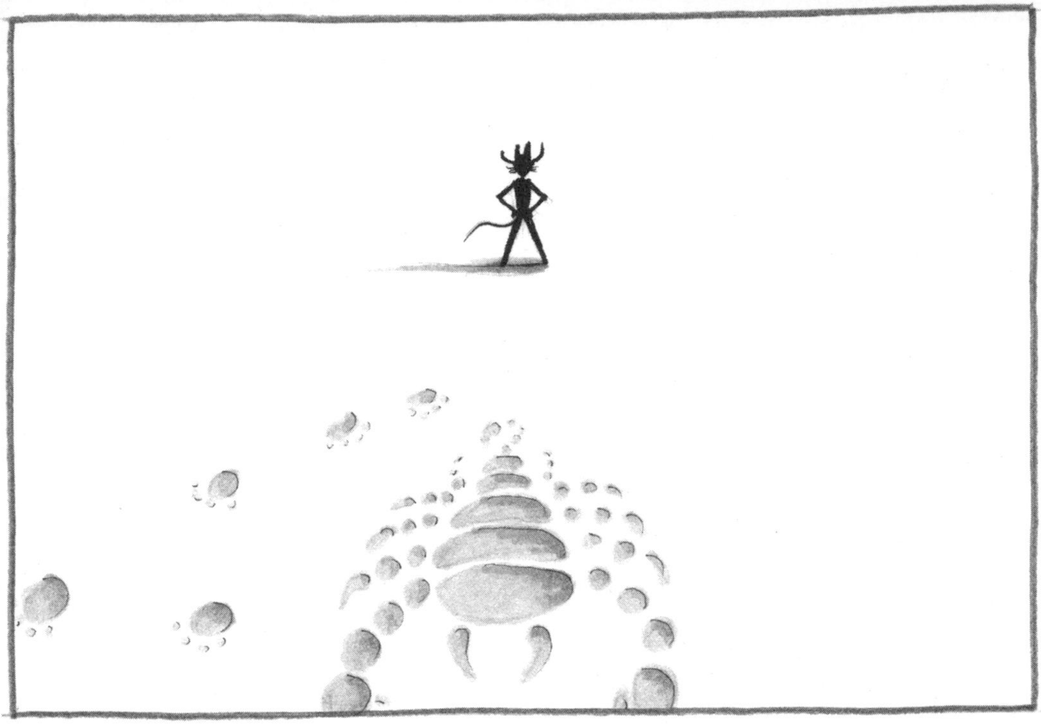

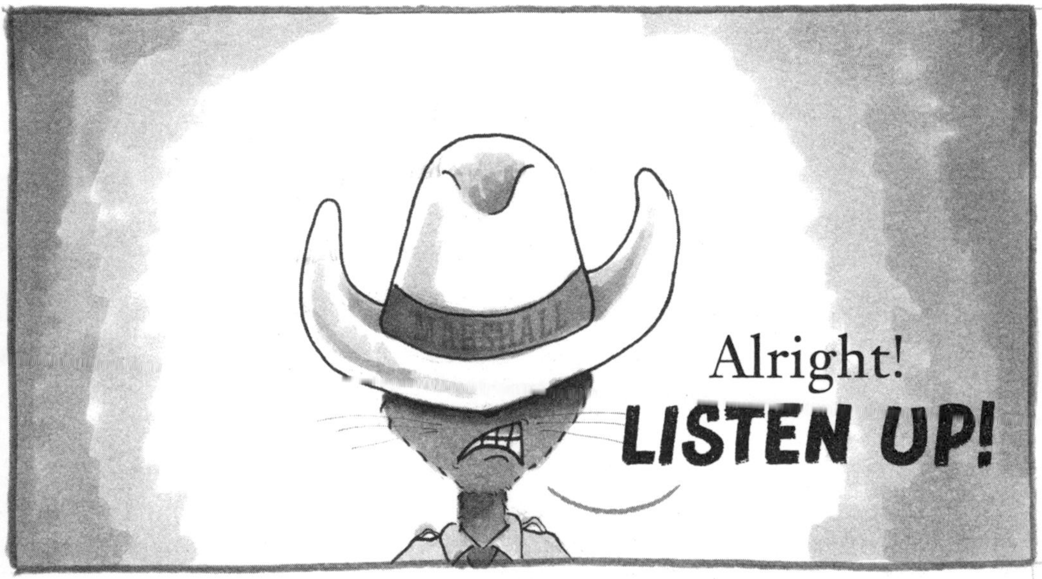

Alright!
LISTEN UP!

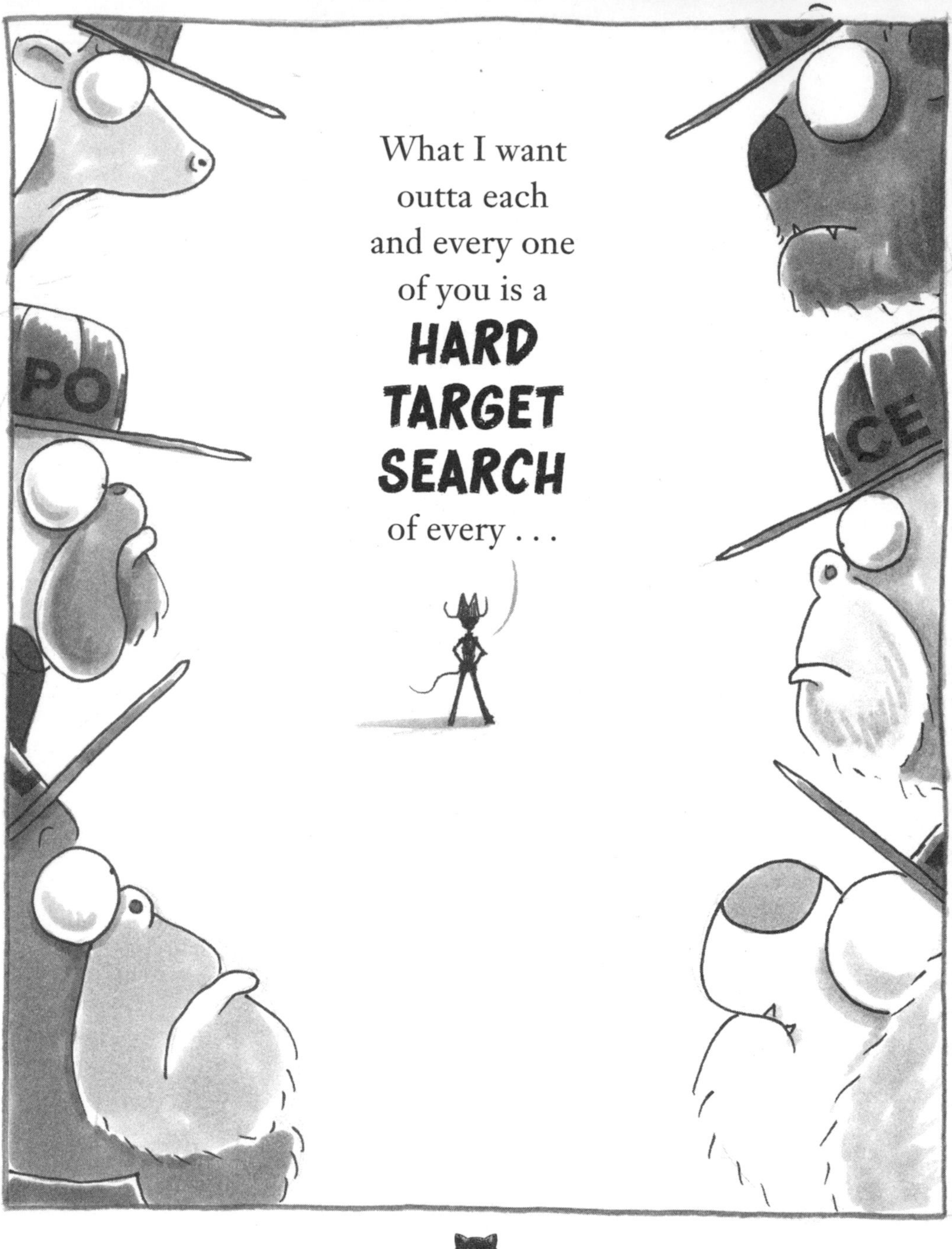
What I want outta each and every one of you is a
HARD TARGET SEARCH
of every . . .

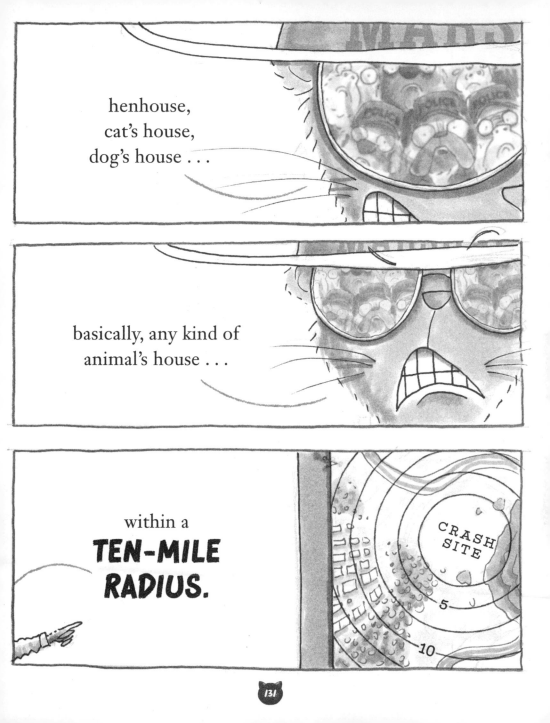

henhouse,
cat's house,
dog's house . . .

basically, any kind of
animal's house . . .

within a
**TEN-MILE
RADIUS.**

CRASH
SITE

5

10

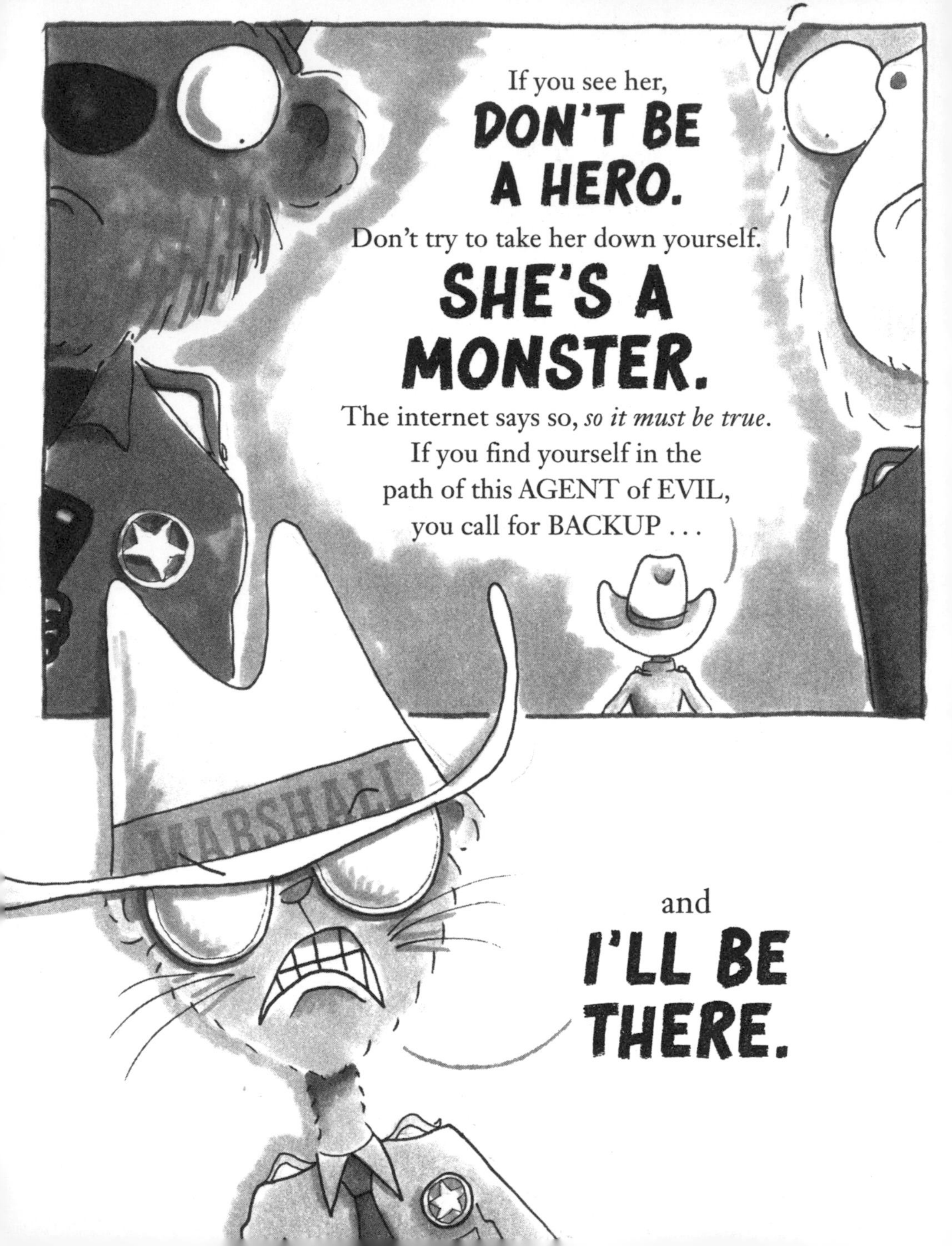

If you see her,
DON'T BE A HERO.
Don't try to take her down yourself.
SHE'S A MONSTER.
The internet says so, *so it must be true*.
If you find yourself in the path of this AGENT of EVIL, you call for BACKUP . . .
MARSHALL
and
I'LL BE THERE.

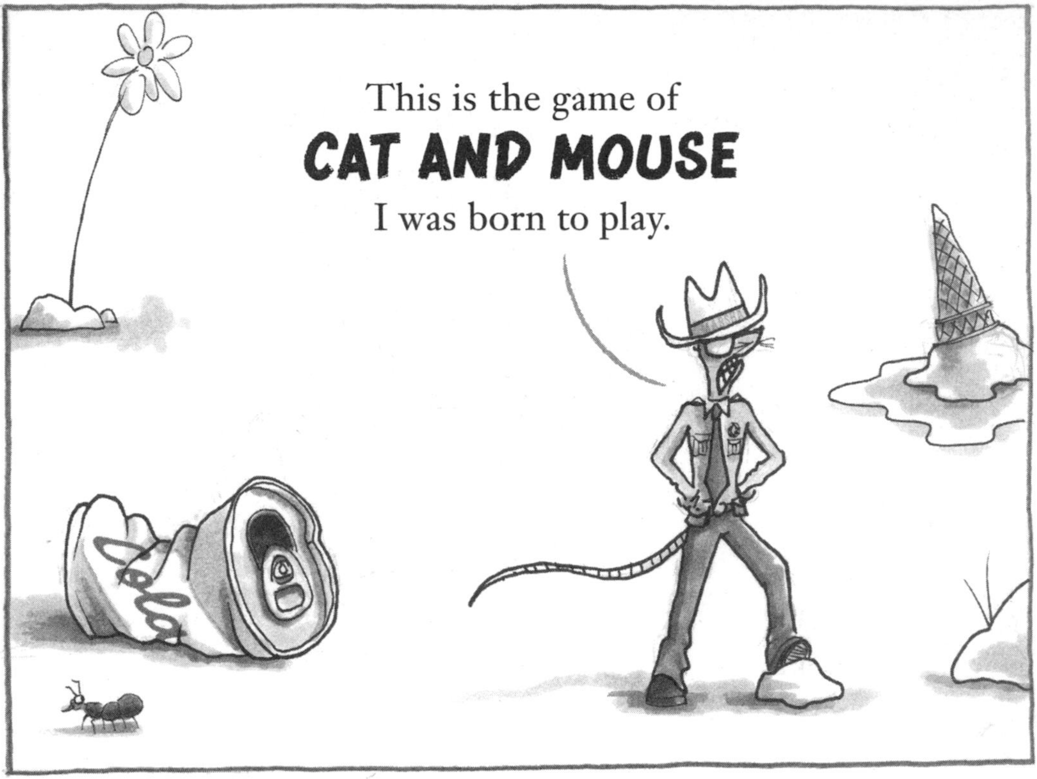
This is the game of
CAT AND MOUSE
I was born to play.
Cola

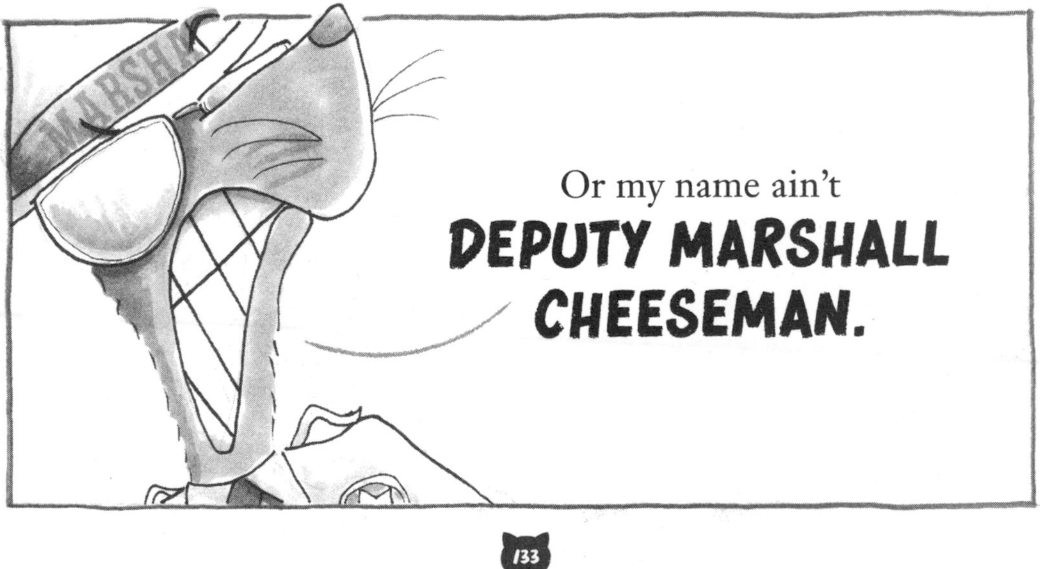
MARSHA
Or my name ain't
DEPUTY MARSHALL
CHEESEMAN.

Seven
SHE WALKS AMONG US

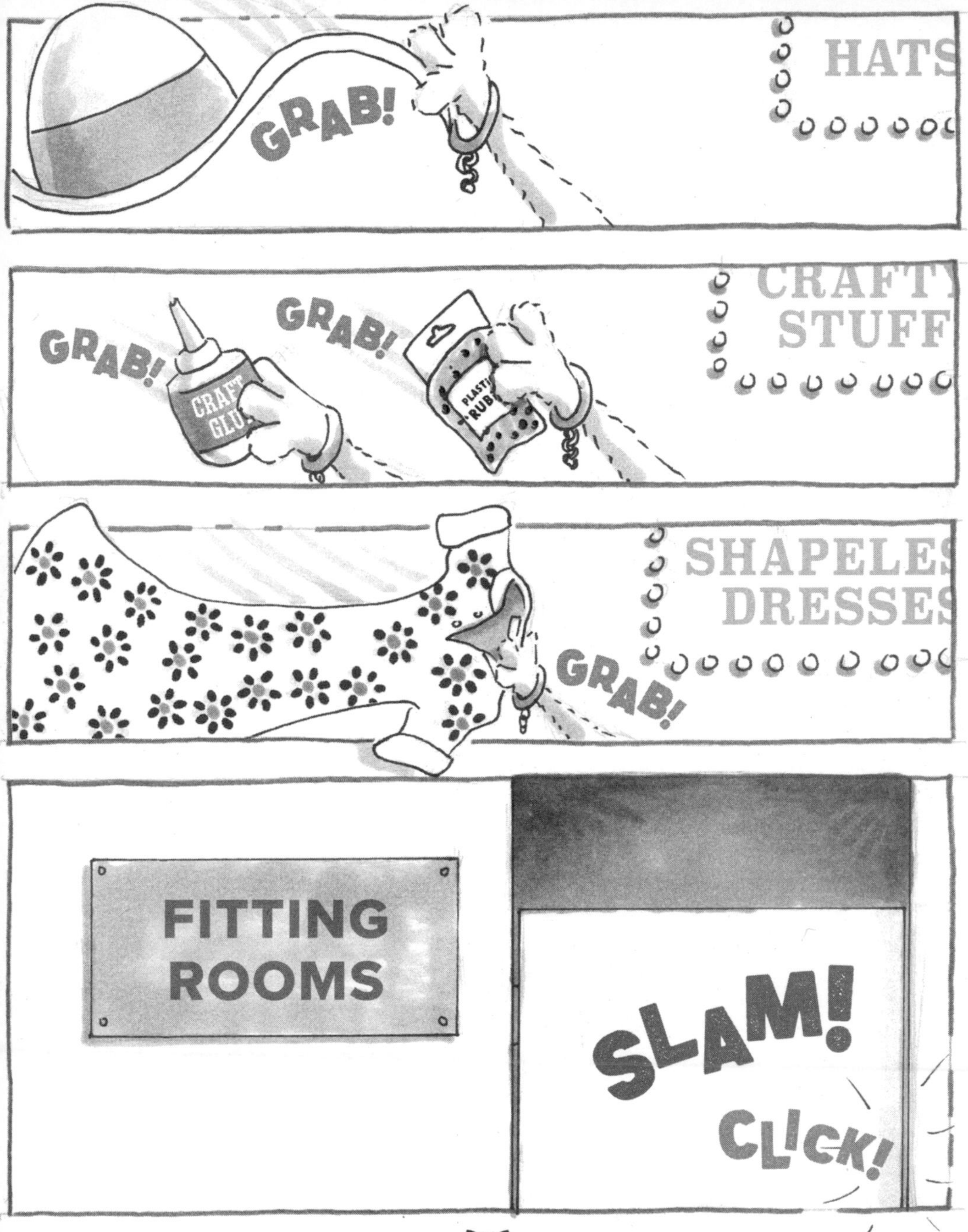

GRAB!
HATS
GRAB!
GRAB!
CRAFT GLU
PLASTI RUB
CRAFTY STUFF
SHAPELESS DRESSES
GRAB!
FITTING ROOMS
SLAM!
CLICK!

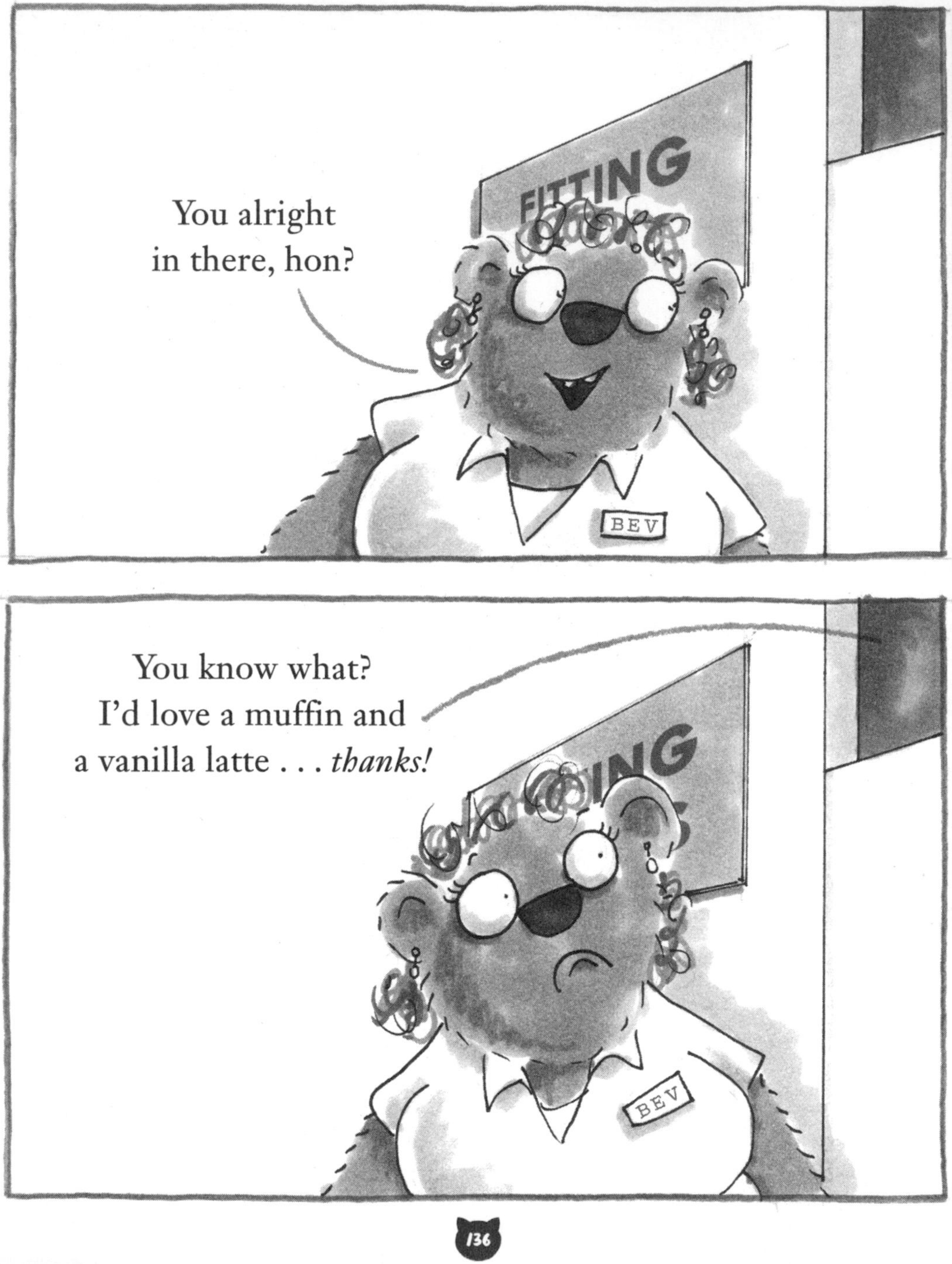
FITTING
You alright in there, hon?
BEV
You know what? I'd love a muffin and a vanilla latte . . . *thanks!*
ING
BEV

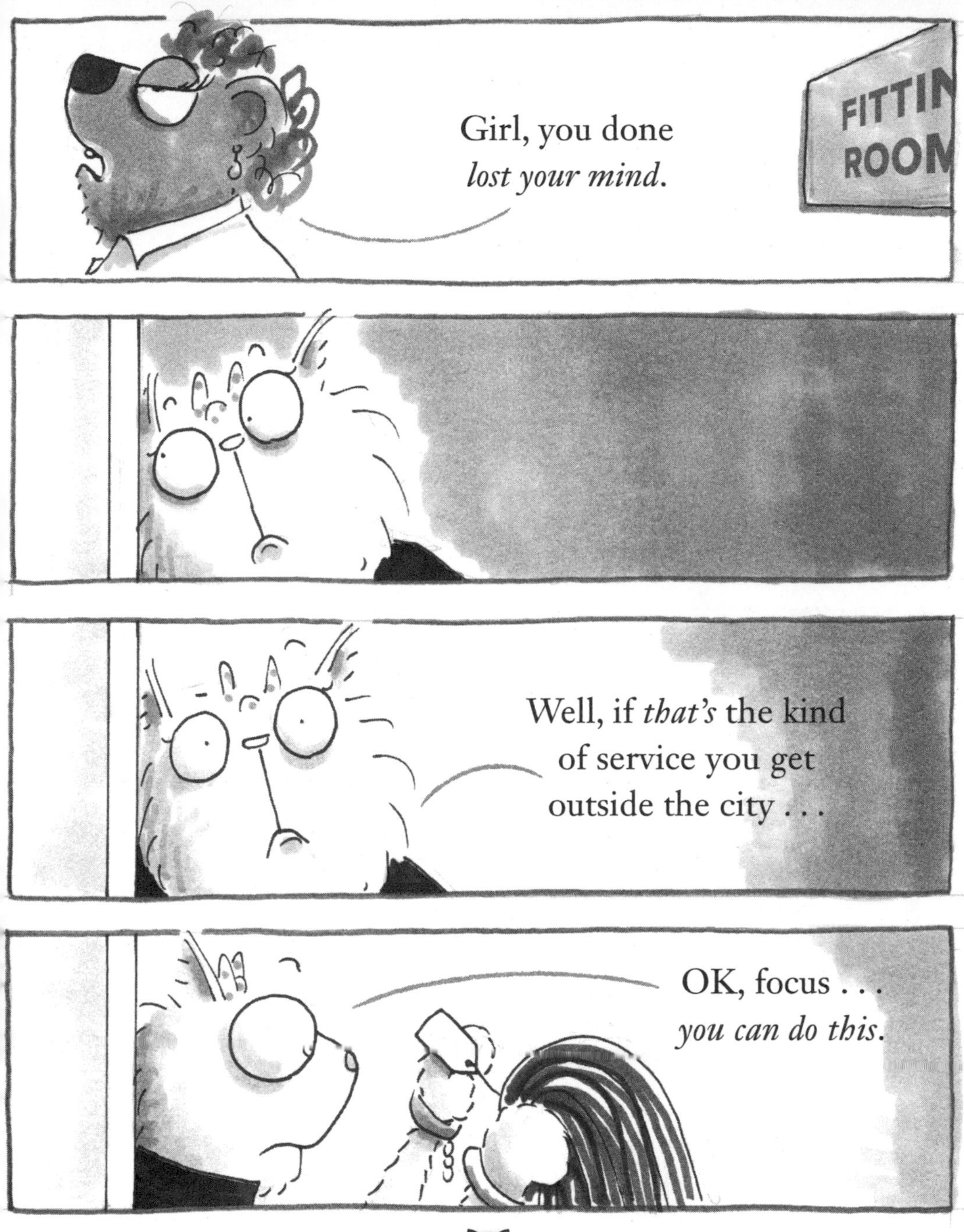
FITTIN
ROOM
Girl, you done *lost your mind*.
Well, if *that's* the kind of service you get outside the city . . .
OK, focus . . . *you can do this*.

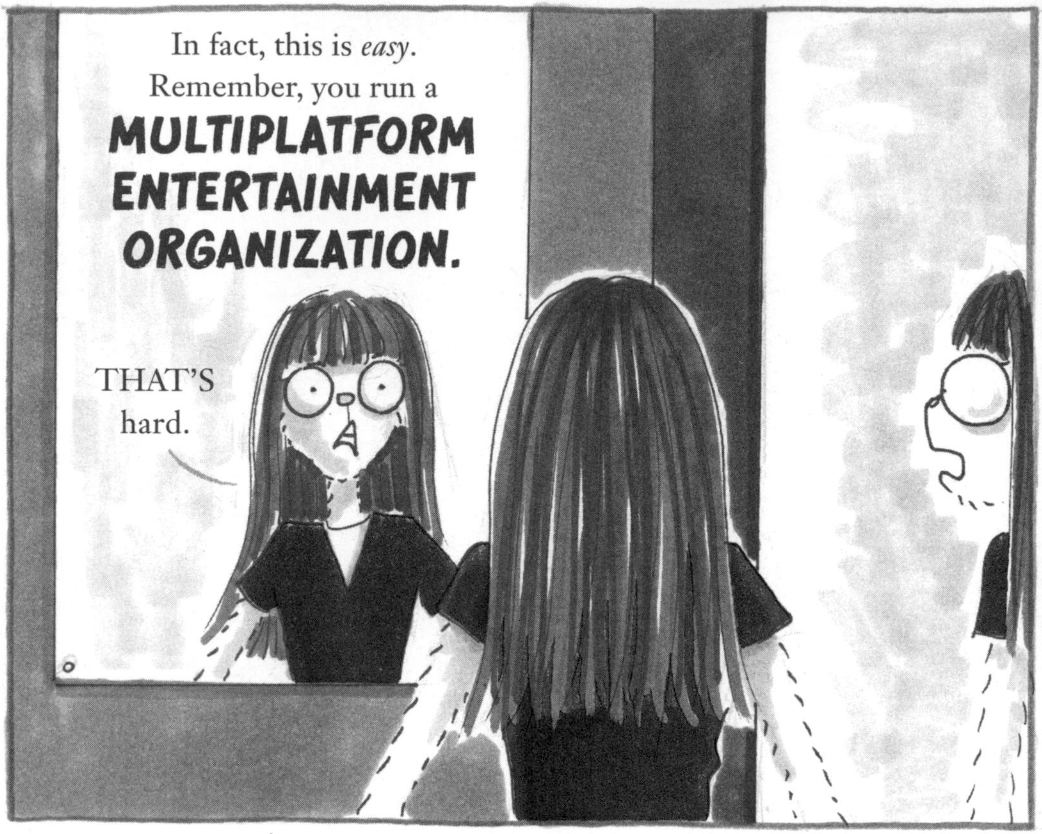
In fact, this is *easy*.
Remember, you run a
MULTIPLATFORM ENTERTAINMENT ORGANIZATION.
THAT'S hard.

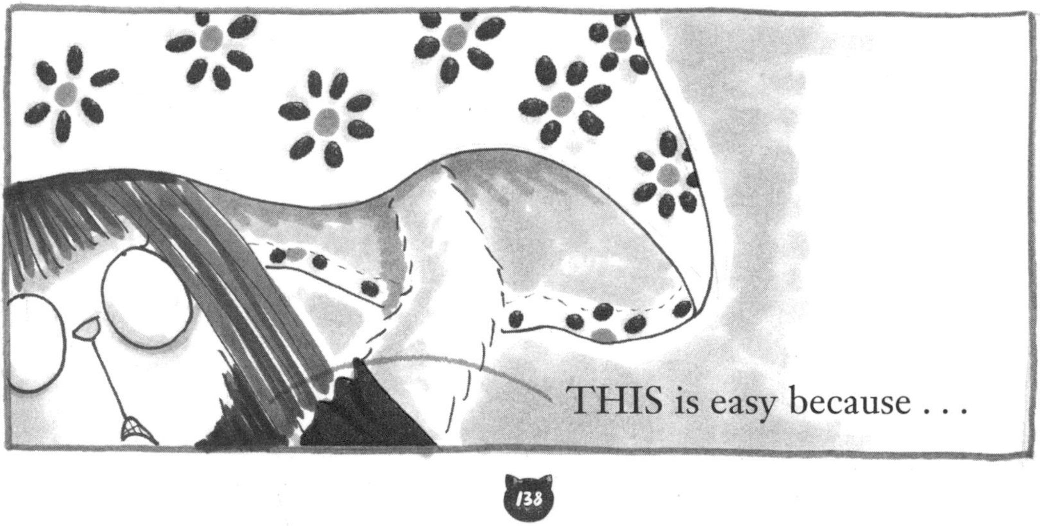
THIS is easy because . . .

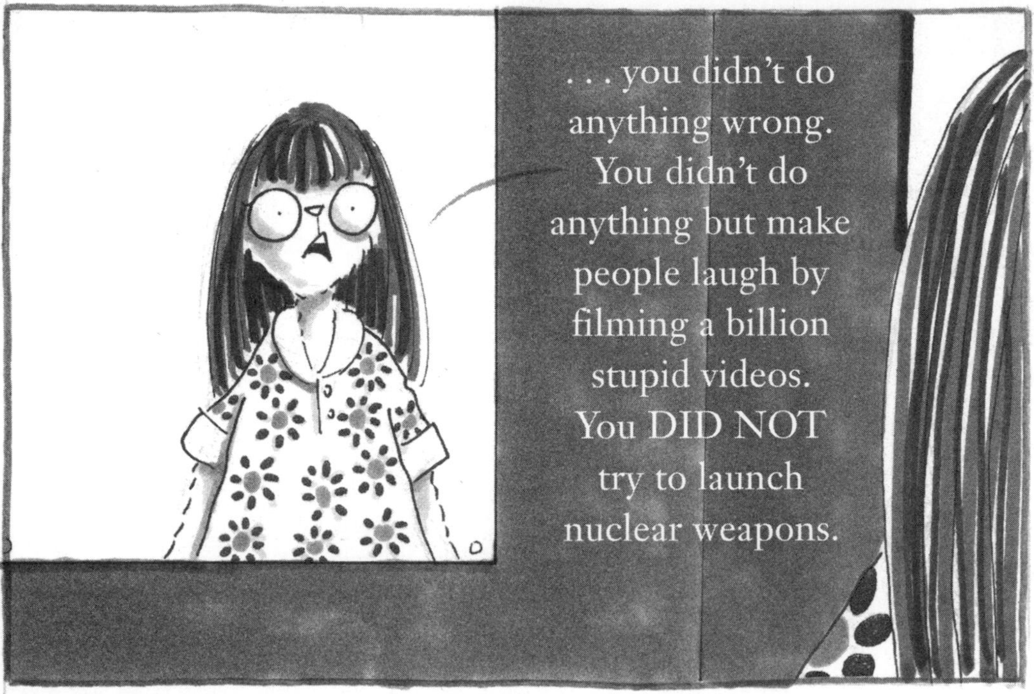
. . . you didn't do anything wrong. You didn't do anything but make people laugh by filming a billion stupid videos. You DID NOT try to launch nuclear weapons.

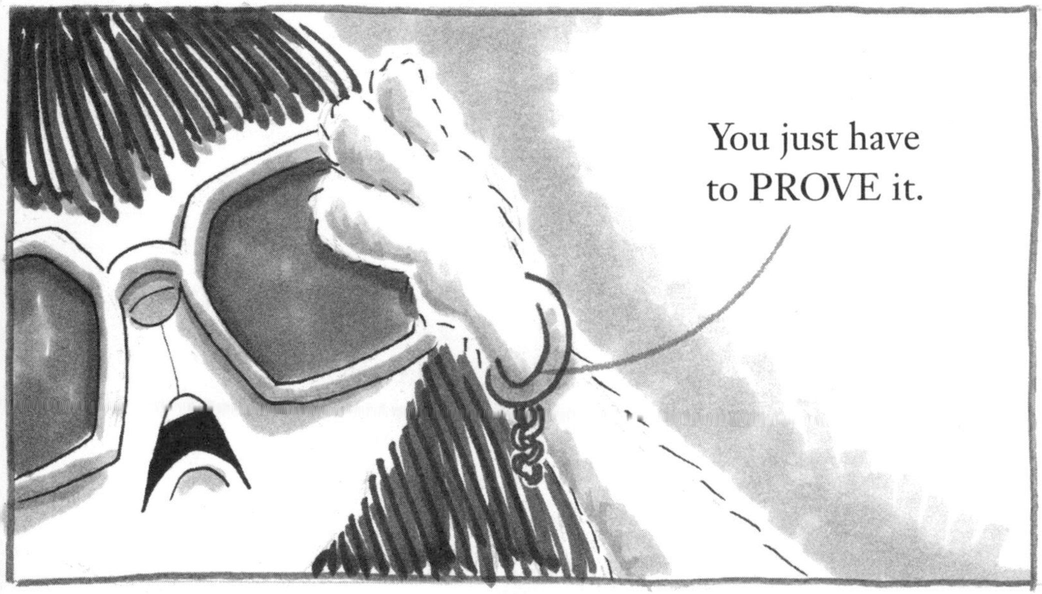
You just have to PROVE it.

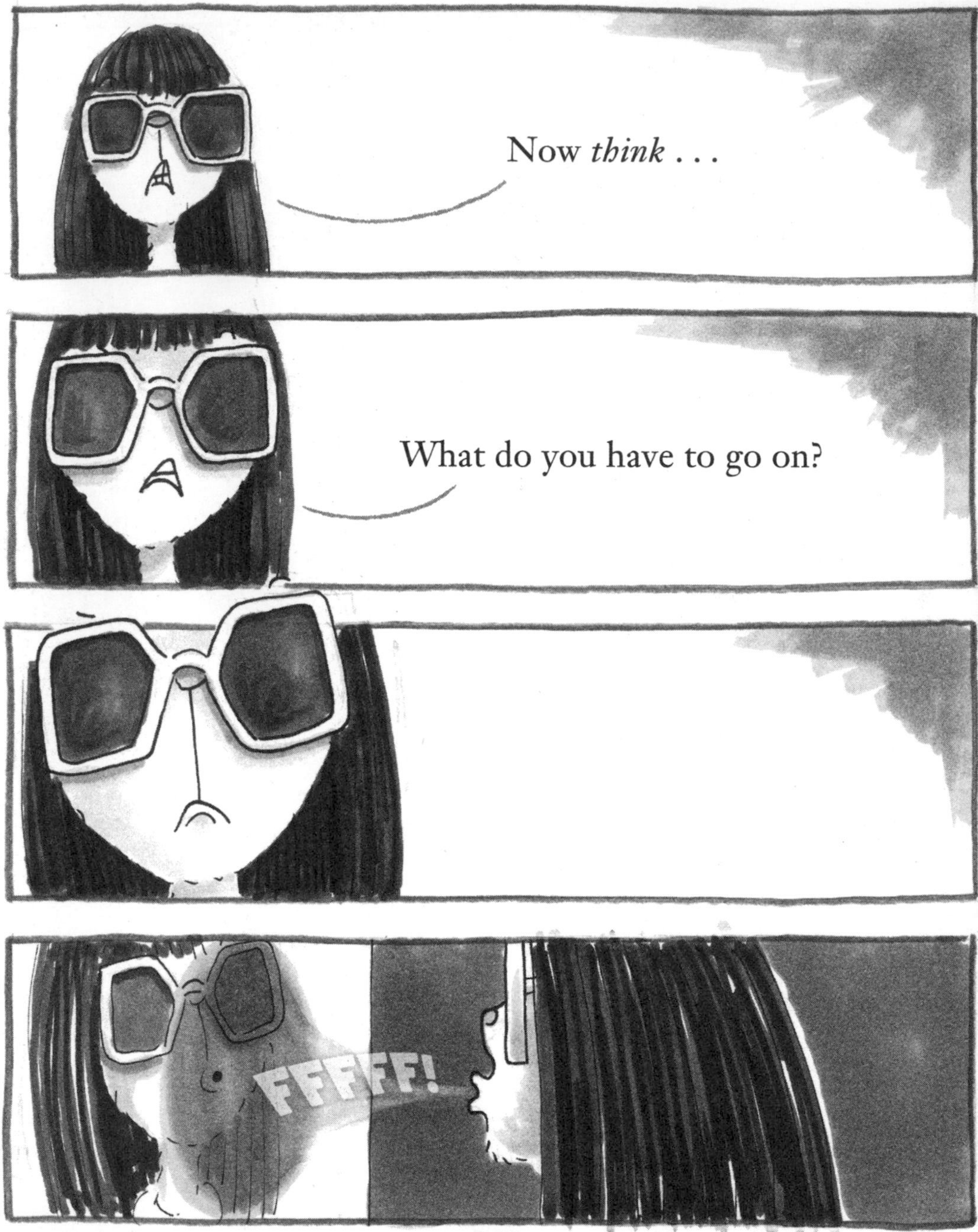
Now *think* . . .
What do you have to go on?
FFFFF!

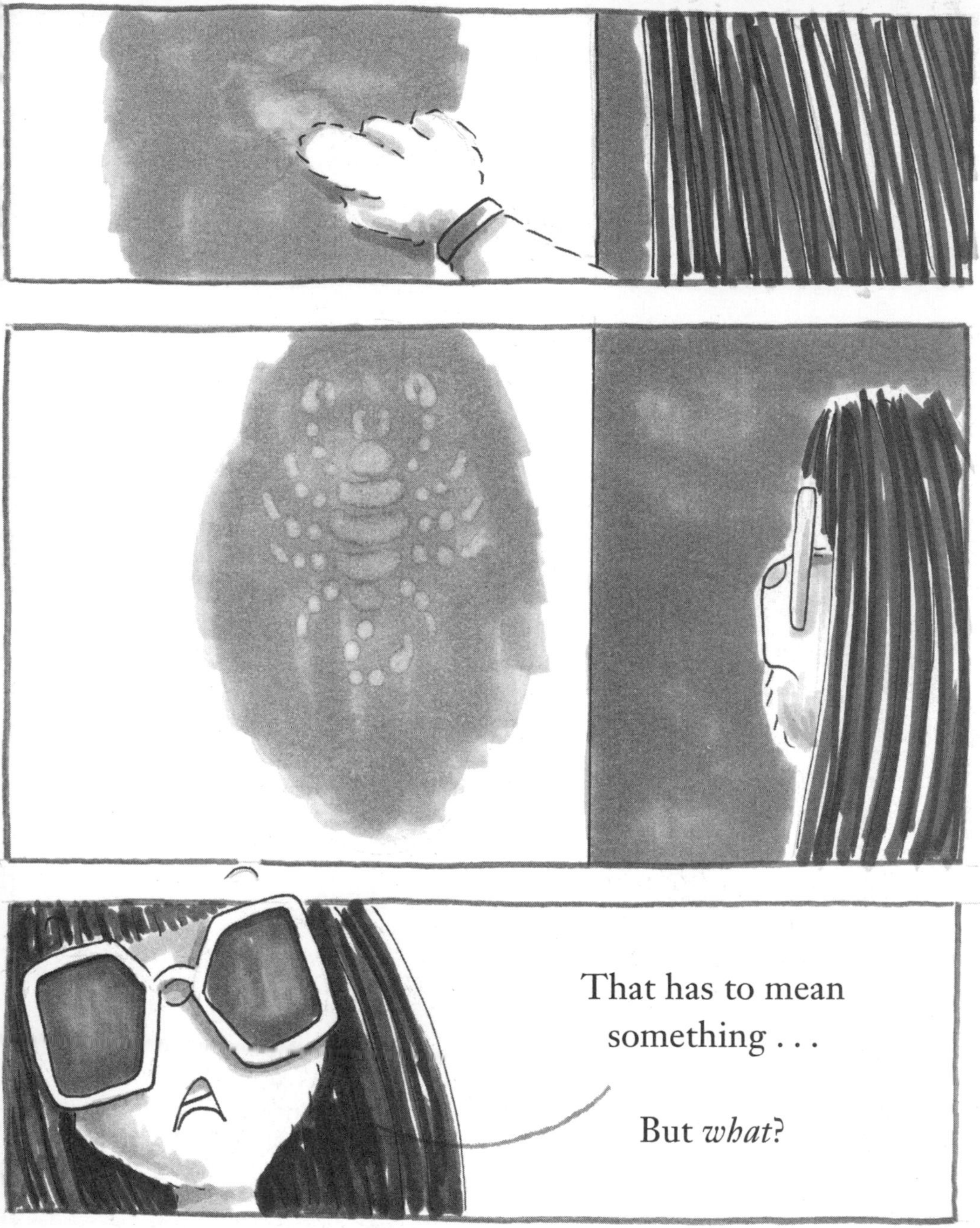
That has to mean something . . .
But *what*?

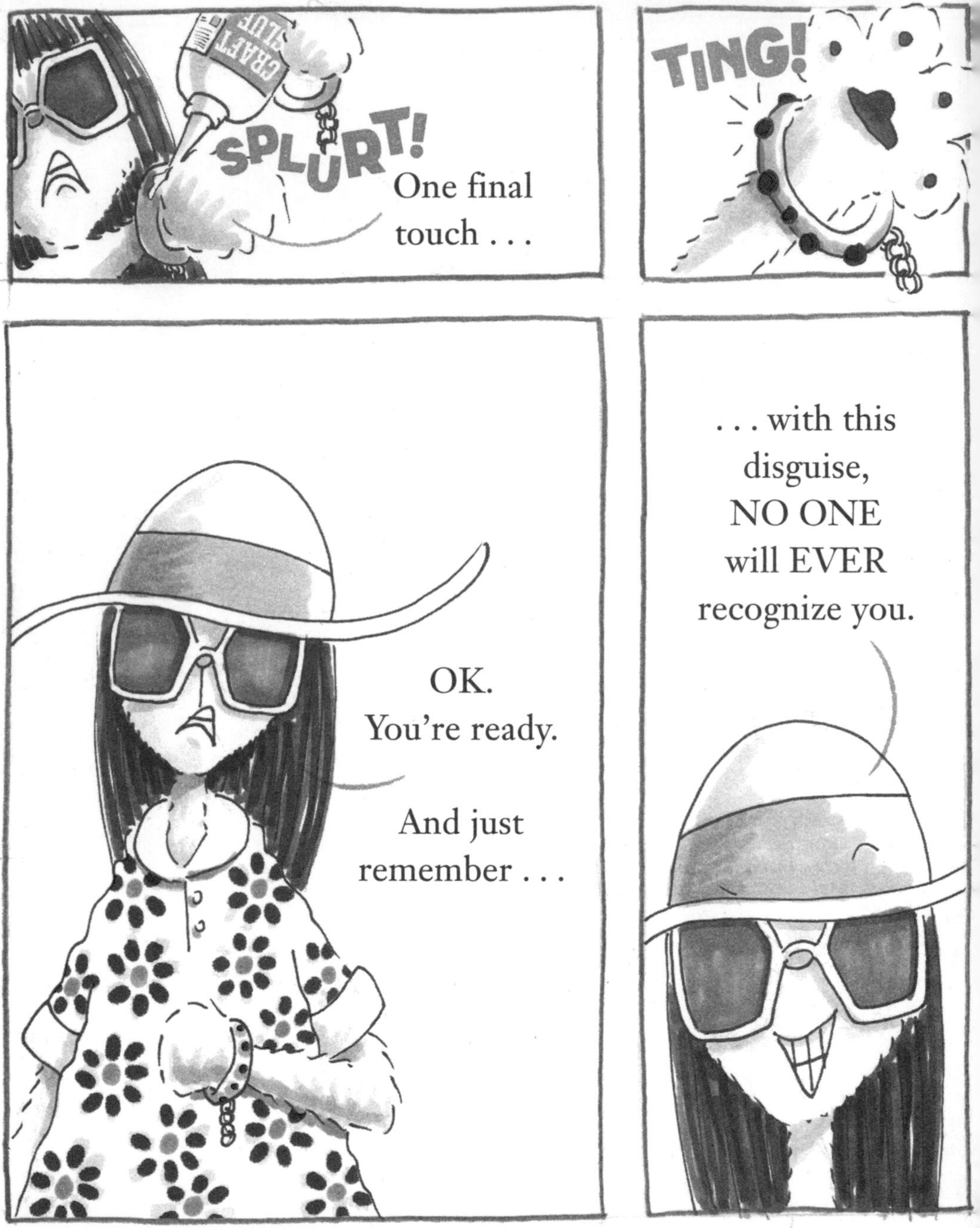
SPLURT!
One final touch . . .
TING!
OK.
You're ready.
And just remember . . .
. . . with this disguise, NO ONE will EVER recognize you.

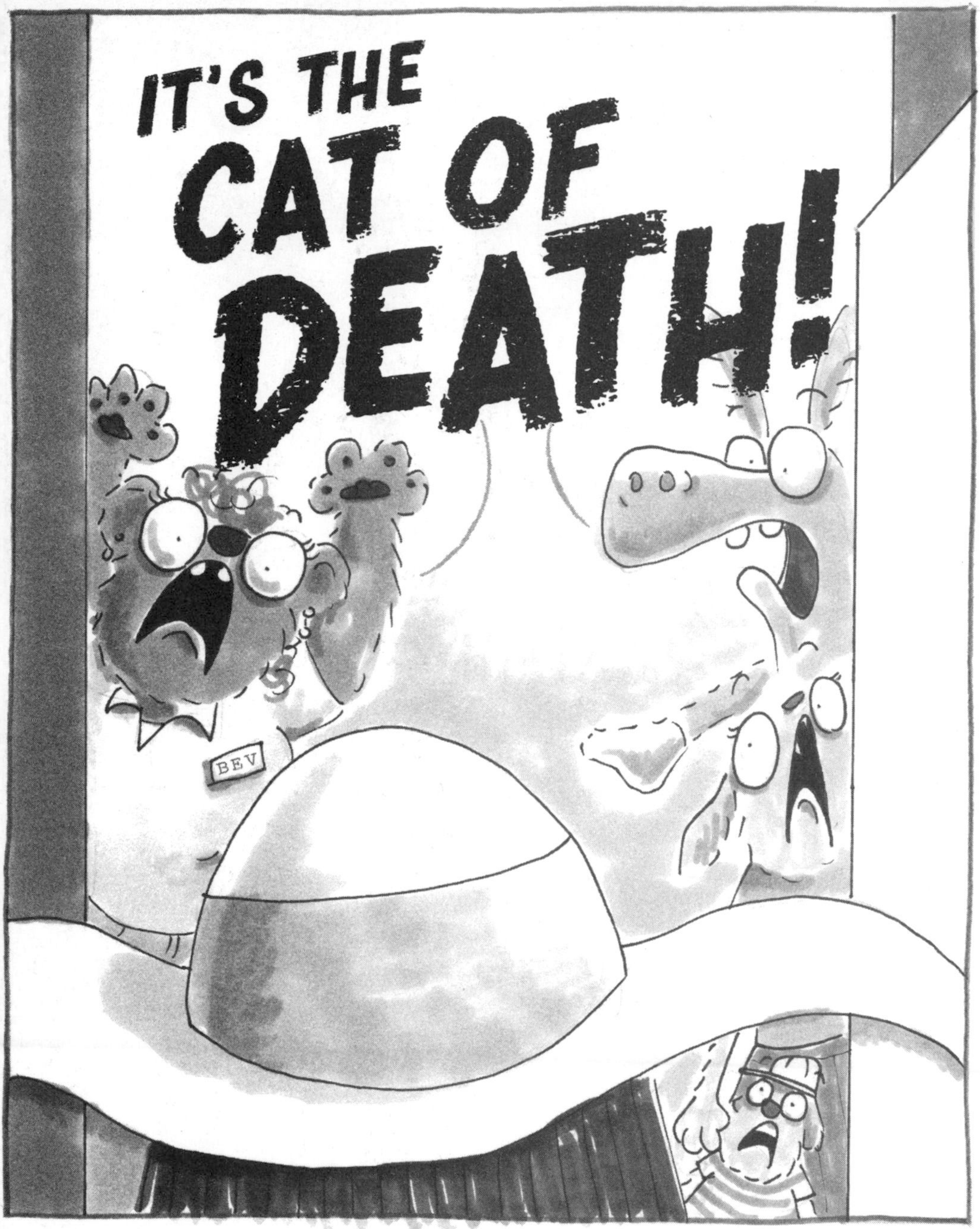
IT'S THE CAT OF DEATH!
BEV

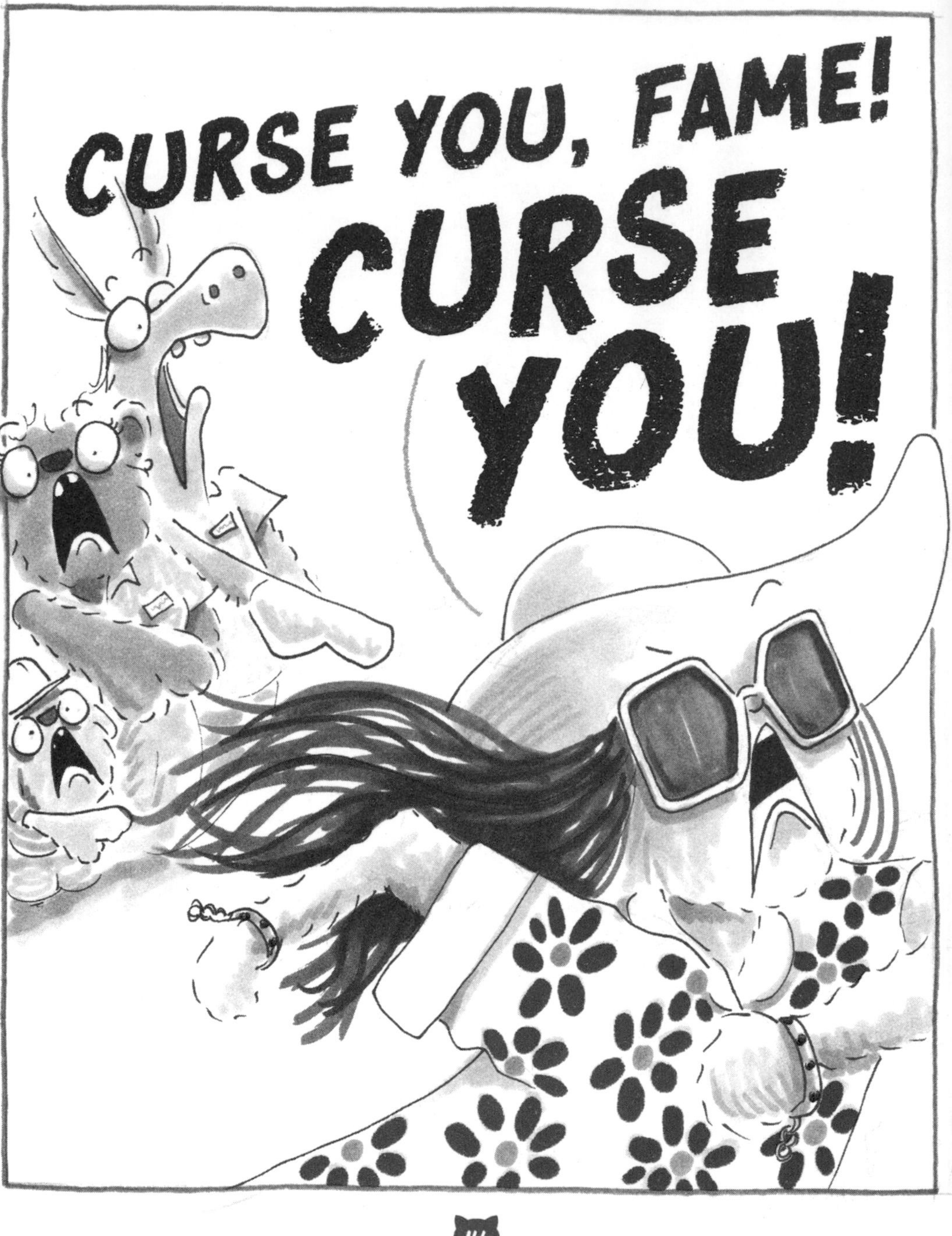
CURSE YOU, FAME! CURSE YOU!

Eight
FOLLOW THE SCORPION

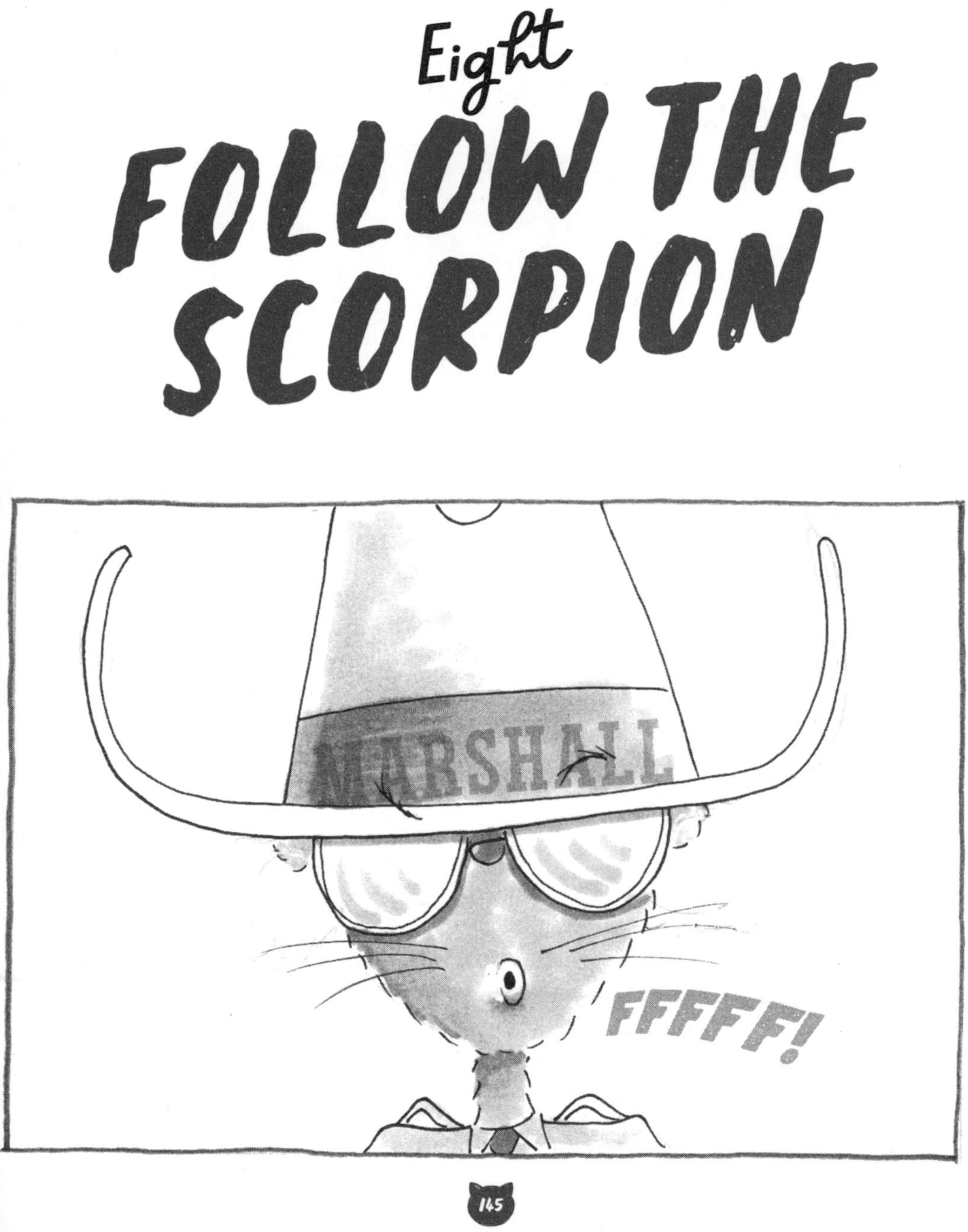
MARSHALL
FFFFF!

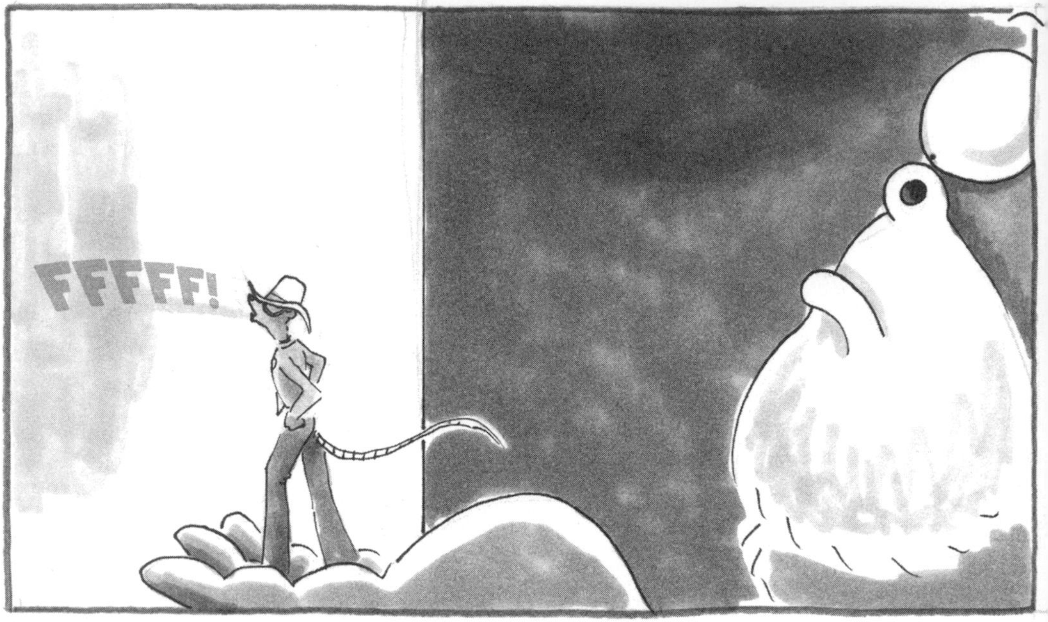
FFFFF!

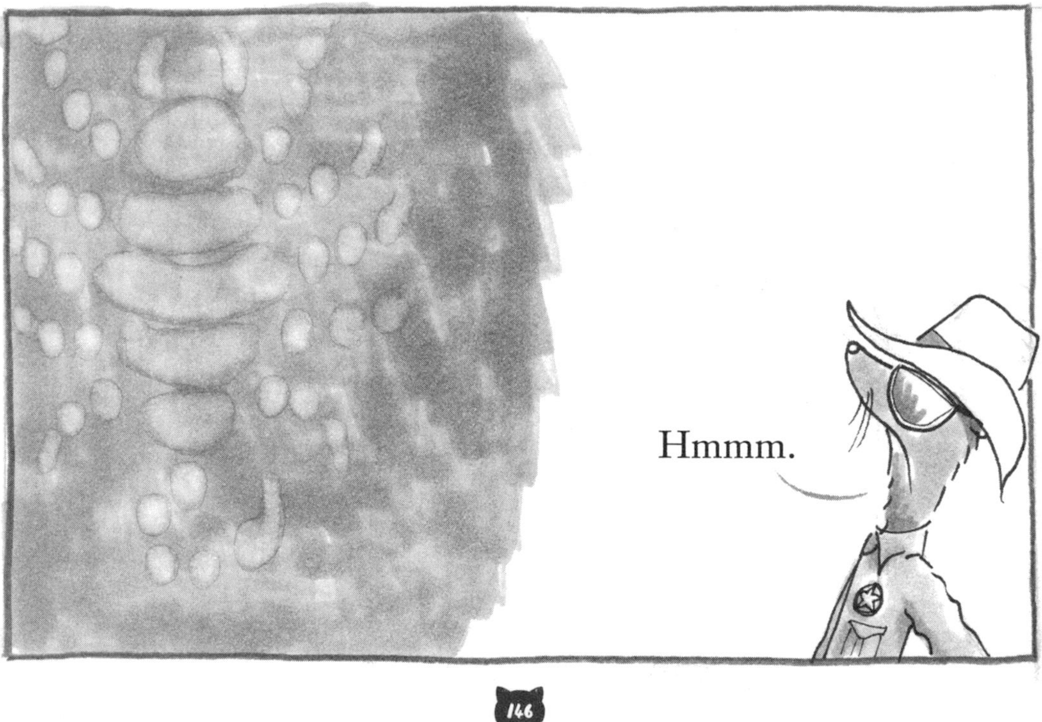
Hmmm.

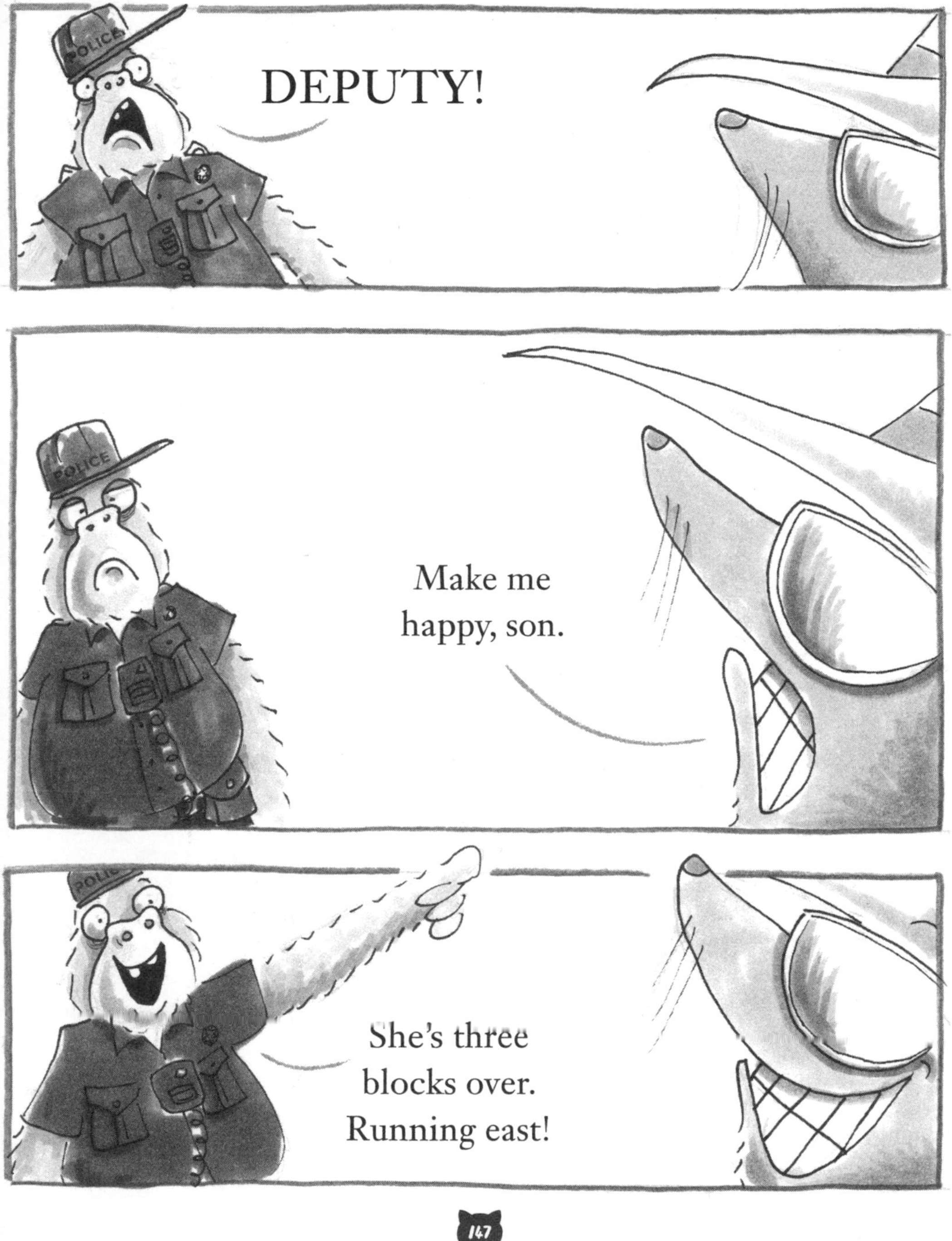
DEPUTY!
Make me happy, son.
She's three blocks over. Running east!

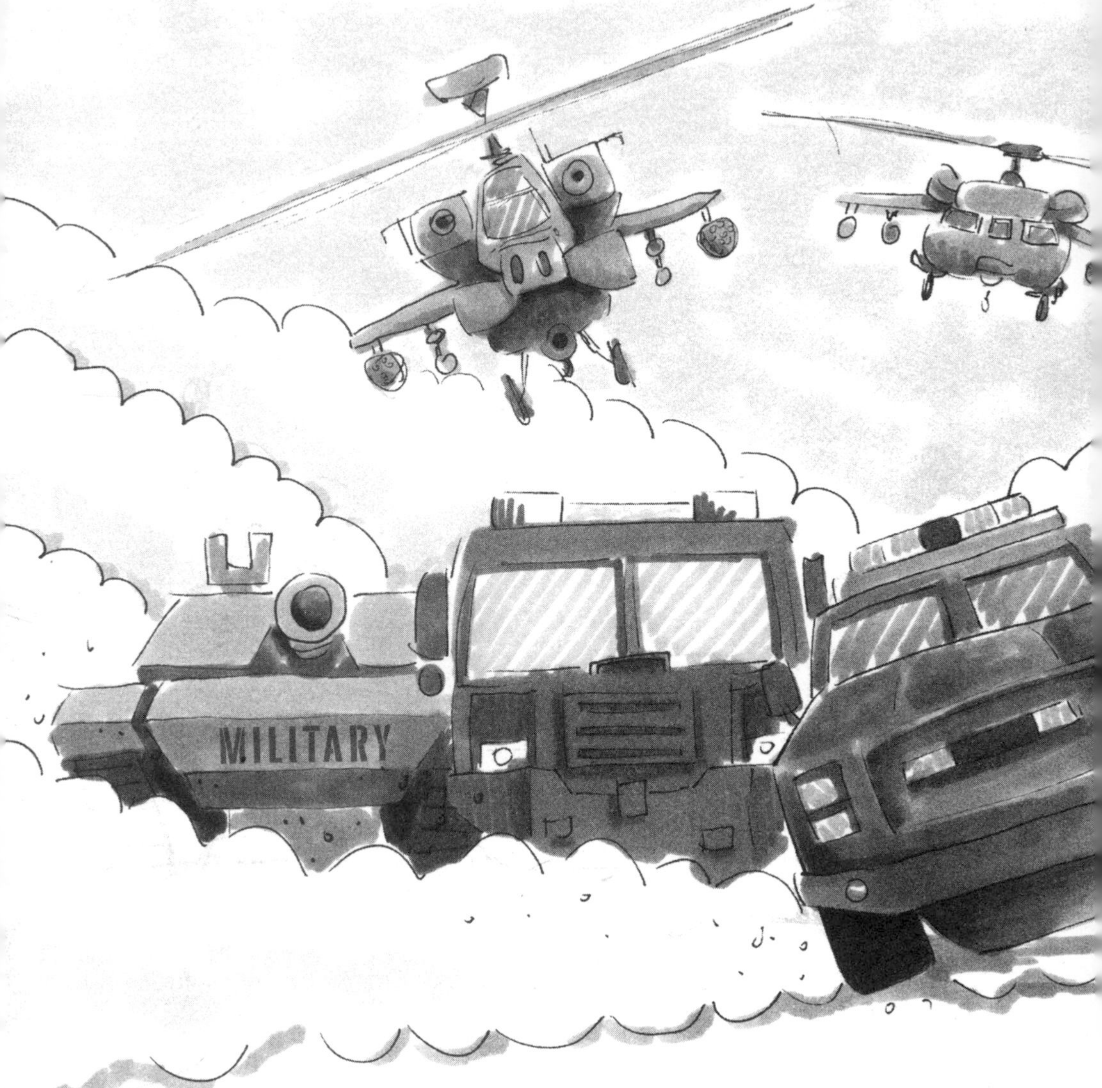
MILITARY

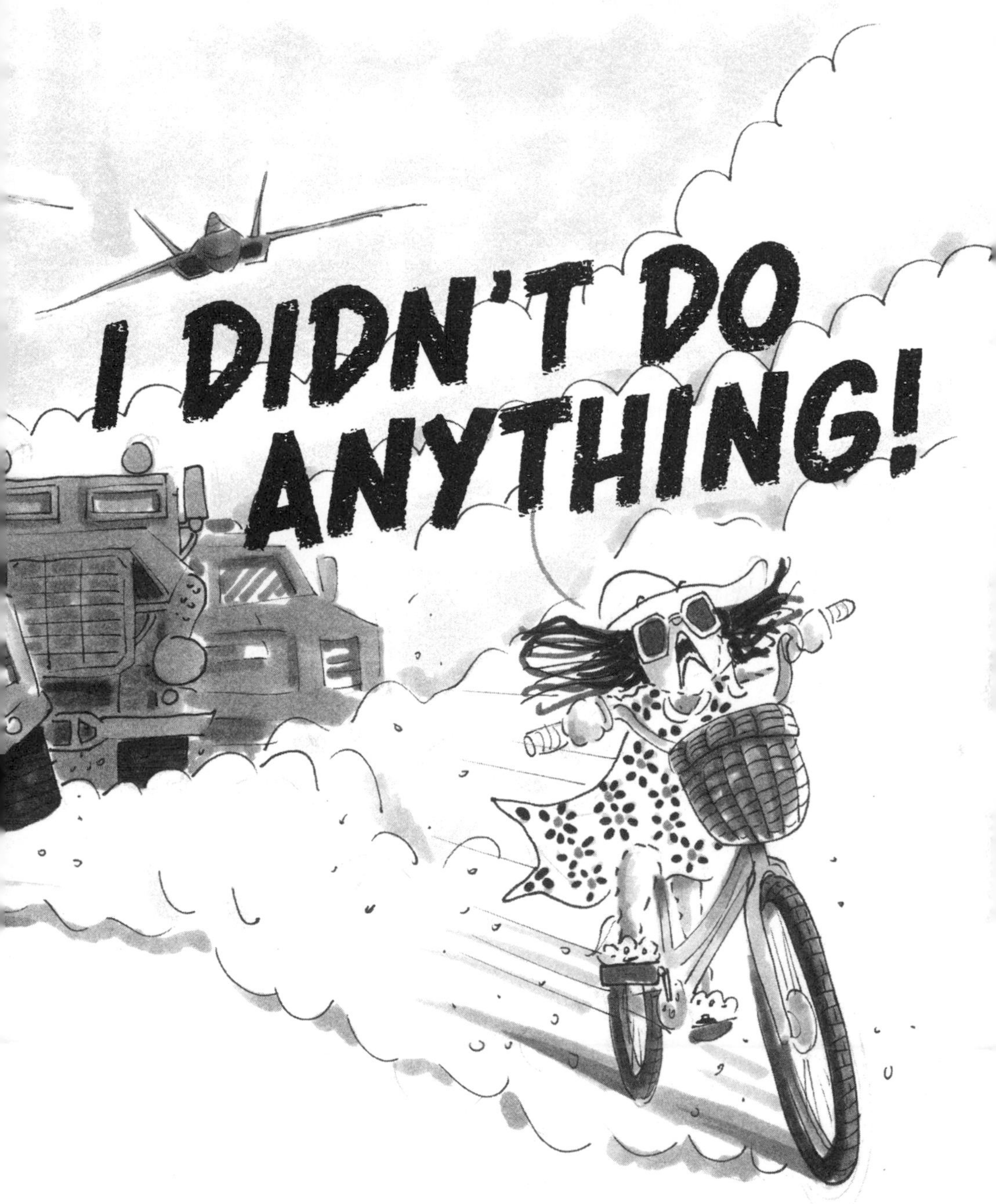
I DIDN'T DO ANYTHING!

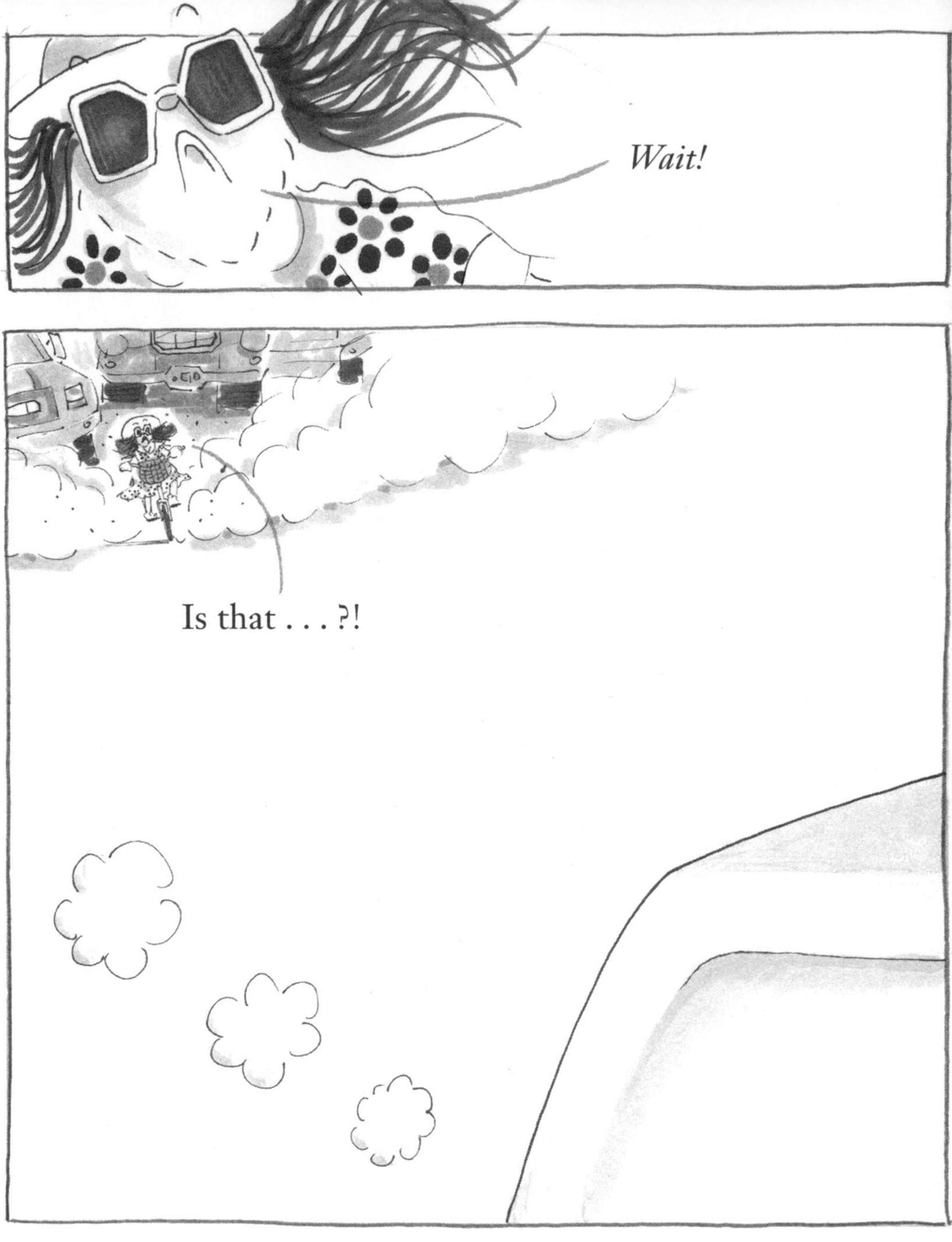
Wait!
Is that . . . ?!

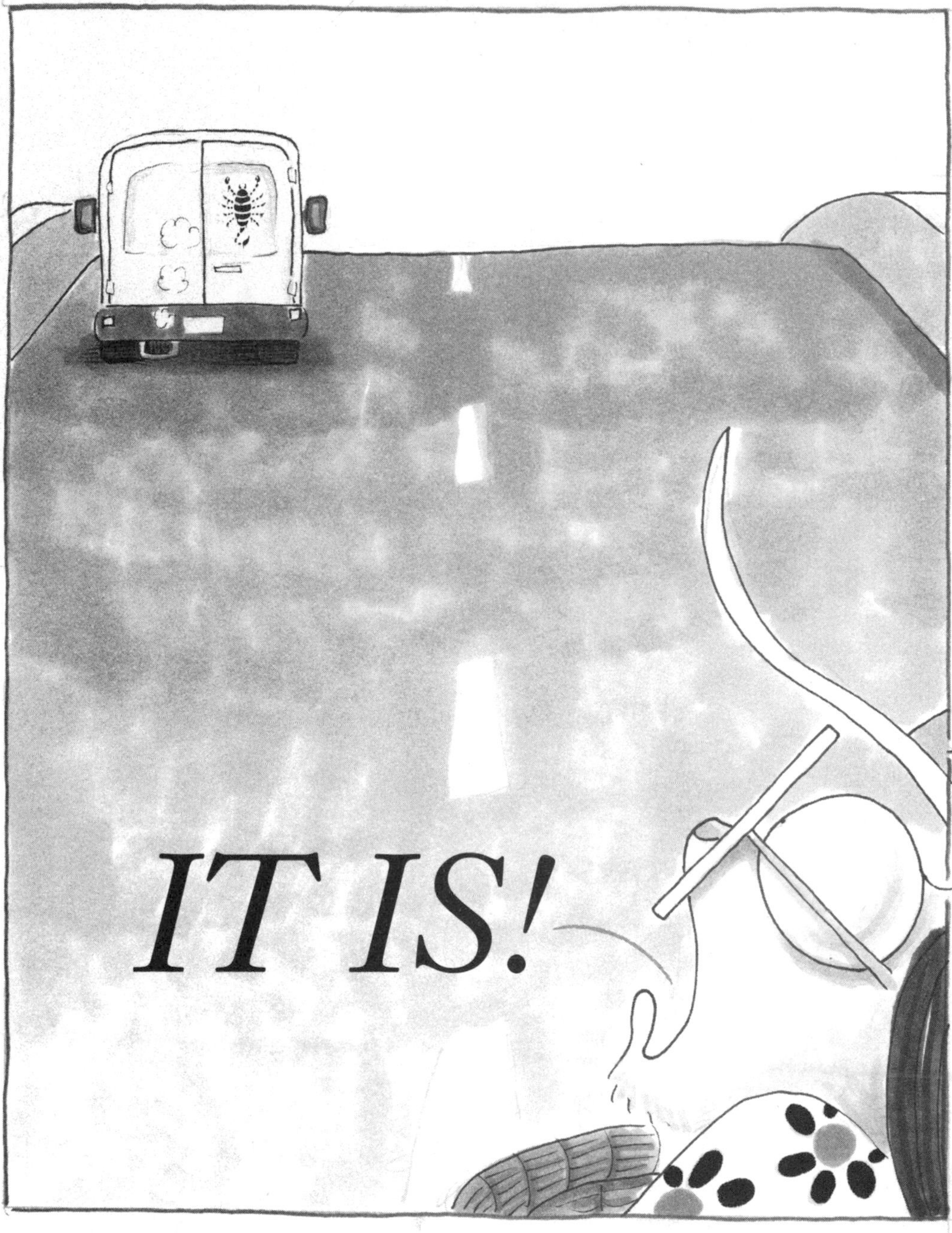
IT IS!

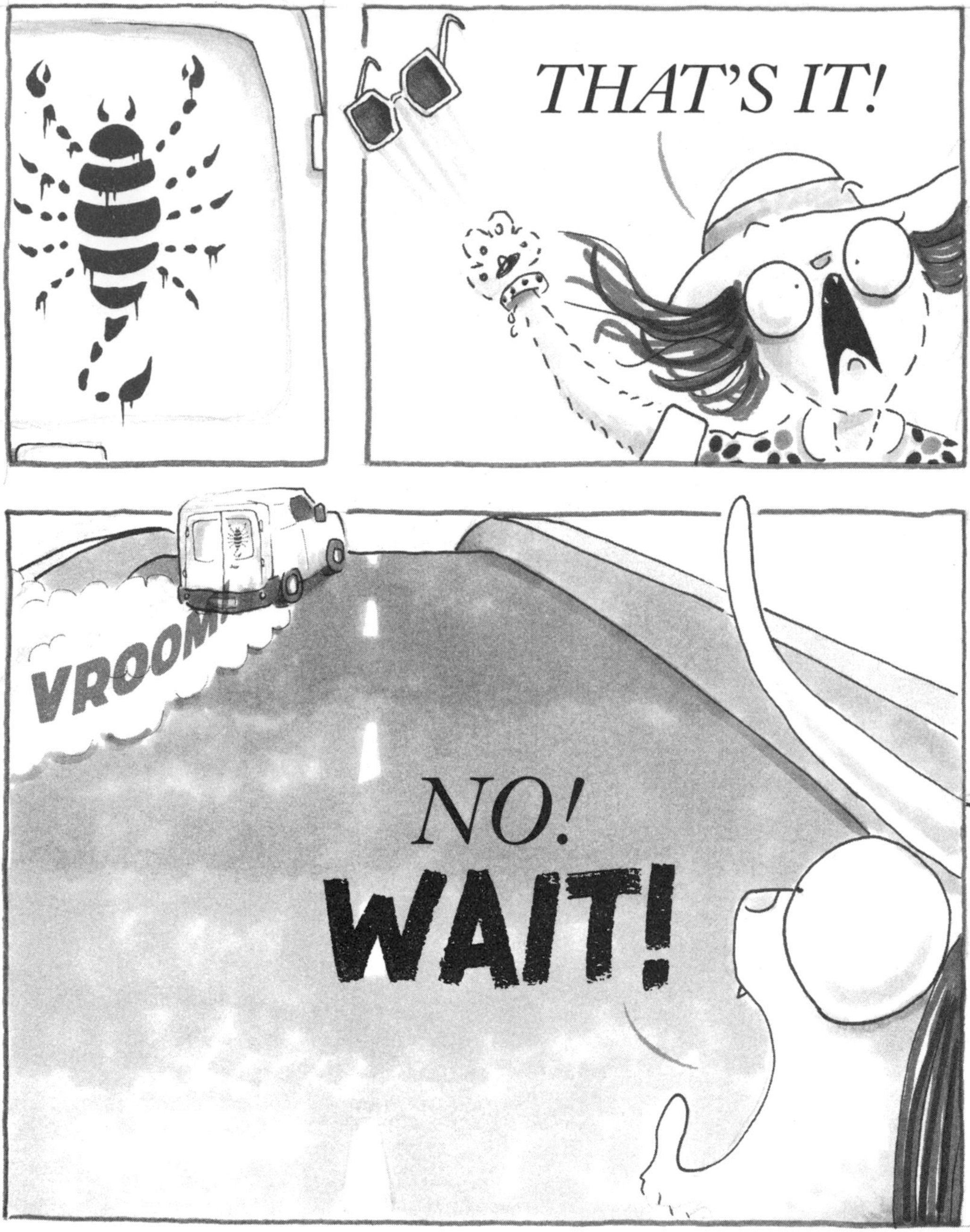
THAT'S IT!
VROOM!
NO!
WAIT!

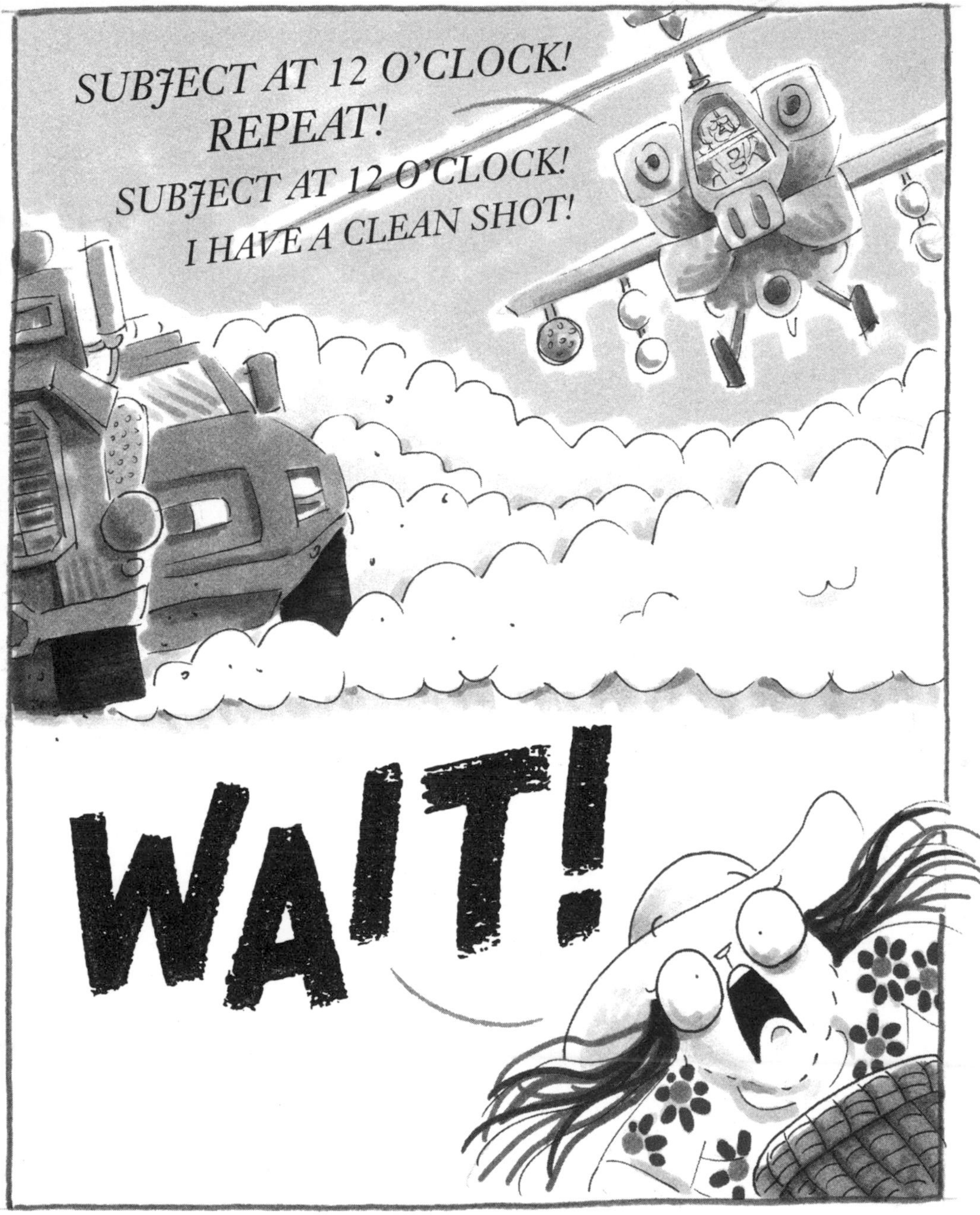
SUBJECT AT 12 O'CLOCK! REPEAT! SUBJECT AT 12 O'CLOCK! I HAVE A CLEAN SHOT!
WAIT!

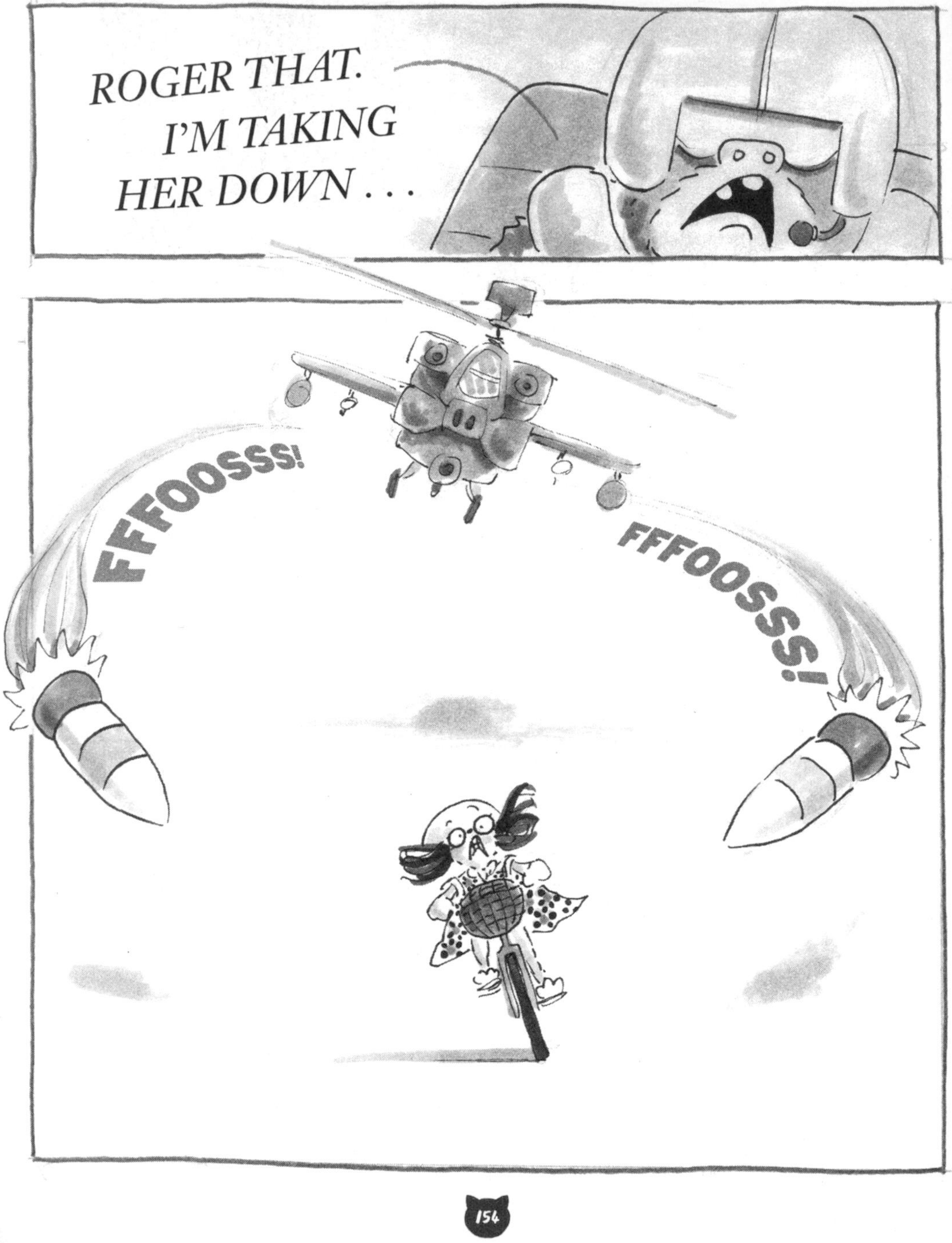
ROGER THAT. I'M TAKING HER DOWN . . .
FFFOOSSS!
FFFOOSSS!

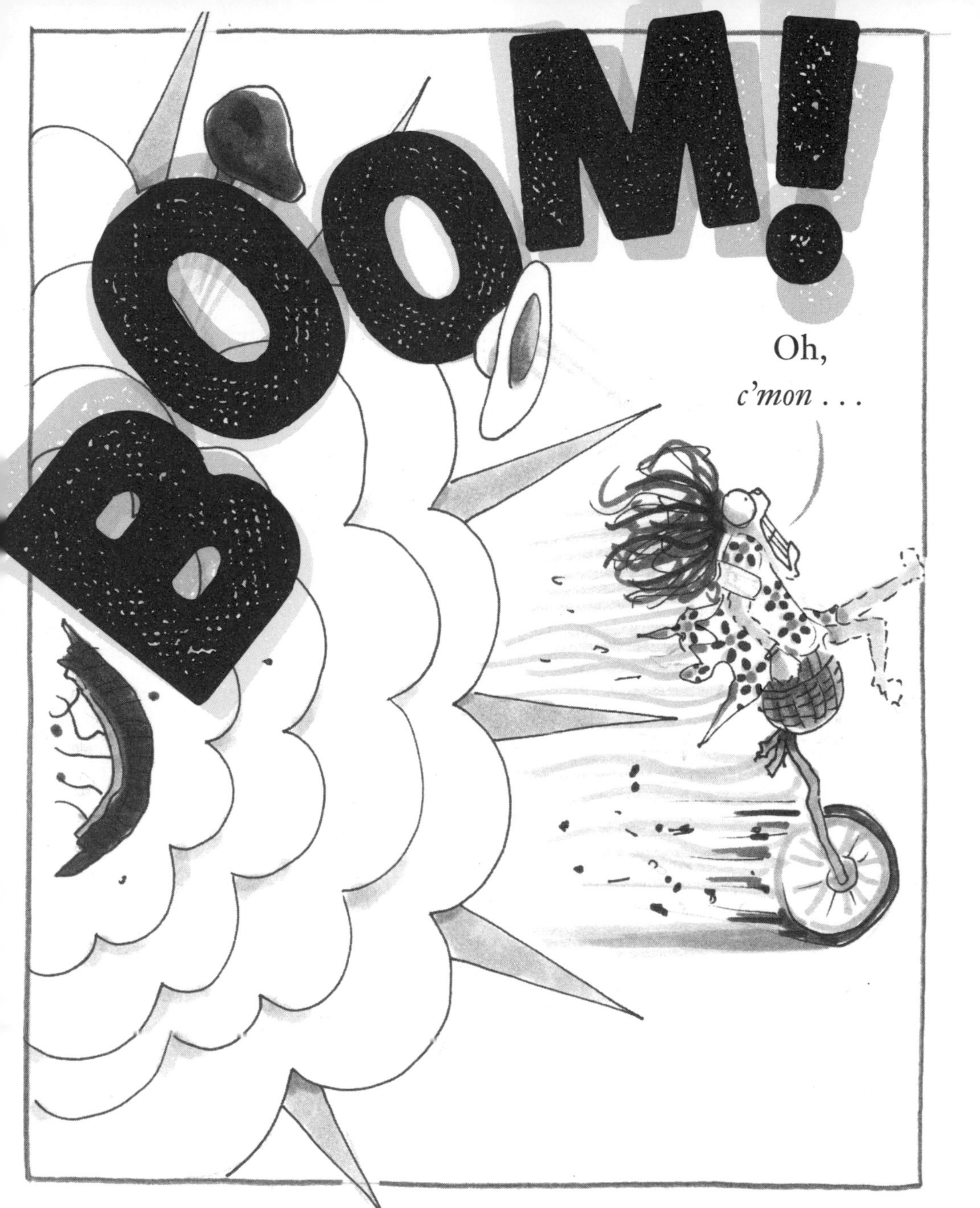
BOOM!
Oh,
c'mon . . .

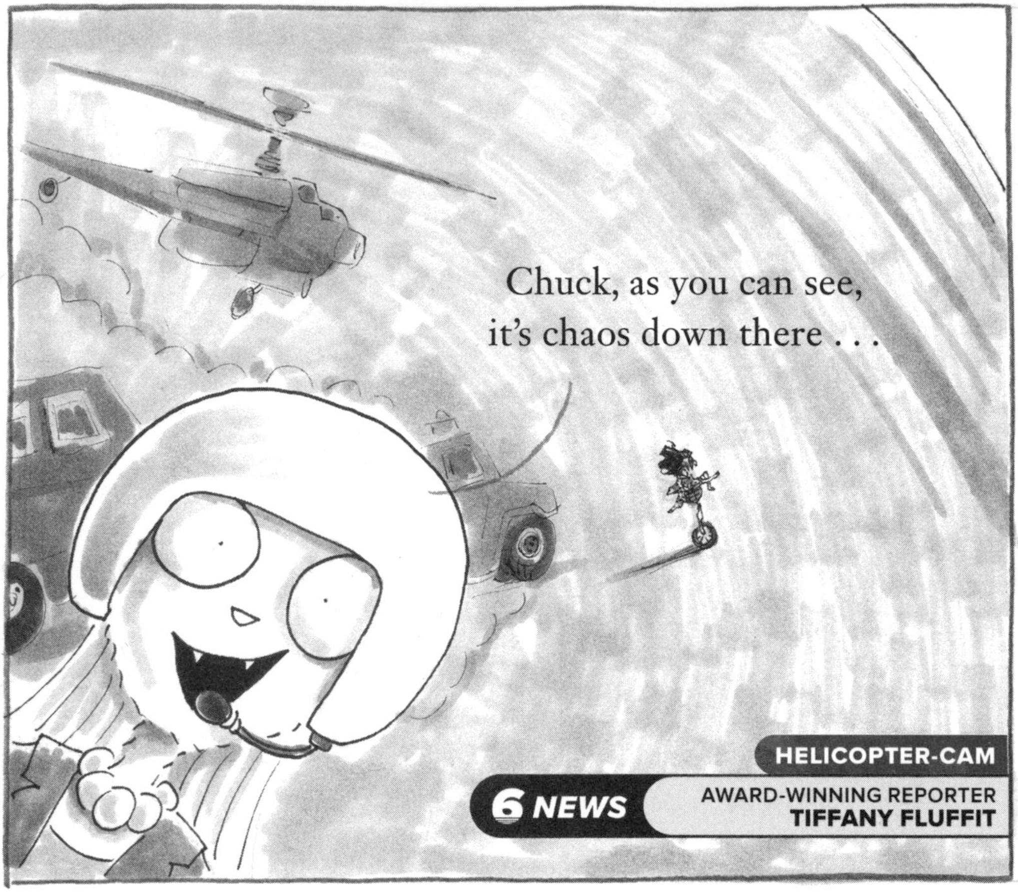
Chuck, as you can see, it's chaos down there . . .
HELICOPTER-CAM
6 NEWS
AWARD-WINNING REPORTER
TIFFANY FLUFFIT

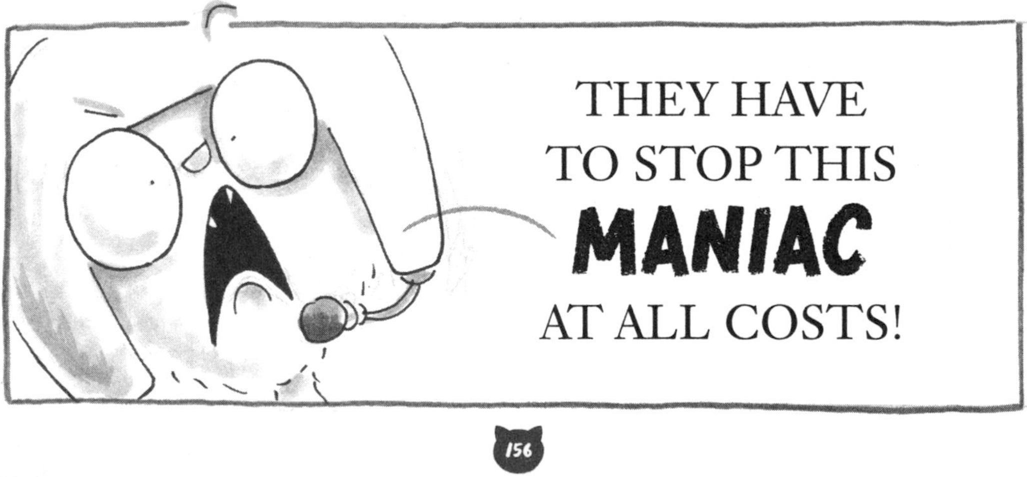
THEY HAVE TO STOP THIS MANIAC AT ALL COSTS!

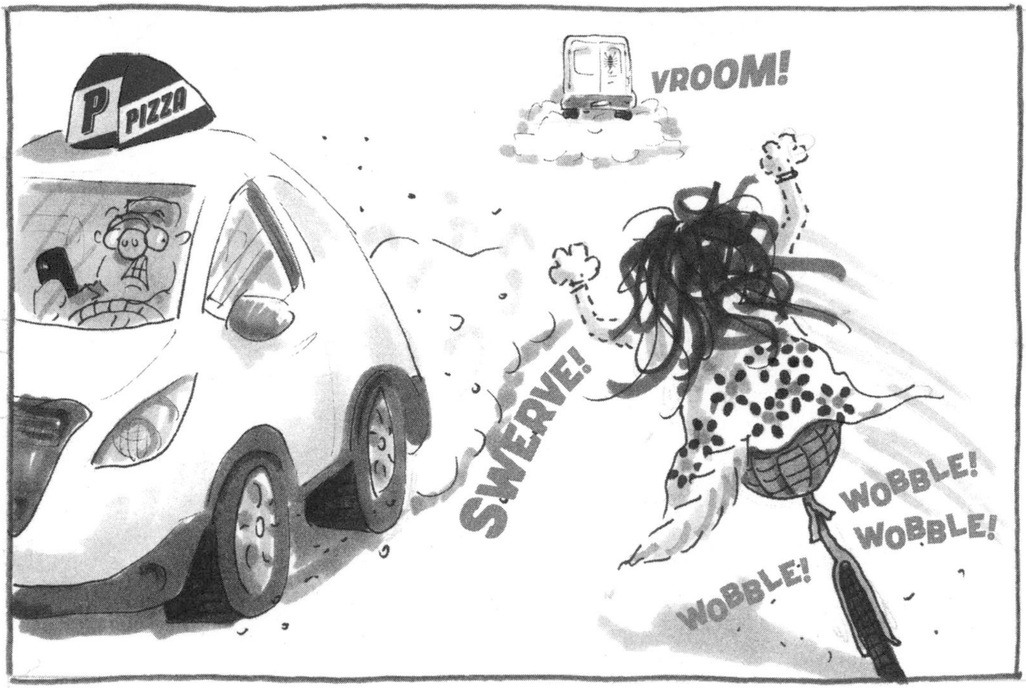

PIZZA
VROOM!
SWERVE!
WOBBLE!
WOBBLE!
WOBBLE!

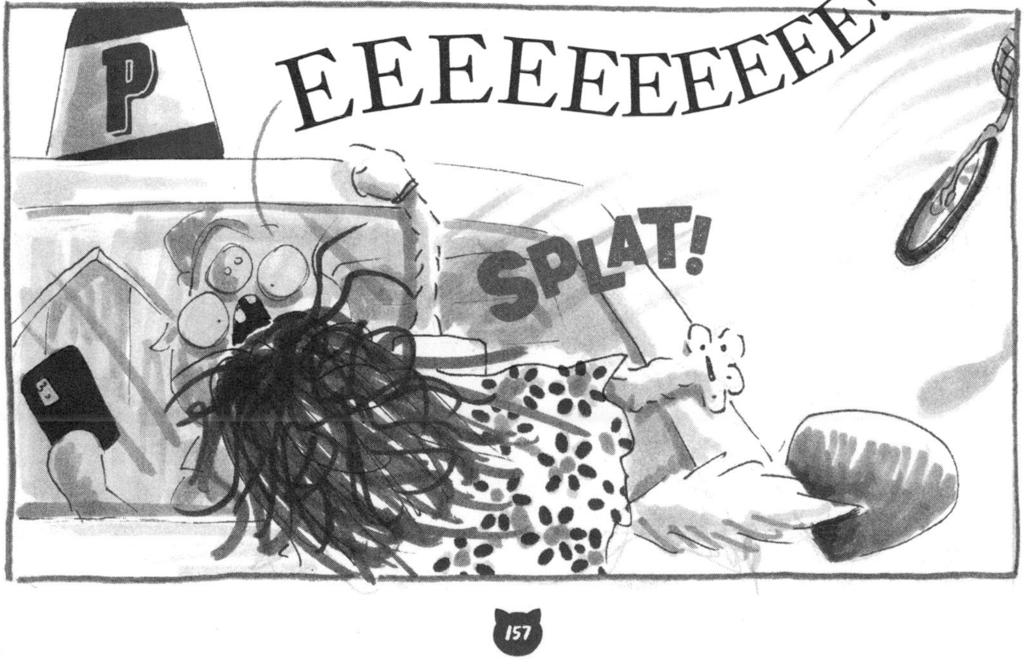

EEEEEEEEEEEE!
SPLAT!

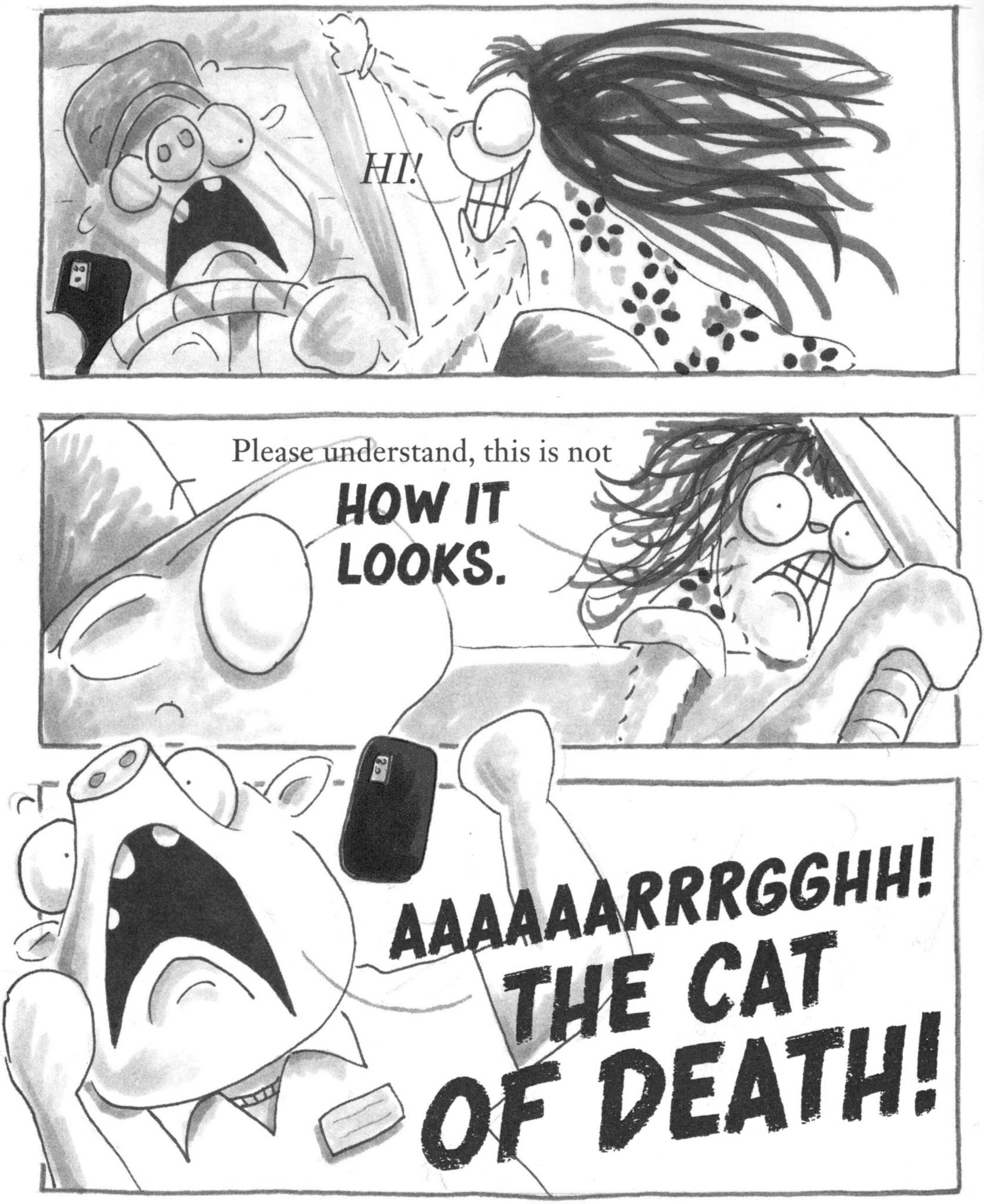

HI!
Please understand, this is not
HOW IT LOOKS.
AAAAAARRRRGGHH!
THE CAT OF DEATH!

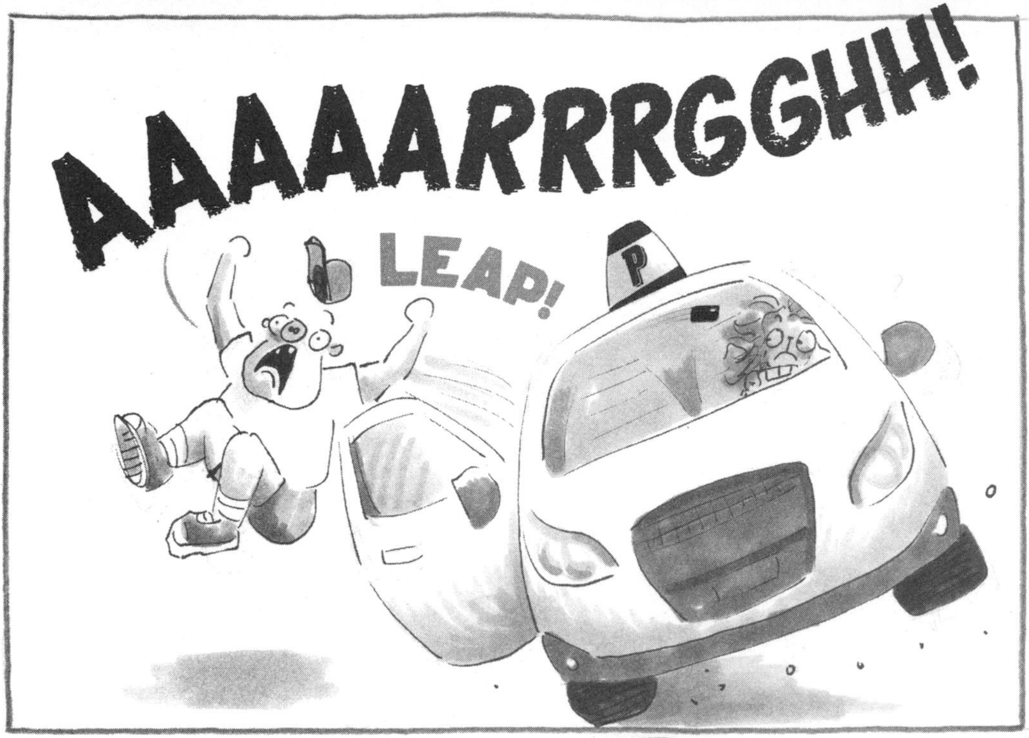
AAAAARRRGGHH!
LEAP!
P

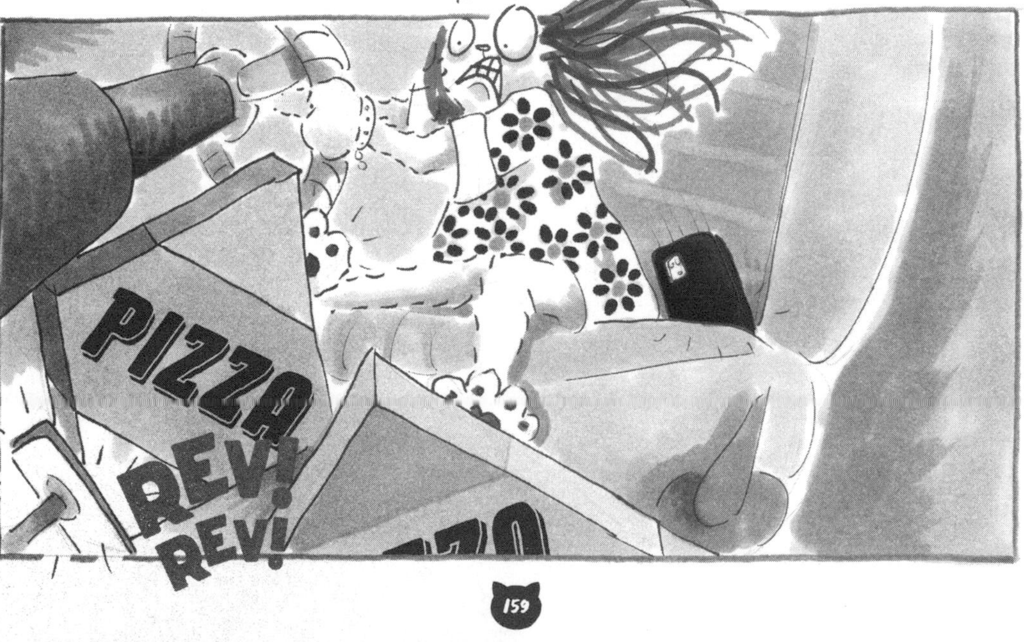
PIZZA
REV!
REV!

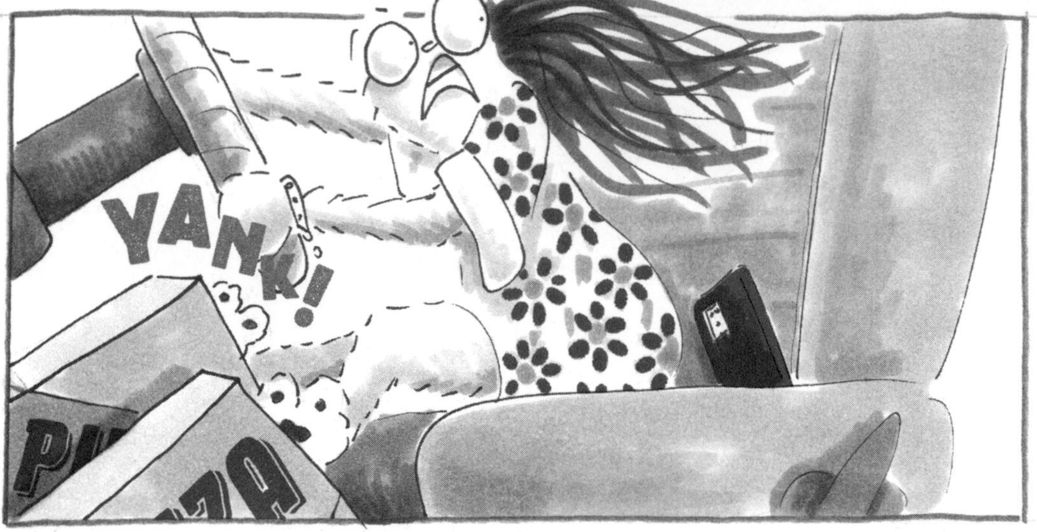
YANK!
PIZZA

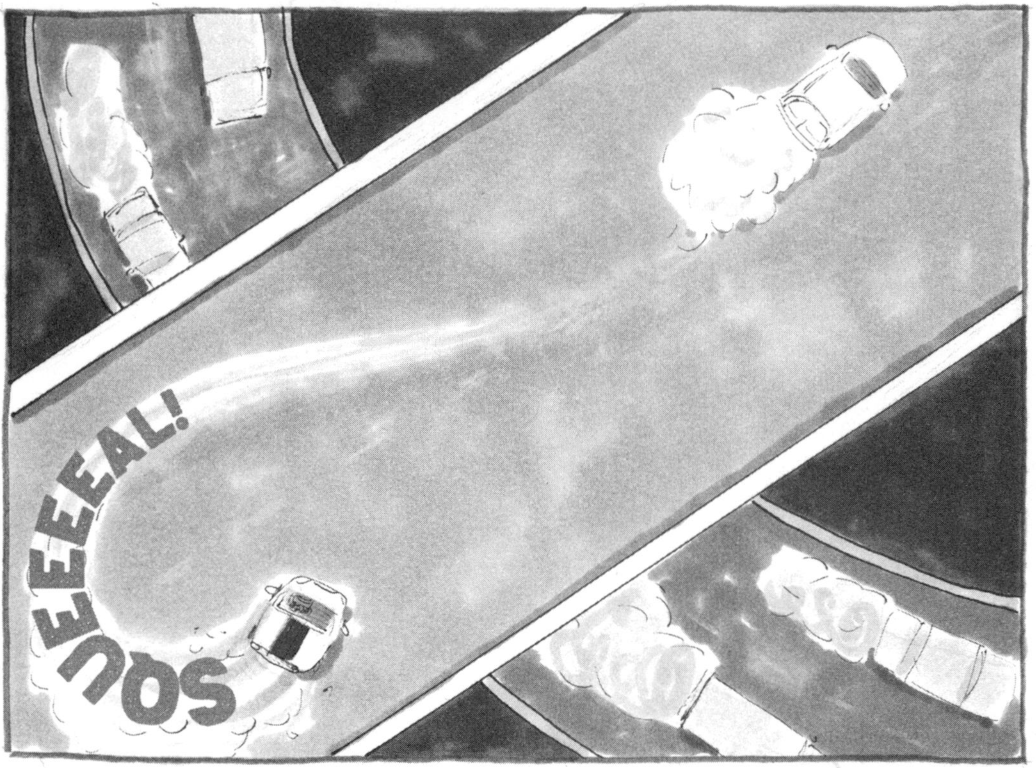
SQUEEEEEAL!

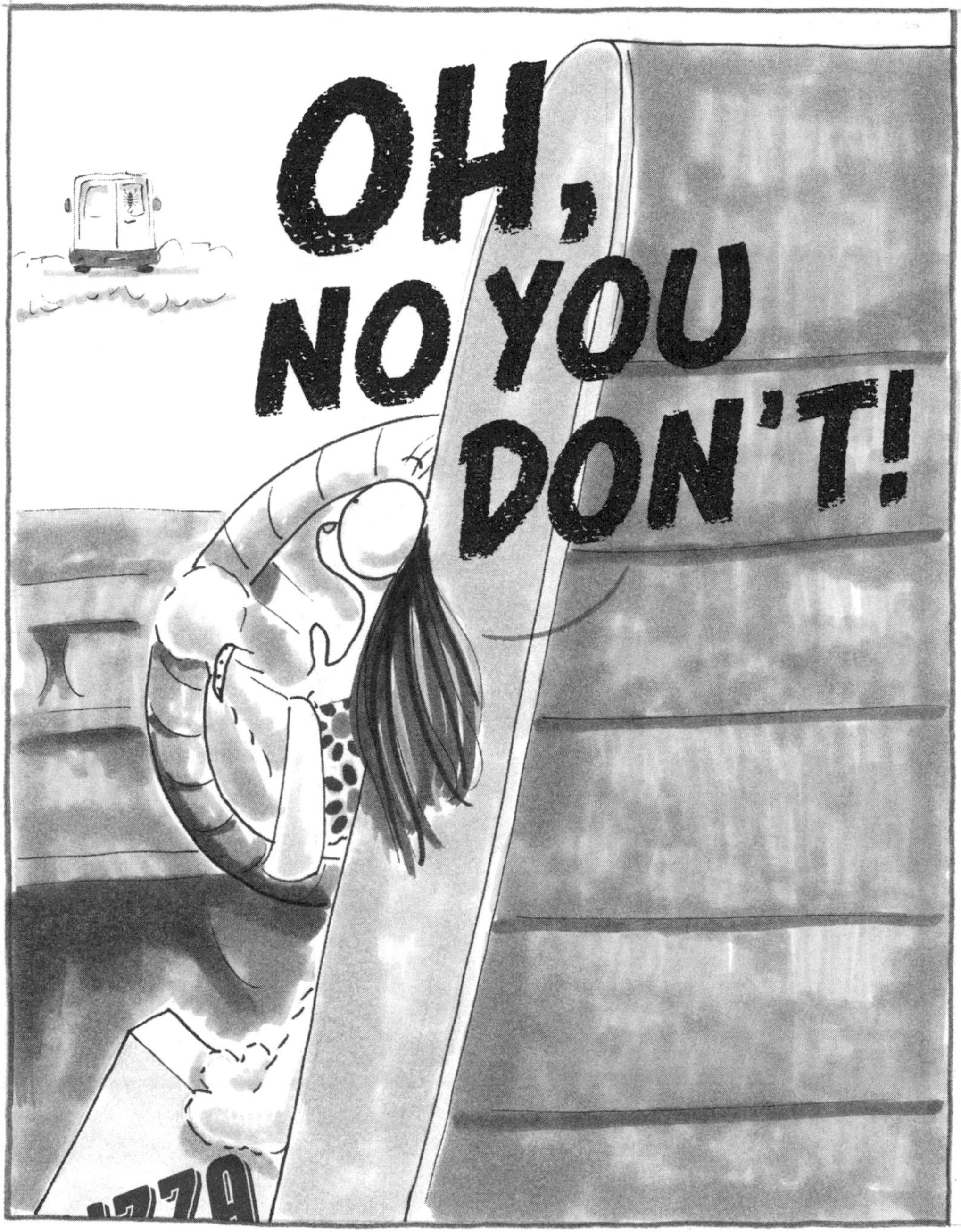
OH, NO YOU DON'T!

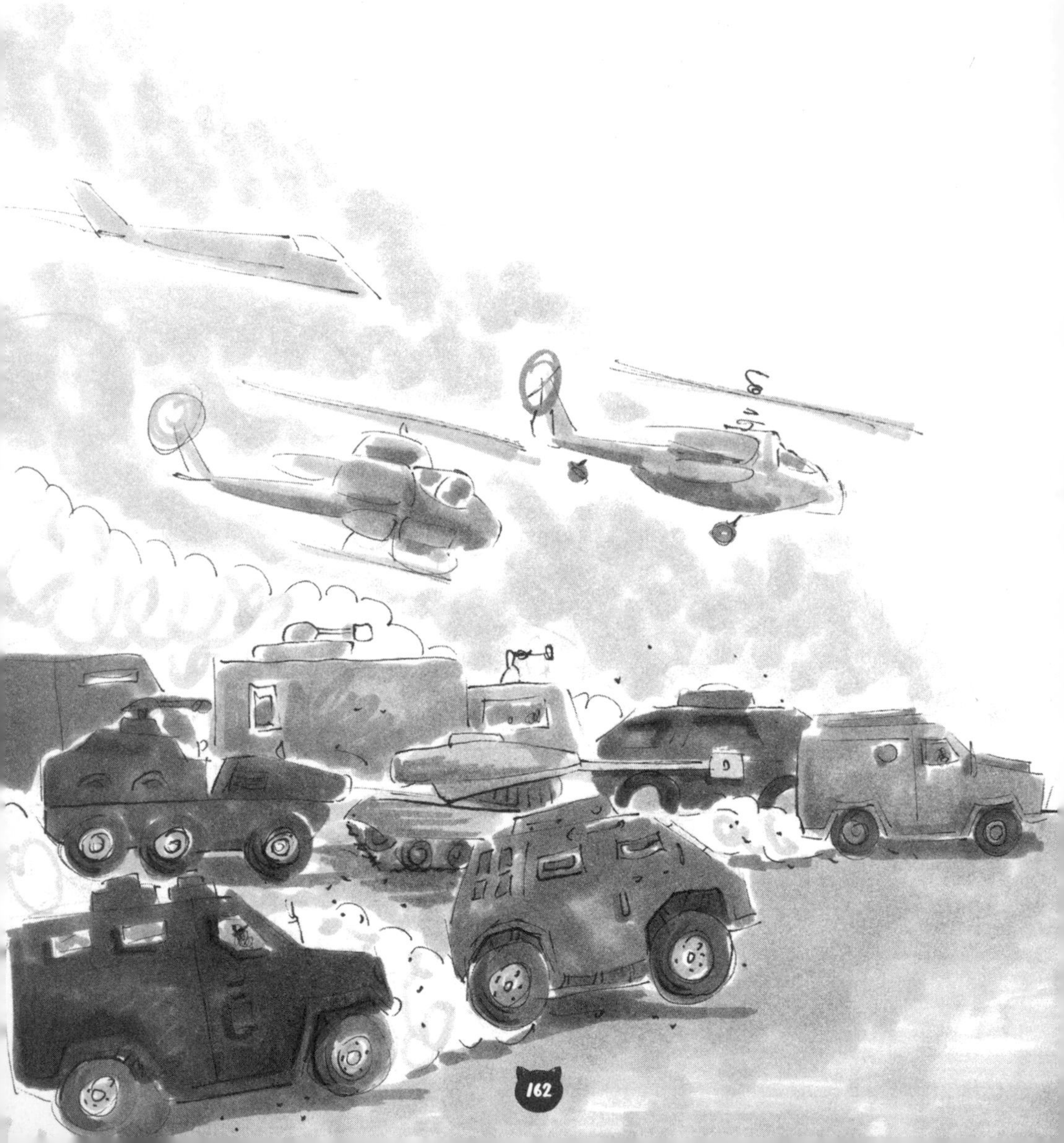

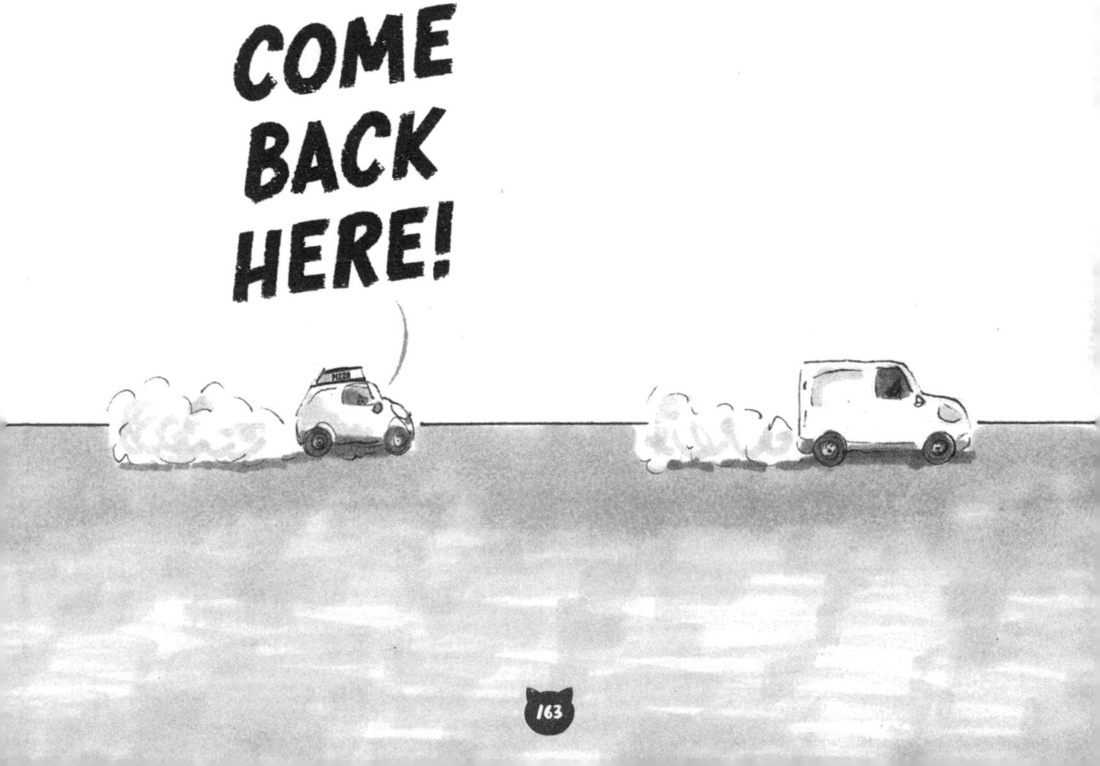
COME BACK HERE!

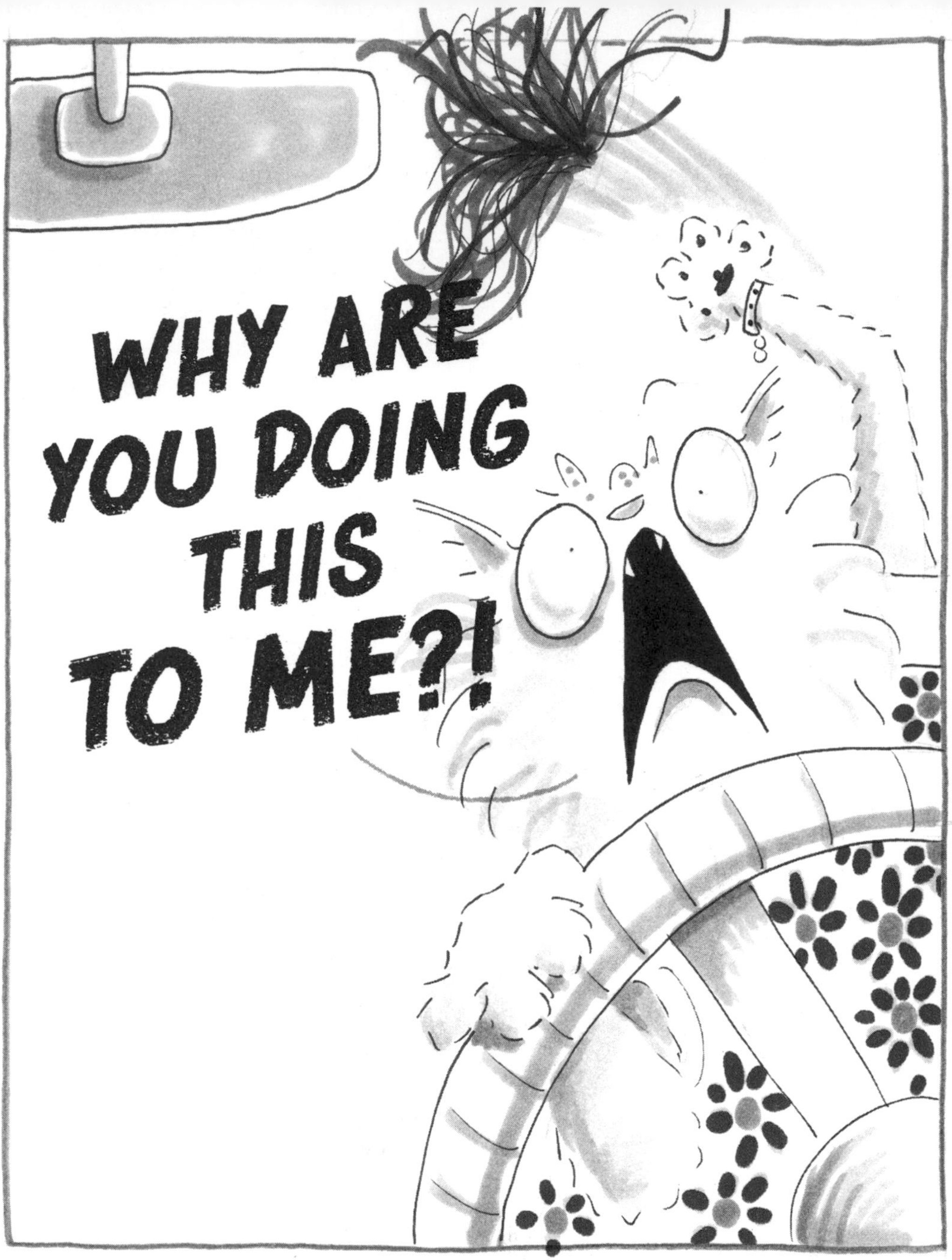
WHY ARE YOU DOING THIS TO ME?!

Nine
THE ABYSS

The pizza guy's **PHONE!**

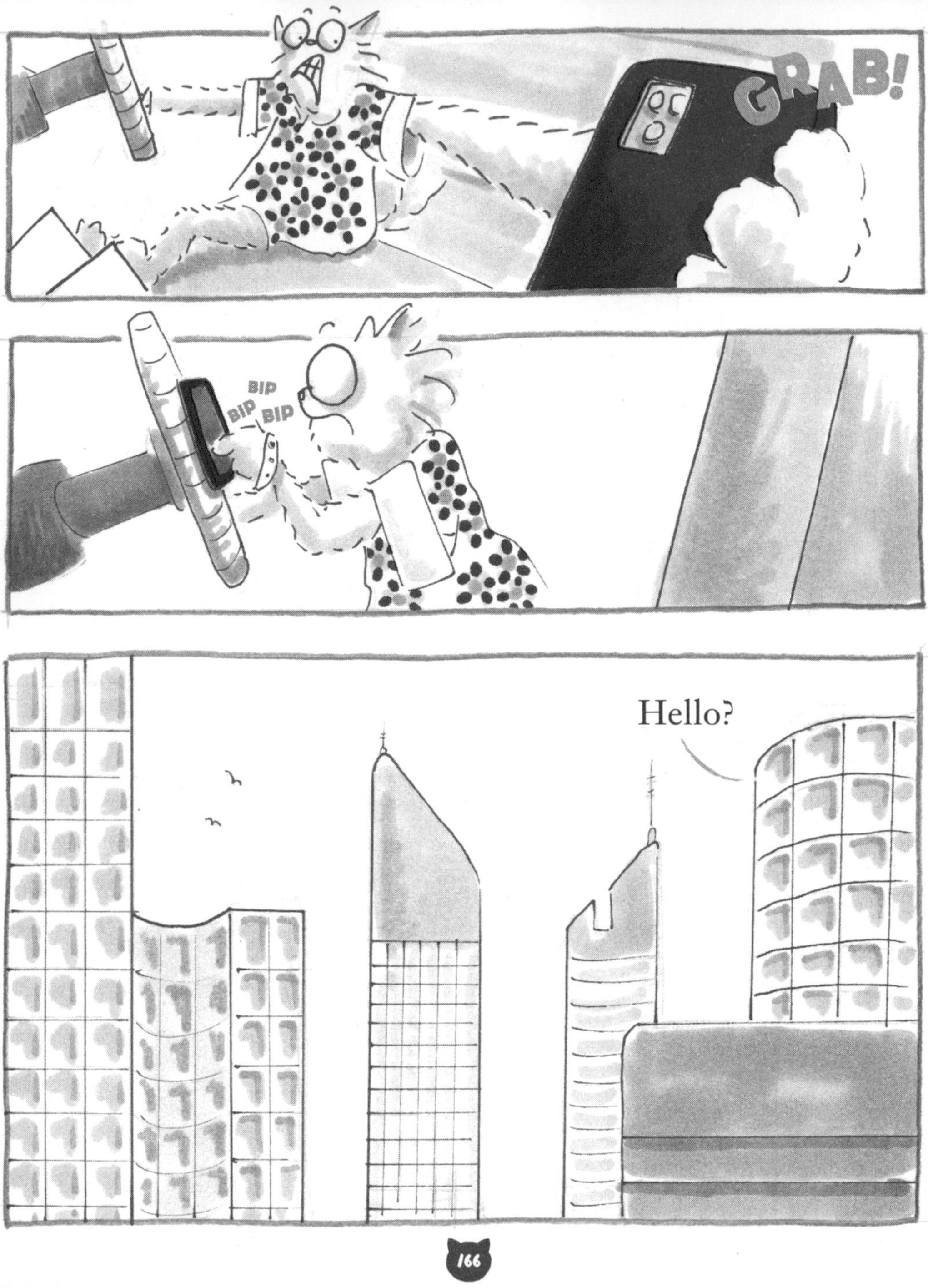
GRAB!
BIP
BIP
BIP
Hello?

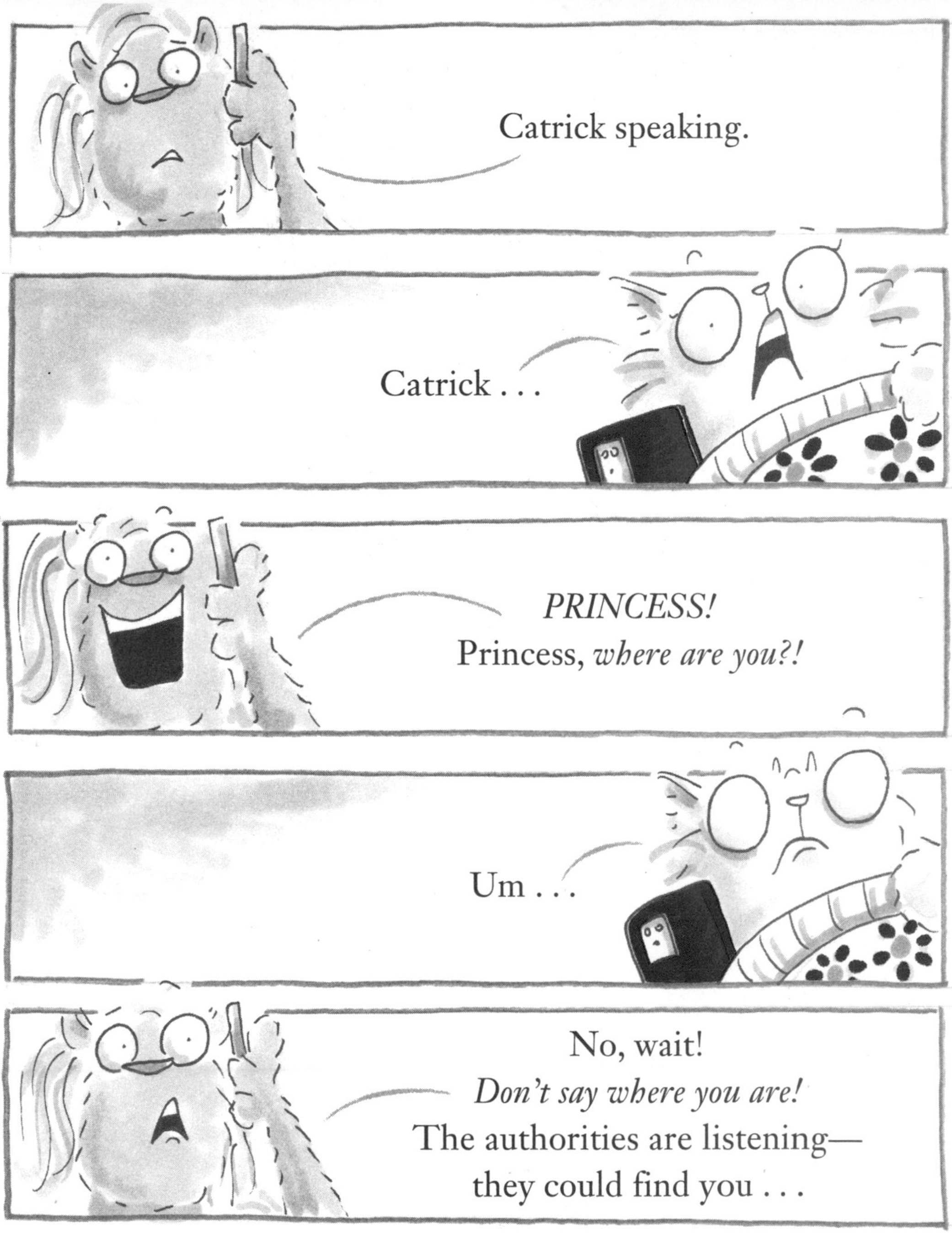
Catrick speaking.
Catrick . . .
PRINCESS!
Princess, *where are you?!*
Um . . .
No, wait!
Don't say where you are!
The authorities are listening—
they could find you . . .

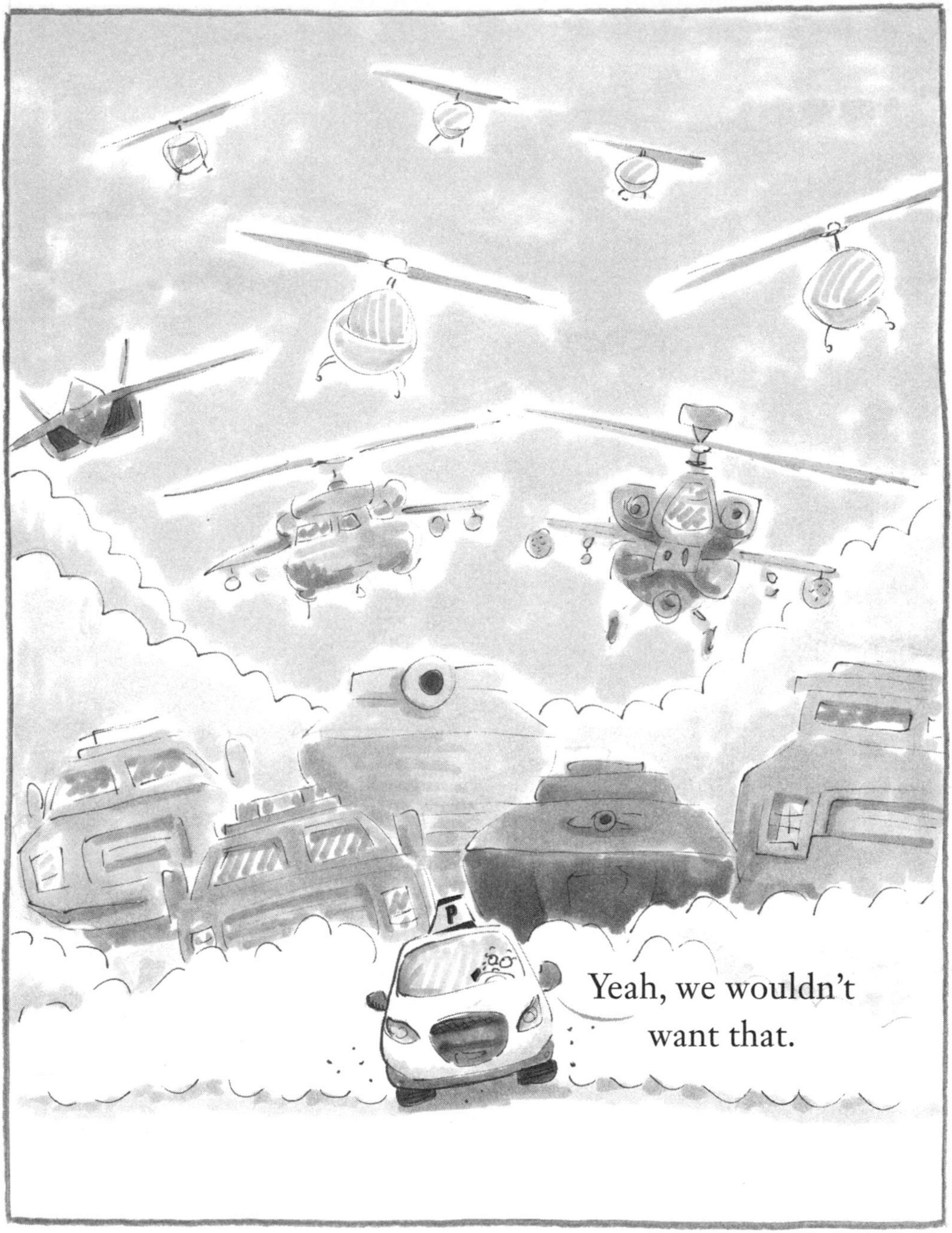
P
Yeah, we wouldn't want that.

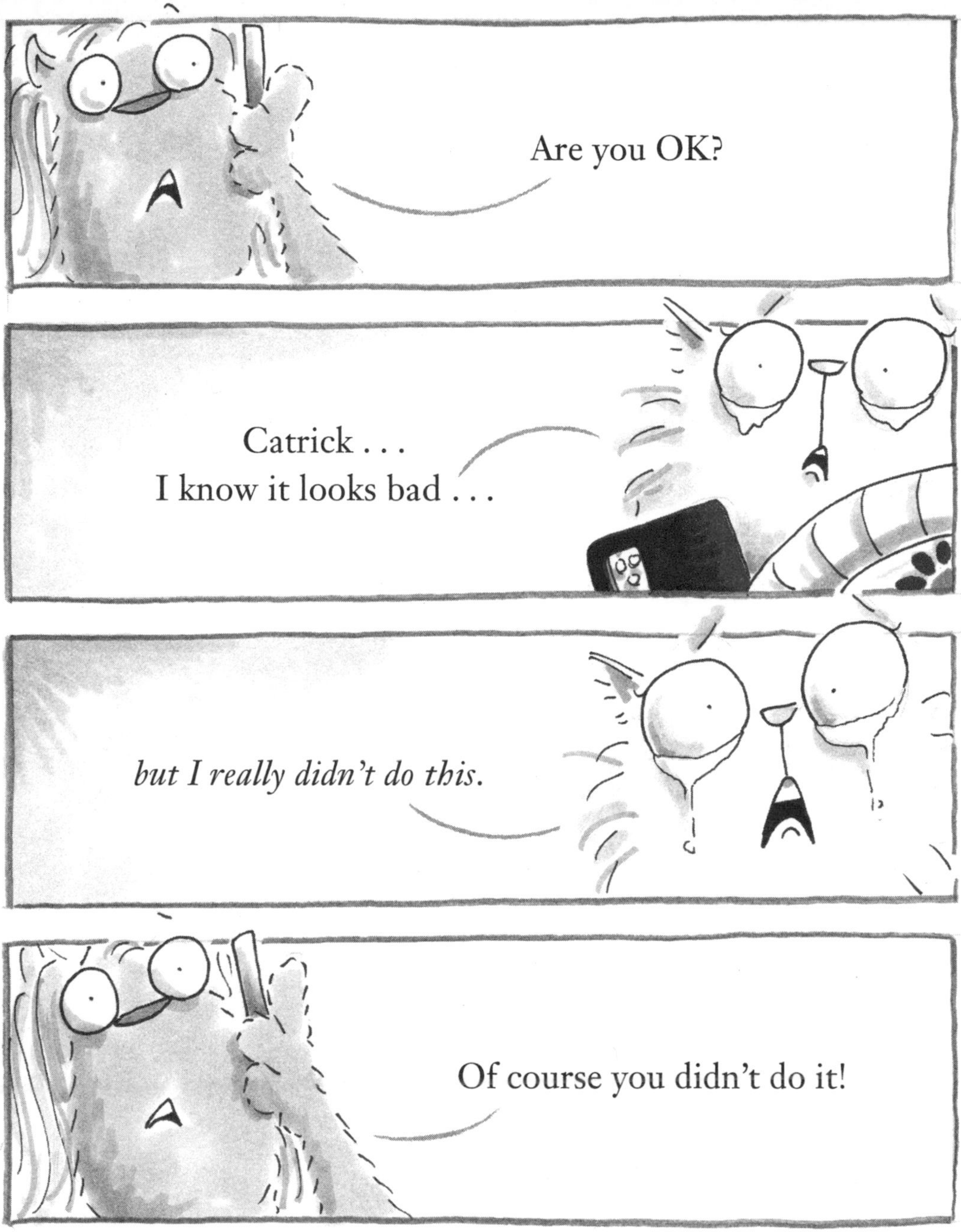
Are you OK?
Catrick . . .
I know it looks bad . . .
but I really didn't do this.
Of course you didn't do it!

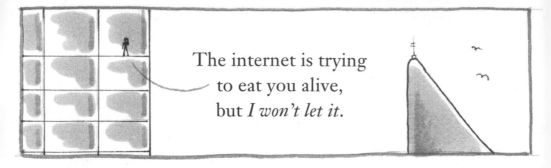

The internet is trying to eat you alive, but *I won't let it.*

I want you to hear this—
I BELIEVE YOU. MY FAMILY BELIEVES YOU . . .

and we are going to do everything we can to show the world that
YOU ARE INNOCENT.

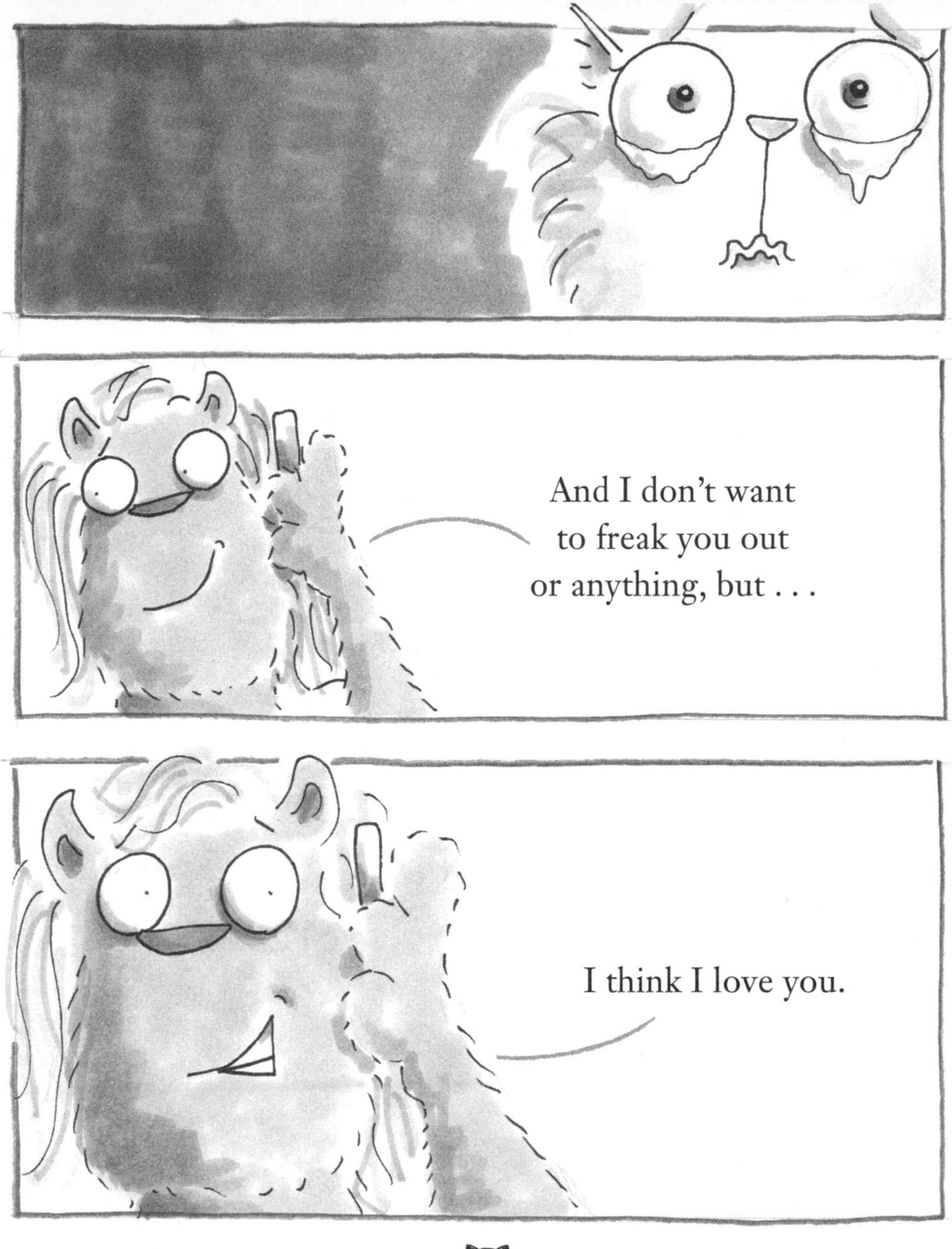
And I don't want to freak you out or anything, but . . .
I think I love you.

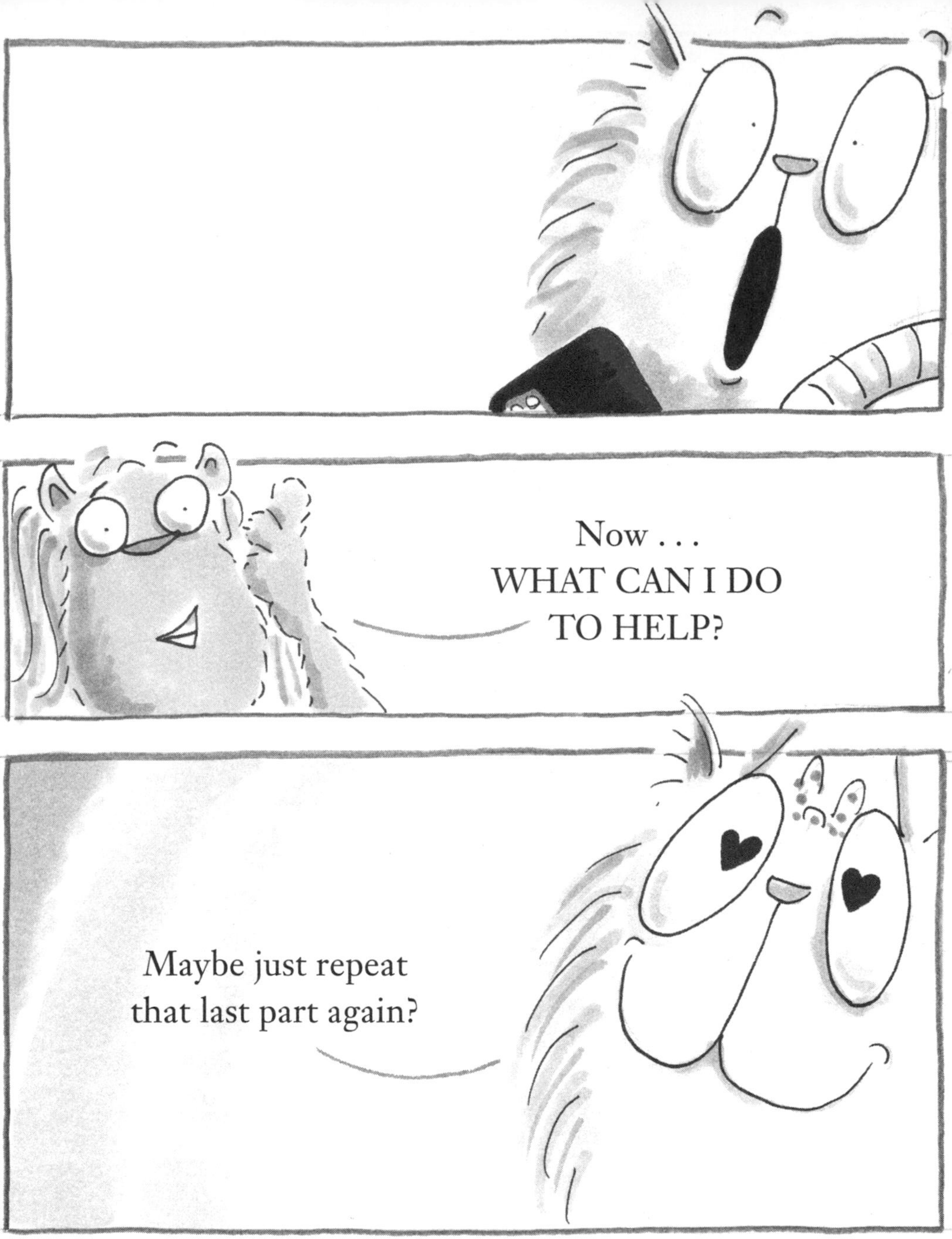
Now . . .
WHAT CAN I DO
TO HELP?
Maybe just repeat
that last part again?

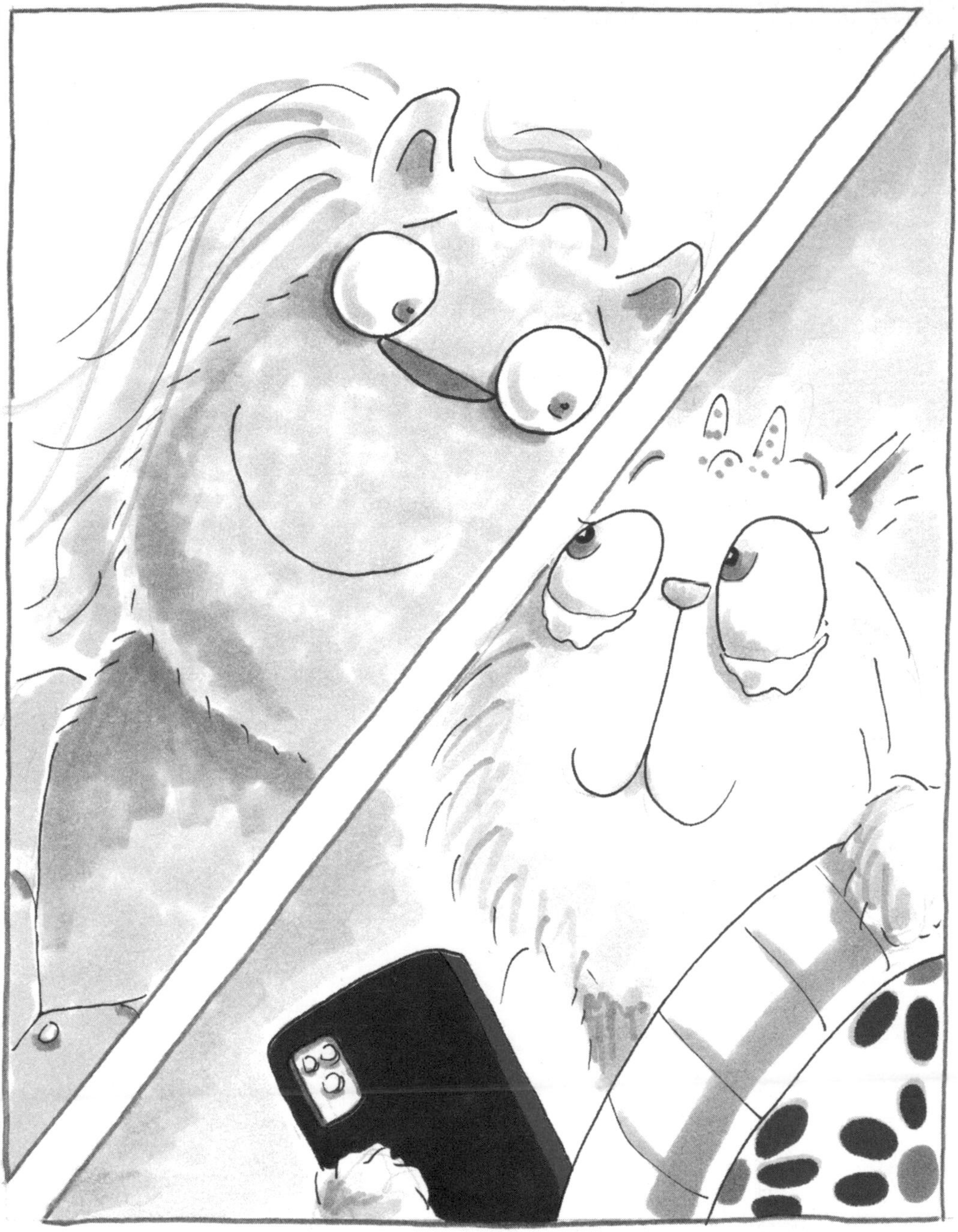

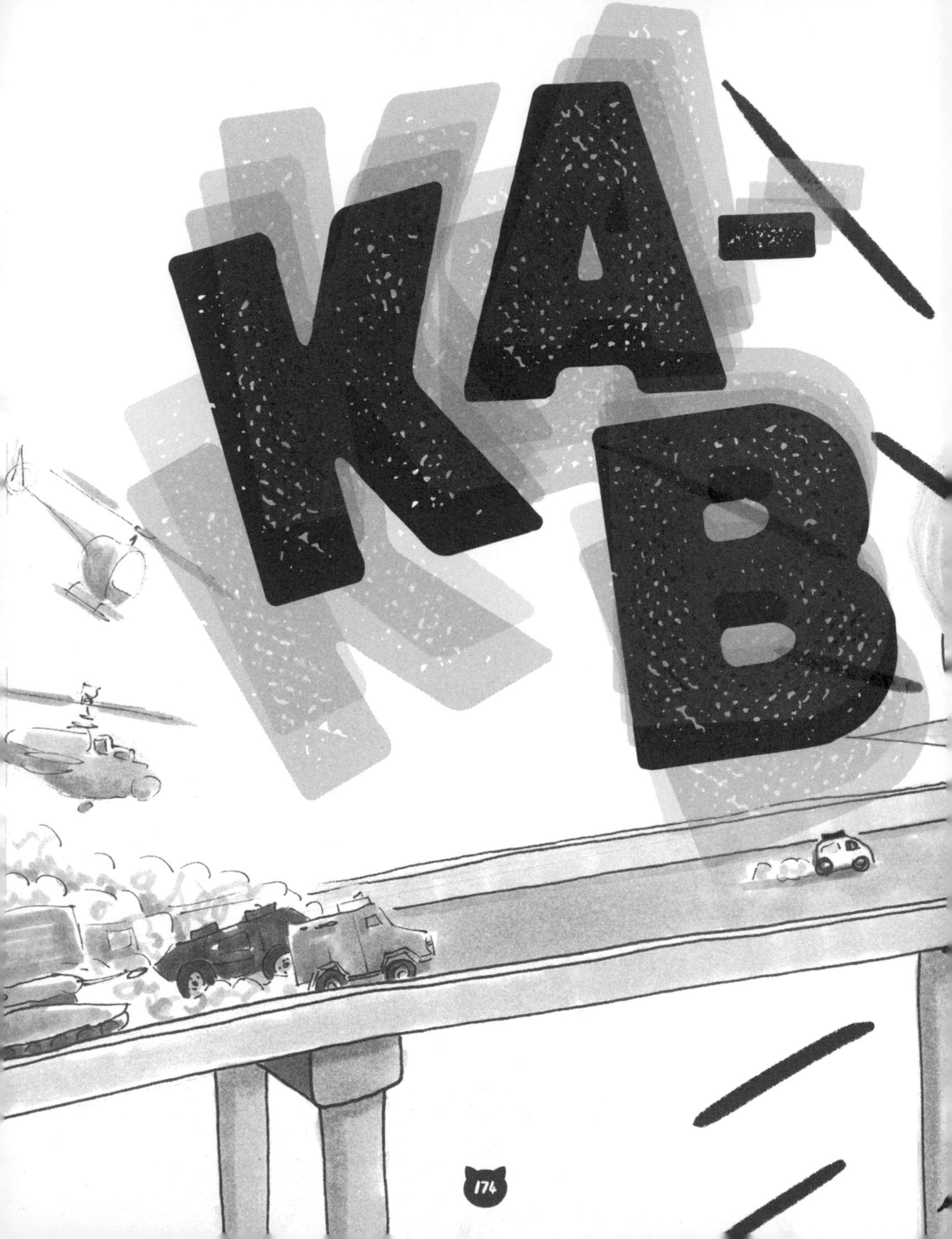
KA-B

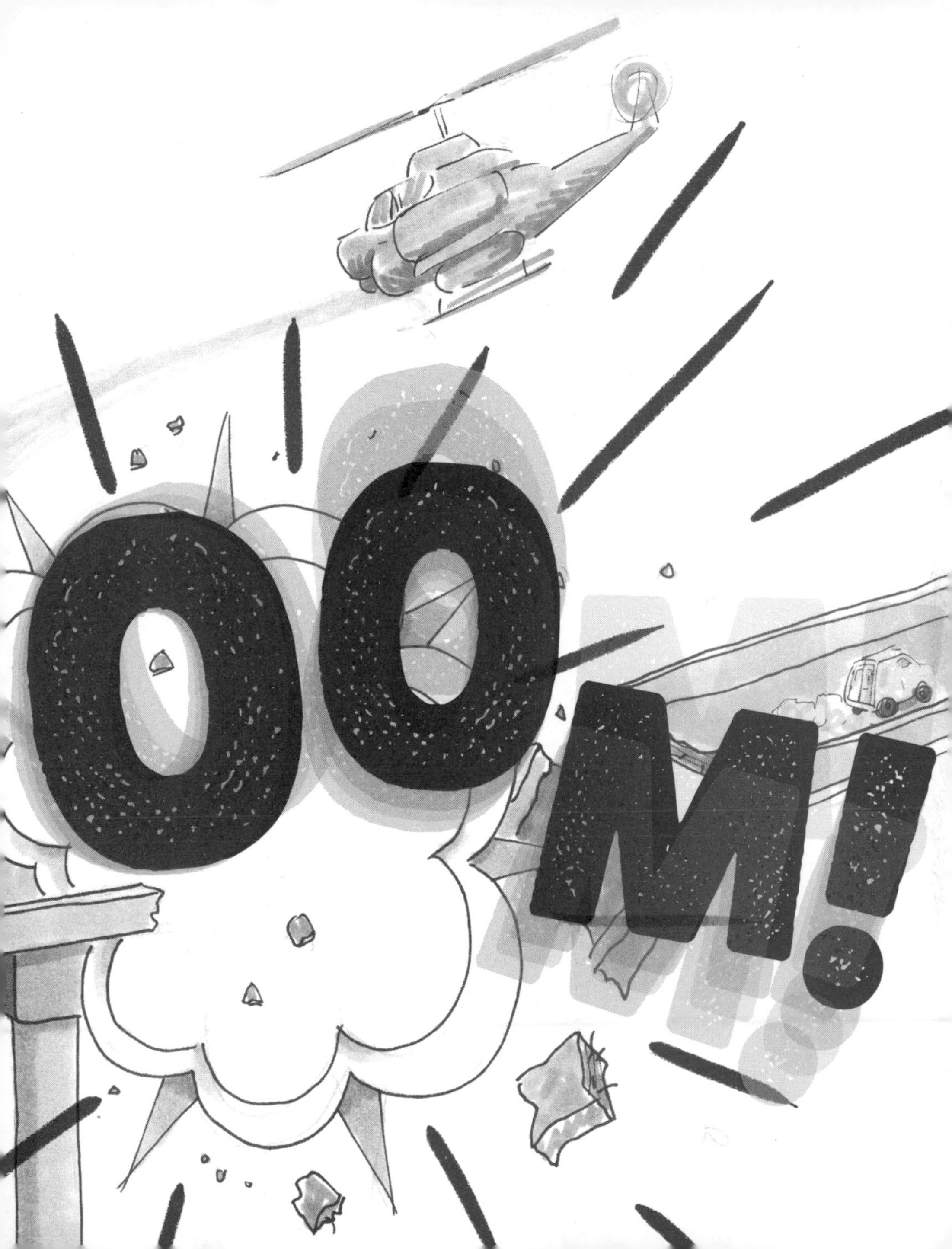
OOM!

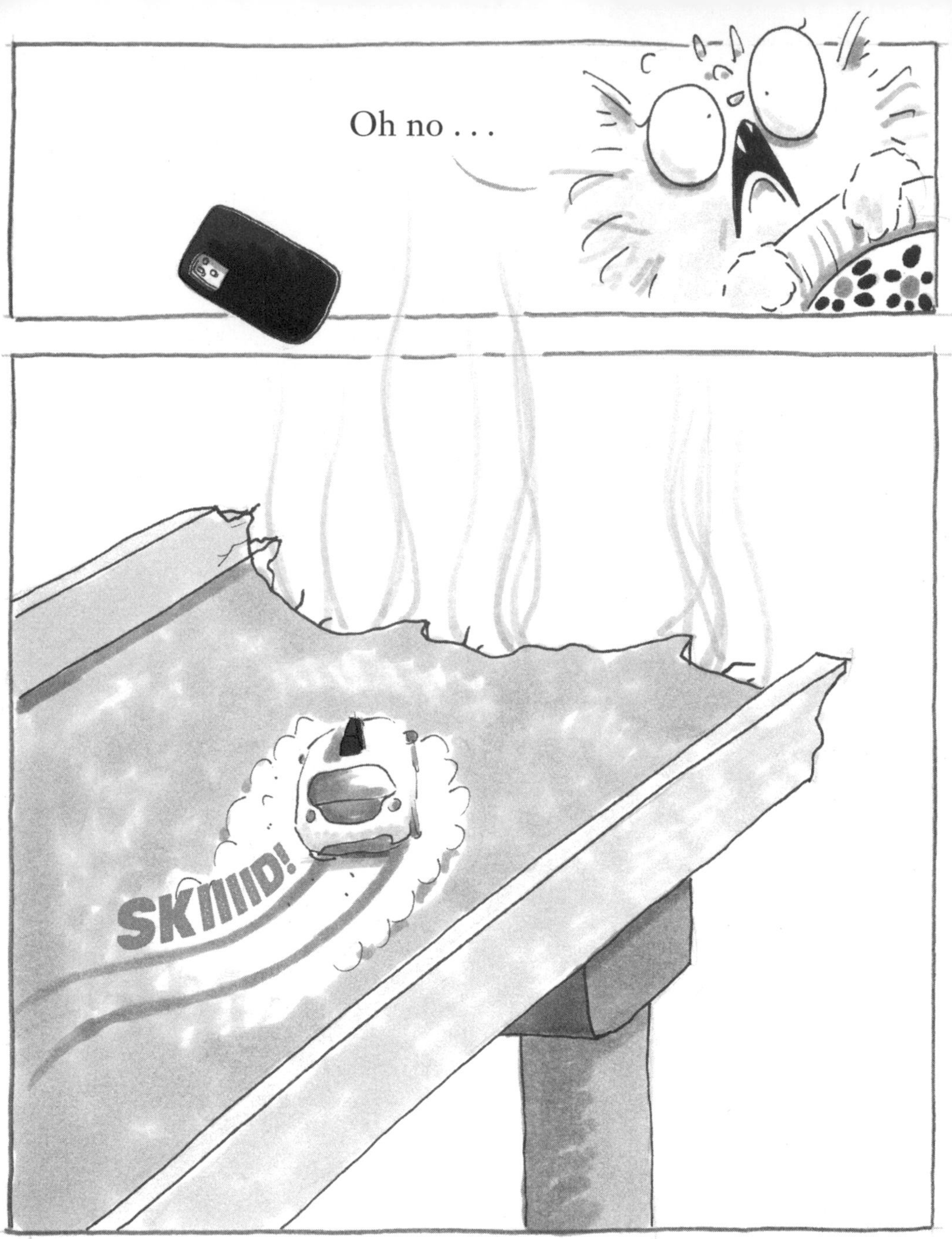
Oh no . . .
SKIIIID!

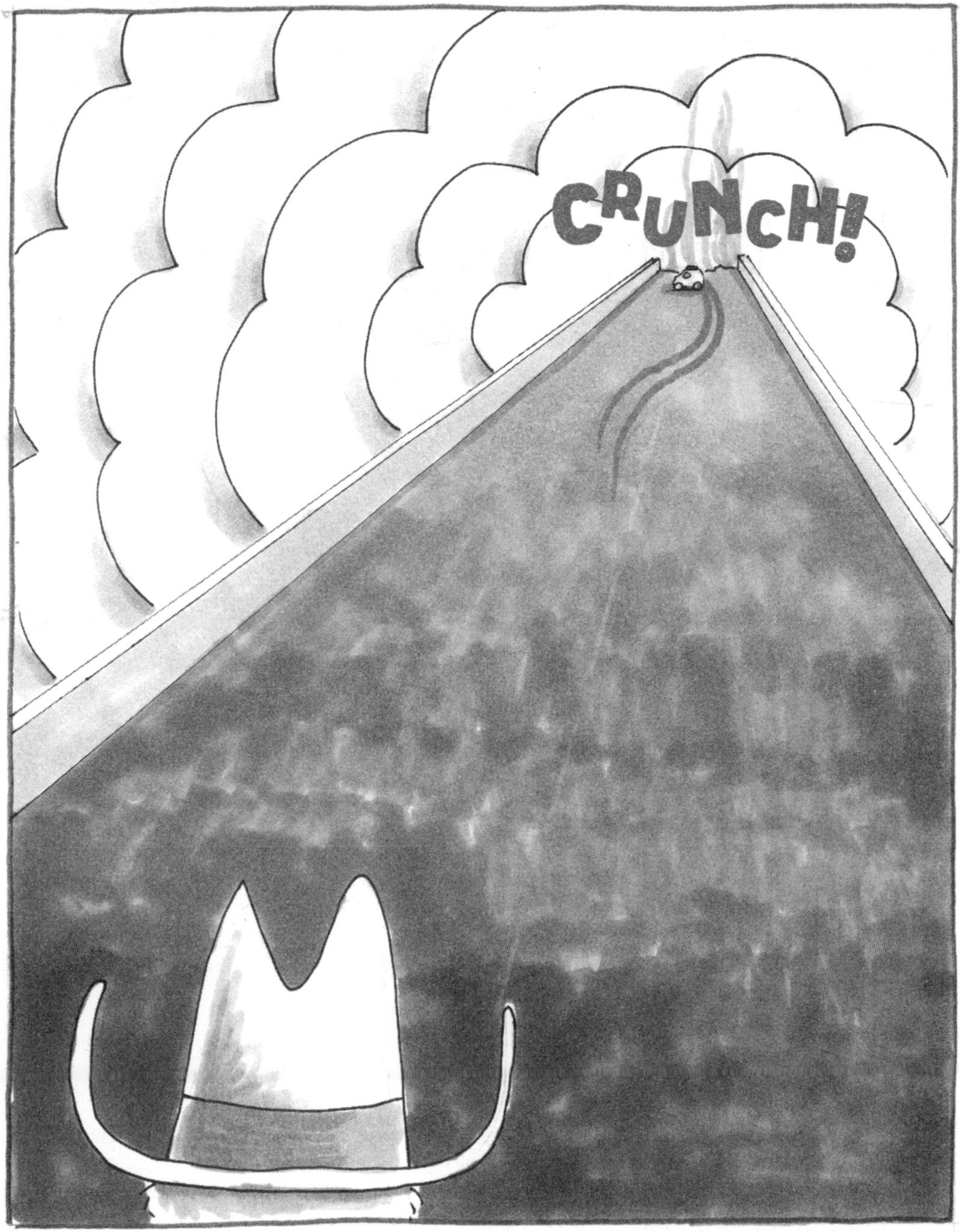
CRUNCH!

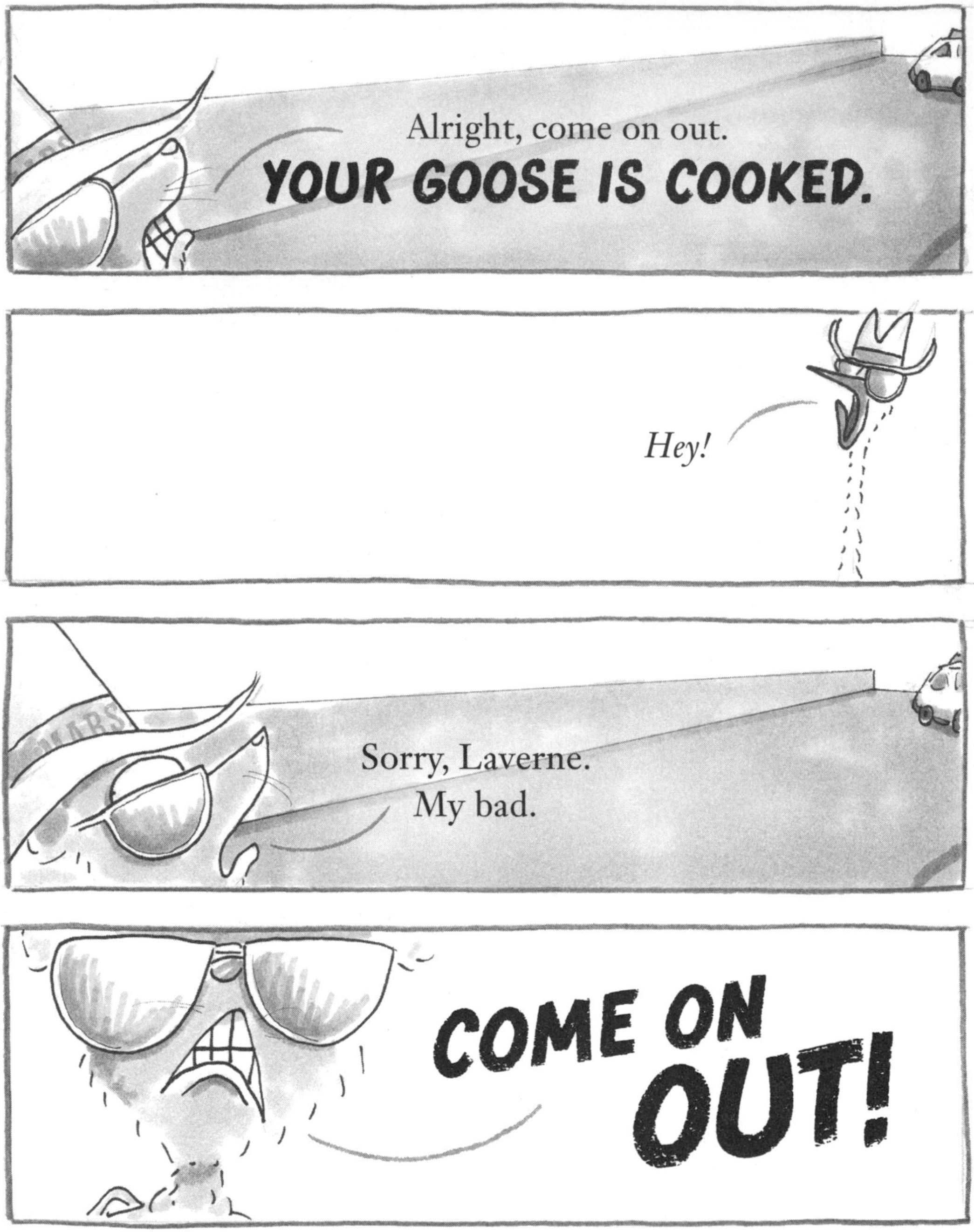
Alright, come on out.
YOUR GOOSE IS COOKED.
Hey!
Sorry, Laverne.
My bad.
COME ON OUT!

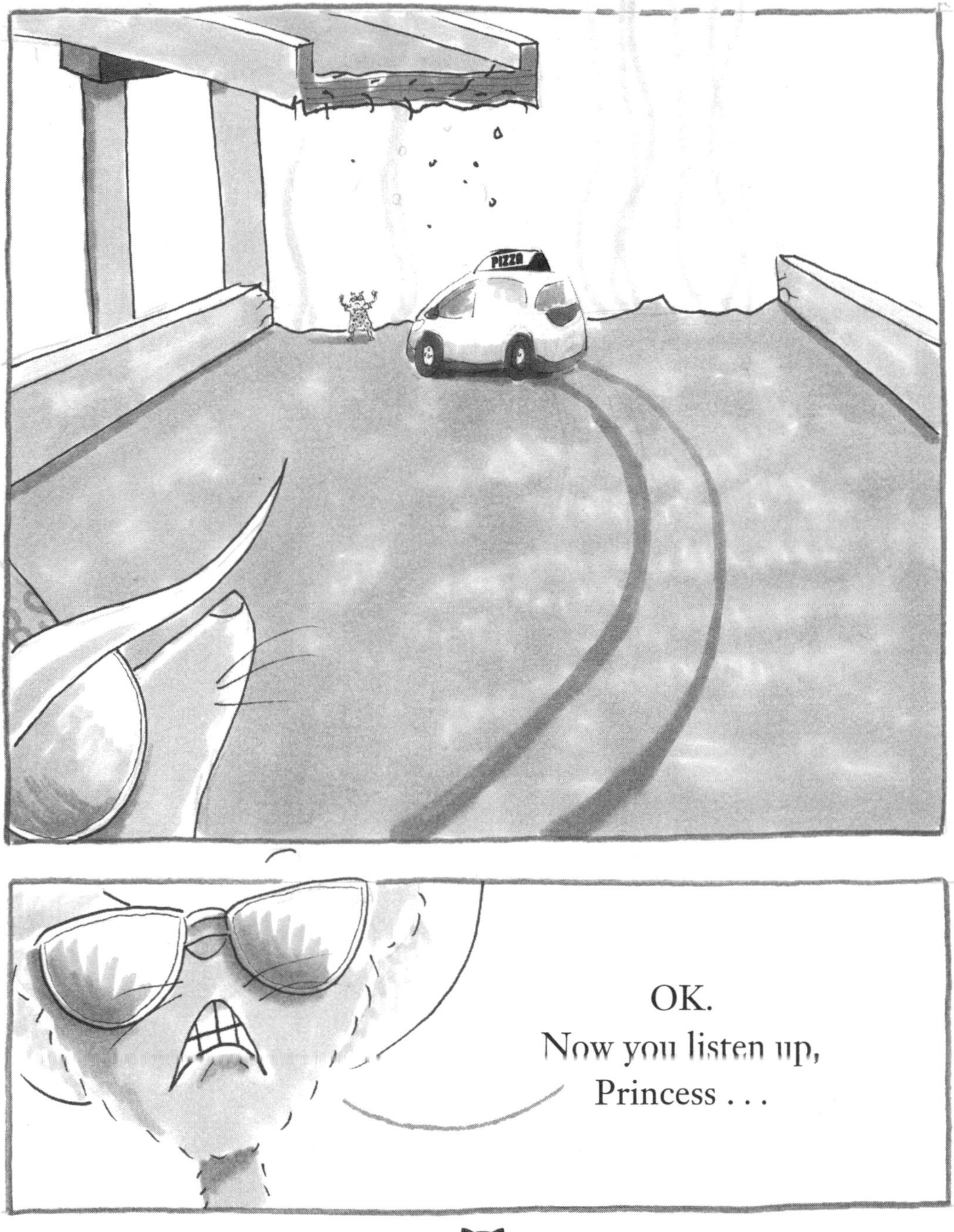
PIZZA
OK.
Now you listen up,
Princess . . .

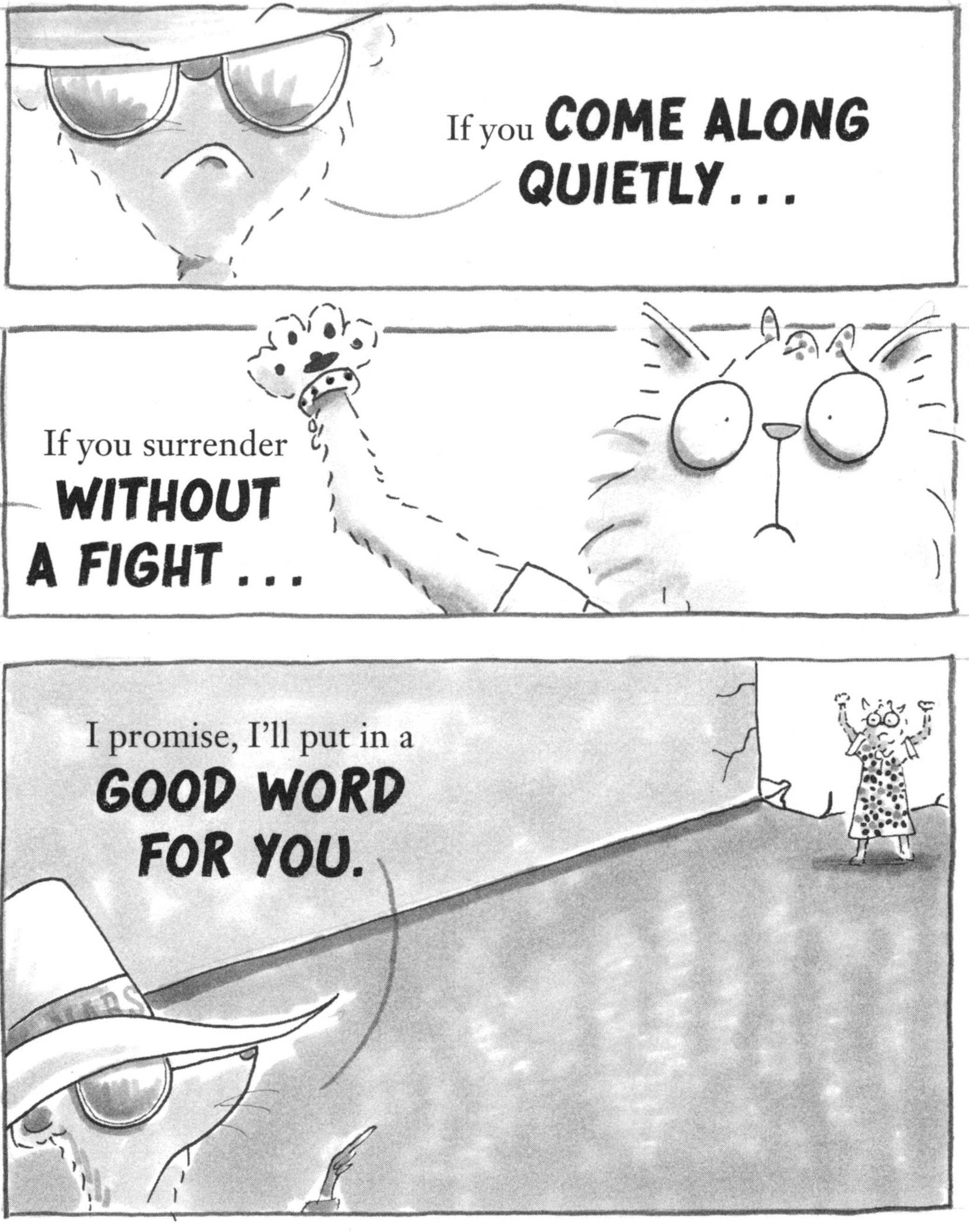
If you COME ALONG QUIETLY . . .
If you surrender WITHOUT A FIGHT . . .
I promise, I'll put in a GOOD WORD FOR YOU.

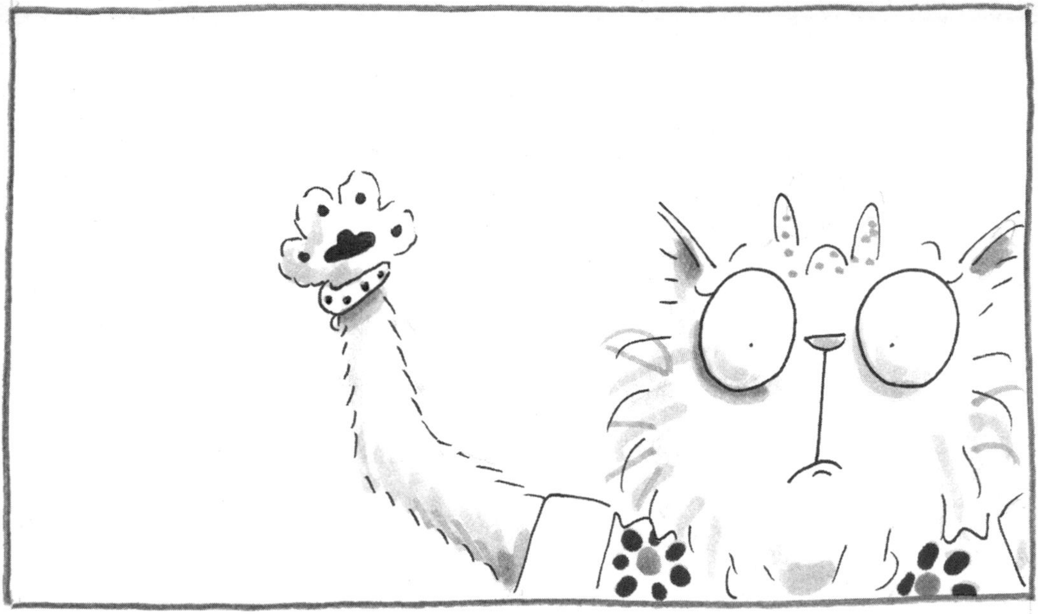

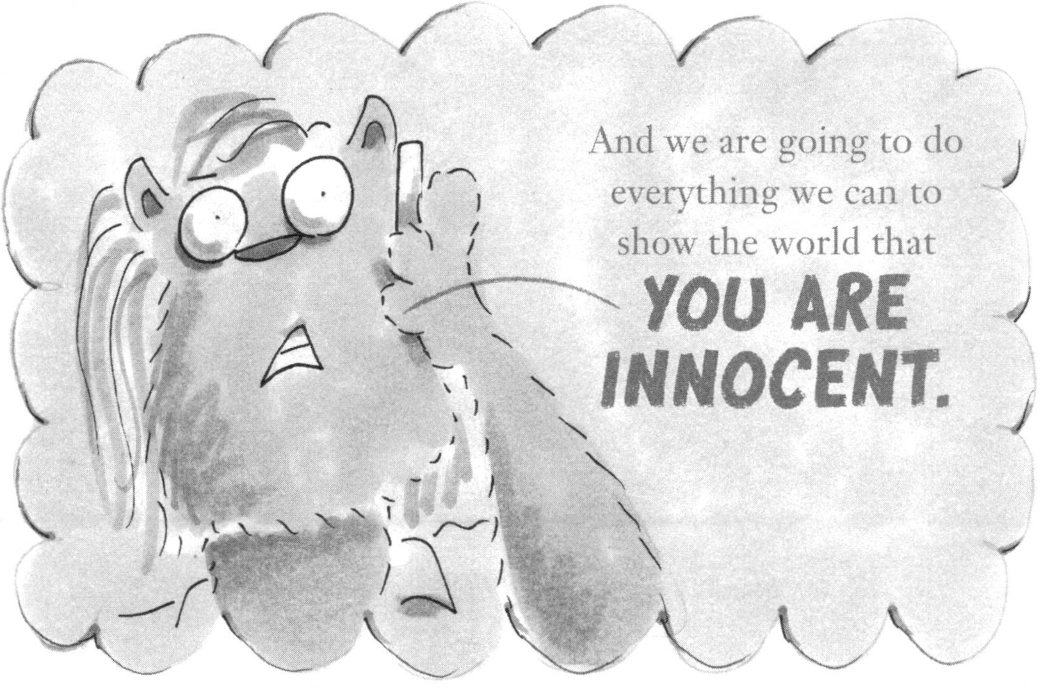
And we are going to do everything we can to show the world that
YOU ARE INNOCENT.

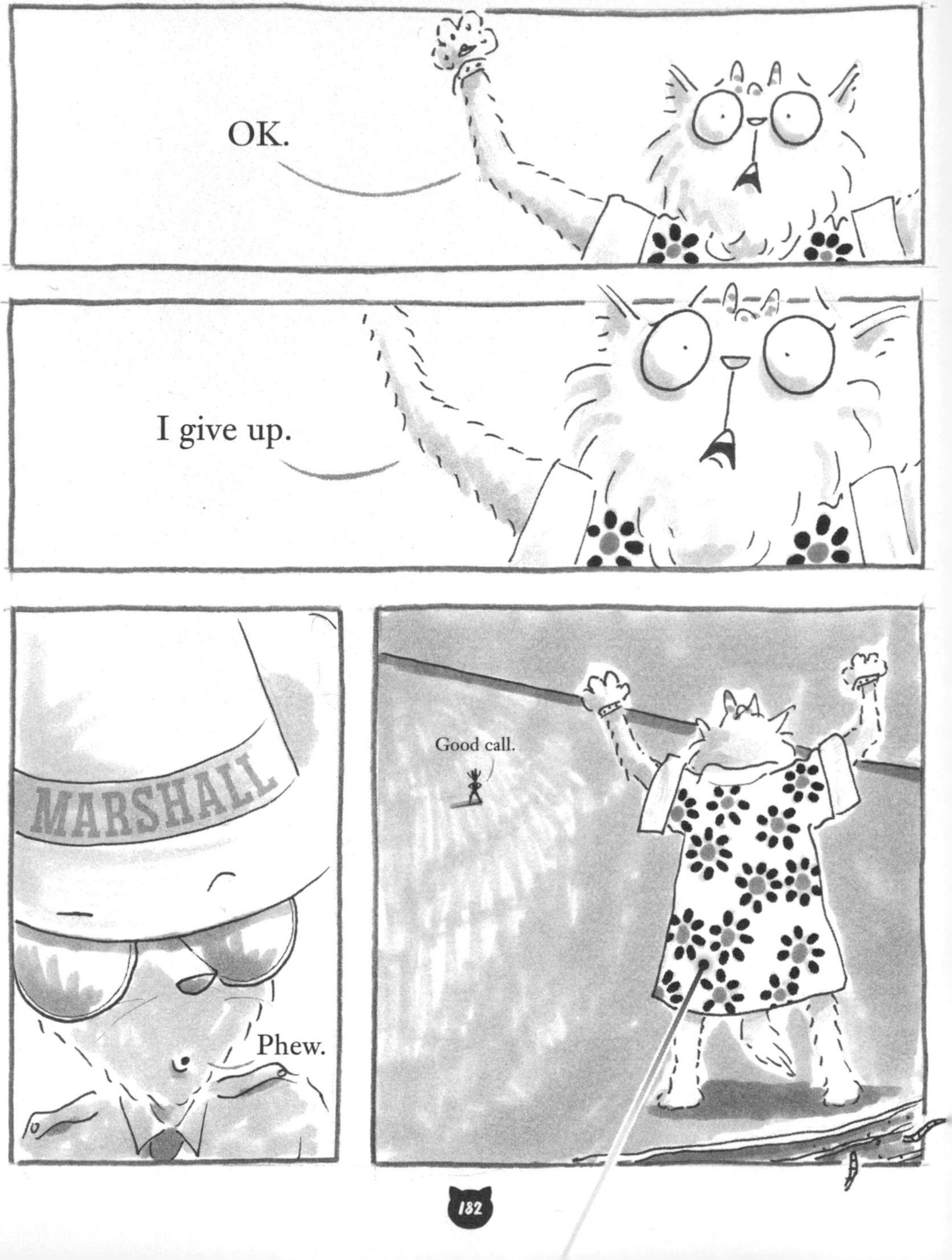
OK.
I give up.
MARSHALL
Phew.
Good call.

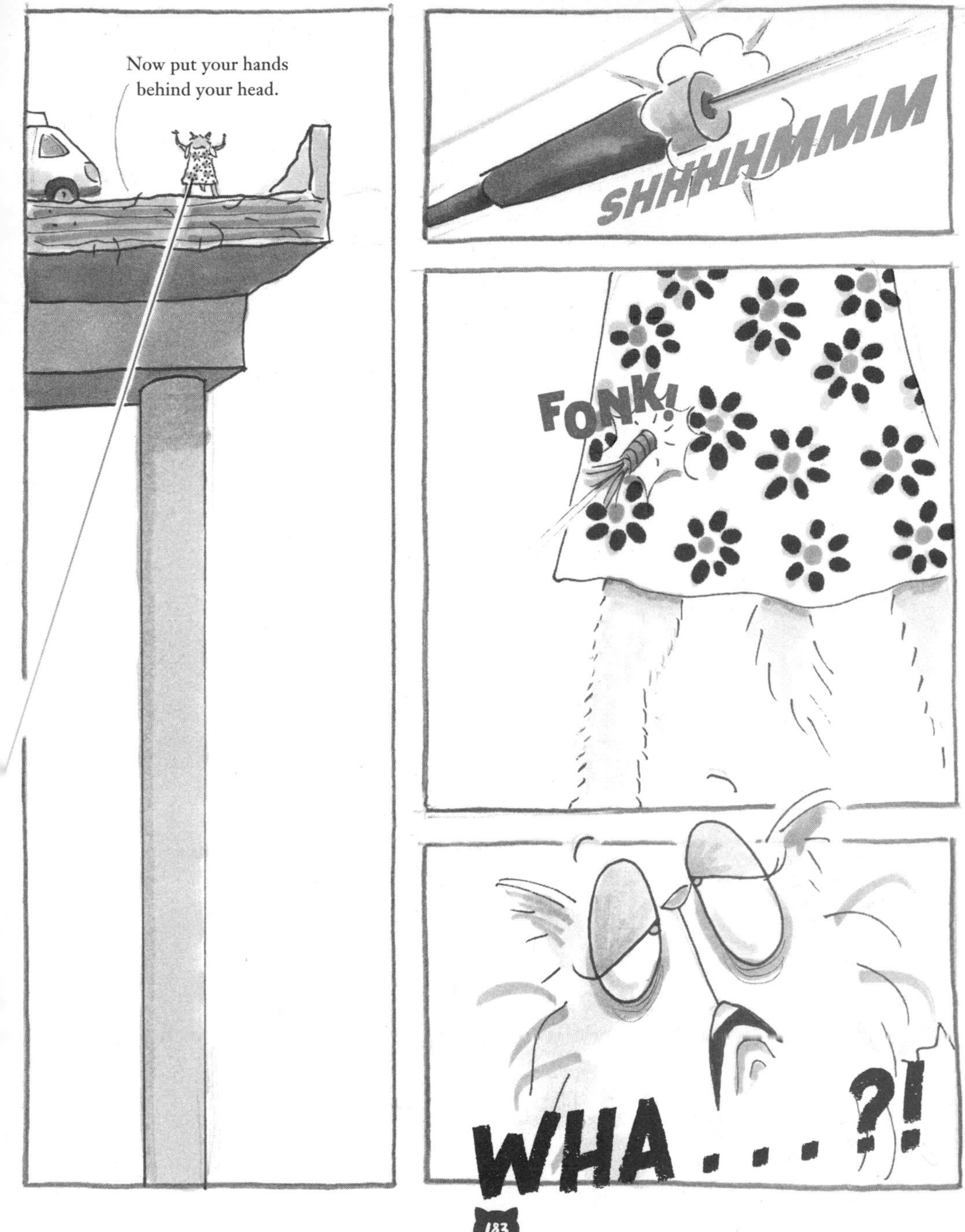
Now put your hands behind your head.
SHHHHMMMM
FONK!
WHA . . . ?!

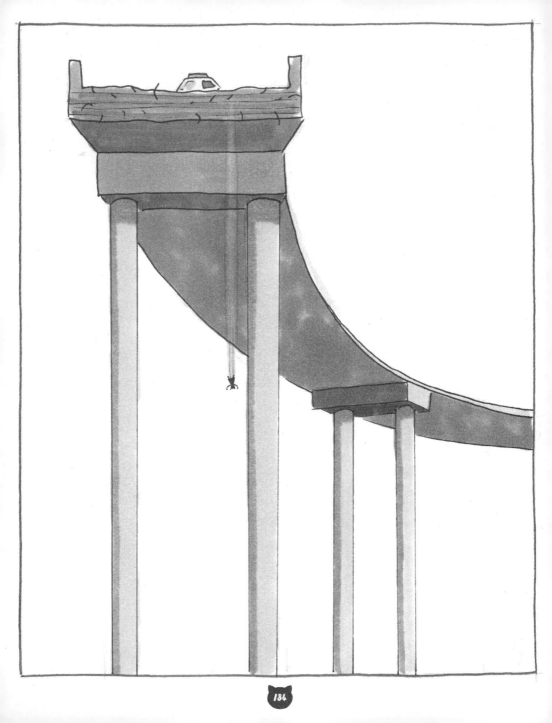

Ten
FOOF!

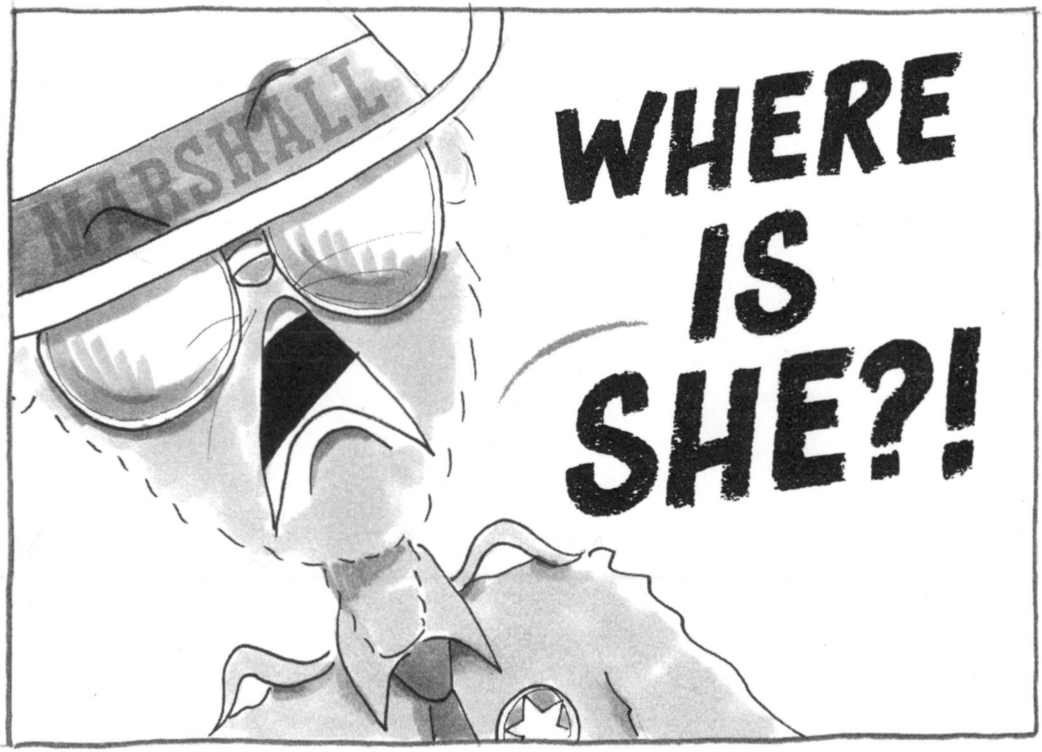
MARSHALL
WHERE IS SHE?!

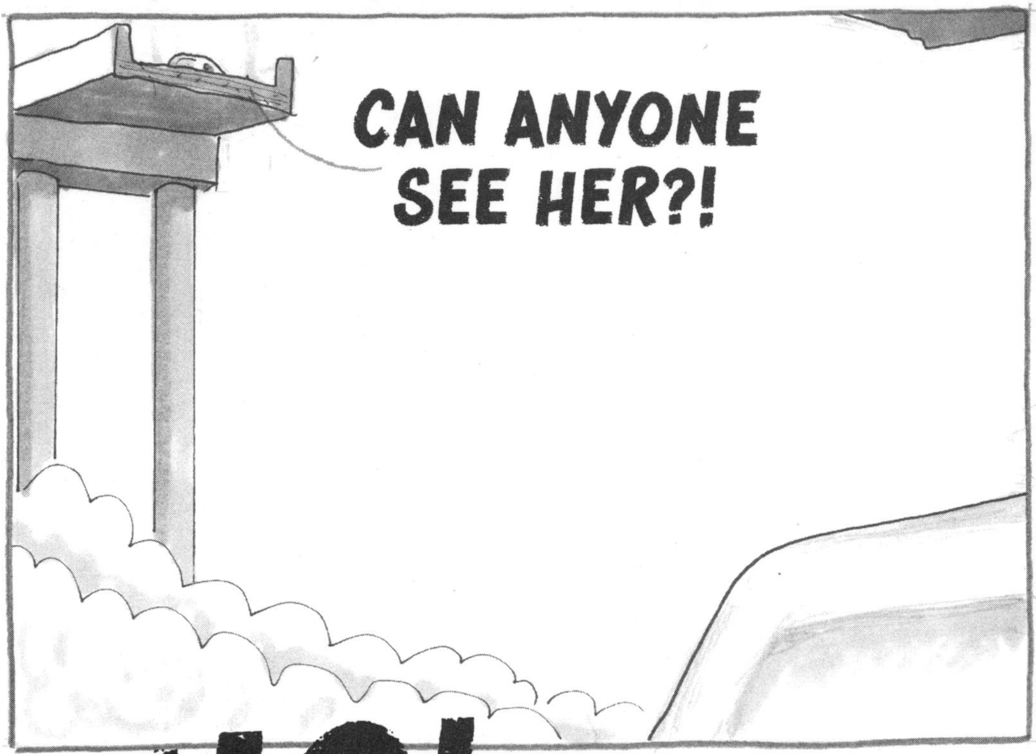
CAN ANYONE
SEE HER?!

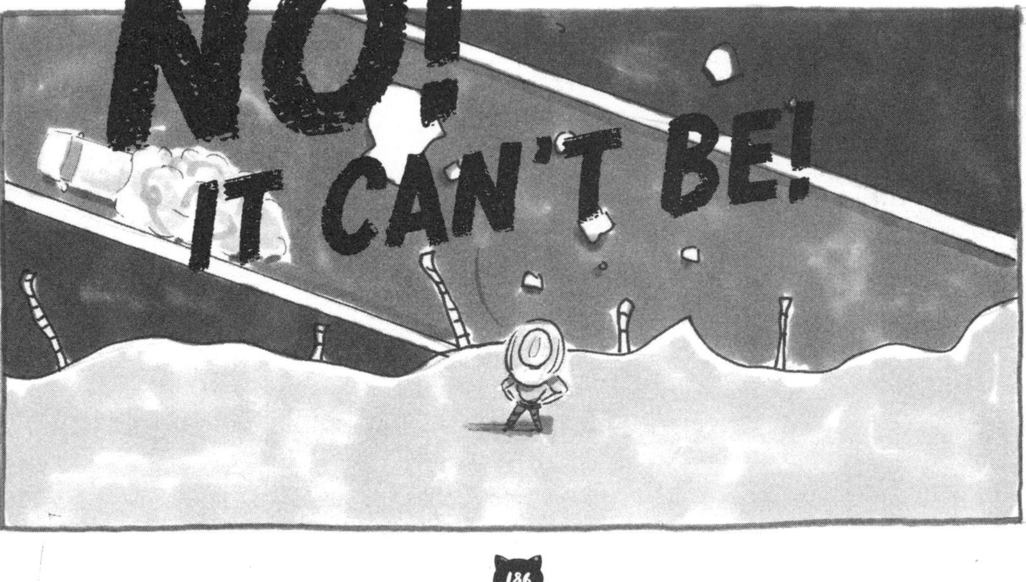
NO!
IT CAN'T BE!

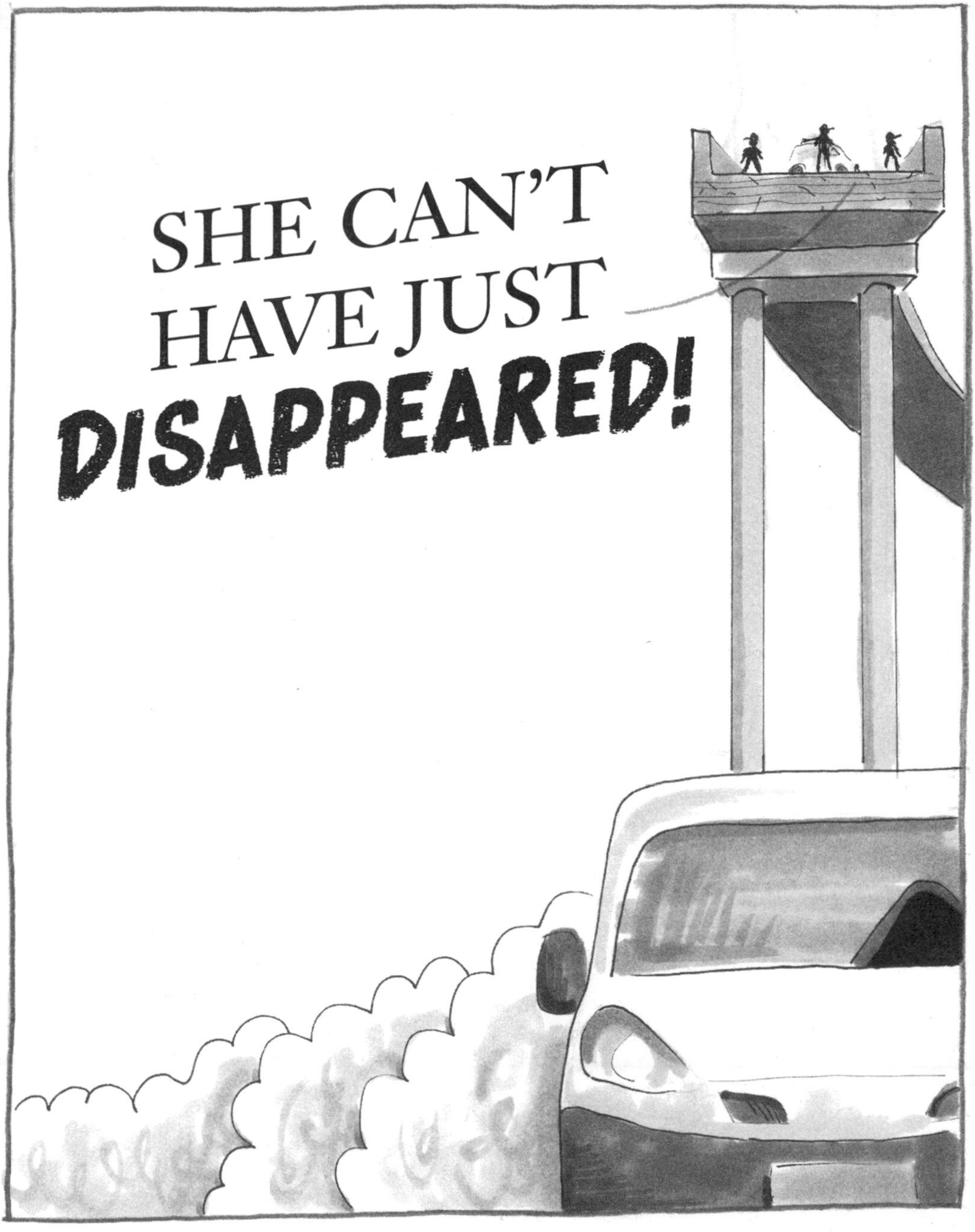
SHE CAN'T HAVE JUST DISAPPEARED!

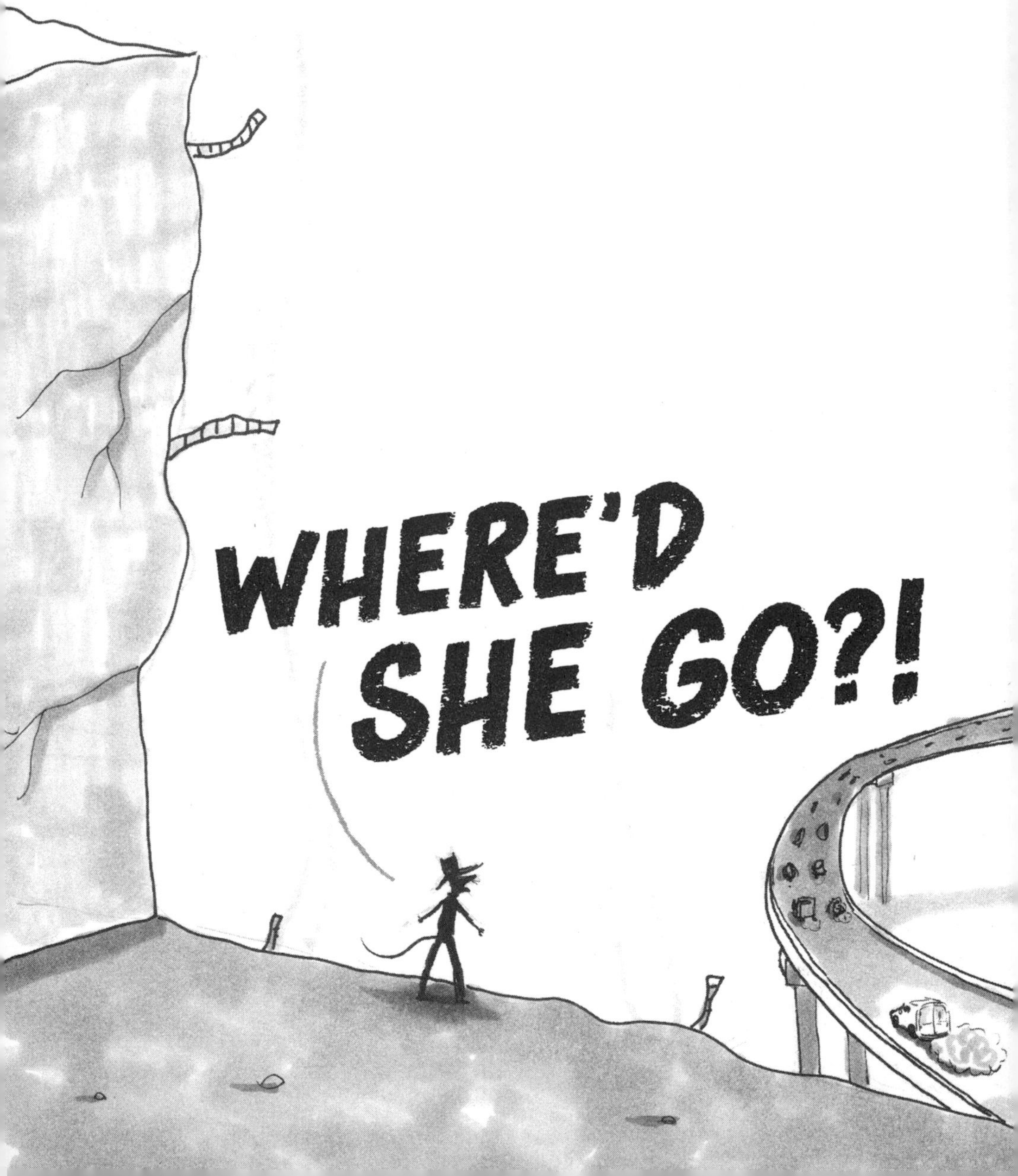
WHERE'D SHE GO?!

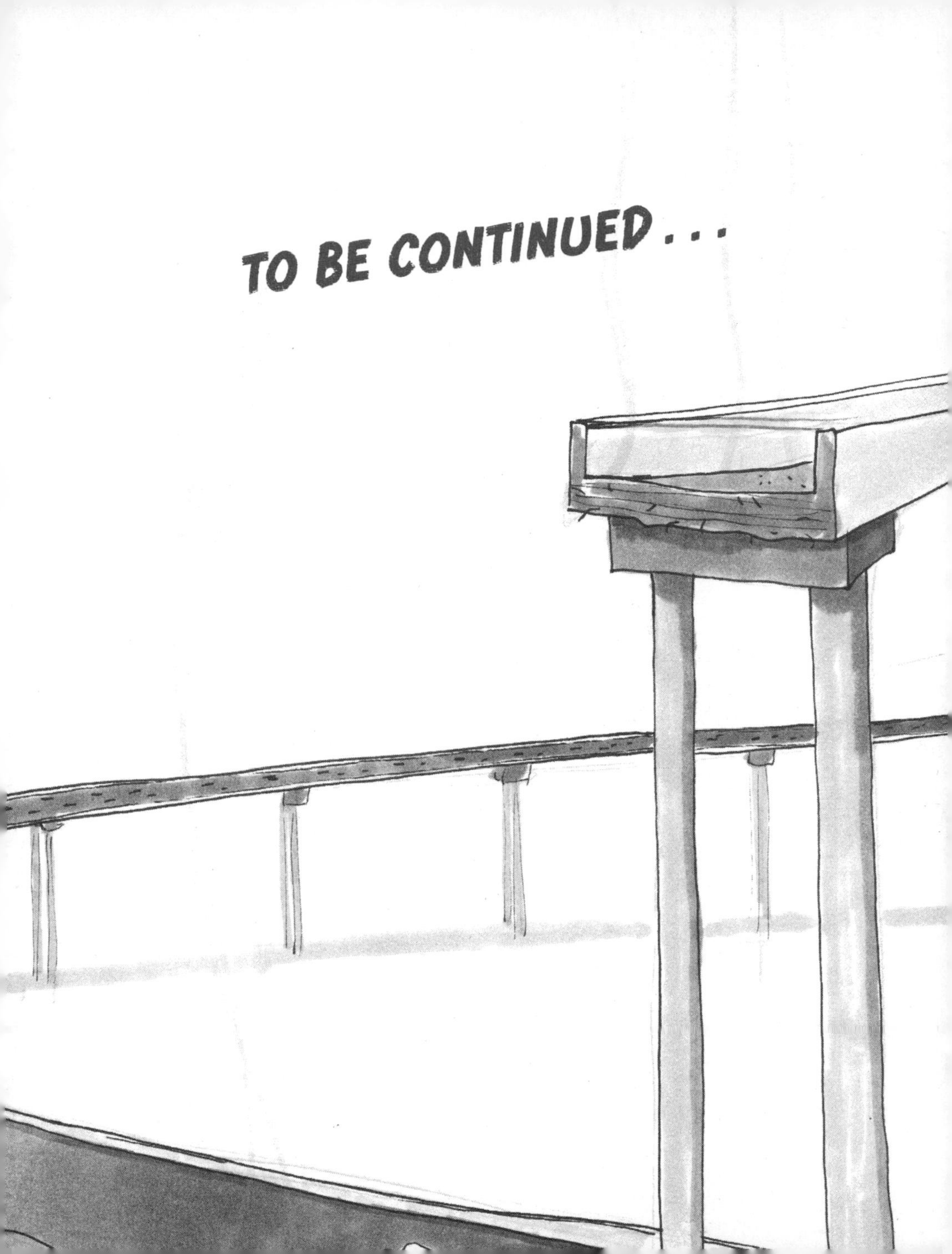
TO BE CONTINUED . . .

CAT on the RUN

BOOK #2
COMING
SOON!